SCIENCE FICTION
OF THE THIRTIES

SCIENCE FICTION
OF THE THIRTIES

Edited and with an Introduction by

DAMON KNIGHT

AVON
PUBLISHERS OF BARD, CAMELOT, DISCUS, EQUINOX AND FLARE BOOKS

To Jacques Sadoul

AVON BOOKS
A division of
The Hearst Corporation
959 Eighth Avenue
New York, New York 10019

ISBN: 0-380-00904-8

Designed by Paula Wiéner

First Avon Printing, March, 1977

Acknowledgments

"Out Around Rigel," by Robert H. Wilson, copyright © 1931, 1958 by Street & Smith Publications, Inc.; reprinted by permission of the publisher.

"The Fifth-Dimension Catapult," by Murray Leinster, copyright © 1931, 1958 by Street & Smith Publications, Inc.; reprinted by permission of the publisher.

"Into the Meteorite Orbit," by Frank K. Kelly, copyright 1933 by Teck Publications, Inc.; reprinted by permission of Forrest J Ackerman.

"The Battery of Hate," by John W. Campbell, Jr., copyright 1933 by Teck Publications, Inc.; reprinted by permission of Scott Meredith Literary Agency, Inc.

"The Wall," by Howard W. Graham, PhD., copyright 1934 by Street & Smith Publications, Inc.; reprinted by permission of Donald Wandrei.

"The Lost Language," by David H. Keller, M.D., copyright 1934 by Teck Publications, Inc.

"The Last Men," by Frank Belknap Long, Jr., copyright 1934 by Street & Smith Publications, Inc.; reprinted by permission of Forrest J Ackerman.

"The Other," by Howard W. Graham, Ph.D., copyright 1934 by Street & Smith Publications, Inc.; reprinted by permission of Donald Wandrei.

"The Mad Moon," by Stanley G. Weinbaum, copyright 1935 by Street & Smith Publications, Inc.; reprinted by permission of Forrest J Ackerman.

"Davey Jones' Ambassador," by Raymond Z. Gallun, copyright 1935 by Street & Smith Publications, Inc.; reprinted by permission of Forrest J Ackerman.

"Alas, All Thinking," by Harry Bates, copyright 1935 by Street & Smith Publications, Inc.; reprinted by permission of Forrest J Ackerman.

"The Time Decelerator," by A. Macfadyen, Jr., copyright 1936 by Street & Smith Publications, Inc.

"The Council of Drones," by W. K. Sonnemann, copyright 1936 by Teck Publications, Inc.

"Seeker of Tomorrow," by Eric Frank Russell and Leslie T. Johnson, copyright 1937 by Street & Smith Publications, Inc.; reprinted by permission of Eric Frank Russell.

"Hyperpilosity," by L. Sprague de Camp, copyright © 1938, 1965 by L. Sprague de Camp; reprinted by permission of the author.

"Pithecanthropus Rejectus," by Manly W. Wellman, copyright 1938 by Street & Smith Publications, Inc.; reprinted by permission of Forrest J Ackerman.

"The Merman," by L. Sprague de Camp, copyright © 1938, 1965 by L. Sprague de Camp; reprinted by permission of the author.

"The Day Is Done," by Lester del Rey, copyright © 1939, 1967 by Street & Smith Publications, Inc.; reprinted by permission of the publisher.

Contents

FOREWORD

In compiling this volume I have partially fulfilled an old ambition, one which I thought I had given up years ago—to reread all the old science fiction magazines I loved when I was young and write their critical history. I wrote about this in an essay called "Goodbye, Henry J. Kostkos, Goodbye" (*Clarion II*, edited by Robin Scott Wilson), where I said the project was no longer possible because there was no audience for the old stories, and, in addition, because they were all junk. This was sour grapes. In fact, as you will see, many of the forgotten stories of the thirties are neglected gems. Only a few of these have been previously reprinted; most exist only in the original magazine versions in the hands of collectors and in libraries. Jacques Sadoul, who undertook my project when I announced I had given it up, remarks in *Les Meilleurs Récits de Astounding Stories* (Editions J'ai Lu, Paris, 1974) that only ninety percent of the stories are worthless and that this conforms to Sturgeon's Rule ("Ninety percent of *everything* is crud"). He is exactly right. I owe grateful appreciation to him, to Howard DeVore, who lent me hundreds of magazines from his immense collection, and to my editor, Barbara Norville.

DAMON KNIGHT

Madeira Beach, August 28, 1974

I

THE EARLY YEARS

The earliest science fiction anthologists, surveying the field as they knew it, found most of the s.f. of the thirties inferior in style and content to the new science fiction pioneered by John Campbell in the forties. Groff Conklin, in *The Best of Science Fiction*, and Healy and McComas, in *Adventures in Time and Space* (both 1946), used a few stories from the thirties and earlier; Conklin continued to use a few, and so did August Derleth, but most of the younger anthologists assumed that everything before 1937 had been well picked over. They were quite wrong.

Many of these forgotten stories, including some that were too poorly written to be included, contain ideas usually thought to have appeared much later; some of them now seem startlingly modern, even prophetic. In "The World of a Hundred Men," by Walter Kately (*Science Wonder Stories*, February 1930), there is a discussion of zero population growth. "Creatures of the Light," by Sophie Wenzel Ellis (*Astounding Stories of Super-Science*, February 1930), mentions "vertical rising aircraft" and speed reading. "A Rescue from Jupiter," by Gawain Edwards (*Science Wonder*, February-March 1930), mentions fusion power and contains a lecture on ecology. "The Power and the Glory," by Charles W. Diffin (*Astounding*, July 1930), is about a device that produces atomic power from thorium, and "The Dark Side of Antri," by Sewell Peaslee Wright (*Astounding*, January 1931), mentions "crude atomic bombs" as weapons of the past. "Beyond the Vanishing Point," by Ray Cummings (*Astounding*, March 1931), refers to an "electric-microscope"; "If the Sun Died," by R. F. Starzl (*Astounding*, August 1931), has "a tiny computing machine about as large as the palm of a man's hand." "Morale," by Murray Leinster (*Astounding*, December 1931), has eddy-current electric stoves, and is subtitled "A Story of the War of 1941-43"; the plot involves a military assault not directed at conventional targets, but intended to destroy civilian morale.

In "Exiles of the Moon" (*Wonder*, January 1932) Nathan Schachner and Arthur Leo Zagat show that an unprotected man would not explode in vacuum and could survive a brief exposure—a device used later by Stanley G. Weinbaum in "The Red Peri" (and still later in the film *2001*). "Slaves of Mercury," by Nathan Schachner (*Astounding*, September 1932), has moving belts with graduated speeds for pedestrian travel. Murray Leinster's "Invasion" (*Astounding*, March 1933), has the United Nations founded in 1987; it also mentions "electric anesthesia." "The Moon Tragedy," by Frank K. Kelly (*Wonder*, October 1933), contains a pretty good description of the Japanese attack on the U.S., and the author gives its date as 1940—not bad. "The Lunar Consul," by Sidney Patzer (*Wonder*, November-December 1933), forecasts the abdication of Edward VIII, and dates it 1947 (eleven years late).

The early development of magazine science fiction was shaped by two men, Hugo Gernsback and Frank R. Paul. In 1926 Gernsback, an immigrant from Luxembourg, founded *Amazing Stories*, the first science fiction magazine in the world. He had already published the first radio magazine, *Modern Electrics*, had established the first mail-order radio company, etc. (and, in his teens, had wired the Luxembourg Carmelite convent for electric bells). A visionary at heart, he was passionately dedicated to the belief that science and technology would transform the world into an earthly paradise. He found the man who could make his dreams manifest in Frank R. Paul, another immigrant (from Austria), whose endlessly fertile imagination produced paintings and drawings of alien landscapes, futuristic cities, gigantic machines, in a creative stream that flowed without remission for thirty-five years. His interpretations of the stories he illustrated inspired other stories, and his vision of the future, with its bright colors and hard edges, stirred the imagination of countless s.f. writers.

By 1930 Gernsback's original magazine had proliferated into five. Gernsback had lost *Amazing* and all his other magazines in bankruptcy proceedings in 1929, but had returned with the same publications under new titles—*Science and Invention* reappeared as *Everyday Mechanics, Radio News* as *Radio-Craft*, and *Amazing Stories* as *Science Wonder Stories* (and *Science Wonder Quarterly*). He also launched *Air Wonder Stories*, devoted to stories about futuristic aircraft; it survived a little less than a year.

Meanwhile Gernsback's old *Amazing* had been sold to a Chicago firm, and it continued under T. O'Conor Sloane, who had been Gernsback's associate editor. In the same year, William F. Clayton brought out still another magazine, *Astounding Stories of Super-Science*. Clayton's magazine was a landmark because it was published in the same format (7″ × 10″) as his other pulps, and appeared on the stands among western, detective and sports magazines. Gernsback's and Sloane's magazines continued to be published in a larger size (8½″ × 11″).

The significance of this was that under Clayton and his editors, science fiction for the first time was treated as just another kind of pulp. The first few issues of *Astounding* placed a heavy emphasis on horror and the occult, as if the publishers were not quite sure yet what science fiction was; before long, however, they began to see the possibilities of s.f. as a branch of adventure fiction, and the lead stories in *Astounding* were peopled with square-jawed young men in riding breeches, swooning girls and bug-eyed monsters.

T. O'Conor Sloane, Thomas Edison's son-in-law, was in his late seventies when he became editor of *Amazing*. Courtly, white-bearded, patient, he utterly lacked Gernsback's crusading fervor; he considered science fiction a harmless amusement at best, and announced more than once in the pages of his magazine that he doubted that space travel would ever become a reality. To replace Frank R. Paul he brought in Leo Morey, whose muddy drawings and bilious green-and-brown cover paintings disfigured *Amazing* until 1938.

In these Depression years, all the magazines were in trouble. Gernsback, hoping for a share of the general pulp market, changed the title of *Science Wonder* to *Wonder Stories* in June 1930 and folded *Air Wonder*. In November he tried the pulp size, but the results were disappointing, and a year later he went back to the larger format. After a brief experiment with slick paper, he lowered the price of the magazine to 15¢ (undercutting *Astounding* by a nickel) and reduced the number of pages. This didn't work either; he restored the magazine to its former thickness and raised the price to 25¢ again. (He continued to publish *Wonder Stories Quarterly* in its extra-large size, 9″ × 12″, until it was discontinued in 1933.) The frequent changes in size, price, and number of pages were symptoms of the magazine's increasing trouble, and must have hurt its newsstand sales.

Amazing, in little better shape, went to the pulp size in October 1933. *Astounding*, in spite of the vigorous editing of Harry Bates, was also feeling the pinch. But in these four years the magazines had published the early work of E. E. Smith, David H. Keller, Jack Williamson, Fletcher Pratt, Philip Francis Nowlan, Murray Leinster, and John W. Campbell, Jr. Science fiction as a commercial medium was established and would live.

Illustrated by H. W. Wesso

I caught his hand and pulled him to safety.

Out Around Rigel

By Robert H. Wilson

T HE SUN had dropped behind the Grimaldi plateau, although for
a day twilight would linger over the Oceanus Procellarum. The
sky was a hazy blue, and out over the deeper tinted waves the full
Earth swung. All the long half-month it had hung there above the
horizon, its light dimmed by the sunshine, growing from a thin
crescent to its full disk three times as broad as that of the sun at
setting. Now in the dusk it was a great silver lamp hanging over
Nardos the Beautiful, the City Built on the Water. The light
glimmered over the tall white towers, over the white ten-mile-long
adamantine bridge running from Nardos to the shore, and lit up the
beach where we were standing, with a brightness that seemed almost
that of day.

"Once more, Garth," I said. "I'll get that trick yet."

The skin of my bare chest still smarted from the blow of his
wooden fencing sword. If it had been the real two-handed Lunarian
dueling sword, with its terrible mass behind a curved razor edge, the
blow would have produced a cut deep into the bone. It was always
the same, ever since Garth and I had fenced as boys with crooked
laths. Back to back, we could beat the whole school, but I never had
a chance against him. Perhaps one time in ten—

"On guard!"

The silvered swords whirled in the Earth-light. I nicked him on
one wrist, and had to duck to escape his wild swing at my head. The
wooden blades were now locked by the hilts above our heads. When
he stepped back to get free, I lunged and twisted his weapon. In a
beautiful parabola, Garth's sword sailed out into the water, and he
dropped to the sand to nurse his right wrist.

"Confound your wrestling, Dunal. If you've broken my arm on the
eve of my flight—"

"It's not even a sprain. Your wrists are weak. And I supposed
you've always been considerate of me? Three broken ribs!"

"For half a cent—"

He was on his feet, and then Kelvar came up and laid her hand on his shoulder. Until a few minutes before she had been swimming in the surf, watching us. The Earth-light shimmered over her white skin, still faintly moist, and blazed out in blue sparkles from the jewels of the breastplates and trunks she had put on.

When she touched Garth and he smiled, I wanted to smash in his dark face and then take the beating I would deserve. Yet, if she preferred him— And the two of us had been friends before she was born. I put out my hand.

"Whatever happens, Garth, we'll still be friends?"

"Whatever happens."

We clasped hands.

"Garth," Kelvar said, "it's getting dark. Show us your ship before you go."

"All right." He had always been like that—one minute in a black rage, the next perfectly agreeable. He now led the way up to a cliff hanging over the sea.

"There," said Garth, "is the *Comet.* Our greatest step in conquering distance. After I've tried it out, we can go in a year to the end of the universe. But, for a starter, how about a thousand light-years around Rigel in six months?" His eyes were afire. Then he calmed down. "Anything I can show you?"

I had seen the *Comet* before, but never so close. With a hull of shining helio-beryllium—the new light, inactive alloy of a metal and a gas—the ship was a cylinder about twenty feet long by fifteen in diameter, while a pointed nose stretched five feet farther at each end. Fixed in each point was a telescopic lens, while there were windows along the sides and at the top—all made, Garth informed us, of another form of the alloy almost as strong as the opaque variety. Running halfway out each end were four "fins" which served to

Editor's Note: The manuscript, of which a translation is here presented, was discovered by the rocket-ship expedition to the moon three years ago. It was found in its box by the last crumbling ruins of the great bridge mentioned in the narrative. Its final translation is a tribute at once to the philological skill of the Earth and to the marvelous dictionary provided by Dunal, the Lunarian. Stars and lunar localities will be given their traditional Earth names; and measures of time, weight, and distance have been reduced, in round numbers, to terrestrial equivalents. Of the space ship described, the *Comet*, no trace has been found. It must be buried under the rim of one of the hundreds of nearby Lunar craters—the result, as some astronomers have long suspected and as Dunal's story verifies, of a great swarm of meteors striking the unprotected, airless moon.

apply the power driving the craft. A light inside showed the interior to be a single room, ten feet high at the center of its cylindrical ceiling, with a level floor.

"How do you know this will be the bottom?" I asked, giving the vessel a shove to roll it over. But it would not budge. Garth laughed.

"Five hundred pounds of mercury and the disintegrators are under that floor, while out in space I have an auxiliary gravity engine to keep my feet there.

"You see, since your mathematical friends derived their identical formulas for gravity and electro-magnetism, my job was pretty easy. As you know, a falling body follows the line of least resistance in a field of distortion of space caused by mass. I bend space into another such field by electromagnetic means, and the *Comet* flies down the track. Working the mercury disintegrators at full power, I can get an acceleration of two hundred miles per second, which will build up the speed at the midpoint of my trip to almost four thousand times that of light. Then I'll have to start slowing down, but at the average speed the journey will take only six months or so."

"But can anyone stand that acceleration?" Kelvar asked.

"I've had it on and felt nothing. With a rocket exhaust shoving the ship, it couldn't be done, but my gravitational field attracts the occupant of the *Comet* just as much as the vessel itself."

"You're sure," I interrupted, "that you have enough power to keep up the acceleration?"

"Easily. There's a two-thirds' margin of safety."

"And you haven't considered that it may get harder to push? You know the increase of mass with velocity. You can't take one-half of the relativity theory without the other. And they've actually measured the increase of weight in an electron."

"The electron never knew it; it's all a matter of reference points. I can't follow the math, but I know that from the electron's standards it stayed exactly the same weight. Anything else is nonsense."

"Well, there may be a flaw in the reasoning, but as they've worked it out, nothing can go faster than light. As you approach that velocity, the mass keeps increasing, and with it the amount of energy required for a new increase in speed. At the speed of light the mass would be infinite, and hence no finite energy could get you any further."

"Maybe so. It won't take long to find out."

A few of the brightest stars had begun to appear. We could just see the parallelogram of Orion, with red Betelgeuse at one corner, and across from it Rigel, scintillant like a blue diamond.

"See," Garth said, pointing at it. "Three months from now, that's where I'll be. The first man who dared to sail among the stars."

"Only because you don't let anyone else share the glory and the danger."

"Why should I? But you wouldn't go, anyway."

"Will you let me?"

I had him there.

"On your head be it. The *Comet* could hold three or four in a pinch, and I have plenty of provisions. If you really want to take the chance—"

"It won't be the first we've taken together."

"All right. We'll start in ten minutes." He went inside the ship.

"Don't go," Kelvar whispered, coming into the *Comet*'s shadow. "Tell him anything, but don't go."

"I've got to. I can't go back on my word. He'd think I was afraid."

"Haven't you a right to be?"

"Garth is my friend and I'm going with him."

"All right. But I wish you wouldn't."

From inside came the throb of engines.

"Kelvar," I said, "you didn't worry when only Garth was going."

"No."

"And there's less danger with two to keep watch."

"I know, but still . . ."

"You are afraid for *me?*"

"I am afraid for you."

My arm slipped around her, there in the shadow.

"And when I come back, Kelvar, we'll be married?"

In answer, she kissed me. Then Garth was standing in the doorway of the *Comet.*

"Dunal, where are you?"

We separated and came out of the shadow. I went up the plank to the door, kicking it out behind me. Kelvar waved, and I called something or other to her. Then the door clanged shut. Seated before the control board at the front of the room, Garth held the switch for the two projectors.

"Both turned up," he yelled over the roar of the generators. His hands swung over and the noise died down, but nothing else seemed to have happened. I turned back again to look out the little window fixed in the door.

Down far below, I could see for a moment the city of Nardos with its great white bridge, and a spot that might be Kelvar. Then there was only the ocean, sparkling in the Earth-light, growing smaller, smaller. And then we had shot out of the atmosphere into the glare of the sun and a thousand stars.

On and up we went, until the moon was a crescent with stars around it. Then Garth threw the power forward.

"Might as well turn in," he told me. "There'll be nothing interesting until we get out of the solar system and I can put on real speed. I'll take the first trick."

"How long watches shall we stand?"

"Eighteen hours ought to match the way we have been living. If you have another preference—"

"No, that will be all right. And I suppose I might as well get in some sleep now."

I was not really sleepy, but only dazed a little by the adventure. I fixed some things on the floor by one of the windows and lay down, switching out the light. Through a top window the sunlight slanted down to fall around Garth, at his instrument board, in a bright glory. From my window I could see the Earth and the gleaming stars.

The Earth was smaller than I had ever seen it before. It seemed to be moving backward a little, and even more, to be changing phase. I closed my eyes, and when I opened them again, sleepily, the bright area was perceptibly smaller. If I could stay awake long enough, there would be only a crescent again. If I could stay awake— But I could not. . . .

Only the rattling of dishes as Garth prepared breakfast brought me back to consciousness. I got to my feet sheepishly.

"How long have I slept?"

"Twenty hours straight. You looked as if you might have gone on forever. It's the lack of disturbance to indicate time. I got in a little myself, once we were out of the solar system."

A sandwich in one hand, I wandered over the vessel. It was reassuringly solid and concrete. And yet there was something lacking.

"Garth," I asked, "what's become of the sun?"

"I thought you'd want to know that." He led me to the rear telescope.

"But I don't see anything."

"You haven't caught on yet. See that bright yellowish star on the edge of the constellation Scorpio. That's it."

Involuntarily, I gasped. "Then—how far away are we?"

"I put on full acceleration fifteen hours ago, when we passed Neptune, and we have covered thirty billion miles—three hundred times as far as from the moon to the sun, but only one half of one percent of a light-year."

I was speechless, and Garth led me back to the control board. He pointed out the acceleration control, now turned up to its last notch forward; he also showed me the dials which were used to change our direction.

"Just keep that star on the cross hairs. It's Pi Orionis, a little out of our course, but a good target since it is only twenty-five light-years away. Half the light is deflected on this screen, with a delicate photo-electric cell at its center. The instant the light of the star slips off it, a relay is started which lights a red lamp here, and in a minute sounds a warning bell. That indicator over there shows our approach to any body. It works by the interaction of the object's gravitational field with that of my projector, and we can spot anything sizable an hour away. Sure you've got everything?"

It all seemed clear. Then I noticed at the top three clocklike dials; one to read days, another to record the speeds of light, and the third to mark light-years traveled.

"These can't really work?" I said. "We have no way to check our speed with outer space."

"Not directly. This is geared with clockwork to represent an estimate based on the acceleration. If your theory is right, then the dials are all wrong."

"And how long do you expect to go ahead without knowing the truth?"

"Until we ought to be at Pi Orionis. At two weeks and twenty-five light-years by the dials, if we aren't there we'll start back. By your figuring, we shouldn't be yet one light-year on the way. Anything more?"

"No, I think I can manage it."

"Wake me if anything's wrong. And look out for dark stars." Then he left me there at the controls. In five minutes he was asleep and the whole ship was in my hands.

For hours nothing happened. Without any control of mine, the ship went straight ahead. I could get up and walk about, with a weather eye on the board, and never was there the flash of a danger light. But I was unable to feel confident, and went back to look out through the glass.

The stars were incredibly bright and clear. Right ahead were Betelguese and Rigel, and the great nebula of Orion still beyond. There was no twinkling, but each star a bright, steady point of light. And if Garth's indicators were correct, we were moving toward them at a speed now seventy-five times that of light itself. If they were correct . . . How could one know, before the long two weeks were over?

But before I could begin to think of any plan, my eye was caught by the red lamp flashing on the panel. I pressed the attention button before the alarm could ring, then started looking for the body we were in danger of striking. The position indicators pointed straight ahead, but I could see nothing. For ten minutes I peered through the telescope, and still no sign. The dials put the thing off a degree or so to the right now, but that was too close. In five more minutes I would swing straight up and give whatever it was a wide berth.

I looked out again. In the angle between the cross hairs, wasn't there a slight haze? In a moment it was clear. A comet, apparently, the two of us racing toward each other. Bigger it grew and bigger, hurtling forward. Would we hit?

The dials put it up a little and far off to the right, but it was still frightening. The other light had come on, too, and I saw that we had been pulled off our course by the comet's attraction. I threw the nose over, passed on the other side for leeway, then straightened up as the side-distance dial gave a big jump away. Though the gaseous globe, tailless of course away from the sun, showed as big as the full Earth, the danger was past.

As I watched, the comet vanished from the field of the telescope. Five minutes, perhaps, with the red danger light flickering all the time. Then, with a ghastly flare through the right hand windows, it passed us.

Garth sat straight up. "What happened?" he yelled.

"Just a comet. I got by all right."

He settled back, having been scarcely awake, and I turned to the board again. The danger light had gone out, but the direction indicator was burning. The near approach of the comet had thrown us off our course by several degrees. I straightened the ship up easily, and had only a little more difficulty in stopping a rocking motion. Then again the empty hours of watching, gazing into the stars.

Precisely at the end of eighteen hours, Garth awakened, as if the consummation of a certain number of internal processes had set off a little alarm clock in his brain. We were forty-one hours out, with a speed, according to the indicator, of one hundred and twenty-eight times that of light, and a total distance covered of slightly over one quarter of a light-year. A rather small stretch, compared to the 466 light-years we had to go. But when I went back for a look out of the rear telescope, the familiar stars seemed to have moved the least bit closer together, and the sun was no brighter than a great number of them.

I slept like a log, but awakened a little before my trick was due.

Exactly on schedule, fourteen days and some hours after we had started off, we passed Pi Orionis. For long there had been no doubt in my mind that, whatever the explanation, our acceleration was holding steady. In the last few hours the star swept up to the brilliance of the sun, then faded again until it was no brighter than Venus. Venus! Our sun itself had been a mere dot in the rear telescope until the change in our course threw it out of the field of vision.

At sixty-five light-years, twenty-three days out, Beta Eridani was almost directly in our path for Rigel. Slightly less than a third of the distance to the midpoint, in over half the time. But our speed was still increasing, 200 miles a second every second, almost four times the speed of light in an hour. Our watches went on with a not altogether disagreeable monotony.

There was no star to mark the middle of our journey. Only, toward the close of one of my watches, a blue light which I had never noticed came on beside the indicator dials, and I saw that we had covered 233 light-years, half the estimated distance to Rigel. The speed marker indicated 3,975 times the speed of light. I wakened Garth.

"You could have done it yourself," he complained, sleepily, "but I suppose it's just as well."

He went over to the board and started warming up the rear gravity projector.

"We'll turn one off as the other goes on. Each take one control, and go a notch at a time." He began counting, "One, two, three . . ."

On the twentieth count, my dial was down to zero, his up to maximum deceleration, and I pulled out my switch. Garth snapped sideways a lever on the indicators. Though nothing seemed to happen, I knew that the speed dial would creep backward, and the distance dial progress at a slower and slower rate. While I was trying to see the motion, Garth had gone back to bed. I turned again to the glass and looked out at Rigel, on the cross hairs, and Kappa Orionis, over to the left, and the great nebula reaching over a quarter of the view with its faint gaseous streamers.

And so we swept on through space, with Rigel a great blue glory ahead, and new stars, invisible at greater distances, flaring up in front of us and then fading into the background as we passed. For a long time we had been able to see that Rigel, as inferred from spectroscopic evidence, was a double star—a fainter, greener blue companion revolving with it around their common center of gravity. Beyond Kappa Orionis, three hundred light-years from the sun, the space between the two was quite evident. Beyond four hundred light-years, the brilliance of the vast star was so great that it dimmed all the other stars by comparison, and made the nebula seem a mere faint gauze. And yet even with this gradual change, our arrival was a surprise.

When he relieved me at my watch, Garth seemed dissatisfied with our progress. "It must be farther than they've figured. I'll stick at twenty-five times light speed, and slow down after we get there by taking an orbit."

"I'd have said it was nearer than the estimate," I tried to argue, but was too sleepy to remember my reasons. Propped up on one elbow, I looked around and out at the stars. There was a bright splash of light, I noticed, where the telescope concentrated the radiation of Rigel at one spot on the screen. I slept, and then Garth was shouting in my ear:

"We're there!"

I opened my eyes, blinked, and shut them again in the glare.

"I've gone around three or four times trying to slow down. We're there, and there's a planet to land on."

At last I could see. Out the window opposite me, Rigel was a blue-white disk half the size of the sun, but brighter, with the companion star a sort of faint reflection five or ten degrees to the side. And still beyond, as I shaded my eyes, I could see swimming in the black a speck with the unmistakable glow of reflected light.

With both gravity projectors in readiness, we pulled out of our orbit and straight across toward the planet, letting the attraction of Rigel fight against our still tremendous speed. For a while, the pull of the big star was almost overpowering. Then we got past, and into the gravitational field of the planet. We spiraled down around it, looking for a landing place and trying to match our speed with its rotational velocity.

From rather unreliable observations, the planet seemed a good deal smaller than the moon, and yet so dense as to have a greater gravitational attraction. The atmosphere was cloudless, and the surface a forbidding expanse of sand. The globe whirled at a rate that gave it, we figured, a day of approximately five hours. We angled down, picking a spot just within the lighted area.

A landing was quite feasible. As we broke through the atmosphere, we could see that the sand, although blotched with dark patches here and there, was comparatively smooth. At one place there was a level outcropping of rock, and over this we hung. It was hard work, watching through the single small port in the floor as we settled down. Finally the view was too small to be of any use. I ran to the side window, only to find my eyes blinded by Rigel's blaze. Then we had landed, and almost at the same moment Rigel set. Half overlapped by the greater star, the faint companion had been hidden in its glare. Now, in the dusk, a corner of it hung ghostlike on the horizon, and then it too disappeared.

I flashed on our lights, while Garth cut out the projector and the floor gravity machine. The increase in weight was apparent, but not particularly unpleasant. After a few minutes of walking up and down, I got used to it.

Through a stopcock in the wall, Garth had drawn in a tube of gas from the atmosphere outside, and was analyzing it with a spectroscope.

"We can go out," he said. "It's unbreathable, but we'll be able to use the space suits. Mostly fluorine. It would eat your lungs out like that!"

"And the suits?"

"Fortunately, they've been covered with helio-beryllium paint, and the helmet glass is the same stuff. Not even that atmosphere can touch it. I suppose there can be no life on the place. With all this sand, it would have to be based on silicon instead of carbon—and it would have to breathe fluorine!"

He got out the suits—rather like a diver's with the body of metal-painted cloth, and the helmet of the metal itself. On the shoulders was an air supply cylinder. The helmets were fixed with radio, so we could have talked to each other even in airless space. We said almost anything to try it out.

"Glad you brought two, and we don't have to explore in shifts."

"Yes, I was prepared for emergencies."

"Shall we wait for daylight to go out?"

"I can't see why. And these outfits will probably feel better in the cool. Let's see."

We shot a searchlight beam out the window. There was a slight drop down from the rock where we rested, then the sandy plain stretching out. Only far off were those dark patches that looked like old seaweed on a dried-up ocean bed, and might prove dangerous footing. The rest seemed hard packed.

My heart was pounding as we went into the air-lock and fastened the inner door behind us.

"We go straight out now," Garth explained. "Coming back, it will be necessary to press this button and let the pump get rid of the poisonous air before going in."

I opened the outer door and started to step out, then realized that there was a five-foot drop to the ground.

"Go ahead and jump," Garth said. "There's a ladder inside I should have brought, but it would be too much trouble to go back through the lock for it. Either of us can jump eight feet at home, and we'll get back up somehow."

I jumped, failing to allow for the slightly greater gravity, and fell sprawling. Garth got down more successfully, in spite of a long package of some sort he carried in his hand.

Scrambling down from the cliff and walking out on the sand, I tried to get used to the combination of greater weight and the awkward suit. If I stepped very deliberately it was all right, but an attempt to run sank my feet in the sand and brought me up staggering. There was no trouble seeing through the glass of my helmet over wide angles. Standing on the elevation by the *Comet*, his space suit shining in the light from the windows, Garth looked like a metallic monster, some creature of this strange world. And I must have presented to him much the same appearance, silhouetted dark and forbidding against the stars.

The stars! I looked up, and beheld the most marvelous sight of the whole trip—the Great Nebula of Orion, seen from a distance of less than one hundred and fifty light-years its own width.

A great luminous curtain, fifty degrees across, I could just take it all in with my eye. The central brilliancy as big as the sun, a smaller one above it, and then the whole mass of gas stretching over the sky. The whole thing aglow with the green light of nebulium and blazing with the stars behind it. It was stupendous, beyond words.

I started to call Garth, then saw that he was looking up as well. For almost half an hour I watched, as the edge of the nebula sank below the horizon. Then its light began to dim. Turning, I saw that the sky opposite was already gray. The dawn!

Why, the sun had just set. Then I realized. It was over an hour since we had landed, and a full night would be scarcely two hours and a half. If we were in a summer latitude, the shorter period of darkness was natural enough. And yet it was still hard to believe as, within ten minutes, it was as bright as Earth-light on the moon. Still clearer and clearer grew the light. The stars were almost gone, the center of the nebula only a faint wisp. There were no clouds to give the colors of sunrise, but a bluish white radiance seemed to be trembling on the eastern horizon.

And then, like a shot, Rigel came up into the sky. The light and heat struck me like something solid, and I turned away. Even with my suit reflecting most of the light away, I felt noticeably warm. The *Comet* shone like a blinding mirror, so that it was almost impossible to see Garth on the plain below it. Stumbling, and shielding my eyes with my hand, I made my way toward him.

He was standing erect, in his hands two old Lunarian dueling swords. There was hate in his voice as the radio brought it in my ears.

"Dunal, only one of us is going back to the moon."

I stared. Was the heat getting him? "Hadn't we better go inside?" I said quietly and somewhat soothingly.

He made no reply, but only held out one of the hilts. I took it dumbly. In that instant he could have struck my head from my body, if he wished.

"But, Garth, old friend—"

"No friend to you. You shall win Kelvar now, or I. I'm giving you a sporting chance. One of your light cuts letting the fluorine inside will be as deadly as anything I can do. The one who goes back will tell of an accident, making repairs out in space. Damn you, if you don't want me to kill you where you stand, come on and fight."

"Garth, you've gone mad."

"I've been waiting ever since I got you to leave the moon. On guard!"

With a rush of anger I was upon him. He tried to step back, stumbled, had one knee on the ground, then hurled himself forward with a thrust at my waist that I dodged only by an inch. I had to cover, and in spite of myself, with the cool work of parrying, my animosity began to disappear.

And so began one of the strangest battles that the Universe has seen. Lumbering with our suits and the extra gravity, we circled each other under the blazing sky. The blue-white of Rigel shimmered off our suits and the arcs of our blades as we cut and guarded—each wary now, realizing that a touch meant death. As that terrible sun climbed upward in the sky, its heat was almost overpowering. The sweat poured off every inch of my body, and I gasped for breath. And still we fought on, two glittering metal monsters under the big blue star sweeping up to its noon.

I knew now that I could never kill Garth. I could not go back to Kelvar with his blood. Yet if I simply defended, sooner or later he would wear me down. There was just one chance. If I could disarm him, I could wrestle him into submission. Then he might be reasonable, or I could take him home bound.

I began leading for the opening I wanted, but with no result. He seemed resolved to tire me out. Either I must carry the fight to him, or I would be beaten down. I made a wide opening, counting on dodging his slow stroke. I did, but he recovered too soon. Again on the other side, with no better result. Still again, just getting in for a light tap on Garth's helmet. Then I stepped back, with guard low, and this time he came on. His sword rose in a gleaming arc and hung high for a moment. I had him. There were sparks of clashing, locked steel.

"Damn you, Dunal!" He took a great step back, narrowly keeping his balance on the sand. On another chance, I would trip him. My ears were almost deafened by his roar, "Come on and *fight.*"

I took a step in and to the side, and had him in the sun. He swung blindly, trying to cover himself with his whirling point but I had half a dozen openings to rip his suit. When he moved to try to see, I would lock with him again. I watched his feet.

And as I watched, I saw an incredible thing. Near one of Garth's feet the sand was moving. It was not a slide caused by his weight; rather—why, it was being pushed up from below. There was a little hump, and suddenly it had burst open, and a stringy mass like seaweed was crawling toward his leg.

"Look out, Garth," I yelled.

How he could see through that terrible sun I do not know, but Garth swung through my forgotten guard with a blow square across my helmet glass. The force threw me to the ground, and I looked up, dazed. The beryllium glass had not broken to let in the fluorine-filled air, but Garth was standing over me.

"That's your last trick, Dunal." His blade rose for the kill.

I was unable even to get up, but with one hand I pointed to the ground.

"Look!" I shouted again, and on the instant the thing wound itself around Garth's foot.

He swung down, hacking it loose. I had got to my feet. "Run for the ship," I cried, and started off.

"Not that way."

I looked back, and saw that I had run in the wrong direction. But it made no difference. Over a whole circle around us the sand was rising, and directly between us and the *Comet* there was a great green-brown mass. We were surrounded.

We stood staring at the creatures. Spread out to full dimensions, each one made a sphere about four feet in diameter. In the center, a solid mass whose outlines were difficult to discern; and spreading out from this a hundred long, thin, many-jointed arms or legs or branches or whatever one could call them.

The things were not yet definitely hostile—only their circle, of perhaps fifty yards radius, grew continually thicker and more impenetrable. Within the enclosed area, the only ripples we could see in the sand were heading outward. There was to be no surprise attack from below, at least; only one in mass. What, I wondered, might be a sign of friendship, to persuade them to let us go?

And then the circle began to close in. The things rolled over and over on themselves, like gigantic tumbleweeds. At one point, to the right of the direct route to the *Comet*, the line seemed thinner. I pointed the place out to Garth.

"Break through there, and make a run for it."

We charged into the midst of them with swinging blades. The very suddenness of our rush carried us halfway through their midst. Then something had my legs from behind. I almost fell, but succeeded in turning and cutting myself free. The creatures from the other side of the circle must have made the hundred yards in four or five seconds. And the rest had now covered the breach in front. It was hopeless.

And so we stood back to back, hewing out a circle of protection against our enemies. They seemed to have no fear, and in spite of the destruction our blades worked among them, they almost overcame us by sheer numbers and weight. It was a case of whirling our swords back and forth interminably in the midst of their tentacles. Against the light, the long arms were a half-transparent brown. Our swords broke them in bright shivers. Formed from the predominant silicon of the planet, the creatures were living glass!

For perhaps a quarter of an hour we were in the thick of them, hewing until I thought my arms must fall, slashing and tearing at the ones that had got underfoot and were clamping their tentacles around our legs. Except for the space suits, we should have, by this time, been overpowered and torn into bits—and yet these garments could not be expected to hold indefinitely.

But at last there was a breathing space. The crippled front ranks dragged themselves away, and there was left around us a brief area of sand, covered with coruscating splinters of glass. Garth got the breath to say something or other encouraging. It was like old days at school.

Only this time the odds were all against us. We were still a good hundred yards from the *Comet*, and in our path stood a solid wall of the creatures. Even if we got free, they could outrace us to the goal. And with our limited strength, we could not hope to kill them all. In a minute or two, they would attack us again.

Somehow we must fight our way as long as we lasted. Perhaps they might be frightened. We threw ourselves at the side blocking us from our goal. The line gave perhaps a yard, then stiffened, and we found ourselves swallowed up in a thick cloud of brown smoke.

Poison gas! It must be shot out of their bodies, at a cost so great that it was kept as a last resort. Through the rolling vapor it was just possible to see our opponents, but they made no forward move. They were waiting for us to be overcome. Suppose their compound could eat through even our helio-beryllium? But it did not. We were safe.

"Stand still, Garth," I whispered, counting on the radio to carry my voice. "Let them think we're dead, and then give them a surprise."

"All right."

Long, long minutes . . . If only they did not know that it was the customary thing for a dead man to fall. . . . Slowly they began to move in.

Then Garth and I were upon them. They halted as if stupefied. We had hacked our way half through their mass. The rest fled, and we began running toward the *Comet*, praying that we might reach the ship before they could get organized again. How we floundered through the sand in wild and desperate haste.

Before we had covered half the distance, the pursuit began. There was no attempt to drag us down directly, but the two wings raced past to cut us off in front. At the base of the little cliff where the *Comet* lay, the circle closed.

"Jump," I called, and threw myself up over them toward the stone. Garth would have fallen back, but I caught his hand and pulled him to safety. We had won.

But had we? Joined by reinforcements from somewhere, the creatures were packed all around the base of the cliff and had begun to climb its walls, to cut us off from the ship. We rushed separately toward the two sides, and they backed away. But those in front were now established on the top. We stepped backward, and the whole line came on. But now we turned and ran for the *Comet*.

We were just able to turn again and clear them away with our swords. In a moment others would be climbing up from behind over the ship. And the door to safety was on a level with our heads.

There was just one chance. Stamping threateningly, we cleared the things out for ten feet in front of us. But once we turned our backs for a running start they were at us again.

"Boost you up, Dunal," said Garth, panting.

"No, you first."

But in the midst of my words, he almost threw me into the doorway. I turned to pull him up after me. They were around his legs, and one had jumped down upon his helmet. And he must have known it would happen.

"Go back to her," he cried, and slammed shut the door.

There was no time to help him, to interfere with the way of expiation he had chosen. I tried to look away, but a sort of fascination kept me watching him through the glass. He had been dragged to his knees. Then he was up again, whirling to keep them away on all sides in a mad, gallant fight. But the creatures knew it was the kill. Now they were around his knees, now up to his waist in their overpowering mass. It was only a matter of minutes.

Garth took a staggering step backward, dragging them all with him. He was facing me, and swung up his sword in the old Lunar salute. "Good luck, Dunal." The words, coming clearly over the radio, had a note of exaltation.

Then, flashing his blade over his head, he hurled it into the midst of the accursed things. With a tremendous effort, Garth tore the protecting helmet from his head, and plunged backward over the cliff. . . .

There was nothing to do but get in out of the lock and start for home, and little on the trip is worthy of recounting. Without unsurpassable difficulty, I was able to operate the machinery and steer, first for Betelguese, then for the sun. Counting on the warning bells to arouse me, I managed to get in snatches of sleep at odd intervals. At times the strain of the long watches was almost maddening.

By the time the midpoint had been passed, I was living in a sort of waking dream; or rather, a state of somnambulism. I ate; my hands moved the controls. And yet all the while my mind was wandering elsewhere—out to Garth's body under the blazing light of Rigel, back to the moon and Kelvar, or else in an unreal, shadowy world of dreams and vague memories.

With perfect mechanical accuracy I entered the solar system and adjusted the projectors for the sun's attraction. Running slower and slower, I watched Venus glide by. And then, gradually, everything faded, and I was walking along the great Nardos bridge with Kelvar. The ocean was so still that we could see mirrored in it the reflection of each white column, and our own faces peering down, and beyond that the stars.

"I shall bring you a handful for your hair," I told her, and leaned over farther, farther, reaching out. . . . Then I was falling, with Kelvar's face growing fainter, and in my ears a horrible ringing like the world coming to an end.

Just before I could strike the water, I wakened to find the alarm bell jangling and the object-indicator light flashing away. Through the telescope, the moon was large in the sky.

It was an hour, perhaps two, before I approached the sunlit

surface and hovered over the shore by Nardos. Try as I would, my sleep-drugged body could not handle the controls delicately enough to get the *Comet* quite in step with the moon's rotation. Always a little too fast or too slow. I slid down until I was only ten or fifteen feet off the ground that seemed to be moving out from under me. In another minute I should be above the water. I let everything go, and the *Comet* fell. There was a thud, a sound of scraping over the sand, a list to one side. I thought for an instant that the vessel was going to turn over, but with the weight of the reserve mercury in the fuel tanks it managed to right itself on a slope of ten or fifteen degrees.

From the angle, I could barely see out the windows, and everything looked strange. The water under the bridge seemed too low. The half-full Earth had greenish black spots on it. And the sky?

So dead with sleep that I could scarcely move, I managed to crane my neck around to see better. There was no sky, only a faint gray haze through which the stars shone. And yet the sun must be shining. I stretched still farther. There the sun burned, and around it was an unmistakable corona. It was like airless space.

Was I dreaming again?

With a jerk, I got to my feet and climbed up the sloping floor to the atmosphere tester. My fingers slipped off the stopcock, then turned it. And the air-pressure needle scarcely moved. It was true. Somehow, as the scientists had always told us would be the case eventually, the air of the moon, with so little gravity to hold it back, had evaporated into space.

But in six months? It was unthinkable. Surely someone had survived the catastrophe. Some people must have been able to keep themselves alive in caves where the last of the atmosphere would linger. Kelvar *must* be still alive. I could find her and bring her to the *Comet*. We would go to some other world.

Frantically, I pulled on my space suit and clambered through the airlock. I ran, until the cumbersome suit slowed me down to a staggering walk through the sand beside the Oceanus Procellarum.

Leaden and dull, the great sea lay undisturbed by the thin atmosphere still remaining. It had shrunk by evaporation far away from its banks, and where the water once had been there was a dark incrustation of impurities. On the land side, all was a great white plain of glittering alkali without a sign of vegetation. I went on toward Nardos the Beautiful.

Even from afar, I could see that it was desolate. Visible now that the water had gone down, the pillars supporting it rose gaunt and skeletal. Towers had fallen in, and the gleaming white was dimmed. It was a city of the dead, under an Earth leprous-looking with black spots where the clouds apparently had parted.

I came nearer to Nardos and the bridge, nearer to the spot where I had last seen Kelvar. Below the old water level, the columns showed a greenish stain, and halfway out the whole structure had fallen in a great gap. I reached the land terminus of the span, still glorious and almost beautiful in its ruins. Whole blocks of stone had fallen to the sand, and the adamantine pillars were cracked and crumbling with the erosion of ages.

Then I knew.

In our argument as to the possible speed of the *Comet*, Garth and I had both been right. In our reference frame, the vessel had put on an incredible velocity, and covered the nine-hundred-odd light-years around Rigel in six months. But from the viewpoint of the moon, it had been unable to attain a velocity greater than that of light. As the accelerating energy pressed the vessel's speed closer and closer toward that limiting velocity, the mass of the ship and of its contents had increased toward infinity. And trying to move laboriously with such vast mass, our clocks and bodies had been slowed down until to our leaden minds a year of moon time became equivalent to several hours.

The *Comet* had attained an average velocity of perhaps 175,000 miles per second, and the voyage that seemed to me six months had taken a thousand years. A thousand years! The words went ringing through my brain. Kelvar had been dead for a thousand years. I was alone in a world uninhabited for centuries.

I threw myself down and battered my head in the sand.

More to achieve, somehow, my own peace of mind, than in any hope of its being discovered, I have written this narrative. There are two copies, this to be placed in a helio-beryllium box at the terminus of the bridge, the other within the *Comet*. One at least should thus be able to escape the meteors which, unimpeded by the thin atmosphere, have begun to strike everywhere, tearing up great craters in the explosion that follows as a result of the impact.

My time is nearly up. Air is still plentiful on the *Comet*, but my provisions will soon run short. It is now slightly over a month since I collapsed on the sands into merciful sleep, and I possess food and water for perhaps another. But why go on in my terrible loneliness?

Sometimes I waken from a dream in which they are all so near—Kelvar, Garth, all my old companions—and for a moment I cannot realize how far away they are. Beyond years and years. And I, trampling back and forth over the dust of our old life, staring across the waste, waiting—for what?

No, I shall wait only until the dark. When the sun drops over the Grimaldi plateau, I shall put my manuscripts in their safe places, then tear off my helmet and join the other two.

An hour ago, the bottom edge of the sun touched the horizon.

Illustrated by H. W. Wesso

The Fifth-Dimension Catapult

By Murray Leinster

FOREWORD

THIS story has no normal starting place, because there are too many places where it might be said to begin. One might commence when Professor Denham, Ph.D., M.A., etc., isolated a metal that scientists have been talking about for many years without ever being able to smelt. Or it might start with his first experimental use of that metal with entirely impossible results. Or it might very

The globe leaped upward into the huge coil, which whirled madly.

plausibly begin with an interview between a celebrated leader of gangsters in the city of Chicago and a spectacled young laboratory assistant who had turned over to him a peculiar heavy object of solid gold and very nervously explained, and finally managed to prove, where it came from. With also impossible results, because it turned "King" Jacaro, lord of vice-resorts and rum-runners, into a passionate enthusiast in non-Euclidean geometry. The whole story might be said to begin with the moment of that interview.

But that leaves out Smithers, and especially it leaves out Tommy Reames. So, on the whole, it is best to take up the narrative at the moment of Tommy's first entrance into the course of events.

CHAPTER I

He came to a stop in a cloud of dust that swirled up to and all about the big roadster and surveyed the gate of the private road. The gate was rather impressive. At its top was a sign, "Keep Out!" Halfway down was another sign, "Private Property. Trespassers Will Be Prosecuted." On one gate-post was another notice, "Live Wires Within," and on the other a defiant placard, "Savage Dogs At Large Within This Fence."

The fence itself was all of seven feet high and made of the heaviest of woven-wire construction. It was topped with barbed wire, and went all the way down both sides of a narrow right of way until it vanished in the distance.

Tommy got out of the car and opened the gate. This fitted the description of his destination, as given him by a brawny, red-headed filling-station attendant in the village some two miles back. He drove the roadster through the gate, got out and closed it piously, got back in the car and shot it ahead.

He went humming down the narrow private road at forty-five miles an hour. That was Tommy Reames's way. He looked totally unlike the conventional description of a scientist of any sort—as much unlike a scientist as his sport roadster looked unlike a scientist's customary means of transit—and ordinarily he acted quite unlike one. As a matter of fact, most of the people Tommy associated with hadn't the faintest inkling of his taste for science as an avocation. There was Peter Dalzell, for instance, who would have held up his hands in holy horror at the idea of Tommy Reames's being the author of that article in the *Philosophical Journal*, "On the Mass and Inertia of the Tesseract," which had caused such a controversy.

And there was one Mildred Holmes—of no importance in the matter of the Fifth-Dimension Catapult—who would have lifted beautifully arched eyebrows in bored unbelief if anybody had suggested that Tommy Reames was that Thomas Reames whose

"Additions to Herglotz's Mechanics of Continua" produced such diversities of opinion in scientific circles. She intended to make Tommy propose to her some day, and thought she knew all about him. And everybody, everywhere, would have been incredulous of his present errand.

Gliding down the narrow, fenced-in road, Tommy was a trifle dubious about this errand himself. A yellow telegraph-form in his pocket read rather like a hoax, but was just plausible enough to have brought him away from a rather important tennis match. The telegram read:

PROFESSOR DENHAM IN EXTREME DANGER THROUGH EXPERIMENT BASED ON YOUR ARTICLE ON DOMINANT COORDINATES YOU ALONE CAN HELP HIM IN THE NAME OF HUMANITY COME AT ONCE.

> A. VON HOLTZ.

The fence went on past the car. A mile, a mile and a half of narrow lane, fenced in and made as nearly intruder-proof as possible.

"Wonder what I'd do," said Tommy Reames, "if another car came along from the other end?"

He deliberately tried not to think about the telegram any more. He didn't believe it. He couldn't believe it. But he couldn't ignore it, either. Nobody could; few scientists, and no human being with a normal amount of curiosity. Because the article on dominant coordinates had appeared in the *Journal of Physics* and had dealt with a state of things in which the normal coordinates of everyday existence were assumed to have changed their functions; when the coordinates of time, the vertical, the horizontal and the lateral changed places and a man went east to go up and west to go down and ran his street numbers in a fourth dimension. It was mathematical foolery, from one standpoint, but it led to some fascinating if abstruse conclusions.

But his brain would not remain away from the subject of the telegram, even though a chicken appeared in the fenced-in lane ahead of him and went flapping wildly on before the car. It rose in midair, the car overtook it as it rose above the level of the hood, and there was a rolling, squawking bundle of shedding feathers tumbling over and over along the hood until it reached the slanting windshield. There it spun wildly upward, left a cloud of feathers fluttering about Tommy's head, and fell still squawking into the road behind.

By the back-view mirror, Tommy could see it picking itself up and staggering dizzily back to the side of the road.

"My point was," said Tommy vexedly to himself, speaking of the article the telegram referred to, "that a man can only recognize three dimensions of space and one of time. So that if he got shot out of this cosmos altogether he wouldn't know the difference. He'd still seem to be in a three-dimensioned universe. And what is there in that stuff to get Denham in trouble?"

A house appeared ahead. A low, rambling sort of bungalow with a huge brick barn behind it. The house of Professor Denham, very certainly, and that barn was the laboratory in which he made his experiments.

Instinctively, Tommy stepped on the gas. The car leaped ahead. And then he was braking frantically. A pipe-framed gate with thinner, unpainted wire mesh filling its surface loomed before him, much too late for him to stop. There was a minor shock, a crashing and squeaking, and then a crash and shattering of glass. Tommy bent low as the top bar of the gate hit his windshield. The double glass cracked and crumpled and bent, but did not fly to bits. And the car came to a halt with its wheels intricately entangled in torn-away fence wire. The gate had been torn from its hinges and was draped rakishly over the roadster. A tire went flat with a loud hissing noise, and Tommy Reames swore softly under his breath and got out to inspect the damage.

He was deciding that nothing irreparable was wrong when a man came bursting out of the brick building behind the house. A tall, lean, youngish man who waved his arms emphatically and approached shouting, "You had no right to come in here! You must go away at once! You have damaged property! I will tell the Professor! You must pay for the damage! You must—"

"Damn!" said Tommy Reames. He had just seen that his radiator was punctured. A spout of ruddy, rusty water was pouring out on the grass.

The youngish man came up furiously. A pale young man, Tommy noticed. A young man with bristling, close-cropped hair and horn-rimmed spectacles before weak-looking eyes. His mouth was very full and very red, in marked contrast to the pallor of his cheeks.

"Did you not see the sign upon the gate?" he demanded angrily, in curiously stilted English. "Did you not see that trespassers are forbidden? You must go away at once! You will be prosecuted! You will be imprisoned! You—"

Tommy said irritably, "Are you Von Holtz? My name is Reames. You telegraphed me."

The waving, lanky arms stopped in the middle of an excited gesture. The weak-looking eyes behind the lenses widened. A pink tongue licked the too-full, too-red lips.

"Reames? The Herr Reames?" Von Holtz stammered. Then he said suspiciously, "But you are not—you cannot be the Herr Reames of the article on dominant coordinates!"

"I don't know why not," said Tommy annoyedly. "I'm also the Herr Reames of several other articles, such as on the mechanics of continua and the mass and inertia of the tesseract. And I believe the current *Philosophical Journal*—"

He surveyed the spouting red stream from the radiator and shrugged ruefully.

"I wish you'd telephone the village to have somebody come out and fix my car," he said shortly, "and then tell me if this telegram is a joke or not."

He pulled out a yellow form and offered it. He had taken an instinctive dislike to the lean figure before him, but suppressed the feeling.

Von Holtz took the telegram and read it, and smoothed it out, and said agitatedly, "But I thought the Herr Reames would be—would be a venerable gentleman! I thought—"

"You sent that wire," said Tommy. "It puzzled me just enough to make me rush out here. And I feel like a fool for having done it. What's the matter? Is it a joke?"

Von Holtz shook his head violently, even as he bit his lips.

"No! No!" he protested. "The Herr Professor Denham is in the most terrible, most deadly danger! I—I have been very nearly mad, Herr Reames. The Ragged Men may seize him! . . . I telegraphed to you. I have not slept for four nights. I have worked! I have racked my brains! I have gone nearly insane, trying to rescue the Herr Professor! And I—"

Tommy stared. "Four days?" he said. "The thing, whatever it is, has been going on for four days?"

"Five," said Von Holtz nervously. "It was only today that I thought of you. Herr Reames. The Herr Professor Denham had praised your articles highly. He said that you were the only man who would be able to understand his work. Five days ago—"

Tommy grunted. "If he's been in danger for five days," he said skeptically, "he's not in such a bad fix or it'd have been over. Will you phone for a repairman? Then we'll see what it's all about."

The lean arms began to wave again as Von Holtz said desperately, "But Herr Reames, it is urgent! The Herr Professor is in deadly danger!"

"What's the matter with him?"

"He is marooned," said Von Holtz. Again he licked his lips. "He is marooned, Herr Reames, and you alone—"

"Marooned?" said Tommy more skeptically still. "In the middle of New York State? And I alone can help him? You sound more and more as if you were playing a rather elaborate and not very funny practical joke. I've driven sixty miles to get here. What is the joke, anyhow?"

Von Holtz said despairingly, "But it is true, Herr Reames! He is marooned. He has changed his coordinates. It was an experiment. He is marooned in the fifth dimension!"

There was dead silence. Tommy Reames stared blankly. Then his gorge rose. He had taken an instinctive dislike to this lean young man, anyhow. So he stared at him, and grew very angry, and would undoubtedly have gotten into his car and turned it about and driven it away again if it had been in any shape to run. But it wasn't. One tire was flat, and the last ruddy drops from the radiator were dripping slowly on the grass. So he pulled out a cigarette case and lighted a cigarette and said sardonically, "The fifth dimension? That seems rather extreme. Most of us get along very well with three dimensions. Four seems luxurious. Why pick on the fifth?"

Von Holtz grew pale with anger in his turn. He waved his arms, stopped, and said with stiff formality, "If the Herr Reames will follow me into the laboratory I will show him Professor Denham and convince him of the Herr Professor's extreme danger."

Tommy had a sudden startling conviction that Von Holtz was in earnest. He might be mad, but he was in earnest. And there was undoubtedly a Professor Denham, and this was undoubtedly his home and laboratory.

"I'll look, anyway," said Tommy less skeptically. "But it is rather incredible, you know."

"It is impossible," said Von Holtz stiffly. "You are right, Herr Reames. It is quite impossible. But it is a fact."

He turned and stalked toward the big brick barn behind the house. Tommy went with him, wholly unbelieving and yet beginning to wonder if, just possibly, there was actually an emergency of a more normal and ghastly nature in being. Von Holtz might be a madman. He might . . .

Gruesome, grisly thoughts ran through Tommy's head. A madman dabbling in science might do incredible things, horrible things, and then demand assistance to undo an unimaginable murder. . . .

Tommy was tense and alert as Von Holtz opened the door of the barnlike laboratory. He waved the lean young man on ahead.

"After you," he said curtly.

He felt almost a shiver as he entered. But the interior of the laboratory displayed no gruesome scene. It was a huge, high-ceilinged room with a concrete floor. A monster dynamo stood in one corner, coupled to a matter-of-fact four-cylinder crude-oil engine, to which was also coupled by a clutch an inexplicable windlass-drum with several hundred feet of chain wrapped around it. There were ammeters and voltmeters on a control panel, and one of the most delicate of dynamometers on its own stand, and there were work benches and a motor-driven lathe and very complete equipment for the working of metals. And there was an electric furnace, with splashes of solidified metal on the floor beside it, and there was a miniature casting-floor, and at the far end of the monster room was a gigantic solenoid which evidently had once swung upon gymbals and just as evidently was now broken, because it lay toppled askew upon its supports.

The only totally unidentifiable piece of apparatus in the place was one queer contrivance at one side. It looked partly like a machine gun because of a long brass barrel projecting from it. But the brass tube came out of a bulging casing of cast aluminum, and there was no opening through which shells could be fed.

Von Holtz moved to that contrivance, removed a cap from the end of the brass tube, looked carefully into the opening, and waved stiffly for Tommy to look in.

Again Tommy was suspicious, watching until Von Holtz was some distance away. But the instant he put his eye to the end of the brass tube he forgot all caution, all suspicion, all his doubts. He forgot everything in his amazement.

There was a lens in the end of the brass tube. It was, in fact, nothing more or less than a telescope, apparently looking at something in a closed box. But Tommy was not able to believe that he looked at an illuminated miniature for even the fraction of a second. He looked into the telescope, and he was seeing out-of-doors. Through the aluminum casting that enclosed the end of the tube. Through the thick brick walls of the laboratory. He was gazing upon a landscape such as should not—such as could not—exist upon the earth.

There were monstrous, feathery tree-ferns waving languid fronds in a breeze that came from beyond them. The telescope seemed to be pointing at a gentle slope, and those tree-ferns cut off a farther view, but there was an impenetrable tangle of breast-high foliage between the instrument and that slope, and halfway up the incline there rested a huge steel globe.

Tommy's eyes fixed themselves upon the globe. It was man-made, of course. He could see where it had been bolted together. There were glassed-in windows in its sides, and there was a door.

As Tommy looked, that door opened partway, stopped as if someone within had hesitated, and then opened fully. A man came out. And Tommy said dazedly, "My God!"

Because the man was a perfectly commonplace sort of individual, dressed in a perfectly commonplace fashion, and he carried a perfectly commonplace briar pipe in his hand. Moreover, Tommy recognized him. He had seen pictures of him often enough, and he was Professor Edward Denham, entitled to put practically all the letters of the alphabet after his name, the author of "Polymerization of the Pseudo-Metallic Nitrides" and the proper owner of this building and its contents. But Tommy saw him against a background of tree-ferns such as should have been extinct upon this earth since the Carboniferous Period, some millions of years ago.

He was looking hungrily at his briar pipe. Presently he began to hunt carefully about on the ground. He picked together half a handful of brownish things which had to be dried leaves. He stuffed them into the pipe, struck a match, and lighted it. He puffed away gloomily, surrounded by wholly monstrous vegetation. A butterfly fluttered over the top of the steel globe. Its wings were fully a yard across. It flittered lightly to a plant and seemed to wait, and abruptly a vivid carmine blossom opened wide; wide enough to admit it.

Denham watched curiously enough, smoking the rank and plainly unsatisfying dried leaves. He turned his head and spoke over his shoulder. The door opened again. Again Tommy Reames was dazed. Because a girl came out of the huge steel sphere—and she was a girl of the most modern and most normal sort. A trim sport frock, slim silken legs, bobbed hair . . .

Tommy did not see her face until she turned, smiling, to make some comment to Denham. Then he saw that she was breathtakingly pretty. He swore softly under his breath.

The butterfly backed clumsily out of the gigantic flower. It flew lightly away, its many-colored wings brilliant in the sunshine. And the huge crimson blossom closed slowly.

Denham watched the butterfly go away. His eyes returned to the girl, who was smiling at the flying thing, now out of the field of vision of the telescope. And there was utter discouragement visible in every line of Denham's figure. Tommy saw the girl suddenly reach out her hand and put it on Denham's shoulder. She patted it, speaking in an evident attempt to encourage him. She smiled, and talked coaxingly, and presently Denham made a queer, arrested gesture and went heavily back into the steel globe. She followed him, though she looked wearily all about before the door closed behind her, and when Denham could not see her face, her expression was tired and anxious indeed.

Tommy had forgotten Von Holtz, had forgotten the laboratory, had forgotten absolutely everything. If his original suspicions of Von Holtz had been justified, he could have been killed half a dozen times over. He was oblivious to everything but the sight before his eyes.

Now he felt a touch on his shoulder and drew his head away with a jerk. Von Holtz was looking down at him, very pale, with his weak-looking eyes anxious.

"They are still all right?" he demanded.

"Yes," said Tommy dazedly. "Surely. Who is that girl?"

"That is the Herr Professor's daughter, Evelyn," said Von Holtz uneasily. "I suggest, Herr Reames, that you swing the dimensoscope about."

"The—what?" asked Tommy, still dazed by what he had seen.

"The dimensoscope. This." Von Holtz shifted the brass tube. The whole thing was mounted so that it could be swung in any direction. The mounting was exactly like that of a normal telescope. Tommy instantly put his eye to the eyepiece again.

He saw more tree-ferns, practically the duplicates of the background beyond the globe. Nothing moved save small, fugitive creatures among their fronds. He swung the telescope still farther. The landscape swept by before his eyes. The tree-fern forest drew back. He saw the beginning of a vast and noisome morass, over which lay a thick haze as of a stream raised by the sun. He saw something move in that morass; something huge and horrible with a long and snakelike neck and the tiniest of heads at the end of it. But he could not see the thing clearly.

He swung the telescope yet again. And he looked over miles and miles of level, haze-blanketed marsh. Here and there were clumps of taller vegetation. Here and there were steaming, desolate pools. And three or four times he saw monstrous objects moving about clumsily in the marsh-land.

But then a glitter at the skyline caught his eye. He tilted the telescope to see more clearly, and suddenly he caught his breath. There, far away at the very horizon, was a city. It was tall and gleaming and very strange. No earthly city ever flung its towers so splendidly high and soaring. No city ever built by man gave off the fiery gleam of gold from all its walls and pinnacles. It looked like an artist's dream, hammered out in precious metal, with its outlines softened by the haze of distance.

And something was moving in the air near the city. Staring, tense, again incredulous, Tommy Reames strained his eyes and saw that it was a machine. An aircraft; a flying machine of a type wholly unlike anything ever built on the planet Earth. It swept steadily and swiftly toward the city, dwindling as it went. It swooped downward toward one of the mighty spires of the city of golden gleams, and vanished.

It was with a sense of shock, of almost physical shock, that Tommy came back to realization of his surroundings to feel Von Holtz's hand upon his shoulder and to hear the lean young man saying harshly, "Well, Herr Reames? Are you convinced that I did not lie to you? Are you convinced that the Herr Professor Denham is in need of help?"

Tommy blinked dazedly as he looked around the laboratory again. Brick walls, an oil-spattered crude-oil engine in one corner, a concrete floor and an electric furnace and a casting-box . . .

"Why—yes . . . ," said Tommy dazedly. "Yes. Of course!" Clarity came to his brain with a jerk. He did not understand at all, but he believed what he had seen. Denham and his daughter were somewhere in some other dimension, yet within range of the extraordinary device he had looked through. And they were in trouble. So much was evident from their poses and their manner. "Of course," he repeated. "They're—there, wherever it is, and they can't get back. They don't seem to be in any imminent danger. . . ."

Von Holtz licked his lips. "The Ragged Men have not found them yet," he said in a hushed, harsh voice. "Before they went into the globe we saw the Ragged Men. We watched them. If they do find the Herr Professor and his daughter, they will kill them very slowly, so that they will take days of screaming agony to die. It is that that I am afraid of, Herr Reames. The Ragged Men roam the tree-fern forests. If they find the Herr Professor, they will trace each nerve to its root of agony until he dies. And we will be able only to watch. . . ."

CHAPTER II

"The thing is," said Tommy feverishly, "that we've got to find a way to get them back. Whether it duplicates Denham's results or not. How far away are they?"

"A few hundred yards, perhaps," said Von Holtz wearily, "or ten million miles. It is the same thing. They are in a place where the fifth dimension is the dominant coordinate."

Tommy was pacing up and down the laboratory. He stopped and looked through the eyepiece of the extraordinary vision apparatus. He tore himself away from it again.

"How does this thing work?" he demanded.

Von Holtz began to unscrew two wing-nuts which kept the top of the aluminum casting in place.

"It is the first piece of apparatus which Professor Denham made," he said precisely. "I know the theory, but I cannot duplicate it. Every dimension is at right angles to all other dimensions, of course. The Herr Professor has a note, here—"

He stopped his unscrewing to run over a heap of papers on the work bench—papers over which he seemed to have been poring desperately at the time of Tommy's arrival. He handed a sheet to Tommy, who read:

"If a creature who was aware of only two dimensions made two right-angled objects and so placed them that all the angles formed by the combination were right angles, he would contrive a figure represented by the corner of a box; he would discover a third dimension. Similarly, if a three-dimensioned man took three right angles and placed them so that all the angles formed were right angles, he would discover a fourth dimension. This, however, would probably be the time dimension, and to travel in time would instantly be fatal. But with four right angles he could discover a fifth dimension, and with five right angles he could discover a sixth. . . ."

Tommy Reames put down the paper impatiently.

"Of course!" he said brusquely. "I know all that stuff. But up to the present time nobody has been able to put together even three right angles, in practice."

Von Holtz had returned to the unscrewing of the wing-nuts. He lifted off the cover of the dimensoscope.

"It is the thing the Herr Professor did not confide to me," he said bitterly. "The secret. The one secret! Look in here."

Tommy looked. The objective-glass at the end of the telescope faced a mirror, which was inclined to its face at an angle of forty-five degrees. A beam of light from the objective would be reflected to a second mirror, twisted in a fashion curiously askew. Then the light would go to a third mirror. . . .

Tommy looked at that third mirror, and instantly his eyes ached. He closed them and opened them again. Again they stung horribly. It was exactly the sort of eyestrain which comes of looking through a lens which does not focus exactly, or through a strange pair of eyeglasses. He could see the third mirror, but his eyes hurt the instant they looked upon it, as if that third mirror were distorted in an impossible fashion. He was forced to draw them away. He could see, though, that somehow that third mirror would reflect his imaginary beam of light into a fourth mirror of which he could see only the edge. He moved his head—and still saw only the edge of a mirror. He was sure of what he saw, because he could look into the wavy, bluish translucency all glass shows upon its edge. He could even see the thin layer of silver backing. But he could not put himself into a position in which more than the edge of that mirror was visible.

"Good Lord!" said Tommy Reames feverishly. "That mirror—"

"A mirror at forty-five degrees," said Von Holtz precisely, "reflects light at a right angle. There are four mirrors, and each bends a ray of light through a right angle which is also a right angle to all the others. The result is that the dimensoscope looks into what is a fifth dimension, into which no man ever looked before. But I cannot move other mirrors into the positions they have in this instrument. I do not know how."

Tommy shook his head impatiently, staring at the so-simple, yet incredible device whose theory had been mathematically proven numberless times, but never put into practice before.

"Having made this device," said Von Holtz, "the Herr Professor constructed what he termed a catapult. It was a coil of wire, like the large machine there. It jerked a steel ball first vertically, then horizontally, then laterally, then in a fourth-dimensional direction, and finally projected it violently off in a fifth-dimensional path. He made small hollow steel balls and sent a butterfly, a small sparrow, and finally a cat into that other world. The steel balls opened of themselves and freed those creatures. They seemed to suffer no distress. Therefore he concluded that it would be safe for him to go, himself. His daughter refused to permit him to go alone, and he was so sure of his safety that he allowed her to enter the globe with him. She did. I worked the catapult which flung the globe in the fifth dimension, but his device for returning failed to operate. Hence he is marooned."

"But the big catapult—"

"Can you not see that the big catapult is broken?" demanded Von Holtz bitterly. "A special metal is required for the missing parts. That, I know how to make. Yes. I can supply that. But I cannot shape it! I cannot design the gears which will move it as it should be moved! I cannot make another dimensoscope. I cannot, Herr Reames, calculate any method of causing four right angles to be all at right angles to one another. It is my impossibility! It is for that that I have appealed to you. You see it has been done. I see that it is done. I can make the metal which alone can be moved in the necessary direction. But I cannot calculate any method of moving it in that direction! If you can do so, Herr Reames, we can perhaps save the Herr Professor Denham. If you cannot—Gott! The death he will die is horrible to think of!"

"And his daughter," said Tommy grimly. "His daughter, also."

He paced up and down the laboratory again. Von Holtz moved to the work bench from which he had taken Denham's note. There was a pile of such memoranda, thumbed over and over. And there were papers in the angular, precise handwriting which was Von Holtz's own, and calculations and speculations and the remains of frantic efforts to work out, somehow, the secret which as one manifestation had placed one mirror so that it hurt the eyes to look at it, and one other mirror so that from every angle of a normal existence, one could see only the edge.

"I have worked, Herr Reames," said Von Holtz drearily. "Gott! How I have worked! But the Herr Professor kept some things secret, and that so-essential thing is one of them."

Presently he said tiredly, "The dimension-traveling globe was built in this laboratory. It rested here." He pointed. "The Herr Professor was laughing and excited at the moment of departure. His daughter smiled at me through the window of the globe. There was an under-carriage with wheels upon it. You cannot see those wheels through the dimensoscope. They got into the globe and closed the door. The Herr Professor nodded to me through the glass window. The dynamo was running at its fullest speed. The laboratory smelled of hot oil, and of ozone from the sparks. I lifted my hand, and the Herr Professor nodded again, and I threw the switch. This switch, Herr Reames! It sparked as I closed it, and the flash partly blinded me. But I saw the globe rush toward the giant catapult yonder. It leaped upward into the huge coil, which whirled madly. Dazed, I saw the globe hanging suspended in midair, two feet from the floor. It shook! Once! Twice! With violence! Suddenly its outline became hazy and distorted. My eyes ached with looking at it. And then it was gone!"

Von Holtz's arms waved melodramatically. "I rushed to the dimensoscope and gazed through it into the fifth dimension. I saw the globe floating onward through the air, toward that bank of glossy ferns. I saw it settle and turn over, and then slowly right itself as it came to rest. The Herr Professor got out of it. I saw him, through the instrument which could look into the dimension into which he had gone. He waved his hand to me. His daughter joined him, surveying the strange cosmos in which they were. The Herr Professor plucked some of the glossy ferns, took photographs, then got back into the globe.

"I awaited its return to our own world. I saw it rock slightly as he worked upon the apparatus within. I knew that when it vanished from the dimensoscope it would have returned to our own universe. But it remained as before. It did not move. After three hours of anguished waiting, the Herr Professor came out and made signals to me of despair. By gestures, because no sound could come through the dimensoscope itself, he begged me to assist him. And I was helpless! Made helpless by the Herr Professor's own secrecy! For four days and nights I have toiled, hoping desperately to discover what the Herr Professor had hidden from me. At last I thought of you. I telegraphed to you. If you can assist me . . ."

"I'm going to try it, of course," said Tommy shortly.

He paced back and forth. He stopped and looked through the brass-tubed telescope. Giant tree-ferns, unbelievable but real. The steel globe resting partly overturned upon a bank of glossy ferns. Breast-high, incredible foliage between the point of vision and that extraordinary vehicle.

While Tommy had been talking and listening, while he had been away from the eyepiece, one or other of the occupants of the globe had emerged from it. The door was open. But now the girl came bounding suddenly through the ferns. She called, though it seemed to Tommy that there was a curious air of caution even in her calling. She was excited, hopefully excited.

Denham came out of the globe with a clumsy club in his hand. But Evelyn caught his arm and pointed up into the sky. Denham stared, and then began to make wild and desperate gestures as if trying to attract attention to himself.

Tommy watched for minutes, and then swung the dimensoscope around. It was extraordinary, to be sitting in the perfectly normal brick-walled laboratory, looking into a slender brass tube, and seeing another universe entirely, another wild and unbelievable landscape.

The tree-fern forest drew back, and the vast and steaming morass was again in view. There were distant bright golden gleams from the city. But Tommy was searching the sky, looking in the sky of a world in the fifth dimension for a thing which would make a man gesticulate hopefully.

He found it. It was an aircraft, startlingly close through the telescope. A single figure was seated at its controls, motionless as if bored, with exactly the air of a weary truck driver piloting a vehicle along a roadway he does not really see. And Tommy, being near enough to see the pilot's pose, could see the aircraft clearly. It was totally unlike a terrestrial airplane. A single huge and thick wing supported it. But the wing was angular and clumsy-seeming, and its form was devoid of the grace of an earthly aircraft wing, and there was no tail whatever to give it the appearance of a living thing. There was merely a long, rectangular wing with a framework beneath it, and a shimmering thing which was certainly not a screw propeller, but which seemed to draw it.

It moved on steadily and swiftly, dwindling in the distance, with its motionless pilot seated before a mass of corded bundles. It looked as if this were a freight plane of some sort, and therefore made in a strictly utilitarian fashion.

It vanished in the haze above the monster swamp, going in a straight line for the Golden City at the world's edge.

Tommy stared at it, long after it had ceased to be visible. Then he saw a queer movement on the earth near the edge of the morass. Figures were moving. Human figures. He saw four of them, shaking clenched fists and capering insanely, seeming to bellow insults after the oblivious and now invisible flying thing. He could see that they were nearly naked, and that one of them carried a spear. But the indubitable glint of metal was reflected from one of them for an instant, when some metal accouterment about him glittered in the sunlight.

They moved from sight behind thick, feathery foliage, and Tommy swung back the brass tube to see the globe again. Denham and his daughter were staring in the direction in which Tommy had seen those human figures. Denham clutched his clumsy club grimly. His face was drawn and his figure tensed. And suddenly Evelyn spoke quietly, and the two of them dived into the fern forest and disappeared. Minutes later they returned, dragging masses of tree-fern fronds with which they masked the globe from view. They worked hastily, desperately, concealing the steel vehicle from sight. And then Denham stared tensely all about, shading his eyes with his hand. He and the girl withdrew cautiously into the forest.

It was minutes later that Tommy was roused by Von Holtz's hand on his shoulder.

"What has happened, Herr Reames?" he asked uneasily. "The— Ragged Men?"

"I saw men," said Tommy briefly, "shaking clenched fists at an aircraft flying overhead. And Denham and his daughter have hidden the globe behind a screen of foliage."

Von Holtz licked his lips fascinatedly.

"The Ragged Men," he said in a hushed voice. "The Herr Professor called them that because they cannot be of the people who live in the Golden City. They hate the people of the Golden City. I think that they are bandits; renegades, perhaps. They live in the tree-fern forests and scream curses at the airships which fly overhead. And they are afraid of those airships."

"How long did Denham use this thing to look through, before he built his globe?"

Von Holtz considered. "Immediately it worked," he said at last, "he began work on a small catapult. It took him one week to devise exactly how to make that. He experimented with it for some days and began to make the large globe. That took nearly two months— the globe and the large catapult together. And also the dimensoscope was at hand. His daughter looked through it more than he did, or myself."

"He should have known what he was up against," said Tommy, frowning. "He ought to have taken guns, at least. Is he armed?"

Von Holtz shook his head. "He expected to return at once," he said desperately. "Do you see, Herr Reames, the position it puts me in? I may be suspected of murder! I am the Herr Professor's assistant. He disappears. Will I not be accused of having put him out of the way?"

"No," said Tommy thoughtfully. "You won't." He glanced through the brass tube and paced up and down the room. "You telephone for someone to repair my car," he said suddenly and abruptly. "I am going to stay here and work this thing out. I've got just the glimmering of an idea. But I'll need my car in running order, in case we have to go out and get materials in a hurry."

Von Holtz bowed stiffly and went out of the laboratory. Tommy looked after him, even moved to make sure he was gone. And then Tommy Reames went quickly to the work bench on which were the littered notes and calculations Von Holtz had been using, and which were now at his disposal. But Tommy did not leaf through them. He reached under the blotter beneath the whole pile. He had seen Von Holtz furtively push something out of sight, and he had disliked and distrusted Von Holtz from the beginning. Moreover, it was pretty thoroughly clear that Denham had not trusted him too much. A trusted assistant should be able to understand, at least, any experiment performed in a laboratory.

A folded sheet of paper came out. Tommy glanced at it:

You messed things up right! Denham marooned and you got nothing. No plans or figures either. When you get them, you get your money. If you don't you are out of luck. If this Reames guy can't fix up what you want it'll be just too bad for you.

There was no salutation nor any signature beyond a scrawled and sprawling "J."

Tommy Reames's jaw set grimly. He folded the scrap of paper and thrust it back out of sight again.

"Pretty!" he said harshly. "So a gentleman named 'J' is going to pay Von Holtz for plans or calculations it is hoped I'll provide! Which suggests—many things! But at least I'll have Von Holtz's help until he thinks my plans or calculations are complete. So that's all right. . . ."

Tommy could not be expected, of course, to guess that the note he had read was quite astounding proof of the interest taken in non-Euclidean geometry by a vice king of Chicago, or that the ranking beer baron of that metropolis was the man who was so absorbed in abstruse theoretic physics.

Tommy moved toward the great solenoid which lay askew upon its wrecked support. It had drawn the steel globe toward it, had made that globe vibrate madly, twice, and then go hazy and vanish. It had jerked the globe in each of five directions, each at right angles to all the others, and had released it when started in the fifth dimension. The huge coil was quite nine feet across and would take the steel globe easily. It was pivoted in concentric rings which made up a set of gimbals far more elaborate than were ever used to suspend a mariner's compass aboard ship.

There were three rings, one inside the other. And two rings will take care of any motion in three dimensions. These rings were pivoted, too, so that an unbelievably intricate series of motions could be given to the solenoid within them all. But the device was broken, now. A pivot had given away, and shaft and socket alike had vanished. Tommy became absorbed. Some oddity bothered him. . . .

He pieced the thing together mentally. And he exclaimed suddenly. There had been four rings of metal! One was gone! He comprehended, very suddenly. The third mirror in the dimensoscope was the one so strangely distorted by its position, which was at half of a right angle to all the dimensions of human experience. It was the third ring in the solenoid's supports which had vanished. And Tommy, staring at the gigantic apparatus and summoning all his theoretic knowledge and all his brain to work, saw the connection between the two things.

"The time dimension and the world-line," he said sharply, excited in spite of himself. "Revolving in the time dimension means telescoping in the world-line. . . . It would be a strain no matter could endure. . . ."

The mirror in the dimensoscope was not pointing in a fourth dimension. It did not need to. It was reflecting light at a right angle, and hence needed to be only at half of a right angle to the two courses of the beam it reflected. But to whirl the steel globe into a fifth dimension, the solenoid's support had for one instant to revolve in time! For the fraction of a second it would have literally to pass through its own substance. It would be required to undergo precisely the sort of strain involved in turning a hollow seamless metal globe inside out! No metal could stand such a strain. No form of matter known to man could endure it.

"It would explode!" said Tommy excitedly to himself, alone in the great bare laboratory. "Steel itself would vaporize! It would wreck the place!"

And then he looked blank. Because the place had very obviously not been wrecked. And yet a metal ring had vanished, leaving no trace. . . .

Von Holtz came back. He looked frightened.

"A—a repairman, Herr Reames," he said, stammering, "is on the way. And—Herr Reames . . ."

Tommy barely heard him. For a moment, Tommy was all scientist, confronted with the inexplicable, yet groping with a blind certainty toward a conclusion he very vaguely foresaw. He waved his hand impatiently. . . .

"The Herr Jacaro is on the way here," stammered Von Holtz.

Tommy blinked, remembering that Von Holtz had told him he could make a certain metal, the only metal which could be moved in the fourth dimension.

"Jacaro?" he said blankly.

"The—friend of the Herr Professor Denham. He advanced the money for the Herr Professor's experiments."

Tommy heard him with only half his brain, though that half instantly decided that Von Holtz was lying. The only Jacaro Tommy knew of was a prominent gangster from Chicago, who had recently cemented his position in Chicago's underworld by engineering the amalgamation of two once-rival gangs. Tommy knew, in a vague fashion, that Von Holtz was frightened, that he was terrified in some way. And that he was inordinately suspicious of someone, and filled with a queer desperation.

"Well?" said Tommy abstractedly. The thought he needed was coming. A metal which would have full tensile strength up to a certain instant, and then disrupt itself without violence into a gas, a vapor . . . It would be an alloy, perhaps. It would be . . .

He struck at his own head with his clenched fist, angrily demanding that his brain bring forth the thought that was forming slowly. The metal that could be revolved in time without producing a disastrous explosion and without requiring an impossible amount of power . . .

He did not see Von Holtz looking in the eyepiece of the dimensoscope. He stared at nothing, thinking concentratedly, putting every bit of energy into sheer thought. And suddenly, like the explosion he sought a way to avoid, the answer came, blindingly clear.

He surveyed that answer warily. A tremendous excitement filled him.

"I've got it!" he said softly to himself. "By God, I know how he did the thing!"

And as if through a mist the figure of Von Holtz became clear before his eyes. Von Holtz was looking into the dimensoscope tube. He was staring into that other, extraordinary world in which Denham and his daughter were marooned. And Von Holtz's face was utterly, deathly white, and he was making frantic, repressed gestures, and whispering little whimpering phrases to himself. They were unintelligible, but the deathly pallor of his cheeks, and the fascinated, dribbling fullness of his lips brought Tommy Reames suddenly down to earth.

"What's happening?" demanded Tommy sharply.

Von Holtz did not answer. He made disjointed, moaning little exclamations to himself. He was twitching horribly as he looked through the telescope into that other world. . . .

Tommy flung him aside and clapped his own eye to the eyepiece. And then he groaned.

The telescope was pointed at the steel globe upon that ferny bank, no more than a few hundred yards away but two dimensions removed from Earth. The screening mass of tree fronds had been torn away. A swarm of ragged, half-naked men was gathered about the globe. They were armed with spears and clubs, in the main, but there were other weapons of intricate design whose uses Tommy could not even guess at. He did not try. He was watching the men as they swarmed about and over the steel sphere. Their faces were brutal and savage, and now they were distorted with an insane hate. It was the same awful, gibbering hatred he had sensed in the caperings of the four he had seen bellowing vituperation at an airplane.

They were not savages. Somehow he could not envision them as primitive. Their features were hard-bitten, seamed with hatred and with vice unspeakable. And they were white. The instant impression any man would have received was that here were broken men; fugitives, bandits, assassins. Here were renegades or worse from some higher, civilized race.

They battered hysterically upon the steel globe. It was not the attack of savages upon a strange thing. It was the assault of desperate, broken men upon a thing they hated. A glass pane splintered and crashed. Spears were thrust into the opening, while mouths opened as if in screams of insane fury. And then, suddenly, the door of the globe flew wide.

The Ragged Men did not wait for anyone to come out. They fought each other to get into the opening, their eyes glaring madly, filled with the lust to kill.

CHAPTER III

A battered and antiquated flivver came chugging down the wire-fenced lane to the laboratory, an hour later. It made a prodigious din, and Tommy Reames went out to meet it. He was still a little pale. He had watched the steel globe turned practically inside out by the Ragged Men. He had seen them bringing out cameras, cushions, and even the padding of the walls, to be torn to bits in a truly maniacal fury. But he had not seen one sign of a human being killed. Denham and his daughter had not been in the globe when it was found and ransacked. So far, then, they were probably safe. Tommy had seen them vanish into the tree-fern forest. They had been afraid, and with good reason. What dangers they might encounter in the fern forest he could not guess. How long they would escape the search of the Ragged Men, he could not know. How he could ever hope to find them if he succeeded in duplicating Denham's dimension-traveling apparatus he could not even think of, just now. But the Ragged Men were not searching the fern forest. So much was sure. They were encamped by the steel sphere, and a scurvy-looking lot they were.

Coming out of the brick laboratory, Tommy saw a brawny figure getting out of the antiquated flivver whose arrival had been so thunderous. That brawny figure nodded to him and grinned. Tommy recognized him. The red-headed, broad-shouldered filling-station attendant in the last village, who had given him specific directions for reaching this place.

"You hit that gate a lick, didn't you?" asked the erstwhile filling-station attendant amiably. "Mr. Von Holtz said you had a flat and a busted radiator. That right?"

Tommy nodded. The red-headed man walked around the car, scratched his chin, and drew out certain assorted tools. He put them on the grass with great precision, pumped a gasoline blow-torch to pressure, and touched a match to its priming-basin, and while the gasoline flamed smokily he made a half-dozen casual movements with a file, and the broken radiator tube was exposed for repair.

He went back to the torch and observed placidly, "The Professor ain't around, is he?"

Tommy shook his head.

"Thought not," said the red-headed one. "He gen'rally comes out and talks a while. I helped him build some of them dinkuses in the barn yonder."

Tommy said eagerly, "Say, which of those things did you help him build? That big thing with the solenoid—the coil?"

"Yeah. How'd it work?" The red-headed one set a soldering iron in place and began to jack up the rear wheel to get at the tire. "Crazy idea, if you ask me. I told Miss Evelyn so. She laughed and said she'd be in the ball when it was tried. Did it work?"

"Too damn well," said Tommy briefly. "I've got to repair that solenoid. How about a job helping?"

The red-headed man unfastened the lugs of the rim, kicked the tire speculatively, and said, "Gone to hell." He put on the spare tire with ease and dispatch.

"Um," he said. "How about that Mr. Von Holtz? Is he goin' to boss the job?"

"He is not," said Tommy, with a shade of grimness in his tone.

The red-headed man nodded and took the soldering iron in hand. He unwound a strip of wire solder, mended the radiator tube with placid ease, and seemed to bang the cooling-flanges with a total lack of care. They went magically back into place, and it took close inspection to see that the radiator had been damaged.

"She's all right," he observed. He regarded Tommy impersonally. "Suppose you tell me how come you horn in on this," he suggested, "an' maybe I'll play. That guy Von Holtz is a crook, if you ask me about him."

Tommy ran his hand across his forehead, and told him.

"Um," said the red-headed man calmly. "I think I'll go break Mr. Von Holtz's neck. I got me a hunch."

He took two deliberate steps forward. But Tommy said, "I saw Denham not an hour ago. So far, he's all right. How long he'll be all right is a question. But I'm going after him."

The red-headed man scrutinized him exhaustively.

"Um. I might try that myself. I kinda like the Professor. An' Miss Evelyn. My name's Smithers. Let's go look through the dinkus the Professor made."

They went together into the laboratory. Von Holtz was looking through the dimensoscope. He started back as they entered, and looked acutely uneasy when he saw the red-headed man.

"How do you do," he said nervously. "They—the Ragged Men—have just brought in a dead man. But it is not the Herr Professor."

Without a word, Tommy took the brass tube in his hand. Von Holtz moved away, biting his lips. Tommy stared into that strange other world.

The steel sphere lay as before, slightly askew upon a bank of glossy ferns. But its glass windows were shattered, and fragments of everything it had contained were scattered about. The Ragged Men had made a camp and built a fire. Some of them were roasting meat—the huge limb of a monstrous animal with a scaly, reptilian hide. Others were engaged in vehement argument over the body of one of their number, lying sprawled out upon the ground.

Tommy spoke without moving his eyes from the eyepiece. "I saw Denham with a club just now. This man was killed by a club."

The Ragged Men in the other world debated acrimoniously. One of them pointed to the dead man's belt, and spread out his hands. Something was missing from the body. Tommy saw, now, three or four other men with objects that looked rather like policemen's truncheons, save that they were made of glittering metal. They were plainly weapons. Denham, then, was armed—if he could understand how the weapon was used.

The Ragged Men debated, and presently their dispute attracted the attention of a man with a huge black beard. He rose from where he sat gnawing at a piece of meat and moved grandly toward the disputatious group. They parted at his approach, but a single member continued the debate against even the bearded giant. The bearded one plucked the glittering truncheon from his belt. The disputatious one gasped in fear and flung himself desperately forward. But the bearded man kept the truncheon pointed steadily. . . . The man who assailed him staggered, reached close enough to strike a single blow, and collapsed. The bearded man pointed the metal truncheon at him as he lay upon the ground. He heaved convulsively, and was still.

The bearded man went back to his seat and picked up the gnawed bit of meat again. The dispute had ceased. The chattering group of men dispersed.

Tommy was about to leave the eyepiece of the instrument when a movement nearby caught his eye. A head peered cautiously toward the encampment. A second rose beside it. Denham and his daughter Evelyn. They were apparently no more than thirty feet from the dimensoscope. Tommy could see them talking cautiously, saw Denham lift and examine a metal truncheon like the bearded man's, and force his daughter to accept it. He clutched a club, himself, with a grim satisfaction.

Moments later they vanished quietly in the thick fern foliage, and though Tommy swung the dimensoscope around in every direction, he could see nothing of their retreat.

He rose from that instrument with something approaching hopefulness. He'd seen Evelyn very near and very closely. She did not look happy, but she did look alert rather than worn. And Denham was displaying a form of competence in the face of danger which was really more than would have been expected in a Ph.D., an M.A., and other academic distinctions running to most of the letters of the alphabet.

"I've just seen Denham and Evelyn again," said Tommy crisply. "They're safe so far. And I've seen one of the weapons of the Ragged

Men in use. If we can get a couple of automatics and some cartridges to Denham, he'll be safe until we can repair the big solenoid."

"There was the small catapult," said Von Holtz bitterly, "but it was dismantled. The Herr Professor saw me examining it, and he dismantled it. So that I did not learn how to calculate the way of changing the position—"

Tommy's eyes rested queerly on Von Holtz for a moment. "You know how to make the metal required," he said suddenly. "You'd better get busy making it. Plenty of it. We'll need it."

Von Holtz stared at him, his weak eyes almost frightened. "You *know?* You know how to combine the right angles?"

"I think so," said Tommy. "I've got to find out if I'm right. Will you make the metal?"

Von Holtz bit at his too-red lips. "But Herr Reames!" he said stridently, "I wish to know the equation! Tell me the method of pointing a body in a fourth or a fifth direction. It is only fair—"

"Denham didn't tell you," said Tommy.

Von Holtz's arms jerked wildly.

"But I will not make the metal! I insist upon being told the equation! I insist upon it! I will not make the metal if you do not tell me!"

Smithers was in the laboratory, of course. He had been surveying the big solenoid-catapult and scratching his chin reflectively. Now he turned.

But Tommy took Von Holtz by the shoulders. And Tommy's hands were the firm and sinewy hands of a sportsman, if his brain did happen to be the brain of a scientist. Von Holtz writhed in his grip.

"There is only one substance which could be the metal I need, Von Holtz," he said gently. "Only one substance is nearly three-dimensional. Metallic ammonium! It's known to exist, because it makes a mercury amalgam, but nobody has been able to isolate it because nobody has been able to give it a fourth dimension—duration in time. Denham did it. You can do it. And I need it, and you'd better set to work at the job. You'll be very sorry if you don't, Von Holtz!"

Smithers said with a vast calmness. "I got me a hunch. So if y'want his neck broke . . ."

Tommy released Von Holtz, and the lean young man gasped and sputtered and gesticulated wildly in a frenzy of rage.

"He'll make it," said Tommy coldly. "Because he doesn't dare not to!"

Von Holtz went out of the laboratory, his weak-looking eyes staring and wild, and his mouth working.

"He'll be back," said Tommy briefly. "You've got to make a small model of that big catapult, Smithers. Can you do it?"

"Sure," said Smithers. "The ring'll be copper tubing, with pin-bearings. Wind a coil on the lathe. It'll be kinda rough, but it'll do. But gears, now . . ."

"I'll attend to them. You know how to work that metallic ammonium?"

"If that's what it was," agreed Smithers. "I worked it for the Professor."

Tommy leaned close and whispered, "You never made any gears of that. But did you make some springs?"

"Uh-huh!"

Tommy grinned joyously.

"Then we're set and I'm right! Von Holtz wants a mathematical formula, and no one on earth could write one, but we don't need it!"

Smithers rummaged around the laboratory with a casual air, acquired this and that and the other thing, and set to work with an astounding absence of waste motions. From time to time he inspected the great catapult thoughtfully, verified some impression, and went about the construction of another part.

And when Von Holtz did not return, Tommy hunted for him. He suddenly remembered hearing his car motor start. He found his car missing. He swore, then, and grimly began to hunt for a telephone in the house. But before he had raised central he heard the deep-toned purring of the motor again. His car was coming swiftly back to the house. And he saw, through a window, that Von Holtz was driving it.

The lean young man got out of it, his face white with passion. He started for the laboratory. Tommy intercepted him.

"I—went to get materials for making the metal," said Von Holtz hoarsely, repressing his rage with a great effort. "I shall begin at once, Herr Reames."

Tommy said nothing whatever. Von Holtz was lying. Of course. He carried nothing in the way of materials. But he had gone away from the house, and Tommy knew as definitely as if Von Holtz had told him, that Von Holtz had gone off to communicate in safety with someone who signed his correspondence with a J.

Von Holtz went into the laboratory. The four-cylinder motor began to throb at once. The whine of the dynamo arose almost immediately after. Von Holtz came out of the laboratory and dived into a shed that adjoined the brick building. He remained in there.

Tommy looked at the trip register on his speedometer. Like most people with methodical minds, he had noted the reading on arriving at a new destination. Now he knew how far Von Holtz had gone. He had been to the village and back.

"Meaning," said Tommy grimly to himself, "that the J who wants plans and calculations is either in the village or at the end of a long-distance wire. And Von Holtz said he was on the way. He'll probably turn up and try to bribe me."

He went back into the laboratory and put his eye to the eyepiece of the dimensoscope. Smithers had his blowtorch going and was busily accumulating an apparently unrelated series of discordant bits of queerly shaped metal. Tommy looked through at the strange, mad world he could see through the eyepiece.

The tree-fern forest was still. The encampment of the Ragged Men was nearly quiet. Sunset seemed to be approaching in this other world, though it was still bright outside the laboratory. The hours of day and night were obviously not the same in the two worlds, so close together that a man could be flung from one to the other by a mechanical contrivance.

The sun seemed larger, too, than the orb which lights our normal earth. When Tommy swung the vision instrument about to search for it, he found a great red ball quite four times the diameter of our own sun, neatly bisected by the horizon. Tommy watched, waiting for it to sink. But it did not sink straight downward as the sun seems to do in all temperate latitudes. It descended, yes, but it moved along the horizon as it sank. Instead of a direct and forthright dip downward, the sun seemed to progress along the horizon, dipping more deeply as it swam. And Tommy watched it blankly.

"It's not our sun. . . . But it's not our world. Yet it revolves, and there are men on it. And a sun that size would bake the earth. . . . And it's sinking at an angle that would only come at a latitude of—"

That was the clue. He understood at once. The instrument through which he regarded the strange world looked out upon the polar regions of that world. Here, where the sun descended slantwise, were the high latitudes, the coldest spaces upon all the whole planet. And if here there were the gigantic growths of a carboniferous era, the tropic regions of this planet must be literal infernos.

And then he saw that in its gradual descent the monster sun was going along behind the Golden City, and the outlines of its buildings, the magnificence of its spires, were limned clearly for him against the dully glowing disk.

Nowhere upon earth had such a city ever been dreamed of. No man had ever envisioned such a place, where far-flung arches interconnected soaring, towering columns, where curves of perfect grace were united in forms of utterly perfect proportion. . . .

The sunlight died, and dusk began and deepened, and vividly brilliant stars began to come out overhead, and Tommy suddenly searched the heavens eagerly for familiar constellations. And found not one. All the stars were strange. These stars seemed larger and much more near than the tiny pinpoints that blink down upon our earth.

And then he swung the instrument again and saw great fires roaring and the Ragged Men crouched about them. Within them, rather, because they had built fires about themselves as if to make a wall of flame. And once Tommy saw twin, monstrous eyes gazing from the blackness of the tree-fern forest. They were huge eyes, and they were far apart, so that the head of the creature who used them must have been enormous. And they were all of fifteen feet above the ground when they speculatively looked over the ring of fires and the ragged, degraded men within them. Then that creature, whatever it was, turned away and vanished.

But Tommy felt a curious shivering horror of the thing. It had moved soundlessly, without a doubt, because not one of the Ragged Men had noted its presence. It had been kept away by the fires. But Denham and Evelyn were somewhere in the tree-fern forest, and they would not dare to make fires. . . .

Tommy drew away from the dimensoscope, shivering. He had been looking only, but the place into which he looked was real, and the dangers that lay hidden there were very genuine, and there was a man and a girl of his own race and time struggling desperately, without arms or hope, to survive.

Smithers was casually fitting together an intricate array of little rings made of copper tubing. There were three of them, and each was fitted into the next largest by pins which enabled them to spin noiselessly and swiftly at the touch of Smithers's finger. He had them spinning now, each in a separate direction, and the effect was bewildering.

As Tommy watched, Smithers stopped them, oiled the pins carefully, and painstakingly inserted a fourth ring. Only this ring was of a white metal that looked somehow more pallid than silver. It had a whiteness like that of ivory beneath its metallic gleam.

Tommy blinked. "Did Von Holtz give you that metal?" he asked suddenly.

Smithers looked up and puffed at a short brown pipe. "Nope. There was some splashes of it by the castin' box. I melted 'em together an' run a ring. Pressed it to shape; y' can't hammer this stuff. It goes to water and dries up quicker'n lightning—an' you hold y'nose an' run. I used it before for the Professor."

Tommy went over to him excitedly. He picked up the little contrivance of many concentric rings. The big motor was throbbing rhythmically, and the generator was humming at the back of the laboratory. Von Holtz was out of sight.

With painstaking care Tommy went over the little device. He looked up.

"A coil?"

"I wound one," said Smithers calmly. "On the lathe. Not so hot, but it'll do, I guess. But I can't fix these rings like the Professor did."

"I think I can," said Tommy crisply. "Did you make some wire for springs?"

"Yeah!"

Tommy fingered the wire. Stout, stiff, and surprisingly springy wire of the same peculiar metal. It was that metallic ammonium which chemists have deduced must exist because of the chemical behavior of the compound NH but which Denham alone had managed to procure. Tommy deduced that it was an allotropic modification of the substance which forms an amalgam with mercury, as metallic tin is an allotrope of the amorphous gray powder which is tin in its normal, stable state.

He set to work with feverish excitement. For one hour, for two, he worked. At the end of that time he was explaining the matter curtly to Smithers, so intent on his work that he wholly failed to hear a motor car outside or to realize that it had also grown dark in this world of ours.

"You see, Smithers, if a two-dimensioned creature wanted to

adjust two right angles at right angles to each other, he'd have them laid flat, of course. And if he put a spring at the far ends of those right angles—they'd look like a T, put together—so that the cross-bar of that T was under tension, he'd have the equivalent of what I'm doing. To make a three-dimensioned figure, that imaginary man would have to bend one side of the cross-bar up. As if the two ends of it were under tension by a spring, and the spring would only be relieved of tension when that cross-bar was bent. But the vertical would be his time dimension, so he'd have to have something thin, or it couldn't be bent. He'd need something 'thin in time.'

"We have the same problem. But metallic ammonium is 'thin in time.' It's so fugitive a substance that Denham is the only man ever to secure it. So we use these rings and adjust these springs to them so they're under tension which will only be released when they're all at right angles to each other. In our three dimensions that's impossible, but we have a metal that can revolve in a fourth, and we reinforce their tendency to adjust themselves by starting them off with a jerk. We've got 'em flat. They'll make a good stiff jerk when they try to adjust themselves. And the solenoid's a bit eccentric—"

"Shut up!" snapped Smithers suddenly.

He was facing the door, bristling. Von Holtz was in the act of coming in, with a beefy, broad-shouldered man with blue jowls. Tommy straightened up, thought swiftly, and then smiled grimly.

"Hullo, Von Holtz," he said pleasantly. "We've just completed a model catapult. We're all set to try it out. Watch!"

He set a little tin can beneath the peculiar device of copper-tubing rings. The can was wholly ordinary, made of thin sheet-iron plated with tin as are all the tin cans of commerce.

"You have the catapult remade?" gasped Von Holtz. "Wait! Wait! Let me look at it!"

For one instant, and one instant only, Tommy let him see. The massed set of concentric rings, each one of them parallel to all the others. It looked rather like a flat coil of tubing; certainly like no particularly obscure form of projector. But as Von Holtz's weak eyes fastened avidly upon it, Tommy pressed the improvised electric switch. At once that would energize the solenoid and release all the tensed springs from their greater tension, for an attempt to reach a permanent equilibrium.

As Von Holtz and the blue-jowled man stared, the little tin can leaped upward into the tiny coil. The small copper rings twinkled one within the other as the springs operated. The tin can was wrenched this way and that, then for the fraction of a second hurt the eyes that gazed upon it—and it was gone! And then the little coil came spinning down to the work bench top from its broken bearings and the remaining copper rings spun aimlessly for a moment. But the third ring of whitish metal had vanished utterly, and so had the coiled-wire springs which Von Holtz had been unable to distinguish. And there was an overpowering smell of ammonia in the room.

Von Holtz flung himself upon the still-moving little instrument. He inspected it savagely, desperately. His full red lips drew back in a snarl.

"How did you do it?" he cried shrilly. "You must tell me! I—I—I will kill you if you do not tell me!"

The blue-jowled man was watching Von Holtz. Now his lips twisted disgustedly. He turned to Tommy and narrowed his eyes.

"Look here," he rumbled. "This fool's no good! I want the secret of that trick you did. What's your price?"

"I'm not for sale," said Tommy, smiling faintly.

The blue-jowled man regarded him with level eyes.

"My name's Jacaro," he said after an instant. "Maybe you've heard of me. I'm from Chicago."

Tommy smiled more widely. "To be sure," he admitted. "You were the man who introduced machine guns into gang warfare, weren't you? Your gunmen lined up half a dozen of the Buddy Haines gang against a wall and wiped them out, I believe. What do you want this secret for?"

The level eyes narrowed. They looked suddenly deadly.

"That's my business," said Jacaro briefly. "You know who I am. And I want that trick y'did. I got my own reasons. I'll pay for it. Plenty. You know I got plenty to pay, too. Or else—"

"What?"

"Something'll happen to you," said Jacaro briefly. "I ain't sayin' what. But it's damn likely you'll tell what I want to know before it's finished. Name your price an' be damn quick!"

Tommy took his hand out of his pocket. He had a gun in it.

"The only possible answer to that," he said suavely, "is to tell you to go to hell. Get out! But Von Holtz stays here. He'd better!"

CHAPTER IV

Within half an hour after Jacaro's leaving, Smithers was in the village, laying in a stock of supplies and sending telegrams that Tommy had written out for transmission. Tommy sat facing an ashen Von Holtz and told him pleasantly what would be done to him if he failed to make the metallic ammonium needed to repair the big solenoid. In an hour Smithers was back, reporting that Jacaro was also sending telegrams but that he, Smithers, had stood over the telegraph operator until his own messages were transmitted. He brought back weapons, too—highly illegal things to have in New York State, where a citizen is only law-abiding when defenseless. And then four days of hectic, sleepless labor began.

On the first day one of Tommy's friends drove in in answer to a telegram. It was Peter Dalzell, with men in uniform apparently festooned about his car. He announced that a placard, warning passersby of smallpox within, had been added to the decorative signs upon the gate, and stared incredulously at the interior of the big brick barn. Tommy grinned at him and gave him plans and specifications of a light steel globe in which two men might be transported into the fifth dimension by a suitably operating device. Tommy had sat up all night drawing those plans. He told Dalzell just enough of what he was up against to enlist Dalzell's enthusiastic cooperation without permitting him to doubt Tommy's sanity. Dalzell had known Tommy as an amateur tennis player, but not as a scientist.

He marveled, refused to believe his eyes when he looked through the dimensoscope, and agreed that the whole thing had to be kept secret or the rescue expedition would be prevented from starting by the incarceration of both Tommy and Smithers in comfortable insane asylums. He feigned to admire Von Holtz, deathly white and nearly frantic with a corroding rage, and complimented Tommy on his taste for illegality. He even asked Von Holtz if he wanted to leave, and Von Holtz snarled insults at him. Von Holtz was beginning to work at the manufacture of metallic ammonium.

It was an electrolytic process, of course. Ordinarily, when—say— ammonium chloride is broken down by an electric current, ammonium is deposited at the cathode and instantly becomes a gas which dissolves in the water or bubbles up to the surface. With a mercury cathode, it is dissolved and becomes a metallic amalgam, which also breaks down into gas with much bubbling of the mercury. But Denham had worked out a way of delaying the breaking-down, which left him with a curiously white, spongy mass of metal which could be carefully melted down and cast, but not under any circumstances violently struck or strained.

Von Holtz was working at that. On the second day he delivered, snarling, a small ingot of the white metal. He was imprisoned in the lean-to shed in which the electrolysis went on. But Tommy had more than a suspicion that he was in communication with Jacaro.

"Of course," he said dryly to Smithers, who had expressed his doubts, "Jacaro had somebody sneak up and talk to him through the walls, or maybe through a bored hole. While there's a hope of finding out what he wants to know through Von Holtz, Jacaro won't try anything. Not anything rough, anyhow. We mustn't be bumped off while what we are doing is in our heads alone. We're safe enough—for a while."

Smithers grumbled.

"We need that ammonium," said Tommy, "and I don't know how to make it. I bluffed that I could, and in time I might, but it would need time and meanwhile Denham needs us. Dalzell is going to send a plane over today, with word of when we can expect our own globe. We'll try to have the big catapult ready when it comes. And the plane will drop some extra supplies. I've ordered a submachine gun. Handy when we get over there in the tree-fern forests. Right now, though, we need to be watching. . . ."

Because they were taking turns looking through the dimensoscope. For signs of Denham and Evelyn. And Tommy was finding himself thinking wholly unscientific thoughts about Evelyn, since a pretty girl in difficulties is, of all possible things, the one most likely to make a man romantic.

In the four days of their hardest working, he saw her three times. The globe was wrecked and ruined. Its glass was broken out and its interior ripped apart. It had been pillaged so exhaustively that there was no hope that whatever device had been included in its design, for its return, remained even repairably intact. That device had not worked, to be sure, but Tommy puzzled sometimes over the fact that he had seen no mechanical device of any sort in the plunder that had been brought out to be demolished. But he did not think of those things when he saw Evelyn.

The Ragged Men's encampment was gone, but she and her father lingered furtively, still near the pillaged globe. The first day Tommy saw her, she was still blooming and alert. The second day she was paler. Her clothing was ripped and torn, as if by thorns. Denham had a great raw wound upon his forehead, and his coat was gone and half his shirt was in ribbons. Before Tommy's eyes they killed a nameless small animal with the truncheonlike weapon Evelyn carried. And Denham carted it triumphantly off into the shelter of the tree-fern forest. But to Tommy that shelter began to appear extremely dubious.

That same afternoon some of the Ragged Men came suspiciously to the globe and inspected it, and then vented a gibbering rage upon it with blows and curses. They seemed half-mad, these men. But then, all the Ragged Men seemed a shade less than sane. Their hatred for the Golden City seemed the dominant emotion of their existence.

And when they had gone, Tommy saw Denham peering cautiously from behind a screening mass of fern. And Denham looked sick at heart. His eyes lifted suddenly to the heavens, and he stared off into the distance again, and then he regarded the heavens again with an expression that was at once of the utmost wistfulness and the uttermost of despair.

Tommy swung the dimensoscope about and searched the skies of that other world. He saw the flying machine, and it was a swallow-winged device that moved swiftly, and now soared and swooped in abrupt short circles almost overhead. Tommy could see its pilot, leaning out to gaze downward. He was no more than a hundred feet up, almost at the height of the tree-fern tops. And the pilot was moving too swiftly for Tommy to be able to focus accurately upon his face, but he could see him as a man, an indubitable man in no fashion distinguishable from the other men of this earth. He was scrutinizing the globe as well as he could without alighting.

He soared upward, suddenly, and his plane dwindled as it went toward the Golden City.

And then, inevitably, Tommy searched for the four Ragged Men who had inspected the globe a little while since. He saw them, capering horribly behind a screening of verdure. They did not shake their clenched fists at the flying machine. Instead, they seemed filled with a ghastly mirth. And suddenly they began to run frantically for the far distance, as if bearing news of infinite importance.

And when he looked back at Denham, it seemed to Tommy that he wrung his hands before he disappeared.

But that was the second day of the work upon our own world, and just before sunset there was a droning in the earthly sky above the laboratory, and Tommy ran out, and somebody shot at him from a patch of woodland a quarter of a mile away from the brick building. Isolated as Denham's place was, the shot would go unnoticed. The bullet passed within a few feet of Tommy, but he paid no attention. It was one of Jacaro's watchers, no doubt, but Jacaro did not want Tommy killed. So Tommy waited until the plane swooped low—almost to the level of the laboratory roof—and a thickly padded package thudded to the ground. He picked it up and darted back into the laboratory as other bullets came from the patch of woodland.

"Funny," he said dryly to Smithers, inside the laboratory again; "they don't dare kill me—yet—and Von Holtz doesn't dare leave or refuse to do what I tell him to do; and yet they expect to lick us."

Smithers growled. Tommy was unpacking the wrapped package. A grim, blued-steel thing came out of much padding. Boxes tumbled after it.

"Submachine gun," said Tommy, "and ammunition. Jacaro and his little pals will try to get in here when they think we've got the big solenoid ready for use. They'll try to get it before we can use it. This will attend to them."

"An' get us in jail," said Smithers calmly, "for forty-'leven years."

"No," said Tommy, and grinned. "We'll be in the fifth dimension. Our job is to fling through the catapult all the stuff we'll need to make another catapult to fling us back again."

"It can't be done," said Smithers flatly.

"Maybe not," agreed Tommy, "especially since we ruin all our springs and one gimbal ring every time we use the thing. But I've got an idea. I'll want five coils with hollow iron cores, and the whole works shaped like this, with two holes bored so. . . ."

He sketched. He had been working on the idea for several days, and the sketch was ready in his mind to be transferred to paper.

"What you goin' to do?"

"Something crazy," said Tommy. "A mirror isn't the only thing that changes angles to right ones."

"You're the doctor," said the imperturbable Smithers.

He set to work. He puzzled Tommy sometimes, Smithers did. So far he hadn't asked how much his pay was going to be. He'd worked unintermittently. He had displayed a colossal, a tremendous calmness. But no man could work as hard as Smithers did without some powerful driving-force. It was on the fourth day that Tommy learned what it was.

The five coils had been made, and Tommy was assembling them with an extraordinary painstaking care behind a screen, to hide what he was doing. He'd discovered a peep-hole bored through the brick wall from the lean-to where Von Holtz worked. He was no longer locked in there. Tommy abandoned the pretense of imprisonment after finding an automatic pistol and a duplicate key to the lock in Von Holtz's possession. He'd had neither when he was theoretically locked up, and Tommy laughed.

"It's a farce, Von Holtz," he said dryly, "this pretending you'll run away. You're here spying now, for Jacaro. Of course. And you don't dare harm either of us until you find out from me what you can't work out for yourself, and know I have done. How much is Jacaro going to pay you for the secret of the catapult, Von Holtz?"

Von Holtz snarled. Smithers moved toward him, his hands closing and unclosing. Von Holtz went gray with terror.

"Talk!" said Smithers.

"A—a million dollars," said Von Holtz, cringing away from the brawny red-headed man.

"It would be interesting to know what use it would be to him," said Tommy dryly. "But to earn that million you have to learn what we know. And to learn that, you have to help us do it again, on the scale we want. You won't run away. So I shan't bother to lock you up hereafter. Jacaro's men come and talk to you at night, don't they?"

Von Holtz cringed again. It was an admission.

"I don't want to have to kill any of them," said Tommy pleasantly, "and we'll all be classed as mad if this thing gets out. So you go and talk to them in the lane when you want to, Von Holtz. But if any of them come near the laboratory, Smithers and I will kill them, and if Smithers is hurt I'll kill you; and I don't imagine Jacaro wants that, because he expects you to build another catapult for him. But I warn you, if I find another gun on you I'll thrash you."

Von Holtz's pallor changed subtly from the pallor of fear to the awful lividness of rage.

"You—*Gott!* You dare threaten—" He choked upon his own fury.

"I do," said Tommy. "And I'll carry out the threat."

Smithers moved forward once more.

"Mr. Von Holtz," he said in a very terrible steadiness, "I aim to kill you some time. I ain't done it yet because Mr. Reames says he needs you a while. But I know you got Miss Evelyn marooned off in them fern-woods on purpose! And—God knows she wouldn't ever look at me, but—I aim to kill you some time!"

His eyes were flames. His hands closed and unclosed horribly. Von Holtz gaped at him, shocked out of his fury into fear again. He went unsteadily back to his lean-to. And Smithers went back to the dimensoscope. It was his turn to watch that other world for signs of Denham and Evelyn, and for any sign of danger to them.

Tommy adjusted the screen before the bench on which he was working, so Von Holtz could not see his task, and went back to work. It was a rather intricate task he had undertaken, and before the events of the past few days he would have said it was insane. But now he was taking it quite casually.

Presently he said, "Smithers."

Smithers did not look away from the brass tube.

"Yeah?"

"You're thinking more about Miss Denham than her father."

Smithers did not reply for a moment. Then he said, "Well? What if I am?"

"I am, too," said Tommy quietly. "I've never spoken to her, and I daresay she's never even heard of me, and she certainly has never seen me, but—"

Smithers said with a vast calmness, "She'll never look at me, Mr. Reames. I know it. She talks to me, an' laughs with me, but she's never sure-'nough looked at me. An' she never will. But I got the right to love her."

Tommy nodded very gravely.

"Yes. You have. So have I. And so, when that globe comes, we both get into it with what arms and ammunition we can pack in, and go where she is, to help her. I intended to have you work the switch and send me off. But you can come, too."

Smithers was silent. But he took his eyes from the dimensoscope eyepiece and regarded Tommy soberly. Then he nodded and turned back. And it was a compact between the two men that they should serve Evelyn, without any rivalry at all.

Tommy went on with his work. The essential defect in the catapult Denham had designed was the fact that it practically had to be rebuilt after each use. And, moreover, the metallic ammonium was so fugitive a substance that it was hard to keep. Once it had been strained by working, it gradually adverted to a gaseous state and was lost. And while he still tried to keep the little catapult in a condition for use, he was at no time sure that he could send a pair of automatics and ammunition through in a steel box at any moment that Denham came close enough to notice a burning smoke-fuse attached.

But he was working on another form of catapult entirely, now. In this case he was using hollow magnets placed at known angles to each other. And they were so designed that each one tended to adjust its own hollow bore at right angles to the preceding one, and each one would take any moving, magnetic object and swing it through four successive right angles into the fifth dimension.

He fitted the first magnet on twin rods of malleable copper, which also would carry the current which energized the coil. He threaded the second upon the same twin supports. When the current was passed through the two of them, the magnetic field itself twisted the magnets, bending the copper supports and placing the magnets in their proper relative positions. A third magnet on the same pair of rods, and a repetition of the experiment, proved the accuracy of the idea. And since this device, like the dimensoscope, required only a forty-five-degree angle to our known dimensions, instead of a right angle as the other catapult did, Tommy was able to work with ordinary and durable materials. He fitted on the last two coils and turned on the current for his final experiment. And as he watched, the twin three-eighths-inch rods twisted and writhed in the grip of the intangible magnetic force. They bent, and quivered, and twisted. . . . And suddenly there seemed to be a sort of inaudible *snap*, and one of the magnets hurt the eyes that looked at it, and only the edge of the last of the series was visible.

Tommy drew in his breath sharply.

"Now we try it," he said tensely. "I was trying to work this as the mirrors of the dimensoscope were fitted. Let's see."

He took a long piece of soft-iron wire and fed it into the hollow of the first magnet. He saw it come out and bend stiffly to enter the hollow of the second. It required force to thrust it through. It went still more stiffly into the third magnet. It required nearly all his strength to thrust it on, and on. . . . The end of it vanished. He pushed two feet or more of it beyond the last place where it was visible. It went into the magnet that hurt one's eyes. After that it could not be seen.

Tommy's voice was strained. "Swing the dimensoscope, Smithers," he ordered. "See if you can see the wire. The end of it should be in the other world."

It seemed an age, an eon, that Smithers searched. Then, "Move it," he said.

Tommy obeyed.

"It's there," said Smithers evenly. "Two or three feet of it."

Tommy drew a deep, swift breath of relief.

"All right!" he said crisply. "Now we can fling anything we need through there, when our globe arrives. We can build up a dump of supplies, all sent through just before we slide through in the globe."

"Yeah," said Smithers. "Uh—Mr. Reames. There's a bunch of Ragged Men in sight, hauling something heavy behind them. I don't know what it's all about."

Tommy went to the brass tube and stared through it. The tree-fern forest, drawing away in the distance. The vast and steaming morass. The glittering city, far, far in the distance.

And then a mob of the Ragged Men, hauling at some heavy thing. They were a long way off. Some of them came capering on ahead, and Tommy swung the dimensoscope about to see Denham and Evelyn dart for cover and vanish amid the tree-ferns. Denham was as ragged as the Ragged Men, by now, and Evelyn's case was little better.

Frightened for them, Tommy swung the instrument about again. But they had not been seen. The leaders who ran gleefully on ahead were merely in haste. And they were followed more slowly by burly men and lean ones, whole men and limping men, who hauled frantically on long ropes of hide, dragging some heavy thing behind them. Tommy saw it only indistinctly as the filthy, nearly naked bodies moved. But it was an intricate device of a golden-colored metal, and it rested upon the crudest of possible carts. The wheels were sections of tree trunks, pierced for wooden axles. The cart itself was made of the most roughly hewed of timbers. And there were fifty or more of the Ragged Men who dragged it.

The men in advance now attacked the underbrush at the edge of the forest. They worked with a maniacal energy, clearing away the long fern fronds while they capered and danced and babbled excitedly.

Irrelevantly, Tommy thought of escaped galley slaves. Just such hard-bitten, vice-ridden men as these, and filled with just such a mad, gibbering hatred of the free men they had escaped from. Certainly these men had been civilized once. As the golden-metal device came nearer, its intricacy was the more apparent. No savages could utilize a device like this one. And there was a queer deadliness in the very grace of its outlines. It was a weapon of some sort, but whose nature Tommy could not even guess.

And then he caught the gleam of metal also in the fern-forest. On the ground. In glimpses and in fragments of glimpses between the swarming naked bodies of the Ragged Men, he pieced together a wholly incredible impression. There was a roadway skirting the edge of the forest. It was not wide; not more than fifteen feet at most. But it was a solid roadbed of metal! The dull silver-white of aluminum gleamed from the ground. Two or more inches thick and fifteen feet wide, there was a seamless ribbon of aluminum that vanished behind the tree-ferns on either side.

The intricate device of golden metal was set up, now, and a shaggy, savage-seeming man mounted beside it grinning. He manipulated its levers and wheels with an expert's assurance. And Tommy saw repairs upon it. Crude repairs, with crude materials, but expertly done. Done by the Ragged Men, past doubt, and so demolishing any idea that they came of a savage race.

"Watch here, Smithers," said Tommy grimly.

He set to work upon the little catapult after Denham's design. His own had seemed to work, but the other was more sure. This would be an ambush the Ragged Men were preparing, and of course they would be preparing it for men of the Golden City. The plane had sighted Denham's steel globe. It had hovered overhead, and carried news of what it had seen to the Golden City. And here was a roadway that must have been made by the folk of the Golden City at some time or another. Its existence explained why Denham remained nearby. He had been hoping that along its length would travel some vehicle containing civilized people to whom he could signal and ultimately explain his plight. And, being near the steel globe, his narrative would have its proofs at hand.

And now it was clear that the Ragged Men expected some ground vehicle, too. They were preparing for it. They were setting a splendid ambush, with a highly treasured weapon they ordinarily kept hidden. Their triumphant hatred could apply to nothing else than an expectation of inflicting injury on men of the Golden City.

So Tommy worked swiftly on the catapult. A new little ring of metallic ammonium was ready, and so were the necessary springs. The Ragged Men would lay their ambush. The men of the Golden City might enter it. They might. But the aviator who had spotted the globe would have seen the shredded contents of the sphere about. He would have known the Ragged Men had found it. And the men who came in a ground vehicle from the Golden City should be expecting just such an ambush as was being laid.

There would be a fight, and Tommy, somehow, had no doubt that the men of the Golden City would win. And when they had cleared the field he would fling a smoking missile through the catapult. The victors should see it and should examine it. And though writing would serve little purpose, they should at least recognize it as written communication in a language other than their own. And mathematical diagrams would certainly be lucid, and proof of a civilized man sending the missile, and photographs. . . .

The catapult was ready, and Tommy prepared his message-carrying projectile. He found snapshots and included them. He tore out a photograph of Evelyn and her father, which had been framed above a work bench in the laboratory. He labored, racking his brain for a means of conveying the information that the globe was of any other world. . . . And suddenly he had an idea. A cord attached to his missile would lead to nothingness from either world, yet one end would be in that other world, and the other end in this. A wire would be better. Tugs upon it would convey the idea of living beings nearby but invisible. The photograph would identify Denham and his daughter as associated with the phenomenon and competent to explain it. . . .

Tommy worked frantically to get the thing ready. He almost prayed that the men of the Golden City would be victors, would find his little missile when the fray was over, and would try to comprehend it. . . .

All he could do was try.

Then Smithers said, from the dimensoscope, "They're all set, Mr. Reames. Y'better look."

Tommy stared through the eyepiece. Strangely, the golden weapon had vanished. All seemed to be exactly as before. The cleared-away underbrush was replaced. Nothing was in any way changed from the normal in that space upon a mad world. But there was a tiny movement and Tommy saw a Ragged Man. He was lying prone upon the earth. He seemed either to hear or see something, because his lips moved as he spoke to another invisible man beside him, and his expression of malevolent joy was horrible.

Tommy swung the tube about. Nothing. . . . But suddenly he saw swiftly moving winkings of sunlight from the edge of the tree-fern forest. Something was moving in there, moving with lightning swiftness along the fifteen-foot roadway of solid aluminum. It drew nearer, and more near. . . .

The carefully camouflaged ambuscade was fully focused and Tommy was watching tensely when the thing happened.

He saw glitterings through the tree fronds come to a smoothly decelerated stop. There was a pause; and suddenly the underbrush fell flat. As if a single hand had smitten it, it wavered, drooped, and lay prone. The golden weapon was exposed, with its brawny and horribly grinning attendant. For one-half a split-second Tommy saw the wheeled thing in which half a dozen men of the Golden City were riding. It was graceful and streamlined and glittering. There was a platform on which the steel sphere would have been mounted for carrying away.

But then there was a sudden intolerable light as the men of the Golden City reached swiftly for peculiar weapons beside them. The light came from the crudely mounted weapon of the Ragged Men, and it was an unbearable actinic glare. For half a second, perhaps, it persisted, and died away to a red flame which leaped upward and was not.

Then the vehicle from the Golden City was a smoking, twisted ruin. Four of the six men in it were blasted, blackened crisps. Another staggered to his feet, struggled to reach a weapon and could not lift it, and twitched a dagger from his belt and fell forward; and Tommy could see that his suicide was deliberate.

The last man, alone, was comparatively unharmed by the blast of light. He swept a pistol-like contrivance into sight. It bore swiftly upon the now surging, yelling horde of Ragged Men. And one—two —three of them seemed to scream convulsively before they were trampled under by the rest.

But suddenly there were a myriad little specks of red all over the body of the man at bay. The pistol-like thing dropped from his grasp as his whole hand became encrimsoned. And then he was buried beneath the hating, blood-lusting mob of the forest men.

CHAPTER V

An hour later, Tommy took his eyes away from the dimensoscope eyepiece. He could not bear to look any longer.

"Why don't they kill him?" he demanded sickly, filled with a horrible, a monstrous rage. "Oh, why don't they kill him?"

He felt maddeningly impotent. In another world entirely, a mob of half-naked renegades had made a prisoner. He was not dead, that solely surviving man from the Golden City. He was bound, and the Ragged Men guarded him closely, and his guards were diverting themselves unspeakably by small tortures, minor tortures, horribly painful but not weakening. And they capered and howled with glee when the bound man writhed.

The prisoner was a brave man, though. Helpless as he was, he presently flung back his head and set his teeth. Sweat stood out in great droplets upon his body and upon his forehead. And he stilled his writhings and looked at his captors with a grim and desperate defiance.

The guards made gestures which were all too clear, all too luridly descriptive of the manner of death which awaited him. And the man of the Golden City was ashen and hopeless and utterly despairing—and yet defiant.

Smithers took Tommy's place at the eyepiece of the instrument. His nostrils quivered at what he saw. The vehicle from the Golden City was being plundered, of course. Weapons from the dead men were being squabbled over, even fought over. And the Ragged Men fought as madly among themselves as if in combat with their enemies. The big golden weapon on its cart was already being dragged away to its former hiding place. And somehow, it was clear that those who dragged it away expected and demanded that the solitary prisoner not be killed until their return.

It was that prisoner, in the agony which was only the beginning of his death, who made Smithers's teeth set tightly.

"I don't see the Professor or Miss Evelyn," said Smithers in a vast calmness. "I hope to Gawd they—don't see this."

Tommy swung on his heel, staring and ashen.

"They were near," he said stridently. "I saw them! They saw what

happened in the ambush! They'll—they'll see that man tortured!"
Smithers's hand closed and unclosed.

"Maybe the Professor'll have sense enough to take Miss Evelyn—
uh—where she—can't hear," he said slowly, his voice level. "I hope
so."

Tommy flung out his hands desperately.

"I want to help that man!" he cried savagely. "I want to do
something! I saw what they promised to do to him. I want to—to kill
him, even! It would be mercy!"

Smithers said, with a queer, stilly shock in his voice, "I see the
Professor now. He's got that gun-thing in his hand. . . . Miss
Evelyn's urging him to try to do something. . . . He's looking at the
sky. . . . It'll be a long time before it's dark. . . . He's gone back
out of sight. . . ."

"If we had some dynamite," said Tommy desperately, "we could
take a chance on blowing ourselves to bits and try to fling it through
and into the middle of those devils. . . ."

He was pacing up and down the laboratory, harrowed by the fate
of that gray-faced man who awaited death by torture; filled with a
wild terror that Evelyn and her father would try to rescue him and be
caught to share his fate; racked by his utter impotence to do more
than watch. . . .

Then Smithers said thickly, "God!"

He stumbled away from the eyepiece. Tommy took his place,
dry-throated with terror. He saw the Ragged Men laughing uproari-
ously. The bearded man who was their leader was breaking the arms
and legs of the prisoner so that he would be helpless when released
from the stake to which he was bound. And if ever human beings
looked like devils out of hell, it was at that moment. The method of
breaking the bones was excruciating. The prisoner screamed. The
Ragged Men rolled upon the ground in their maniacal mirth.

And then a man dropped, heaving convulsively, and then another,
and still another. . . . The grim, gaunt figure of Denham came out of
the tree-fern forest, the queer small golden-metal truncheon in his
hand. A fourth man dropped before the Ragged Men quite realized
what had happened. The fourth man himself was armed—and a
flashing slender body came plunging from the forest and Evelyn
flung herself upon the still-heaving body and plucked away that
weapon.

Tommy groaned, in the laboratory in another world. He could not look away, and yet it seemed that the heart would be torn from his body by that sight. Because the Ragged Men had turned upon Denham with a concentrated ferocity, somehow knowing instantly that he was more nearly akin to the men of the Golden City than to them. But at sight of Evelyn, her garments rent by the thorns of the forest, her white body gleaming through the largest tears, they seemed to go mad. And Tommy's eyes, glazing, saw the look on Denham's face as he realized that Evelyn had not fled, but had followed him in his desperate and wholly hopeless effort.

Then the swarming mass of Ragged Men surged over the two of them. Buried them under reaching, hating, lusting fiends who fought even among themselves to be first to seize them.

Then there was only madness, and Denham was bound beside the man of the Golden City, and Evelyn was the center of a fighting group which was suddenly flung aside by the bearded giant, and the encampment of the Ragged Men was bedlam. And somehow Tommy knew with a terrible clarity that a man of the Golden City to torture was bliss unimaginable to these half-mad enemies of that city. But a woman—

He turned from the instrument, three-quarters out of his head. He literally did not see Von Holtz gazing furtively in the doorway. His eyes were fixed and staring. It seemed that his brain would burst.

Then he heard his own voice saying with an altogether unbelievable steadiness, "Smithers! They've got Evelyn. Get the submachine gun."

Smithers cried out hoarsely. His face was not quite human, for an instant. But Tommy was bringing the work bench on which he had installed his magnetic catapult, close over by the dimensoscope.

"This cannot work," he said in the same incredible calmness. "Not possibly. It should not work. It will not work. But it has to work!"

He was clamping the catapult to a piece of heavy timber.

"Put the gun so it shoots into the first magnet," he said steadily. "The magnet windings shouldn't stand the current we've got to put into them. They've got to."

Smithers's fingers were trembling and unsteady. Tommy helped him, not looking through the dimensoscope at all.

"Start the dynamo," he said evenly—and marveled foolishly at the voice that did not seem to belong to him at all, talking so steadily and so quietly. "Give me all the juice you've got. We'll cut out this rheostat."

He was tightening a vise which would hold the deadly little weapon in place while Smithers got the crude-oil engine going and accelerated it recklessly to its highest speed. Tommy flung the switch. Rubber insulation steamed and stank. He pulled the trigger of the little gun for a single shot. The bullet flew into the first hollow magnet, just as he had beforehand thrust an iron wire. It vanished. The series of magnets seemed unharmed.

With a peculiar, dreamlike steadiness, Tommy put his hand where an undeflected bullet would go through it. He pressed the trigger again. He felt a tiny breeze upon his hand. But the bullet had been unable to elude the compound-wound magnets, each of which now had quite four times the designed voltage impressed upon its coils.

Tommy flung off the switch.

"Work the gun," he ordered harshly. "When I say fire, send a burst of shots through it. Keep the switch off except when you're actually firing, so—God willing—the coils don't burn out. Fire!"

He was gazing through the dimensoscope. Evelyn was struggling helplessly while two Ragged Men held her arms, grinning as only devils could have grinned, and others squabbled and watched with a fascinated attention some cryptic process which could only be the drawing of lots. . . .

Tommy saw, and paid no attention. The machine gun beside him rasped suddenly. He saw a tree-fern frond shudder. He saw a gaping, irregular hole where a fresh frond was uncurling. Tommy put out his hand to the gun.

"Let me move it, bench and all," he said steadily. "Now try it again. Just a burst."

Again the gun rasped. And the earth was kicked up suddenly where the bullets struck in that other world. The little steel-jacketed missiles were deflected by the terribly overstrained magnets of the catapult, but their energy was not destroyed. It was merely altered in direction. Fired within the laboratory upon our own and normal world, the bullets came out into the world of tree-ferns and monstrous things. They came out, as it happened, sidewise instead of point first, which was due to some queer effect of dimension change upon an object moving at high velocity. Because of that, they ricocheted much more readily, and where they struck they made a much more ghastly wound. But the first two bursts caused no effect at all. They were not even noticed by the Ragged Men. The noise of the little gun was thunderous and snarling in the laboratory, but in the world of the fifth dimension there was no sound at all.

"Like this," said Tommy steadily. "Just like this. . . . Now fire!"

He had tilted the muzzle upward. And then with a horrible grim intensity he traversed the gun as it roared.

And it was butchery. Three Ragged Men were cut literally to bits before the storm of bullets began to do real damage. The squabbling group, casting lots for Evelyn, had a swath of dead men in its midst before snarls begun had been completed.

"Again," said Tommy coldly. "Again, Smithers, again!"

And again the little gun roared. The burly bearded man clutched at his throat—and it was a gory horror. A Thing began to run insanely. It did not even look human any longer. It stumbled over the leader of the Ragged Men and died as he had done. The bullets came tumbling over themselves erratically. They swooped and curved and dispersed themselves crazily. Spinning as they were, at right angles to their line of flight, their trajectories were incalculable and their impacts were grisly.

The little gun fired ten several bursts, aimed in a desperate cold-bloodedness, before the smell of burnt rubber became suddenly overpowering and the rasping sound of an electric arc broke through the rumbling of the crude-oil engine in the back.

Smithers sobbed.

"Burnt out!"

But Tommy waved his hand.

"I think," he said savagely, "that maybe a dozen of them got away. Evelyn's staggering toward her father. She'll turn him loose. That prisoner's dead, though. Didn't mean to shoot him, but those bullets flew wild."

He gave Smithers the eyepiece. Sweat was rolling down his forehead in great drops. His hands were trembling uncontrollably.

He paced shakenly up and down the laboratory, trying to shut out of his own sight the things he had seen when the bullets of his own aiming literally splashed into the living flesh of men. He had seen Ragged Men disemboweled by those spinning, knifelike projectiles. He had turned a part of the mad world of that other dimension into a shambles, and he did not regret it because he had saved Evelyn, but he wanted to shut out the horror of seeing what he had done.

"But now," he said uncertainly to himself, "they're no better off, except they've got weapons. . . . If that man from the Golden City hadn't been killed. . . ."

He was looking at the magnetic catapult, burned out and useless. His eyes swung suddenly to the other one. Just a little while since he had made ready a missile to be thrown through into the other world by that. It contained snapshots, and diagrams, and it was an attempt to communicate with the men of the Golden City without any knowledge of their language.

"But—I can communicate with Denham!"

He began to write feverishly. If he had looked out of the laboratory window, he would have seen Von Holtz running like a deer, waving his arms jerkily, and—when out of earshot of the laboratory—shouting loudly. And Von Holtz was carrying a small black box which Tommy would have identified instantly as a motion picture camera, built for amateurs but capable of taking pictures indoors and with a surprisingly small amount of light. And if Tommy had listened, he might possibly have heard the beginnings of those shoutings to men hidden in a patch of woodland about a quarter of a mile away. The men, of course, were Jacaro's, waiting either until Von Holtz had secured the information that was wanted, or until an assault in force upon the laboratory would net them a catapult ready for use—to be examined, photographed, and duplicated at leisure.

But Tommy neither looked nor listened. He wrote feverishly, saying to Smithers at the dimensoscope, "Denham'll be looking around to see what killed those men. When he does, we want to be ready to shoot a smoke-bomb through to him, with a message attached."

Smithers made a gesture of no especial meaning save that he had heard. And Tommy went on writing swiftly, saying who he was and what he had done, and that another globe was being built so that he and Smithers could come with supplies and arms to help. . . .

"He's lookin' around now, Mr. Reames," said Smithers quietly. "He's picked up a ricocheted bullet an' is staring at it."

The crude-oil engine was running at a thunderous rate. Tommy fastened his note in the little missile he had made ready. He placed it under the solenoid of the catapult after Denham's design, with the springs and rings of metallic ammonium. He turned to Smithers.

"I'll watch for him," said Tommy unsteadily. "You know, watch for the right moment to fling it through. Slow up the generator a little. It'll rack itself to pieces."

He put his eye to the eyepiece. He winced as he saw again what the bullets of his aiming had done. But he saw Denham almost at once. And Denham was scratched and bruised and looked very far indeed from the ideal of a professor of theoretic physics, with hardly more than a few shreds of clothing left upon him, and a ten-days' beard upon his face. He limped as he walked. But he had stopped in the task of gathering up weapons to show Evelyn excitedly what it was that he had found. A spent and battered bullet, but indubitably a bullet from the world of his own ken. He began to stare about him, hopeful yet incredulous.

Tommy took his eye from the dimensoscope just long enough to light the fuse of the smoke-bomb.

"Here it goes, Smithers!"

He flung the switch. The missile with its thickly smoking fuse leaped upward as the concentric rings flickered and whirled bewilderingly. The missile hurt the eyes that watched it. It vanished. The solenoid dropped to the floor from the broken small contrivance.

Then Tommy's heart stood still as he gazed through the eyepiece again. He could see nothing but an opaque milkiness. But it drifted away, and he realized that it was smoke. More, Denham was staring at it. More yet, he was moving cautiously toward its source, one of the strange golden weapons held ready. . . .

Denham was investigating.

The generator at the back of the laboratory slowed down. Smithers was obeying orders. Tommy hung close by the vision instrument, his hands moving vaguely and helplessly, as one makes gestures without volition when anxious for someone else to duplicate the movements for which he sets the example.

He saw Denham, very near, inspecting the smoking thing on the ground suspiciously. The smoke-fuse ceased to burn. Denham stared. After an age-long delay, he picked up the missile Tommy had prepared. And Tommy saw that there was a cord attached to it. He had fastened that cord when planning to try to communicate with the men of the Golden City, when he had expected them to be victorious.

But he saw Denham's face light up with pathetic hope. He called to Evelyn. He hobbled excitedly to her, babbling. . . .

Tommy watched, and his heart pounded suddenly as Evelyn turned and smiled in the direction in which she knew the dimensoscope must be. A huge butterfly, its wings a full yard across, fluttered past her head. Denham talked excitedly to her. A clumsy batlike thing swooped by overhead. Its shadow blanketed her face for an instant. A running animal, small and long, ran swiftly in full view from one side of the dimensoscope's field of vision to the other. Then a snake, curiously horned, went writhing past. . . .

Denham talked excitedly. He turned and made gestures as of writing, toward the spot where he had picked up Tommy's message. He began to search for a charred stick where the Ragged Men had built a fire some days now past. A fleeing furry thing sped across his feet, running. . . .

Denham looked up. And Evelyn was staring now. She was staring in the direction of the Golden City. And now what was almost a wave of animals, all wild and all fleeing, swept across the field of vision of the dimensoscope. There were gazelles, it seemed—slender-limbed, graceful animals, at any rate—and there were tiny hoofed things which might have been echippi, and then a monstrous armadillo clanked and rattled past. . . .

Tommy swung the dimensoscope. He gasped. All the animal world was in flight. The insects had taken to wing. Flying creatures were soaring upward and streaking through the clear blue sky, and all in the one direction. And then out of the morass came monstrous shapes; misshapen, unbelievable reptilian shapes, which fled bellowing thunderously for the tree-fern forest. They were gigantic, those things from the morass. They were hideous. They were things out of nightmares, made into flabby flesh. There were lizards and what might have been gigantic frogs, save that frogs possess no tails. And there were long and snaky necks terminating in infinitesimal heads, and vast palpitating bodies following those impossible small braincases, and long tapering tails that thrashed mightily as the ghastly things fled bellowing. . . .

And the cause of the mad panic was a slowly moving white curtain of mist. It was flowing over the marsh, moving with apparent deliberation, but, as Tommy saw, actually very swiftly. It shimmered and quivered and moved onward steadily. Its upper surface gleamed with elusive prismatic colors. It had blotted out the horizon and the Golden City, and it came onward. . . .

Denham made frantic, despairing gestures toward the dimensoscope. The thing was coming too fast. There was no time to write. Denham held high the cord that trailed from the message-bearing missile. He gesticulated frantically, and raced to the gutted steel globe and heaved mightily upon it and swung it about so that Tommy saw a great steel ring set in its side, which had been hidden before. He made more gestures, urgently, and motioned Evelyn inside.

Tommy struck at his forehead.

"It's poison gas," he muttered. "Revenge for the smashed-up vehicle. . . . They knew it by an automatic radio signal, maybe. This is their way of wiping out the Ragged Men. . . . Poison gas. . . . It'll kill Denham and Evelyn. . . . He wants me to do something. . . ."

He drew back, staring, straining every nerve to think. . . . And somehow his eyes were drawn to the back of the laboratory, and he saw Smithers teetering on his feet, with his hands clasped queerly to his body, and a strange man standing in the door of the laboratory with an automatic pistol in his hand. The automatic had a silencer on it, and its clicking had been drowned out, anyhow, by the roaring of the crude-oil engine.

The man was small and dark and natty. His lips were drawn back in a peculiar mirthless grin as Smithers teetered stupidly back and forth and then fell. . . .

The explosion of Tommy's own revolver astounded him as much as it did Jacaro's gunman. He did not even remember drawing it or aiming. The natty little gunman was blotted out by a spouting mass of white smoke—and suddenly Tommy knew what it was that Denham wanted him to do.

There was rope in a loose and untidy coil beneath a work bench. Tommy sprang to it in a queer, nightmarish activity. He knew what was happening, of course. Von Holtz had seen the magnetic catapult at work. That couldn't be destroyed or its workings hidden like the ring catapult of Denham's design. He'd gone out to call in Jacaro's men. And they'd shot down Smithers as a cold-blooded preliminary to the seizure of the instrument Jacaro wanted.

It was necessary to defend the laboratory. But Tommy could not spare the time. That white mist was moving upon Evelyn and her father, in that other world. It was death, as the terror of the wild things demonstrated. They had to be helped. . . .

He knotted the rope to the end of the cord that vanished curiously somewhere among the useless mass of rings. He tugged at the cord—and it was tugged in return. Denham, in another world, had felt his signal and had replied to it. . . .

A window smashed suddenly and a bullet missed Tommy's neck by inches. He fired at that window, and absorbedly guided the knot of the rope past its vanishing point. The knot ceased to exist and the rope crept onward—and suddenly moved more and more swiftly to a place where abruptly it was not. For the length of half an inch, the rope hurt the eyes that looked at it. Beyond that it was not possible to see it at all.

Tommy leaped up. He plunged ahead of two separate spurts of shots from two separate windows. The shots pierced the place where he had been. He was racing for the crude-oil engine. There was a chain wound upon a drum, there, and a clutch attached the drum to the engine.

He stopped and seized the repeating shotgun Smithers had brought as his own weapon against Jacaro's gangsters. He sent four loads of buckshot at the windows of the laboratory. A man yelled.

And Tommy dropped the gun to knot the rope to the chain, desperately, fiercely, in a terrible haste.

The chain began to pay out to that peculiar vanishing point which was here an entryway to another world—perhaps another universe.

A bullet nicked his ribs. He picked up the gun and fired it nearly at random. He saw Smithers moving feebly, and Tommy had a vast compassion for Smithers, but— He shuddered suddenly. Something had struck him a heavy blow in the shoulder. And something else battered at his leg. There was no sound that could be heard above the thunder of the crude-oil motor, but Tommy was queerly aware of buzzing things flying about him, and of something very warm flowing down his body and down his leg. And he felt very dizzy and weak and extremely tired. . . . He could not see clearly, either.

But he had to wait until Denham had the chain fast to the globe. That was the way he had intended to come back, of course. The ring was in the globe, and this chain was in the laboratory to haul the globe back from wherever it had been sent. And Von Holtz had disconnected it before sending away the globe with Denham in it. If the chain remained unbroken, of course it could be hauled in, as it would turn all necessary angles and force the globe to follow those angles, whatever they might be. . . .

Tommy was on his hands and knees, and men were saying savagely, "Where's that thing, hey? Where's th' thing Jacaro wants?"

He wanted to tell them that they should say whether the chain had stopped moving to a place where it ceased to exist, so that he could throw a clutch and bring Denham and his daughter back from the place where Von Holtz had marooned them when he wanted to steal Denham's secret. Tommy wanted to explain that. But the floor struck him in the face, and something said to him, "They've shot you."

But it did not seem to matter, somehow, and he lay very still until he felt himself strangling, and he was breathing in strong ammonia which made his eyes smart and his tired lungs gasp.

Then he saw flames, and heard a motor car roaring away from close by the laboratory.

"They've stolen the catapult and set fire to the place," he remembered dizzily, "and now they're skipping out. . . ."

Even that did not seem to matter. But then he heard the chain clank, next to him on the floor. The white mist! Denham and Evelyn waiting for the white mist to reach them, and Denham jerking desperately on the chain to signal that he was ready. . . .

The flames had released ammonia from the metal Von Holtz had made. That had roused Tommy. But it did not give him strength. It is impossible to say where Tommy's strength came from, when somehow he crawled to the clutch lever, with the engine roaring steadily above him, and got one hand on the lever, and edged himself up, and up, and up, until he could swing his whole weight on that lever. That instant of dangling hurt excruciatingly, too, and Tommy saw only that the drum began to revolve swiftly, winding the chain upon it, before his grip gave way.

And the chain came winding in and in from nowhere, and the tall laboratory filled more and more thickly with smoke, and lurid flames appeared somewhere, and a rushing sound began to be audible as the fire roared upward to the inflammable roof, and the engine ran thunderously. . . .

Then, suddenly, there was a shape in the middle of the laboratory floor. A huge globular shape which it hurt the eyes to look upon. It became visible out of nowhere as if evoked by magic amid the flames of hell. But it came, and was solid and substantial, and it slid along the floor upon small wheels until it wound up with a crash against the winding drum, and the chain shrieked as it tightened unbearably —and the engine choked and died.

Then a door opened in the monstrous globe. Two figures leaped out, aghast. Two ragged, tattered, strangely armed figures, who cried out to each other and started for the door. But the girl stumbled over Tommy and called, choking, to her father. Groping toward her, he found Smithers. And then Tommy smiled drowsily to himself as soft arms tugged bravely at him, and a slender, glorious figure staggered with him to fresh air.

"It's Von Holtz," snapped Denham, and coughed as he fought his way to the open. "I'll blast him to hell with these things we brought back. . . ."

That was the last thing Tommy knew until he woke up in bed with a feeling of many bandages and an impression that his lungs hurt.

Denham seemed to have heard him move. He looked in the door.

"Hullo, Reames. You're all right now."

Tommy regarded him curiously until he realized. Denham was shaved and fully clothed. That was the strangeness about him. Tommy had been watching him for many days as his clothing swiftly deteriorated and his beard grew.

"You are, too, I see," he said weakly. "I'm damned glad." Then he felt foolish, and querulous, and as if he should make some apology, and instead said, "But five dimensions does seem extreme. Three is enough for ordinary use, and four is luxurious. Five seems to be going a bit too far."

Denham blinked, and then grinned suddenly. Tommy had admired the man who could face so extraordinary a situation with such dogged courage, and now he found, suddenly, that he liked Denham.

"Not too far," said Denham grimly. "Look!" He held up one of the weapons Tommy had seen in that other world, one of the golden-colored truncheons. "I brought this back. The same metal they built that wagon of theirs with. All their weapons. Most of their tools—as I know. It's gold, man! They use gold in that world as we use steel here. That's why Jacaro was ready to kill to get the secret of getting there. Von Holtz enlisted him."

"How did you know—" began Tommy weakly.

"Smithers," said Denham. "We dragged both of you out before the lab went up in smoke. He's going to be all right, too. Evelyn's nursing both of you. She wants to talk to you, but I want to say this first: You did a damned fine thing, Reames! The only man who could have saved us, and you just about killed yourself doing it. Smithers saw you swing that clutch lever with three bullets in your body. And you're a scientist, too. You're my partner, Reames, in what we do in the fifth dimension."

Tommy blinked. "But five dimensions does seem extreme. . . ."

"We are the Interdimensional Trading Company," said Denham, smiling. "Somehow, I think we'll find something in this world we can trade for the gold in that. And we've *got* to get there, Reames, because Jacaro will surely try to make use of that catapult principle you worked out. He'll raise the devil; and I think the people of that Golden City would be worth knowing. No, we're partners. Sooner or later, you'll know how I feel about what you've done. I'm going to bring Evelyn in here now."

He vanished. An instant later Tommy heard a voice—a girl's voice. His heart began to pound. Denham came back into the room and with him was Evelyn. She smiled warmly upon Tommy, though as his eyes fell blankly upon the smart sport clothes she was again wearing, she flushed.

"My daughter Evelyn," said Denham. "She wants to thank you."

And Tommy felt a warm soft hand pressing his, and he looked deep into the eyes of the girl he had never before spoken to, but for whom he had risked his life, and whom he knew he would love forever. There were a thousand things crowding to his lips for utterance. He had watched Evelyn, and he loved her—

"H-how do you do?" said Tommy, lamely. "I'm—awfully glad to meet you."

But before he was well he learned to talk more sensibly.

Passengers poured in long lines from the open door-ports of the liner, moving in steady flow through brilliantly lit tubes into the debarking tunnels.

Illustrated by Morey

Into the Meteorite Orbit

By Frank K. Kelly

THE Cape Town liner dropped into the slips at Chicago's Municipal Rocket Port at five minutes after midnight. Circular slabs of stellite slid back silently; thin tongues of metal came out in narrow gangplanks that contacted automatically with the passenger's debarking tunnels. Below, under the ship's rounded belly, freight locks swung swiftly back with a sudden clang of metal, and belched forth a rapid stream of cargo from the Dark Continent into the gravity loading chutes.

Passengers poured in long lines from the open door-ports of the liner, moving in steady flow through brilliantly lit tubes into the debarking tunnels, and from them, coming out in a few minutes into the vast dome of the Central Way-Station. Here long rows of soft-cushioned seats were crowded with people, passengers of all ages, sexes, and descriptions, from all corners of the globe, waiting for the scarlet flash of neon light that would signal the arrival of an outgoing liner. A bell was ringing softly somewhere, in a flicker of deep sound. . . .

Across the floor sparks of green light flowed and flickered on a great luminous board, marking the rapid passage of stratosphere ships, high overhead. Switch operators sat half-crouched before banked televise panels, shifting messages from speeding ships to ground stations and back again: "Strato-ship RX-V2 calling Chicago . . . Strato-Liner calling Chicago . . . RX-V2 calling Chicago. Commercial signals. Channel 1792. One-seven-nine-two. Message begins. . . ."

"Way-Station, Central Berlin. Relay through on 4.33 wavelength. Check. Contacting all Transatlantic rotor ships. Weather bad in the southeast. . . ."

Men in the black-and-gold uniform of the Transport Combine moved quietly through the flowing crowds, some keeping systematic confusion from merging into chaos, others giving information to inquirers on ship schedules, still others directing bewildered individuals in drab metal cloth and the stenciled "Rural" on their name-tabs to seats in their correct debarkation sections; all in all adding a final touch of quiet efficiency to a scene of apparently shifting confusion.

A man, Girand by name, an engineer, came through the debarking tunnel for Section 678-NZ-Africa, and stood hesitantly for an instant at the edge of the vast, crowded room. He glanced about him as though expecting someone. Disappointment crept in behind his gray eyes.

Another man shouldered a way through the crowd and stood before him. This other was tall, more than six feet, so that he towered above the slim height of Ron Girand like a bulky giant, for the engineer, in common with most of the people in the great hall, stood only a little over five feet. There was a curious restrained force about this man, a sense of leashed power and tensed unease, that was almost inhuman. His eyes were hard and glittering; his voice, when he addressed Girand respectfully, held a curious rasp of metal.

"Good evening, M. Girand. I have the 'copter waiting on Z roof, sir. If you will follow me—"

Girand met his impassive, hooded eyes. The engineer spoke, half eagerly, half impatiently: "Mr. Jimmy? He did not come?"

The other shook his great head in a slow, negative gesture. The metallic eyes blinked.

"No, sir. Mister Jimmy is gone. He left soon after you, sir. Arizona, he told me to tell you."

"I see." Girand nodded, attempting without success to conceal his disappointment. He frowned; he did not at all see into it. It had been arranged that Jimmy was to meet him here on this date—without fail. Girand shrugged. After all, he told himself, he could expect no better treatment. This boy—man now—Jimmy Warren by name, with his unguessable wealth from Anton Warren's moon properties, was his ward in name only; in reality he neither had, nor attempted to have, any control over young Warren's actions. And Girand hadn't hesitated to go off on a nine-months' jaunt into Africa for some unknown purpose and unrevealed destination—without giving any explanation to Jimmy Warren. . . .

He wished suddenly that old Anton Warren were still alive. The father had seemed to possess a subtle knack of knowing how to handle Jimmy, headstrong and impulsive though he was. Girand shrugged: there was no helping it. His father was dead, worse luck, and he had been left with the duties of guardian—at thirty-five.

Not that he didn't like Jimmy. . . . He knew that his disappointment was strongly tinged with a desire for the easy comradeship the other had to offer—that, and something else. The game was getting too deep and intricate to continue playing a lone hand; and he'd counted on taking Jimmy into the conflict on returning from this trip. . . .

He shrugged, came out of his abstraction when Denn stepped on the starter, and began turning over the compact, efficient little sun-engines of the helicopter. He had been curiously silent all the way up from the way-station of Z roof, and said nothing even when Denn, the servant, had helped him along with his bags into the 'copter's rear cabin.

Power fed into the ship's six lift propellers from hidden photocell storage units. Through the glass roof of the cabin he could detect the spinning blur of the metal "props," could catch the rising whine of the trembling engines. Then they were in the air, rising straight up from the light-jeweled darkness of the Chicago of A.D. 2163.

Denn spun a control-wheel, straightened out their air course for Girand's roof bungalow on the Victoria Hotel, whose hundred-story tower of berylliumstellite lanced skyward in a blaze of light, a mile in the distance.

Girand leaned forward on sudden impulse and spoke, his mind busy with a comparison between this modern Minotaur and the growing cities of the South African veldt, forgetting for an instant the true nature of the other.

"Denn, you should have been with me this trip. They're doing things, those Africans. Some day the world's going to hear from what it calls the Dark Continent—hear from it in a real way. Washington and London aren't awake yet—but they will be . . . and Power!"

His voice caught, throbbing; came again: "Power unthinkable—and undeveloped! . . . Enough to break the stranglehold the Monopoly's putting on the world. Those miles of sun-mirrors south of Capetown . . ."

Suddenly he stopped, flushed deeply in the darkness of the little cabin, and cursed himself for a fool. Talking to this robot, this thing of delicately fabricated metal, a reasoning piece of animate machinery! As if it could understand. . . .

Denn spoke suddenly from the control seat, his harsh voice rasping: "Yes, sir. We are landing now, sir. Hold on—"

Girand nodded and caught a firm hold of the handle of his cushioned seat. The helicopter dropped straight down, motors humming, and struck softly against something smooth and hard. Denn cut the engines, leaped down from his seat, and came around to open the engineer's door.

Girand was already out. He gestured, and the other reached in and took his bags. Denn went on toward a door set into the smooth, metal wall of the roof bungalow, while Girand closed and locked the mechanism of the little 'copter. The engineer followed in a moment.

He came into a great, comfortable living room with heavy furnishings arranged in a quiet manner that showed good taste backed by unlimited resources. The walls and long windows were paneled in the prevailing style of the day, with modernistic designs of black and white etched in the silvery metal. A great divan was placed before a wide, comfortable fireplace, and Denn had already lit a blaze in the ato-burner.

Girand went over and stood looking down into the quiet, steady atomic flame, which changed color softly as he watched. Green and scarlet and a queer roseate white leaped up against the smooth metal of the grate and died down again while he stared, oblivious to the miracle of controlled utilization of the atom.

He shrugged, a little angry with himself. He should have been exultant, throbbing with the fullness of triumph, tasting the joy of his victory . . . but he was not. He was introspective, more than a little lonesome. His thoughts went back to Capetown, and South Africa. . . .

Raw country, down there. Raw, and new, and still bound by the pains of growth and youth—but with a foresight and a wisdom in its leaders that had not been given to the continents of Asia, America, and Europe. Himself, fighting the strength and resources of the Inter-Allied Power Monopoly. Fighting—and winning. Africa's power belonged to—Africa. A hard glow came to his eyes. . . . The African Power Development Corporation, controlled and regulated by the Governmental Council of United African States.

All of it built up by him, Girand. No room in Africa for the outreaching fingers of the Monopoly—as long as he lived. The Monopoly knew that. It had known it even before himself. . . .

He had won other victories—skirmishes. But this was first blood. The Monopoly was wounded, stricken—and angry. . . . As well as he did, the Group of Five realized that Power struck the keynote of this the twenty-second century. The twentieth had been the age of steel; the twenty-first, the era of transportation; and the twenty-second was fast developing into the power century. . . . Power meant control, and control meant the ruling of the world, not by its peoples, but by—the Group of Five.

If the Monopoly lived, Girand must die. . . . It had been so decided—and the Group had not been idle. They had tried often, with an untiring zeal; Girand knew that it was only a matter of time—unless the battle ended in his victory. . . . That was why he wanted Jimmy behind him. There was an old saying he had read somewhere—"Carry on!" Jimmy could carry on. . . .

He shrugged, and moved a little away from the fire. He had counted so much on finding Jimmy here, after the stark solitude of long nights in the veldt. He missed the constant activity that prevailed in these rooms during Jimmy Warren's brief occupancies of the bungalow.

There would be a party of some kind on now, if Jimmy had been here; flushed, bright-eyed couples locked in the motions of the newest modernistic dance, whirling in the center of the polished floor; Jimmy presiding gaily over the impromptu bar, serving bubbling synthetic concoctions with reckless abandon; someone else mounted on the great mahogany table against the wall, declaiming with intoxicated eloquence upon the evils of oversocialization and the increasing paternalism of the damned government. . . . Where was Jimmy now, Girand wondered? Arizona, Denn had said.

Arizona! Bleak, white desert shining under a hard-gold sun. . . . A yellow moon rising over the sharp ridges of gaunt mountains. . . . Long miles of rolling ranchland, barren, forsaken, ruthless as primeval Nature. Arizona! . . .

Denn came in from Girand's bedroom, closing the door silently behind him. He bowed a little stiffly, and Girand thought he could detect a faint mocking glint in the metallic, hooded eyes. . . . The hard voice came respectfully.

"Your room is ready now, sir. Pajamas on the bed. Sandwiches and coffee on the end-table. A new book sent you by the Communal Library, if you wish to read. And if there is anything else—"

"Nothing," Girand said, nodding dismissal. "Thanks, Denn. You can go now. I won't need you any more tonight. . . . Wait a minute!"

"Yes, sir?"

"Any messages come here since the last group you forwarded to me? From Jimmy—or anyone else?"

The other hesitated. "I think not, sir. . . . But yes. There was one. I accepted it, recorded as usual. The reception disk is there, in the televise cabinet."

Girand stiffened. "You know who sent the message?"

The hidden eyes flickered. "No. That was a strange thing. Visual connection was not given during the reception of the communication. Only audible."

"I see," Girand said, and smiled grimly. "The visa-screen was dark—clouded?"

The metallic glance met the engineer's. "It was, sir. Almost black, as if there was a broadcast interference."

Girand nodded. "That's all. You can go now."

"Yes, sir. Good night, sir." The stiff-jointed, shadowy figure was gone. Girand relaxed and lit a cigarette, staring again into the coruscating flames. . . . After a time he spoke, half aloud, as if there had been a long gap in his thoughts.

"Damn funny fellow, Denn . . . *thing*, I suppose I mean. Hard to think of him as not human. He certainly comes mighty close to the real article. . . . Warren was a genius! To create Denn. . . . I'll never see how he did it. Damn, but I wish Anton were still around somewhere to help me. . . ."

The thought made his eyes tighten. His fingers locked taut together. Anton Warren had fought the Monopoly, laughed when the Group asked for his records of the experiments that had created Denn. . . . He had turned the plans over to the Pan-American Council—and died a month after. Girand always believed he had been murdered. . . .

The engineer jerked his shoulders. Impatiently, he flung the half-smoked tube into the fire, watched it dissolve instantly into bubbling points of disrupted light. . . . He walked into the bedroom, yawning, the televisor record-disk under his arm.

He glanced around at the door, nodded with satisfaction. Denn had been true to his word. Two sandwiches were arranged temptingly on a white plate on the little end-table, sitting beside a smoking cup of black coffee. A book with a gaudy green jacket stamped CL-17 lay near the coffee cup. His pajamas were spread out neatly on the great bed. . . . Denn was very nearly human.

He slid the smooth cylinder of the recording disk into the opening of a translating machine, a square-shaped mechanism with a finely sensitive needle for bringing back recorded sound. Visual recording was possible by a combination of functions. . . .

Girand flicked over a switch. A soft purring sound came from the translator, shifted in a blur of static, and merged into the smooth voice of a man. Girand sat up straight; he recognized the voice. . . . One of the Five.

"The Group extends congratulations, Girand. Once again you have—beaten us. This is the third time, I think. . . . Warnings, with a man like you, are futile and childish. The Group gives no warnings and makes no threats. But it is feared that you will soon die. Your death will not be quick nor crude, Girand. It may take a very long time. . . . We are sorry you have decided to allow Jimmy Warren to risk himself in your own foolhardy manner. Warren has been withdrawn from—the conflict between us. *The space between you will remain unchanged.* When you hear this message, the meaning of that will not be clear; but understanding is coming soon. . . . You will remember that the Group gives no warnings and makes no threats."

The message ended. The name of the speaker was not given. It was unnecessary; Girand knew. . . . He sat silent a long time, thinking deeply. He had been told of his approaching death before, in messages almost exactly duplicating this one. . . . And yet there was a puzzle here, something too vague and formless for his mind to get hold of—and by the same token all the more menacing. "The space between you will remain unchanged. . . ." Queer, cryptical sentence, without apparent meaning. . . . And yet Girand knew that the Group did not deal in meaningless things. If Jimmy was in danger. . . .

He shrugged and reached forward, turned the switch of the translator back to neutral, laid the small record-disk on the end-table. There was nothing he could do—until the time came. And when it came, he would know. . . .

Minutes later he was in the bed, luxuriating between the smooth white sheets, succumbing to a sudden overwhelming feeling of drowsiness and warmth. . . . So different, this, from long nights on the veldt, incased in an uncomfortable sleeping bag under the stars, constantly tormented by hordes of vicious insects. . . . So much better, this; safer and better. . . . But if Jimmy was in danger—it was there again, digging at the corner of his brain, mingling uneasiness with queer uncertainty. He was very tired. . . . Body triumphed over mind. He dozed, forgetting the reading lamp above his head, the gaudy green volume on the little end-table. . . .

Then suddenly he was awake again, sitting straight upright in the great bed, his eyes puzzled, half-startled. He had heard nothing, seen nothing—yet he could have sworn someone had called him. A faint voice fingering softly deep within his brain, it was—calling.

It came again. Louder now, with an undertone of sudden, urgent insistence.

"Ron Girand! Ron Girand! Do you hear me? Answer me if I have made contact. . . . Granton calling. Granton calling. Answer if you get this. Ron Girand! Ron Girand—!"

"I hear you," Girand said quietly, fighting down an instinctive feeling of panic at this uncanny thing. "What do you want? How are you able to speak to me this way? Who—"

"Girand! This is Granton; Dr. Richard Granton." The silent inner voice throbbed strongly. "You remember? Anton Warren was my friend; he must have told you of me. We have never met, you and I; but we both know a friend. . . . His name is Jimmy Warren."

"Jimmy!"

Girand's brain was rioting. But he remembered; there *had* been a Dr. Richard Granton of which Anton Warren had spoken often. A lifelong friend of Warren's who had gone to Arizona to delve into private researches of his own. Jimmy must have gone out there to see him. . . .

"Jimmy!" Girand exclaimed then. "Jimmy Warren! I remember you, Granton—but what's the meaning of this, man? What—"

"There is no time to explain it to you this way," the voice answered him coolly. "My mind is already growing weak. It is exhausting, this thought-contact, even with the aid of my transference mechanism. You've got to trust me, Girand, take my unsupported word for what I say. Jimmy's in trouble. We believe you're the only man who can help him. . . . I have tried, Girand, and failed. But together we might do something. Will you come where I direct you?"

Girand hesitated, his mind suspicious, seething with turmoil. Yet this other seemed honest, straightforward, frank. And Jimmy was in trouble. . . . This strange thing!

"What do you mean, man? How—"

"We're wasting precious time," the voice cut in immediately. "Answer me, and don't play the fool. Will you obey me, put your will under my control? I know what I'm asking; and believe me, it is absolutely necessary. . . . For Jimmy. I swear it. Quick, Girand; what's your answer? Power is—getting low. . . ."

The thought impulses were coming disconnectedly now, in short stabs of forced effort that brought sudden striking pain into Girand's temples. He made a quick decision.

"All right, Granton. I'm game. . . . But if this is a hoax—"

"No hoax," the voice answered swiftly. "Get out of your bed. Hurry!"

Girand obeyed wonderingly.

"Step into the center of the carpet. Now hold your body very still. Keep your mind blank. . . . Sleep."

Girand's eyes closed slowly, and his body relaxed, arms hanging limply at his sides. The room glowed then, was abruptly suffused with a roseate nimbus of whirling light that crystallized into a thickly luminous sphere about the motionless body of the engineer. . . . The sphere darkened, thickened, spun feverishly on an invisible axis. . . . And suddenly exploded, with a soundless concussion.

Denn, lying silently on his bed in the next room, staring out with sleepless eyes at the night sky, heard no sound.

But Ron Girand had gone.

CHAPTER II

Granton opened a door cut into the rock, and stepped out upon the floor of the Arizona desert. On all sides of him desolation, barren and complete, stretched away to the far horizon. He yawned slowly and glanced up along the steep side of the overhanging cliffs; the first dawnlight was just beginning to gild the edges of the hills.

The man behind him spoke, in a quick clipped voice. "Tired, Chief?"

Granton grinned. "Dead—from the neck up."

He yawned, and flexed tired muscles. His eyes were shadowed, reddened; he had spent sixteen hours of labor without rest in the cave laboratory behind the door in the rock. But his brain was not tired; something, sharp and vibrating within him, knew that he was close to the end of a long trail. And success would mean—something that he dared not think about. . . .

The man behind watched him, a queer look in narrowed eyes, head and shoulders shifted a little forward. A thin man this, with lean lips and a lean face, a tall well-knit body. Quick, agile, intelligent with a flashing brilliance that leaped, like a flame, to heights untouched by Granton's plodding genius . . . Barclay, Granton's assistant.

Granton jerked his strong head suddenly, startled, curious. A low humming quivered through the thin air over the desert; the shape of a fast-flying helicopter came into view, sharply etched in gold against the background of the rising sun. The little ship came on until it was directly above Granton's hills; then the engines died, and lifting blades fell off to half speed. The 'copter settled slowly down past the side of the cliff, struck the desert not twenty feet from where Granton stood.

For once his curiosity was stirred. He had chosen this spot from all others, because of its isolation and quiet; and it had proved ideal for the work he was doing. Interruption he did not want. But he was human, and just then a little lonesome, tired of constant rubbing elbows with Barclay and Barclay alone. . . . He moved toward the little ship almost eagerly. Barclay followed with a kind of reluctance, a half-frown gathering on his thin face.

The door in the side of the ship's cabin opened abruptly, and a man's figure climbed down to the floor of the desert. Even at the distance, and despite the shapelessness of the flying clothes, Granton caught something familiar in the tall litheness of the other. Recognition came dimly, merged into certainty . . . Jimmy Warren!

Granton's heartbeat jumped; he quickened pace. The sun struck down on a mass of yellow hair and a square brown face; there could be only one head like that in the world—and it belonged to Jimmy Warren.

Granton came up panting, eyes eager, half incredulous at seeing the other here. "Jimmy! . . . You got my message?"

"I did that." The other laughed, the sound clear and keen in the desert air. Confidence and capability in that laugh, strong and alert. Jimmy Warren caught Granton's hand.

"In the name of seven devils, Granton, what ever possessed you to hide yourself away from the world in this place? Letting me hear from you once in five years! If Dad were alive—"

Granton grinned; and then, eyes darkening an instant: "I heard about Anton. . . . I'm sorry, Jimmy. You're on your own, now."

"Not quite," he said a little queerly. "I've a guardian, you remember: Ron Girand. . . . But he never bothers about what I do, so that doesn't cramp my style much."

"I see," Granton said, nodding. He swung, jerked a hand at Barclay, standing silently behind him. "My assistant, Mark Barclay . . . Mark, Jimmy Warren."

"I've heard of you enough." Barclay smiled and shook hands with the other; his face changed when he smiled, lips curling in a little twist, eyes lighting. . . . Jimmy nodded and grinned.

"Sorry to know that. You'll probably have me cut out for a half-brained lounge lizard—if you listened to Granton!"

The older man chuckled. "You always were a liar!" He turned, put an arm across Jimmy's shoulders. "Come up to my den . . . I can't promise you anything—but I have got a laboratory that's pretty much of a mess. And I suppose you're wondering why I sent for you?"

"I was, a little," Warren echoed, face suddenly sober; he turned from locking the cabin of the little ship. "That's why I've come out here to see you, really. . . . I know what you're trying to do—and I've got to tell you about a few ideas of my own—afterwards."

Granton looked at him an instant in silence. "I see. Come along, then. We'll talk that over—later. . . . Tell me all about yourself now. And Girand—how is he?"

They walked together up the rock slope that led to Granton's cave laboratory. He swung open the door cut into the cliff, and stood aside. Jimmy entered first, stopped a minute inside, eyes still a little dazzled from the sun-glare of the desert. Then he saw, and exclaimed softly, breath caught in his throat.

Granton put a hand on Barclay's shoulder, jerked his head. "Talk to you later, Mark. . . . Come back in half an hour."

The other shrugged, nodded, and swung away, disappearing through a door at one side of the laboratory. . . . Jimmy was standing silently on the metal floor of a vast room, whose arched irregular roof lost itself somewhere in distant shadow and vagueness. Yet the place, however vast, was crowded, filled almost to capacity by unending rows of apparatus. Some of it he knew and recognized: tubes and coils and banked condensers; but there was much of complexity and uses unguessable. A flame rose and fell in a great arched globe, fading and growing with a faint soft hissing sound. Hot sparks smashed in crackling crescendo across the gap of an electron power circuit. . . . Granton waved a careless hand to indicate it all.

"My laboratory," he said inadequately. "You like it?"

Jimmy swung and faced him. "Like it? . . . It's not in you to ask fool questions, Granton—but that comes close to being idiotic. I can't describe how I feel about it; but I think it's what I had a picture of in my mind. . . . You're close to your—objective?"

Granton's eyes lit up with a sudden, intense fire. He nodded slowly. "Very close. That was why I sent for you. There's power here. . . . I'm closer than ever I had expected to be. I've been working all night, with Barclay, on a model of the first generator. I know now my idea is right; all that remains is to prove it practical."

"I get it," Jimmy said, straight eyes upon him, lean body tense. "Anton told me you had a dream—and what you were doing to make it real . . . and you've done it now: made a dream real!"

Granton nodded quietly. "You might call it that. . . . I suppose we all have our dreams."

Warren's head lifted with sudden determination; the straight eyes met those of Granton. "You're right, Doctor. Even I have . . . Oh, I know—you've always believed I was shallow, foolish, impractical, a spoiled fool, with too much money to worry about having brains; but I've had my dream so long that it begins to get vague, fade in my mind. . . . Should I fight to hold it?"

The other met the hard glance with serious eyes. "You should . . . always."

"And if I told you what it was?"

"It would make no difference. If you believe with all your soul that you can make it real, if it's like a fire in you—carry on, no matter what I, or anyone else, might tell you."

Warren hesitated, eyes a little queer. Then, slowly, "I've had it ever since—I saw the moon. My dream depends on yours. . . . I want to go out into space—and reach the moon."

Granton stood an instant with the breath strangling in his throat; he caught the other's shoulders in a harsh grip. "Good God! Jimmy,

I didn't mean what I said. . . . I must have been insane, for a little. There are some dreams that are—follies."

The other stood straight and calm—hesitancy gone.

"Mine isn't . . . because I'm going, some day. And you're going to make it possible, Dick. . . . We're not always to be earthbound, tied to a pebble for infinity! I can't believe that; something in me . . . If your motor can give power unthinkable—why can't I use it?"

He gave Granton, standing astounded, no chance to answer. "I'm going to! Oh, all my life I've thought about it, and planned—and dreamed. . . . To be the first to go out across space! It would be worth living for! And why hasn't it been done? Because men have always been afraid; afraid to face the thought of going out into infinity alone! They've been contenders with their rocketships and their 'copters and their sun-motors; content to stay earthbound! Well, *I'm* not!"

Slowly the white heat of his intensity caught fire within Granton's soul, blazed up in flame. He must have been a little mad, to give in, to promise that when the motor was complete they would build a ship of space and go voyaging into infinity—but then he was a dreamer, and he had been alone, a long time.

"You win, Jimmy," Granton said, a little huskily. "When the generator is finished, and I'm satisfied with the power of it, and we've *proved* that power—why, we'll go out to the moon together!"

Warren's face changed all at once, in a bright glow. He came close, held out a hand. "Anton was right! You're an ace! . . . When do we start?"

"Not for a long time yet." Granton laughed. "But we've made a beginning! Just now we'll shake hands on it. . . ."

And Jimmy crushed his fingers in sheer exultance. . . .

Behind them a door opened; Barclay came across the floor. "You're all in, Chief. You'd better get some rest. . . . I'll fix Warren up with a room while you get a little sleep. All right?"

"Yes," Granton said. He hesitated. . . . "I'll go now. But not before we've taken you in on this, Mark. . . . How long have we been together?"

The other's eyes looked queer, as if startled. "Why—it's been four years. . . ."

"Long enough." Granton nodded. "Long enough to make me sure of you. . . . Mark, Jimmy and I are working together—on the motor.

And when it's done, we're going to build a ship. A space ship . . . that will take us out across space to the moon."

Barclay's face stiffened, became impassive. "You'll let me in—I'll go with you?"

Granton made a slow motion of the head. "I hoped you'd say that. . . . The answer is yes—if you want to go."

Barclay's voice came, clipped and straight. "I'm going."

And Jimmy and Granton shook hands on it again. . . .

So they built the Granton motor. Jimmy called it that, but Granton said that he and Barclay had as much to do with it as himself. It was a beautiful little thing, though, when Granton had finished; compact and efficient, and almost indestructible. The principle of it was simple: gravital radiation.

Granton had never been able to understand why gravitation had always been called a "pull"; every phenomenon known concerning the force of gravity would fit as well into the framework of a repulsive theory. He had gone on that principle: that gravity is *not* a pull, but a pressure pervading all space. The Granton motor was attuned to the matter-radiations of the earth, and it was insulated against the influences of the other worlds of space. It acted as a super-transformer unit, infinitely sensitive in its receiving cells to the pressure of the earth; the result was tremendous propulsive power. In operation tests it proved to be nearly ninety-nine percent efficient—as close to perfect as any manbuilt mechanism could come; harnessed to a space ship, it would be just about the ideal thing for interplanetary travel.

And the ship was fast becoming a reality. The day arrived when Granton and Mark Barclay, who had taken over the duties of superintendent of construction on the little vessel, fitted the first full-power Granton generator into the hull. Jimmy had called the ship "The Anton Warren." It was a little beauty; long and slim and silvery, with the exhaust jets of the Granton force-streams built snugly into the rounded end of the lean hull. . . . Jimmy was half mad about it.

There came the night that the ship was finished. Jimmy and Granton were standing close beside the sleek hull of "The Anton Warren," very near a patch of shadow that the moonlight did not penetrate. The desert lay silent under the stars, stretching out before them.

The other was queer tonight, Granton thought; half troubled, and half exultant. He spoke, breaking a long silence.

"How well do you really know Barclay, Granton?"

"Barclay! . . . I don't understand what you mean," Granton said, his eyes disturbed. "He came to me four years ago. He's worked hard. He's been faithful. And he's a good scientist. . . . I don't know what more I could ask."

Warren nodded. "I see. . . . I like the man myself. He's brainy, even brilliant—keen on details. . . . But I meant—before he came out here with you. What he'd been, what he'd done, what connections he'd had."

The older man shrugged. "I never asked. I didn't bother much about what he'd *been*. . . . It's what he *was* that counted."

Warren was silent an instant. He was thinking, hesitant, uncertain of how to put his thoughts into words. And yet . . . memory came back to him of the talk he'd had with Barclay that morning, out here near the ship. Barclay had been brusque, and cryptical, and sensitive—but he had gotten a meaning across. . . . Barclay, brilliant, a research scientist in the first city of Arizona; the world of silent delving into forbidden things spread out before him—and temptation, temptation that led into a trap. Shady, crooked dealings. Stolen money. . . . And caught. Threatened with exposure, with ruin. . . .

What would Barclay have done if an offer had come to him from the Directory Board of the Arizona Power Corporation—and if the offer was a thinly veiled threat of what would happen if he refused? . . . The offer had come, with orders. He was to follow Granton to the desert; become the other's assistant; do nothing, say nothing, act the straightforward research scientist he claimed to be. But to watch Granton, always—every move the older man made. And report, when the time came to act. . . .

Barclay had put the case to him that way, sketching it out with quick words and nervous gestures, but carefully keeping before Warren's mind the fact that it was *another* who stood in the dilemma. And Barclay had asked him what that other man should do—when the time came. Hold to his science and the faith of his friend—or yield to the command of those who had the power to destroy him by a refusal? Warren had given him a quick answer, brain rife with suspicion. . . .

"You're sure, then, Granton? You're confident that Barclay is all you think he is. . . . You believe he's—honest with you?"

Granton frowned. "I wish you'd make yourself clear. Of course I believe in him!"

Warren looked up at him in the moonlight. "Then so do I. . . . I'm on edge. Tomorrow—we're going out *there*. . . ."

He jerked a head toward the star-sprinkled blackness of the night sky, with a white moon riding high on the horizon. Thought of Barclay was gone from his mind, in a sudden sweep of exultance. He leaned forward, put a hand on Granton's shoulder.

"Granton—*I'm* going tonight!"

The other caught his arm, the breath dry in his throat. Granton said impatiently, angrily, "Don't be a fool!"

Warren was looking up again at the full moon, driving through a scattered wrack of clouds. "I can't wait any longer! Why not—tonight? The ship is ready; and we were going in the morning. . . . I can't ask you to go, Granton—you and Barclay; it's my game. You're too big; you're worth too much to the world. But somebody like me—who'd never be missed, if anything broke wrong—I *ought* to go . . . I can go; I will!"

Granton looked at him then with frozen intensity, their glances locked. "Get this: I'd see the ship wrecked first, before I'd let you go out there—alone. What kind of fool do you think I am? We'll go together—tomorrow. . . . No! I'll take the ship up myself . . . tonight."

That startled him. "You wouldn't, Granton! . . . I'll wait, then, if you will. Until tomorrow—but no longer."

Granton believed him. The older man said with relief, "Of course. And we'll go together—tomorrow."

They moved off side by side, away from the ship, up the slope of rock leading to the door of Granton's laboratory. There were rooms on either side of the laboratory, caves carved out of the hills, furnished austerely; Warren was staying in one near the door, and Barclay had that on the other side of Granton. Granton and Warren separated in the doorway, with one last look at the slim, silver beauty of the ship, cradled on steel trestlework rising out of the sand.

Granton went directly to his room. He was just beginning to doze, when he heard the scrape as the outside door opened, and caught the soft scuffling sound of someone's feet moving quietly along the corridor. He called out, "Barclay?"

"Yes. Sorry I made the noise. I'd hoped not to wake you up. You'll need your sleep—for tomorrow."

"Right," Granton said. "Good night." He turned over in bed and went to sleep. Later, he was to remember that Barclay's voice had been hoarse and trembling. . . .

He did not sleep very long. It seemed to him that he had just gotten well into a doze again, when he felt a soft voice calling in his brain, fingering gently deep within his consciousness. He sat up sharply in the bed. . . . It was Warren.

"Granton, are you awake? Can you hear me?"

Granton had a sharp foreboding of disaster. "Yes . . . what in the name of the seven veiled devils do you mean by using the telepath at this time of night?"

The answer struck him into paralyzed disbelief; but the words came crystal-clear in his brain: "I'm using the telepath in the ship. Can you hear me? I'm at five thousand feet altitude, directly over you. Granton, the motor is perfect! Working like a charm! . . . You're a genius."

"Good God!" Granton cried, his tongue released from paralysis. "Jimmy! You're not serious?"

He was faintly amused. "Of course. I thought I'd let you know before I headed for the moon. I'm not even getting a thrill out of this; it's almost too easy! Granton, you don't know the feel of this ship! It's grand!"

Granton fought for self-control. The room whirled before him; Jimmy—out there, alone! "Jimmy, I'm begging you now, understand? . . . For God's sake come back before you run into something you can't handle! You're not dealing with theories now, you know; you're up against reality. God knows what's out—*there!*"

The other's answer came back, a little contemptuous. "I didn't know you were a coward, Granton. Haven't you faith in the motor you built, the ship you created? *I* have! . . . I'm cutting off. The next you'll hear from me will be from—space!"

"No, no!" Granton cried, struggling to hold contact, the sweat beading over his forehead. "My God, Jimmy!"

But there was silence in his brain. The other had gone. . . . Granton was left alone, filled with a queer sort of empty panic, and a feeling that something unguessable impended. . . .

He went at once and got Barclay. The two of them hurried into the laboratory together, to try to get in touch with Warren through the giant telepath-transmitter.

Granton was too upset to pay much attention to Barclay, though he did notice that the other was queerly pale; there was a muscle jerking nervously in a corner of the thin mouth. . . . Barclay could not face the older man, but kept his glance on the floor or flickering over the apparatus in the room. His eyes swung from the tele-transmitter along the room to the vibra-screen and back again, incessantly. But Granton believed it was fear for Warren, increased by his friendship for the other to the point of frenzy.

Then while Granton was frantically adjusting the distance dials of the transmitter, fitting the telepath-helmet on his head, Barclay spoke hoarsely, voice trembling.

"It's my fault, Granton. My fault. Good God, I must have been insane! . . . I listened to you two tonight, when you were talking about taking the ship up. I went into the engine room after you left, and jammed the second circuit of condenser coils. . . . The generator is going to break down somewhere out in space—and Warren in the ship! . . . Granton, Warren was right. I got in wrong, before I came to you. I sold you out—for a price. . . ."

"You mean," Granton asked with an unnatural coolness, "you've been taking orders from the Group? They want—the motor?"

Barclay dropped his glance. "I mean that . . . God knows, I'm a fool! I reported yesterday the ship was finished; they gave me orders to hold you off another day. . . . After that—it wouldn't be necessary. They'd have the motor."

"They're coming here?"

"They're here now. In the desert. They've got a fleet of helicopters, and flash paralysis guns. . . . They were planning to take the laboratory tomorrow—before the sun. . . ."

The clipped voice broke. "I was a damned louse! Selling you out, and the motor, because I was afraid . . . God!"

A rage rose within Granton slowly, freezing the sudden hatred at the back of his brain. He could have killed Barclay where he stood, but something about the man was so wretched and broken that the lust to murder went out of him, and he was simply contemptuous.

"I won't tell you what I think of you, Mark. There aren't words for it in the language."

The other nodded, all the life and confidence gone out of his eyes.

"I know. You're right. But anything you might call me wouldn't come near to what I think of myself. I've sweat blood, thinking about that ship out there in space. . . . If you'll just let me *do* something, anything that might pull him through! I might help, some way."

Granton believed he was sincere, suddenly. After all, the other was a *scientist*—and that was something that meant more than fear of death. . . . Granton nodded in a curt motion.

"All right. First, we've got to handle the Group. . . . You thought about the beam-shields—put them out of hookup?"

"No!" Barclay said in sudden exultance. "No! I'd forgotten, completely. . . . We can hold the Group off—until we reach Warren. I'll get the shields up. . . ."

Granton caught his shoulder for an instant in a crushing grip. And spoke grimly: "See that you *do*."

Barclay nodded speechlessly, swung to the banked control-panel that held within it the interleading conduits of electric force that created fan-beams of crackling force-shields. His fingers played rapidly over gleaming studs, building up voltage and charged power, blanketing in the hill of the laboratory with a silent, shimmering screen of electric energy. He grunted in sudden satisfaction, set a quick glance along steadying dials. . . . "Set, Chief. They'll sweat some, breaking through that!"

Granton shot the board a swift look, nodded, swung on the other. "Get over here and shut up. We've got a chance of reaching Warren before it's too late."

They worked in a kind of frozen silence, each of them thinking of the man in the little silvery ship, speeding unconsciously toward an unguessable doom—to be an occupant of a new satellite, a human being in an eternal tomb, endlessly circling . . . or to fall back in a long screaming slant to the hard breast of earth. Granton cursed the other inwardly to relieve pent-up feelings, but outwardly the two of them were that many machines, working with frantic fingers to build up contact with the ship.

They got it. Faint, it was, and flickering and uncertain—but contact. Granton called Jimmy's name softly, and he came into their field of vision, appearing as a shadowy, half-materialized wraith standing there in the center of the energized screen.

Granton spoke rapidly, quietly, but with a solemn steadiness that drove home the earnest reality of what he said. He urged, concluding a brief summary of what Barclay had confessed.

"Get it straight, Jimmy . . . you've got to turn back at once. If you do, you have a chance. If not—well, we'll try to save you, but it will be long odds, that's all."

The other's face paled, and all the conscious stubbornness faded out of his eyes. Granton realized then the inner boyishness of the other, taking everything he wanted as his just right. . . . But he was a little afraid, now.

"I'm turning back, Granton."

He vanished for an instant, and the two taut men in the laboratory could visualize him working frantically at the ship's controls, swinging the little vessel about in a wide circle to bring it back to earth.

Then he was before them again, eyes dulled with sudden despair. "I can't turn back, Granton! The controls are jammed somehow! I can't move them!"

His face was dead-white, subtly pleading with Granton to find for him a way out of this queer trap into which his own willfulness had plunged him. Granton was in agony.

"My God! Jimmy—try it again. Jam against them hard; they might work this time. . . ."

The other nodded, suddenly calm, self-controlled again. He vanished. . . . Barclay spoke, voice harsh with horror, "Granton, couldn't we materialize him? We've tried it before; and we've got the transmitter. . . ."

Granton nodded, hope coming back behind his eyes. It looked possible. The other had already been half materialized. Matter was vibration; what could be simpler than to dematerialize him, bring him back through space to the laboratory, and reintegrate the atoms of his body?

Warren came back into their field of vision, eyes hopeless. "It won't work, Granton. The controls are jammed; I can't move them."

"Never mind," Granton said, forcing cheerfulness into his voice. "Barclay's suggested using this transmitter to bring you back to the laboratory. We'll have to cut off for a while, and make some changes in the coil setup; you'll be all right till then, of course. You're not in immediate danger, you know. And the ship—we supplied it for several months, Jimmy."

He nodded slowly, resignation in his face. "I see. . . . Then it may be months before you can reach me. I'll wait, of course—the view is grand! I've got a front seat for the biggest show of infinity!"

Granton laughed, forcing his mirth. "You have that! And it won't be months either, Jimmy. A few hours, that's all. . . . I'll cut off now; every minute saved will get you out of this that much quicker."

"I'll be waiting," the other said, a faint smile at the corner of his lips. . . . Granton and Barclay went to work, then; they changed the coil setup and condenser arrangement of the transmitter a dozen times, and tried sending experimental animals from one end of the laboratory to the other, and return. They succeeded, hours later. They had done it before; but never with a human subject. . . .

Granton got connection with Warren again, and tried it. He failed, time and again. The transmitter was helpless outside the atmosphere of the earth, apparently; they could see and hear the other plainly enough, but beyond that they could not go. Always it was the same; the ship swinging endlessly in a long orbit, between the earth and moon—and Warren waiting, hope dying within him. . . .

Then he thought of Girand. Granton was working wearily at the transmitter, forcing tired fingers to move.

"Granton! If you could get Ron Girand—"

"Girand?" the older man echoed, a little puzzled; then: "I see. Your guardian. Where is he?"

The hope rising in Warren's face faded away. "No—you couldn't reach him. He's in South Africa somewhere. . . . Wait! How long has it been since I came there?"

Granton considered. "Seven months."

Warren spoke slowly, hesitantly. "Granton—do you think, with Barclay and men from Tucson to help, you could build another ship in two months? Girand will be back in Chicago, before then. You could get him; he would come, I know."

Granton nodded decisively. His eyes lightened, met Barclay's. "The only way out—and you thought of it! Barclay—you and I are going to work!"

Barclay's eyes were on the control-panel of the beam shields. Dials quivered and jerked under the impact of a sudden flow of counter-acting power. . . . "Have you forgotten—the Group? *They're here.* . . . We couldn't get through to Tucson or anywhere else. Build another ship like that one in two months? It can't be done!"

Granton's face was grim as steel. He glanced once all around the clicking rhythm of the great laboratory. "It can. We've got the material—and the power, power that can't be tapped from the outside. We can set up beam protection on the desert here. . . . Barclay, it's *going* to be done!"

CHAPTER III

Ron Girand came out of hypnotic sleep with a startled jerk and lifted bewildered eyes. He met the straight, grave glance of another man, a man in a close-fitting laboratory smock that came down over the knees of his thin body, covered his whole form from his square chin and unruly shock of dark gray hair to the rubber tops of his heavy boots. Girand opened his mouth to speak, but felt a sudden subtle tingling in his bare feet, and looked down. He gaped amazed.

He stood, still in the pajamas he had worn in the prosaic safety of his Chicago bedroom, upon a circular plate of smooth, hard metal, flanked on either side by the banked tubes and massed dials of some strange apparatus, his position directly under the steady glare of a great blue-flaming dome light. Amazement struck him again, and overwhelming curiosity. He stared again at the man in the acid-spotted smock, his eyes taking in the curious costume, half that of the confined sedentary scientist, half that of an outdoor huntsman.

"Where am I?" Girand demanded at last, after a moment of mutual appraisal. "What's this mean? You told me Jimmy—"

"I did," the man answered in a grave, pleasant voice, extending a firm hand. His eyes looked unutterably tired, as if he had been driving himself incessantly for a very long time. "I told you he was in trouble, and I wasn't lying, Girand. He *is* in danger. Serious danger. And we've got to get him out of it—quickly. . . . Step down here, and put these on."

He was holding forward a small pile of clothes; Girand obeyed and found himself standing on the cool metal floor of a huge room, whose distant roof lost itself in shadowy vagueness high above. The room was crowded, filled almost to capacity by endless rows of apparatus of complexity and uses unguessable. Granton nodded.

"My laboratory," he said simply. "I suppose you're wondering how you got here. That plate from which you just stepped is the receiving instrument of my vibra-transmitter; I've just finished reintegrating the matter of your body. The beam into which you walked in your bedroom simply reduced your body to vibration which it carried on a returning wave-channel to the plate here. . . . And you came."

Girand shook his head slowly. "I may never understand that part of it, Granton, but I know it works. That's mostly what I'm interested in. Engineering happens to be my line. I don't pretend to know much about anything else."

"Good idea, that," Granton said amusedly, his face relaxing a little. "And now you want to know why I brought you here."

"I do," Girand said, his eyes mirroring his itching curiosity. "That's all that counts. . . . Where's Jimmy?"

The other's face sobered. He gestured toward the long barrel of a telescope that reached up through the roof of the room. He turned toward it, and Girand followed.

"This will tell you better than anything I could say. . . . Use this eye-piece."

Girand looked into the tube and caught a breathless vision of intense black space, dusted with the brilliance of uncounted stars. Nearer and larger than any other body in the interstellar vastness was the huge face of the moon, scarred and pitted with dark craters. . . . And in between, a tiny sliver of light, coming nearer. Girand watched; the breath caught in his throat. He saw it plainly, before it began to grow smaller again: A ship out there in space!

He turned slowly, eyes incredulous. "Jimmy—is there?"

Granton nodded. "Yes . . . in that ship. I built it. He came two months ago with a dream in his brain: of reaching the moon. I suppose I was weak, insane, to give in, but there was a fire in him, Girand, that—well, I helped build that ship and the generator that took it off the earth. We got a few technies from Tucson to help on construction, and Mark Barclay—that's my assistant—superintended the building of the hull. . . . Barclay sold out to Power. . . . You've heard of the Five?"

"Heard of it!" Girand said bitterly. "My God, yes! . . . Now I know what they meant when. . . . *The space between you will remain unchanged!* They *knew* that Jimmy was—out there. Go on, Granton."

"Barclay tampered with the motor, set it so that it would break down, he thought, before the ship could be taken off the ground . . . but it didn't. It held, till mid-space—and then gave out. . . . The night the ship was finished Jimmy took it and headed into space. There isn't much more. And what there is—it's plain enough."

"Yes," Girand said slowly, "I think so. The ship is caught out there, by the forces of the moon and the earth, endlessly circling, a new satellite. Jimmy—out there alone among the worlds of space! Good God, it's unbelievable!"

"But it's true," Granton said softly.

Girand swung on him with a sudden terrible swiftness. "What are we going to do, man? We've got to save him! We've got to!"

"Will you listen to me?" Granton asked, almost impatiently. "We're under siege here—have been for months. We're holding out, by using beam-shields. The Group hasn't brought up enough power *yet* to—break through. But it's a matter of time. You and Barclay have got to go—quickly. We've built another ship, Mark and I. . . . I've forgiven Barclay for what he's done these last weeks. If ever a man worked like a slave—but it makes no difference to you. You see, he feels as if he's been a traitor to something bigger than you or me or the Five—his science. He's trying to make up for it. . . . Girand, are you willing to go out into space to save him?"

The engineer said simply, face grim and taut, "I'd go to hell and back. Jimmy counts a little with me. . . . But I've got something to settle with—the Group."

Granton looked at him for a long time in silence. "Jimmy believed you'd come through. He said something about what you were doing with power. . . . When you come back, Girand—you are coming back—we'll fight together."

The other stared a little queerly. "What do you mean?"

Granton smiled, meeting his eyes. "I think you know. . . . The ship is ready."

The engineer did not hesitate. He extended his hand abruptly. "You're on, Granton. . . . Where is it?"

Granton shook his hand in silence. Then, "Follow me."

They went out through a door in the rock, side by side. Granton gestured toward the slim bulk of a silvery football of metal, resting snugly in the trestlework of a debarking cradle. A vague and shimmering brightness hung above it, in a curving shield: the electric beam-screen, athrob with pulsing power.

"That's the ship."

The red light of the rising sun crept along smooth, curved sides, gleaming soft crimson. Girand sucked in his breath with a soft sound: "My God!" It was that beautiful.

A man was standing silently beside the open airlock in the side of the little vessel, his eyes on the slowly lightening sky. His face was deeply carved with lines of weariness. . . . Girand nodded to him, looked at Granton.

"Barclay?"

"Yes . . . Barclay. He's going with you."

They came up together. The man by the airlock hesitated an instant and held out his hand, something humble in the gesture. "My name is Barclay, Girand."

The engineer stood silent an instant, fighting himself. An urge of fierce anger, of contempt, of anger that would shrivel the humility of the man, and contempt that would destroy him, mingled in hate. . . . But he shook hands, and nodded.

"I know. . . ."

Barclay shot him a silent, grateful glance. Granton moved a little away from them both and spoke softly. He was glancing at his watch. He nodded suddenly, and stepped back from the ship.

"You haven't got very much time. He may need you—now. And the Group won't wait forever. They're trying to break through now. . . . Come back with him, Girand. You understand me?"

Girand smiled grimly. As if this other had to tell him that! "I do."

Granton shot him a long, hard glance, then nodded. "You'd better go, now. . . ."

The other two nodded. Girand stepped through the opening of the airlock and vanished; Barclay followed, moving the mechanism that closed the double doors. . . . They swung shut, fitted snugly into place.

A humming sound throbbed though the thin desert air. Granton stood very still, watching. There was no display of unleashed power; but the ship rose slowly from the grip of the landing cradle, climbed upward through the reddening sky. . . .

In the distance dark shadows stirred, and the purring roar of armored heliships came across the sand. A scarlet fleet of ships struck upward, motors throbbing, beam projectors sparkling angry streaks of yellow light. . . . The Group had begun to fight.

The speed of the silvery football changed, merged into a silent slip of soundless force, driving hard through the thin veil of the earth's air. Power, quivering and unseen, answering the challenge of the red squadron . . . Spinning lift blades fought the fading droop of thinning atmosphere; motors failed and choked, yielding to the frozen rigor of the edge of space. Futile saffron beams stabbed out like angry fingers—but the silver ship climbed onward, vanished. . . .

As so many baffled hawks, the red 'copters resigned the chase, dropped straight down in screaming flight upon the banked shimmering glow of Granton's beam-shields. Yellow beams and purple flared and flashed in counteraction on the glimmering screens; flickered and faded, swung away. . . . The fleet came about, motors humming, and slid low across the desert beyond Granton's hills—was gone.

Granton, crouched before the clicking panel of the beam-control board, straightened suddenly, eyes on the vision pictured in the glow of the receptor visa-plate. He looked up and laughed. . . .

The ship moved upward through the atmosphere with an effortless ease, the Granton generator humming a steady song of power. Girand sat by a porthole, looking down at the world falling away beneath them.

The horizon climbed, and curled upward, and the earth looked concave, distant. They went higher, and convexity came, to round out into a great sphere, cloud-girt, with the Pacific very blue in the far distance. Then they were out of the atmosphere and the whole globe spread out before them, with the continents like etched figures in a small wood puzzle. . . . Barclay sat like an automaton before the simple control board, his eyes unwavering from his instruments.

Except once—when the televise screen glimmered to the bright scarlet of the raiding ships, and flashed and flickered under the yellow stab of ion rays. . . . Then Barclay turned pale about the lips, and drove home the plunger of a master-stud. The ship quivered, shot upward faster, left the red fleet far behind. . . .

"The Group?" Girand asked calmly, almost as if the matter held no great importance. . . . It seemed insignificant and small, out here. Barclay nodded.

"The fleet's been holding us in the laboratory since—just before Warren left. And now we've slipped out between their fingers. . . . The Group will foam."

"I hope so." Girand grinned and turned away. . . . Thought of that faded in a quick exultance from his mind. He felt a thrill rising in his soul. They had dared to go out into space, in this little bubble of steel—man was no longer earthbound! The thought set his heart to pounding. . . .

The feeling passed, and loneliness came in its place, as the ship shot on into infinity, the sky intensely black before them, with the stars like diamond dust scattered with a cosmic hand. And the moon a monstrous world blotting out half the universe, hiding the orange flame of the distant sun. . . .

Girand got up and moved cautiously about the ship, found the locker holding the two space suits, both of which would have to be used. They could take no chances on losing Jimmy; it would be a game of life and death at best, bringing him across space to this ship.

Barclay stiffened suddenly, and cried out: "Here she comes—'The Anton Warren!' Girand—look!"

Girand came behind him quickly, and stared through the glassite plate above the control panel. The tiny sliver of silver light was growing, expanding before them, until they were hurtling through space side by side, circling in an endless orbit, each ship no more than a hundred feet from the other.

Barclay locked the controls and rose, face set. He looked at Girand. "We're in a meteor belt here, Girand. God help us if we get in the way of one of those things!"

Girand shook his head. "We'll hope for the best, that's all. And Jimmy is out there—waiting for us. That counts."

"Yes," the other agreed, "of course . . . Let's go."

They helped each other into the clumsy space suits, with their rocket attachments along the sides and back. Air-tight helmets came down, fitted snugly into the neck segments of the metal fabric. Girand and Barclay stared at each other, caught a vision of ungainly monsters in armor.

Girand led the way to the lock; he was familiar with the mechanism. It was very similar to the emergency ports of the stratosphere lines of earth. . . . The inner panel slid open, and the two men went in together. The panel closed; and the outer slab swung inward.

The engineer and Barclay went out head foremost into space, with a little rush of air from the lock. Girand, an instant later, felt a sensation of unutterable giddiness, watching the universe whirl around him; and then he was himself again. He applied the power to his rocket attachments gingerly, felt himself jerk, watched the other ship draw appreciably nearer. Barclay was moving on the other side of him.

The smooth sides of "The Anton Warren" loomed up before them. Girand's throat was dry; only a little longer, and Jimmy would be with them. . . .

Barclay opened the airlock, and went through. Girand moved alongside, waiting. . . . The other's head and shoulders appeared, with the armored form of Warren in his arms. Barclay's body swung, and Jimmy moved across space, struck against Girand; the engineer caught him hard, looked through the helmet.

He caught a jerk of surprise through the glassite plating; Jimmy's voice came through the radiophone: "Girand! You here! You know—I'd almost begun to think you weren't coming!"

"You knew better than that," Girand said quietly, fighting a queer tightness in his throat. "I came—and I'm here!"

"When you two get through there, I'd like to remind you we haven't got all day," Barclay's voice came abruptly. "Let's get going, Girand. I don't like the thought of those meteorites."

"Right," Girand said. "Come over on the other side; Jimmy's suit hasn't rocket attachments. We'll take him together."

"Coming," Barclay answered. He moved in close and caught Warren's right arm. Girand took the other. They applied power slowly, swung away from the derelict "Anton Warren," and came nearer to their ship.

Girand's heart tightened suddenly, the breath caught in his throat; the power was dying, choking off in his suit! He dropped back slowly, inexorably, felt himself pulling against Warren's arm. With sudden decision he let go, spoke quickly.

"Barclay! The power is going in my suit— It's gone! How's yours?"

The other hesitated. When he answered, his voice was queer: "All O.K. . . . you say yours is *all* gone? You can't move?"

Girand gestured helplessly. "No. There's nothing left. . . . You'll have to keep us all going."

He was falling back steadily. Already a gap had opened between his body and the other two.

"Good God!" Barclay's voice was taut with horror. "Look there, Girand! Coming at us!"

They all three saw it: a meteorite, a jagged chunk of rock and iron, whirling endlessly through space—and now on an orbit even with the three in armor, hurtling toward them! Barclay applied power in a sudden burst; the engineer, frozen, saw lines of flame leap from the rocket jets of the other's suit.

"Girand, get away! Try, man, for God's sake! We can't save you! If I turn back now it'll get us all!"

But the engineer knew, and Warren knew, that that was a lie. There was time yet—if Barclay willed it so. . . . But if he was afraid—

Warren spoke frantically, struggling against Barclay's grip: "Let me go, you yellow scum! I'll stay with him. . . . Let go!"

Barclay's voice came, taut and strained: "All right! . . . Yellow! You think—I'm afraid. . . . I'm coming, Girand!"

He hurled the other from him suddenly; Warren's body shot across space and struck the edge of the airlock in the side of the ship. Then Barclay turned and came down in a swift slant to where Girand struggled helplessly, staring with dazed eyes at the oncoming meteor.

Barclay struck the engineer like a thunderbolt, rocket jets standing out in long plumes of flame behind him; Girand's body turned over twice, hurtling through space, shot past the edge of the jagged mass of oncoming rock. The shock of the collision halted Barclay's headlong flight, flung him off at a tangent—squarely into the path of the ragged bulk of iron and stone. . . .

Warren cried out and turned his eyes away; Girand watched, unable to move, his body flattened against the outer panel of the airlock. . . . It was over quickly. He turned, a little sickened.

"He was right, Girand!" Warren choked hoarsely. "He couldn't have saved us all—and I thought he was leaving you because—"

"So did I," Girand said, still dazed. "But he saved us both . . . at the cost of himself. . . . It was a quick death."

"Yes," Warren whispered, eyes staring into space, "I believe he wanted it that way. . . ."

Girand fumbled at the outside controls of the airlock, felt the panel opening under him; he caught Warren by the arms and drew the other after his body, into the ship. . . . The outer panel closed behind them.

Girand gestured toward the control board. "Can you handle this ship, Jimmy? If not—"

The other did not hesitate. He shrugged out of the ungainly space suit. "But I can. It's a duplicate of the other. . . . We'll go back now, Girand."

The engineer nodded. "Yes. Back . . . Granton will be waiting."

A little later a silver line of light swung round in a long oval near the moon, straightened out, and sped down through nothingness toward the beckoning earth. A ship of space was going home.

The gas plane rose swiftly, and above the electric plane drew quickly nearer. The gravitational altimeter was rising rapidly.

Illustrated by Morey

The Battery of Hate

By John W. Campbell, Jr.

CHAPTER I

BRUCE KENNEDY looked delightedly at the ampere-hour-meter on the laboratory bench, at the voltmeter, and finally at the ammeter. Then he drew out the notebook from the left-hand desk drawer and carefully wrote in the new entries.

"Wednesday, May 28, 1938, nine-thirty A.M. Ampere-hours, five thousand, six hundred seventy-two; watt-hours, twenty-three thousand, eight hundred twenty-two; volts, four-point-two; amperes, eighty-five. Sweet spirits of niter, isn't she a brute for work!" He looked happily at the squat, black case on the floor, two feet long, eighteen inches wide, and two feet high. A small, humped projection at one end seemed the source of a faint whine that filled the cellar-laboratory. A mass of heavy leads ran from two thick copper terminals at the top of the black case, up to the table which served as a laboratory bench. Over on one side of the room, where the angle of the concrete cellar wall joined the wallboard, a pile of unused apparatus of various sorts was heaped in disarray. Inductances, voltmeters, heavy resistance coils, all the apparatus of an experimenter in electrophysics. On the concrete wall, sections of shelves had been placed, holding rows of various chemicals; in a rack on the floor below the window that let a patch of bright golden sunshine on the floor hung a dozen curious rectangles of a black, lustrous material. They were just the shape of the end of the black case on the floor, plates for the battery evidently, black, lustrous plates, soft black graphite.

To one side of the door through the wallboard was a frame of pipes, and, attached to it by porcelain insulators was a network of wires that resembled a gigantic electric toaster. A plate of zinc hung behind it, evidently protecting from the heat the more or less combustible wallboard, which had, nevertheless, been scorched slightly.

The room was terrifically, uncomfortably hot, though both door and window were opened, for it was a warm May day, and the huge heater certainly did nothing to alleviate the temperature. Kennedy wiped the perspiration from his forehead, happily, however, and smiled down at his battery.

"The fuel battery—the ideal source of power! Electricity directly from coal—or graphite. Electricity produced so cheaply nothing can compete! Electric automobiles ten times more powerful and a hundred times simpler than the best today—electric airplanes, noiseless and unfailing, because an electric motor has just two bearings and a magnetic field. These batteries won't fail—they can't.

"Lord, the world will be a better place, I guess." He smiled and stretched himself ecstatically. Some men get more pleasure out of proving the world isn't a bad place, and making their fellows like it better, than from cornering the means to bring what pleasures the world already has to themselves. Bruce Kennedy was one of the first kind. He smiled whimsically at his "toaster" now. "You were all right when I started these experiments last January, but May in New Jersey and you don't get along. Guess it's time to test those batteries on a refrigerating machine." He stopped, as still another thought struck him. Success was here and the thousand and one tiny but irritating problems were ironed out, and now the great problem of its use came before him. "Another thing people will have—home cooling will be worthwhile when electric power comes at ten dollars a ton!"

Bruce Kennedy saw the good his invention of the fuel battery would bring the world. A plate of graphite, cheaper and more plentiful than coal, down there in the Archiazoic Period, oxygen from the air, a plate of copper, plated with a thin layer of gold merely to collect current, and a cheaply made solution. Power. Power, as he said, at "ten dollars a ton," for the air was free; the graphite alone had to be renewed. The little whining motor, run by the battery itself, served to force the bubbles of air through the solution, to keep it saturated with oxygen.

So Bruce Kennedy blithely set about patenting the great invention and making himself an electric automobile to be driven by these super-batteries. Had someone pointed out to him the terrible path of hate and bloodshed that lay ahead of that squat, rounded block of power on his cellar floor, and ahead of him, he would not have believed it, for he was young enough to think that men worked for the good of men, as he himself did.

CHAPTER II

Marcus Charles Gardner, large, very friendly, and popularly known as M. Chas. Gardner, the big power of finance, was looking in some surprise at his secretary.

"What? Who's this wants in? What's he got that's so important and confidential, he can't tell you?"

"I don't know, for of course he didn't say, Mr. Gardner, but he's one of your patent examiners. It might well be important."

"Oh, well. He might have waited till later in the morning anyway. Everybody knows I hate to do or listen to anything important before lunch. Send him in; it probably isn't much."

A small, shrewd-looking man came in. His clothes were very neat and very somber. He looked like a successful lawyer, and was one, a patent lawyer.

"Mr. Gardner?"

"Yes," replied the magnate.

"I'm Peasley Jamison, as you have seen, and I have some news I am sure you will want to hear. Perhaps I should not be certain, perhaps you will certainly *not* want to hear it. At any rate"— he smiled at the bigger man ironically— "there's a new invention. I've been watching for it for the last twenty years, hoping I'd get hold of it. Hardwell and Thomas got it, new firm, not big at all, but they tied it up beautifully. Very skillfully drawn patent. Very pretty work."

"I," said M. Chas. Gardner angrily, "don't give a damn how beautiful it is. *What* is it?"

Still the lawyer did not seem content to disclose his mystery. "I believe you have control of North American Super-power? And proxy-control of most of the oil fields of the country?"

"Yes, what of it?" Gardner was beginning to be wearied.

"If you can, sell out, and do it *quickly*," snapped the little man. Gardner suddenly looked very much more alive.

"Eh, what? What in hell is this invention?"

"You wouldn't know if I told you. It's called a fuel battery, invented by a young man by the name of Bruce Hollings Kennedy. It's a device that can produce power directly from graphite, and it gives it as electricity, the most adaptable of all powers."

"Well, why not buy it?" snapped Gardner.

"Because, my dear man, you haven't money enough to pay adequately for it," smiled the little lawyer.

Gardner looked startled. That was the first time, in some twenty years, anyone had told him he hadn't money enough to buy what he wanted. "What? How— Why I'm worth at least a billion."

"Could you get that billion in cash? No, you could not. Neither could you buy that invention. Even if you could, what would you use it for?"

"Why not in power plants, which is the natural answer? Tear out the boilers and generators?"

"Because it generates *direct* current, which can't be shipped along a line readily; because there won't be any power plants when any man can make his own, as he now owns his own cellar furnace; and lastly because that is only one of the very minor possibilities. Do you know what's going to happen to the oil companies? There won't be one where there are hundreds now. There aren't going to be any gasoline-burning, oil-wasting, smelly, greasy, troublesome gasoline automobiles any more. They'll be electric, and a gasoline motor uses two quarts of oil for every drop an electric motor needs on its two bearings. Gasoline is going to be so cheap they'll pay to have it carted away, and save the insurance."

Gardner laughed. "I hope the rest of your predictions are as empty. I've seen electric automobiles and their batteries. Now and then you can see one having a furious race with some spavined truck horse."

Jamison's tight-lipped smile returned. "Did you ever see a hundred-and-fifty-horsepower electric car? I did; I went to Florida to see it. I was one of the few who saw it and knew what it was. Kennedy built one. He went one hundred and seventy-five miles an hour. He said later he got scared and had to stop."

"One hundred and fifty won't do that," said Gardner keenly.

"One hundred and fifty gasoline won't," Jamison acquiesced, "but one hundred and fifty electric is something different. You've seen electric trucks, haven't you? Some make a good twenty-five miles an hour—with two horsepower.

"A gasoline engine is in a constant state of explosion, which means it wastes ninety-nine percent of its power on noise, heat, friction, and waste motion. An electric motor has two bearings, no explosions, no noise, no waste motion, and almost no heat."

"You mean the automobile is doomed?"

"I said nothing of the sort. It's going to have a new lease on life, but the gasoline car is going out the way wooden battleships did when the *Monitor* and the *Merrimac* called it a draw. Battleships didn't go out, but wooden ones did."

"Gasoline is out, oil isn't needed, power stations won't be wanted; how about iron and steel?"

"Still safe—except that new types of refining will be introduced. Gas for cooking won't be wanted, which will finish the oil fields."

Gardner had been looking at his desk, thinking deeply, his head in his hands. He looked up slowly. "My God, man, he'll ruin the world! It's going to ruin *me*. I won't have a cent left after this panic gets over." His face was going white. "Oil—dead! Power—dead! Automobile corporations—save one—dead!" His voice took on a cold, steely menace.

"I've *got to buy* that patent! Get out." The lawyer left the great man brooding, staring out at New York sweltering in a late September heat. But he didn't see New York; he was seeing the things that would happen if this invention were sold. His comforts would be stripped from him, his yacht, his home, his apartment—and another apartment—everything. He could not get out, for the instant he started selling heavily enough to make a practical retreat, the word would be out, and he would be swamped, the market would drop to zero—everywhere—he'd be cleaned out as his pyramided loans collapsed—

God, but he hated the man who invented that battery!

CHAPTER III

By the next morning Gardner had decided to try his one hope for salvation. He had not slept that night, and his face was lined from lack of sleep; his eyes were bloodshot, and there were patches under them. He knew he stared ruin in the face if he did not succeed today.

At the office he rang for his secretary at once. "Arthurs, I want to locate Bruce Kennedy; try this address, and see if you can get him here before lunch."

Robert Arthurs looked surprised. He had found out quickly that the patent lawyer's visit yesterday had upset his employer badly indeed, but he had not learned how. But now he was again violating his hitherto inviolable rule—he wanted to see someone before lunch!

Nevertheless it was nearly eleven-thirty before Kennedy arrived. Arthurs went into Gardner's office at once. "He has come now, sir," he announced. No need to say who had come—Gardner had been asking him about it all morning.

"Ahhh—send him in! No, wait. What does he look like?"

"About twenty-five, sir, six feet I should say, weighs about one hundred eighty, I should guess, powerfully built, intelligent, well-mannered, soft, deep voice. Clear eyes, brown, and brown hair. Good-looking, and seems very anxious to see you. I took the liberty to mention it was on the matter of an invention of his, and he promised to come at once."

"Damn! Why did you—oh, well, perhaps he'll want to sell. I may be able to get it reasonably—" Gardner seemed lost in thought. "Young you say—probably no more money than he needs?"

"Oh, no sir, he is young, but Bradstreet says he's worth close to a quarter of a million. His father left it. An old mining claim that petered out—that is, gold mining—was reopened shortly before his death. Someone sold him the mine as a gold mine, salted it first, it seems, and shortly Mr. Kennedy found a genuine vein, but when it gave out he left. He had gone west for his health. Five years ago he sold it for a quarter of a million as one of the rich tungsten mines. He would have gotten more, but it was inaccessible."

"Thank you, Arthurs. Excellent. That may help in talking to him. Send him in, please."

Kennedy came in smiling. "I don't know just what this call is for, Mr. Gardner, though your secretary mentioned a patent, and I have only one."

"That was the one; I heard of it through a patent attorney of mine. You seem anxious to get to business." The great man smiled disarmingly.

"I am, I guess. I got the patent only a few days ago, and have been getting ready to attempt marketing it."

"Have you offered it anywhere?"

"Yes, but no one has seen it," Kennedy admitted ruefully. "They didn't believe."

"That is a model?" Gardner asked, noting the small satchel in his hand, not unlike a doctor's bag.

"Right." Kennedy opened it and took from it a miniature battery such as that still working in his home in New Jersey. He pushed a button, and a small motor hummed feebly, rapidly gained power and speed, and finally settled down to a steady whine.

"The blower—air is needed to supply the oxygen for combustion of the graphite. This battery simply burns coal electrically instead of thermically. The energy that would come off as heat in a furnace comes as electricity. Furthermore, it uses graphite, the natural form of free carbon. Coal can be converted to graphite in electric furnaces cheaply, now that electricity will be cheap."

"That might run a flashlight," said Gardner skeptically, "but it wouldn't replace a dynamo."

"That would run an automobile," said Kennedy, "and it, or a larger one, would easily replace a dynamo. The case is steel, with black enamel baked on. It is a strong, tough battery. The solution, which is the real secret, of course, is cheap and, like the solution in the ordinary lead-acid storage battery, lasts practically forever, with the occasional addition of water. The solution in a storage battery is renewed by charging; that is, renewed by the current forced through it."

"How much do they cost?"

"This one cost me five dollars to build, but if you built a hundred thousand they would cost about one hundred thousand dollars."

Gardner whistled softly. "What's the trouble with them?"

"Why—nothing!" replied Kennedy, puzzled and annoyed.

"Lad, there is nothing in this world that's perfect. Automobiles run out of gas, storage battery plates shed, generators overheat and burn their insulation. What's wrong with them?"

"Oh, well—graphite is soft, and somewhat brittle. I've been using very high grade artificial graphite, which leaves practically no ash, but in commercial power plants they would have to use cheap, natural graphite, and add an ashtray of some sort. That would mean draining and refilling at periods. The cheaper the grade of graphite, the more ash."

Gardner nodded slowly. That certainly was not a serious objection. "But in automobiles—don't the plates crack, and break?"

"They were mounted on springs and sponge-rubber in the car, and mine haven't cracked yet."

"I understand the metal plates are gold-plated," said Gardner at length, "and that sounds expensive. How can you make the set for a dollar?"

"They give away gold-plated razors," Kennedy reminded him with a smile.

"Well, I'm convinced. You had a model at the Patent Office, and they accepted it, so it must be O.K. What do you want for your patents?"

"Mr. Gardner, I don't want to sell them. I want backing. I want five million dollars' worth of backing, but I don't want to sell the patents. I want to put this on the market."

Gardner's face did not change, but he was going to have those patents. He *had* to have them.

"I offer you *one million dollars* cash for those patents," he said slowly.

Kennedy's face fell. "I'm sorry, Mr. Gardner. I had hoped we could do business. I am not selling."

He put the bag on the desk and returned the battery to it. Again Gardner made an offer, and though he tried as much as five millions, Kennedy would not sell.

"Good God, man. *Why* won't you sell?" he demanded at length, just as Kennedy started for the door.

"You own heavily in power and oil, Gardner. You are making money in it, and this invention is going to change things. I want to hold these patents, and see that they are *used.* This is an invention that is not going to be suppressed. If necessary I can start in a small way myself." Kennedy went out.

Gardner settled back heavily in his seat. Kennedy had not been angry, simply immovable; he had decided, and the decision would stand. He knew that type of man.

Presently color returned to his face, and he sat there steadily looking out of the window, while his secretary refused all comers. He did not eat, and it was nearly two o'clock before he moved again. Then he hurled himself into action at once.

"Arthurs," he said sharply, hurriedly, "get Jimmy Blake and Bob Hill in here. Tell 'em it's worth their while."

In ten minutes, from other parts of the great building, the two men came. They listened and paled while Gardner talked. In the end, scarcely ten minutes later, they nodded and started for their offices.

Two and a half billion dollars set about crushing certain stocks and bonds, marshaled and directed by three of the keenest minds in the Street. In the short time remaining that day, those stocks were crushed so low that they were almost valueless. They were the stocks in which Kennedy's money was invested.

But there remained some ten thousand dollars in Government bonds, and a few thousand more in some of the finest industrials that even Gardner and his friends had not dared to assail, they were so solid.

CHAPTER IV

The dining room of the very exclusive club was a beautifully furnished place, paneled richly. An air of quiet and impressive dignity, almost of overawing dignity, lent a quieting effect that hushed voices tending toward raucous volume. Lung-power is frequently well developed on the floor of the Exchange.

Gardner was talking to a group of friends at his table, and as he finished the dessert he chuckled to himself. The group of hand-picked friends looked at him admiringly.

"Well, Charlie, what is it? Whom did you fool today?" asked Wainwright, smiling.

"Nobody, Bob, nobody. Somebody tried to fool me." The great man chuckled again. "Come on down to the smoking room, and I'll tell you the story of a patent."

"Well," said Caller, settling himself between Gardner and Wainwright, five minutes later, "here we are, waiting expectantly for your tale." He bit off the end of a cigar, lit it and settled back comfortably.

"A man came in to see me yesterday morning with a great idea. He was going to put all the power plants in the country out of operation. He had invented, and patented, a sort of a wet dry-cell, as far as I could make out from his cautious statements. The only things he said that weren't cautious and as discreet as one should be when selling a patent to the man who is scheming to rob you, as he decided I must be, since I wasn't enthusiastic, were his claims." Gardner permitted himself a hearty laugh.

"Well, he had a battery that was like a big dry-cell, only it was wet, and he wanted to put that in place of generators, just have a lot of big batteries instead of generators."

A general laugh was interrupted by Wainwright. "Well, you bought it up, of course!"

"No, but would you believe it, the fellow was really quite surprised and put out because I didn't. His point was that it was more efficient and didn't require a lot of boilers and generators. He evidently neglected to figure the cost of his metal plates—oh, by the way—the plates had to be gold-plated!"

"Gold-plated batteries for power houses! Good Lord, why didn't you call up the Psychopathic?"

"And direct current at that, you know. He'd have us using cables like those in the George Washington Bridge to ship power!"

"Who was this genius?"

"Ah—let's see—" Gardner pulled out a notebook and consulted it a moment. "Oh, yes, fellow named Bruce Kennedy—the inventor of the gold-plated wet dry-cell for power houses!"

The talk veered after that, and shifted to many other subjects, and Gardner left, to go back to his office and make certain the stocks he had depressed stayed there.

His work had been done, and, he felt, well done. None of those men he had talked to, the most important on the Street, would touch that battery now. That was a clever touch, he felt, mentioning the gold-plated plates of the battery. By tomorrow every man on the Street would know the story and would be laughing at it. Kennedy's stocks would be useless to him. He could not build the things himself. He would try to get help, and help would not be forthcoming. He had turned on that battery the heaviest bombardment he could find—the bombardment of ridicule that will blast asunder the greatest hopes and the wisest plans.

Kennedy sat morosely behind the wheel of his car as he drove slowly along. The Holland Tunnel seemed crowded, and the comet of yellow light he followed and kept pace with seemed as elusive as his hopes of selling that idea to some of the big men who could have supported it.

Out of the tunnel, up the ramp, then up and across the Meadows, past the lights of the Newark Airport. He turned off and cut across country to the southwest, avoiding the city ahead. His low gray coupé hummed softly along the road, and as he got free of the heavy traffic he opened out a bit; the accelerator went toward the floor. The smooth whine of the powerful electric motors mounted in crescendo, and the road began to flash back at higher speed.

Automatically he followed the road back to his home, for in the past week these trips had become automatic. His name had been sent into the sanctums of the great, and it seemed almost as though something discreditable had been known of it, for invariably it came out almost instantly. He had not seen one of the men he had wanted to see, and still his stocks hung so low on the market he could not sell them for the money he needed.

Suddenly he sat straighter, and the swift-moving car swerved slightly under his hands. "And I almost forgot—!" He smiled happily.

Bob Donovan! Just a short while ago he had thought of Bob Donovan as one of his best, and poorest, friends. Bob's father was rich, distinctly so. But he had gotten rich by his own hard work and had every intention that his son should do the same. In fact, the stipulation was that until Bob could gather the sum of ten thousand dollars in one year, by his own efforts, the estate would not be his, and the interest would simply add.

Then Bob had succeeded, and in just one week that year would be up! In that time, he could not have transferred his estate of better than five millions to stocks, which Kennedy was beginning to distrust.

A little town appeared ahead, and the swift gray car slowed down, the motors taking on a peculiar whine as it did so. The car became momentarily warmer, as the motors acted as generators, throwing their current into heating resistance coils.

Before a drugstore the car stopped. Kennedy locked the car and went into the shop.

He telephoned a telegram to the nearest office and came out smiling.

It was an hour later when he reached his house, garaged the car, and went in. A telegram awaited him:

GOT ESTATE AT LAST STOP VERY BUSY AND CAN'T COME STOP WHAT DO YOU WANT BOB.

Another half-hour, and Bob Donovan was looking at a yellow slip with the familiar strips of letters:

NOT HALF AS BUSY AS I AND YOU CAN COME ONLY YOU DON'T KNOW IT STOP LEAVE ESTATE AS IT IS AND COME STOP FOR GOD'S SAKE DON'T BUY STOCKS STOP I NEED CASH AND YOU WANT MORE COME STOP INVENTION BRUCE.

Bob Donovan frowned, finally grinned, and called his lawyer. Then, having gotten that immensely annoyed gentleman out of bed, and arranging to leave the estate as it was, he sent a telegram—collect:

YOU'RE ANNOYING ME STOP COMING TO ANNOY YOU AND WON'T STOP BOB.

Apparently he was very anxious to carry out his threat, for he hired an autogyro and covered the two hundred and thirty miles from Boston in an hour and thirty minutes. It was then after four A.M., and he greatly enjoyed getting Kennedy out of his comfortable bed.

"Well, look who came. I see you lived up to your promise, didn't you?" said Kennedy slowly.

"Such a greeting, such a greeting, and from one who invited me. Don't you know, my lad, that I'm a dignified and important millionaire, and that little boys with inventions should go to the millionaires, and not make the millionaires come to them?"

"Shut up. That's what I've been doing all week. You never wrote me or let me know you'd inherit that estate, and you almost missed out. I've been running to millionaires trying to sell them the idea of backing me, but the only man who would see me wanted to buy it, and it isn't for sale."

"What is it?" demanded Donovan.

Kennedy led him down to the cellar and turned on the lights. "I haven't been connected with the city power for three months now," he explained, and pointed to a long black case against one wall. It was far larger than the small experimental battery he had been working with in May, and leads from it connected to the house wiring. "That's the invention. I've installed electric heaters in every room, and you noticed I turned one on when you came. It's chilly these late summer nights, and already they are useful. That combines my furnace, power and light, and my gas connections."

"What is it?"

"Battery, of course. Do you remember my lectures on that subject before we left school? I've been working on it now for three years, and I got it at last. That's the result."

Donovan started, and wheeled on his friend, his blue eyes opened wide in amazement. "*Fuel battery!* You did it, Bruce! And I'm backing you for all it's worth. How much do you want, why didn't you back it yourself?"

"Bob, I'll tell you. I told Gardner about that—he seemed to have heard I had the patent, and sent for me. He wanted to buy, but I wanted backing, so he wouldn't agree. I told him I could get backing elsewhere and if necessary do it myself. That afternoon my entire group of stocks, save for a few of the biggest companies, where I owned comparatively small amounts, lay down and went to sleep. They are still sleeping. And I haven't seen anybody else."

"Is that so? And what do you think happened?" Bob's eyes squinted slightly at his friend.

"I don't know. I thought Gardner might depress the stocks, but he couldn't keep his enemies from seeing me."

"Couldn't he? Why couldn't Columbus get anybody to back him when he tried to sail to the Asian coast?"

"Everybody laughed at him—but—" Kennedy's quick mind began to understand and see the laughing points. "And do you know, this thing has gold-plated metallic plates."

"That's the answer, Bruce," nodded Donovan. "He probably told them you had some sort of an oversize dry-cell with gold plates that you wanted to replace the power plants with. Tell that to a group of friends as a joke, and the whole financial crowd would know it in a day. The only support you'll get, according to his lights, is from him, and he wants to buy. What are you going to do?"

"Do? Why, build a plant and start manufacturing, if you'll let me. Your estate hasn't been taken out of bonds and banks and real estate, has it? He can't depress the price of Government bonds, and banks still have to pay cash. We can start manufacturing anyway."

"Manufacturing what? Flashlights? We won't be able to borrow; Gardner and his pals have too much influence, and five millions won't do a lot. We need five hundred millions, and we could get it in a day after a few big demonstrations—if Gardner weren't opposing us. If we manufacture flashlights, or anything little, no one will ever believe they will work in a big size."

"No, and by all the planets, I'll wreck Gardner! He can keep banks from loaning, he can keep brokers from investing or offering stock, but he can't keep you from using your own money, if you will. Listen—all we have to do is to make a few thousands of those over there, and sell them to private owners! I can make one of those for about one hundred and twenty-five dollars on a quantity basis, and they cost about five or ten dollars to install. Their one difficulty is that they give D.C., and all modern radio sets use A.C., and the television sets use the A.C. power lines as a third circuit for synchronization.

"But there aren't many television sets yet, and there are lots of D.C. radio sets. We can get G.E. to make some sort of a heater for rooms that works on 110 D.C., and then we are set. We can sell to suburban homes. How many women would like to have electric ranges, if the power were only as cheap as gas? How many men would like to have a heating system that would warm the house in ten minutes in the morning, and could be turned on with an alarm clock that would work every time? Our greatest, in fact only, difficulty will be the electric clocks and radio sets.

"But look what happens. We steal a lot of Gardner's power customers, we bring the battery sharply before the public, not as a flashlight power source, but as a genuine source of practical power. Farms will buy them for power, then small cities will see that the municipal plant could use a big set.

"Then there will be the next step—automobiles. I'll show you one tomorrow—mine. I made better than one hundred seventy down at Daytona Beach, but I got scared, I guess, and cut the power. It has two motors, and a big battery under the hood. The motors are in the wheel. I reversed the usual system and have a revolving field with a stationary armature. The wheel is the field."

"You're right, Bruce. We can—and will!"

"Now let's sleep."

CHAPTER V

M. Chas. Gardner looked up from his work, at a tiny red light that appeared suddenly in the frame of a picture on his desk—He looked across the study toward a long oil painting. He hesitated a moment and punched at something on his desk—the lock, apparently, of one of the drawers. A faint click was the response, and the oil painting opened inward. A slim, black-haired man with sharp black eyes stepped quickly into the room, and the painting returned to its frame.

"Chief, they beat me. Gawd, I never saw anythin' go like that gray coupé of his. He got a friend wid him. I dunno who it was."

Gardner's face flushed quickly. "Cazoni, I told you to put some men on him!"

"Aw, Chief, I did but, hell, the guy went into dreamlan' about two in the A.M., an' the guy was tired as hell, so he pulled out. I had another torp on the job about five, an' it was dark. How'd we know anybody came. They—"

"Fool! I told you to change men so he wouldn't know he was trailed. He found it out, and beat you! Imbecile!"

"Aw, Chief, I did change men—plenty. I dunno how he found out, but anyway, that friend musta slipped in at night, an' how was we to know?"

"What happened this morning?" demanded Gardner.

"About six-thirty, the man on the house—Tony, ya know, he got Chi to take his place and got some chow. It was after seven 'fore he got back, an' Chi was mad an' beat it. Nothin' happened though till about ten, then they—only Tony thought he was still alone, he sent away that housekeeper a while back, and has her come in every other day—well, they got breakfast, then about eleven two guys came out, an' went to his garage and got out that gray car of his. Ya know, it looks like hell, no lines at all. Looks like a model of 1930. Big square-front radiator, posed headlights—got pants on the wheels, though. Well, we didn't think it could move worth talkin' about, and we had a big Packard 16.

"Well, they start out, an' light for the north. They go nice and easy up the Hudson, cross above the Big Town, cut toward the coast again—an' hit the main Route One north. It was early in the afternoon and it was a weekday. They lit out—man how they moved! Tony picked me up, when he saw where they were goin', an' I was with him. That boat of mine will do one hundred and twenty any day easy. But that old gray can was doin' one hundred by the time we could hit eighty, and was so far away we couldn't see it, when we hit better'n a hundred. Chief, I never saw anything move like that did. That boat of mine acted like it was a balky truck beside an airplane.

"We gotta get a boat like that, Chief, before we can keep him in sight. What kind is it, d'ya know?"

"So you lost him. Lost him just after he found some friend. What did the friend look like? Tony say?"

"Tall, blond, good-lookin', looks like a college friend of this guy's. Looks slow, but Tony says he moves fast, dropped somethin' an' it never hit the ground. They had a big black box that made the springs move when they put it in, but this bird handles it easy. Guess he's strong. Kinda slim though. 'Bout five-eleven or six-one, somewhere in there."

"College friend, eh? Headed north on Route One, and just ran away from you? Keep a plane handy after this, and use a shortwave set to keep in touch," ordered Gardner. He paused in thought. "And find out who that friend is, and *locate Kennedy!* Get that? There's more in this than in the rest of our business. The car—he made it! The thing that made it so fast is what I want. It's cost me five million dollars on the market already to keep him from getting some support! Now do you know how important that is?"

Gardner's eyes blazed at his lieutenant. Jimmy Cazoni whistled softly. "Five millions! It's worth that, eh?"

"No. It's worth a hundred times that!" Gardner spoke tensely. *"Don't lose that man when you find him!"*

"We won't, Chief," promised the gangster. "How about an accident to that car—wouldn't that help?"

"No. It would be worse, if anything. He and a friend of his named Robert Donovan made exchange wills, I believe. Neither has any relatives, and they fixed it up a couple of years ago. Some kid stunt, I guess, but it holds. And this Donovan—" Gardner broke off with an exclamation of dismay! "Donovan—Boston—Route One—Good God! That Donovan just came into a fortune of five millions, and he could give that man support!

"Cazoni!" He turned his eyes sharply to the slim, black-eyed man. "Get men on the lookout in Boston. Try first at"—Gardner searched hurriedly through some papers, and found the letter he wanted— "409 Marlboro Street, Boston. This Donovan owns the place—apartment house, I believe, and he's been living there. Keep Tony watching, and if he recognizes the man, send me word. Now beat it, and *move!*"

Cazoni started rapidly toward the painting, but Gardner called him back. "Wait—let Nannery take over the other business, and don't bother me. I'll be busy, so he can handle it himself. This is more important."

Cazoni stepped in front of the picture with a word of agreement, the frame clicked, the picture swung back, and Cazoni disappeared.

"Thank heavens I have an organization I can depend on in time of need," piously declared Gardner. "With those two together, I may be able to get somewhere." He smiled approvingly.

"Well, do you believe in it, Bob?" asked Kennedy, as the gray coupé swung to the curb in Boston. The whine of the motors died, and the parking lights went on.

"Sweet, little brother, sweet. I never heard so pleasant a sound as the hum of those motors. Even when we hit one hundred and forty they hummed, and there was no engine vibration. How long can you go on one set of plates?"

"About three thousand miles, Bob. I carry a spare set, as well. Remember that I get eighty-five percent efficiency from those plates, and an electric motor is better than ninety percent efficient."

"What a thing for an airplane motor!"

"I've been wanting to try it, but I made this first, as easier and safer to experiment with."

They were getting out their bags, and walked across the street, into the apartment. "I have a plane now," said Donovan softly. "Or should have. Lockheed promised it today. It's a special stratosphere racer with high-altitude Diesel. How much would batteries and motor weigh?"

Kennedy's eyes were bright. There was more fun, more enjoyment in the experiments than the constant disappointment of the business. He calculated rapidly. Presently he frowned slightly. "Hard to say. The batteries increase in weight for desired cruising range. I should say eight hundred pounds for one thousand horsepower and ten-thousand-mile cruise, but with every additional two hundred pounds another ten thousand miles of spare plates can be added."

Donovan whistled. "The engine and charger alone weigh one thousand pounds, fuel additional, and the power declines from eight hundred horse at sea level to three hundred at fifty-five thousand feet. Any decline in your scheme?"

"I'll tell you, I don't know. I've never tried it, you see. The composition of the air at fifty-five thousand is about the same, but the density is easily arranged—just a pump, and the batteries use one anyway. Simply make it larger. Or better, have them in the fuselage and keep air there."

"Not so good," replied Donovan, sitting down in a chair, "because air has weight, and it will just mean that many more pounds of thick air to carry with us. But will it work?"

"I'll bet I can get at least nine hundred at any height the plane will fly."

"Let's have supper and then we'll see," suggested Bob.

They reached the field after dark to find that the plane had been delivered, a five-place stratosphere plane, the air-tight cabin with its double walls streamlined with a beauty that seemed to make the plane move even when at rest. The great radial Diesel, surrounded by the Venturi cowling and the bulge of the supercharger, alone seemed to break the lines.

"No cooling on an electric motor," muttered Kennedy, "but that's the prettiest thing I've seen in years."

"It'll be prettier," replied Donovan. "I'm going to take it up now, though, and then you'll be able to see the difference."

"I'll get busy—the Lockheed man is still here," replied Kennedy, and stuck to his decision.

Before they left the field that night, men were at work unshipping the heavy Diesel and the fuel tanks.

The next morning they went to see James Montgomery, of Montgomery, Harrison and Flagg, Donovan's lawyers.

"So what we want," Donovan concluded, "is your advice and help, and perhaps, if you wish, a partnership with us."

Montgomery shook his iron-gray head and laughed. "Couldn't make it—your lawyer. Corporation law. Want to incorporate, don't you? What's the title?"

"Kennedy Fuel Battery, Incorporated," replied Donovan instantly.

"Kennedy and Donovan," said Bruce insistently.

"Kennedy Fuel Battery is better—it's your battery."

"And your money."

"All right, give me a show for my money, will you! I say Kennedy Fuel Battery," grinned Donovan.

"Now the next question," interrupted the lawyer, "is whether you have any money, Bob. If what Kennedy suspects is true, you'd better draw out of banks before they close. I can believe it, because that's Gardner's way of fighting."

"Why—what do you mean?" asked Donovan in surprise.

"About a quarter of a million of your money is still in banks, due to the original trust, and another million due to the fact that it is changing hands. If Gardner suspects you are lending help, he can readily tie up those funds—break the bank if necessary, close it for examination of books, a number of things. Get out of that, and buy—Government bonds, I guess would be the best bet."

"Do it," nodded Donovan.

But it was easier said than done. They acted quickly, taking the largest deposits first, finally coming to the smaller. They did not get four of these, totaling one hundred and seventy-five thousand dollars. The rest were in bonds already, and unassailable.

"He's already moved. How under the sun did he know so soon?" asked Kennedy helplessly as they left the doors which bore the announcement that payment had been temporarily suspended.

A short, heavily built man across the street could have told them. He ducked into a drugstore and telephoned as the gray coupé started down the street, a powerful black touring car following it.

" 'At's him. Mus' be this Donovan, all right. What is he, a cop? No? Soun's like a cop's name," he reported.

Presently he was walking rapidly across the Common and made his way toward Marlboro Street.

M. Chas. Gardner had given another order.

CHAPTER VI

Gardner listened to the somewhat metallic voice from the telephone, and cursed softly to himself. Donovan had beaten him to his banks by minutes only, and now there was practically the whole of his fortune in a condition he could readily use. Further, it was in bonds, bonds that could not be driven down in value, and Gardner realized that no amount of juggling would get those funds frozen again.

Further, the companies with whom Donovan would place orders would accept the orders—but loans—? He would have to have some loans if he wanted to make the batteries on the scale that would be demanded. To manufacture batteries for power plants would require more than a few millions, particularly as only the small, municipal plants would be available to him. Gardner himself controlled the big plants that could have given saving orders. Automobiles—no, he could control that. Laughter! The bomb that would explode any plan among the giants of industry, the men who gave orders in the thousands of units, hundreds of thousands of dollars. Unless he started a new make of car, and that meant months of designing, more months, years, perhaps, before the public accepted it. Flashlights—that was the place for batteries, but there were no millions in that, and it would do enormous damage to Kennedy's invention.

Flashlights and million-horsepower power plants don't come in the same thought.

No, Donovan would be tied for some time yet, and Gardner decided, as he hung up the receiver, that the campaign of ridicule must go on. It must spread to Boston, to other cities. So on that day men from his office went to various cities—to tell a joke!

They were sent to financial centers to do some business, some reasonable excuse was given, but everywhere the tale of the golden battery was told.

But that was not enough. A second report reached him soon after they left. "Kennedy Fuel Batteries" was being incorporated. The next order would have surprised even the not easily surprised Montgomery. Gardner went home to give the order, and he used a private telephone, which was not listed, to call an unlisted number in Boston, and a second unlisted number in New York City.

"And remember, *Cazoni, be careful to have that pen job first and do that second one right!* If you fail me in that, Cazoni—" Gardner's voice was harsh.

Cazoni understood, and assured Gardner things would be "fixed up."

Gardner was worried, horribly worried. He had spent thirty years in building up the colossal machine that he represented to the world, and nearly five years building up that secret, deadly machine which had more than once aided in the smooth passage of the greater machine. It had grown out of one of those rough passages. At the end of the depression in 1933 a certain man had threatened the horizon, a black cloud of storm that seemed about to sweep away those pyramided loans, toppling already. That man had been murdered—mysteriously.

But never before had so serious a menace appeared. This was, he knew, a Hydra of Business. To lop off one head, he knew would be useless, unless he could fasten himself firmly in its place. Those patents—the patents that he must control.

They meant millions to him, if he could get them, but he was growing old, and these younger men were thinking faster than he now, foreseeing his moves. They meant millions if he could get them, but if he didn't—

And all he wanted was peace!

CHAPTER VII

When the large battery in his cellar had been made, dies and patterns for the parts had been cut; and as they were by far the most expensive parts in the construction, Kennedy had made twenty complete sets. As a result, the batteries for the plane were readily put together, a freight plane making the trip down to New Jersey and back with them. In the meantime the powerful, light electric motor was easily obtainable, for that was practically standard equipment obtainable at once.

They ripped out the fuel tanks and the engine during the morning, and in the afternoon the batteries were set up in their place, electric heaters were installed, and electric motors were provided to power the compressors that would maintain atmospheric pressure in the cabin.

Nearly the entire day was spent at the field, working on the ship, and night was falling when at last they were ready for the trial.

Wainwright, the Lockheed engineer, had been a great help in the work, for he knew the plane thoroughly, and the tensile strains the various members could safely resist. And now that the plane must be relicensed, he offered to go with them to testify as to its fitness before the Inspector of Aviation. To reach the Government official, they found they would have to go to his home in Quincy, and the three men crowded into the gray coupé.

Across Boston, out through the Jamaica Parkway, and finally swinging into the Cape Cod Superhighway, the gray coupé moved leisurely.

Behind it a large black sedan with New York plates moved along at an equal pace. As the two cars swung out on the eight-lane concrete superhighway, the powerful sedan spurted ahead, rapidly cutting down the quarter-mile lead. Presently it swung across the round of the speed-lane separation rib. The two-lane, high-speed concrete with its banked curves opened out before it, and almost simultaneously the gray coupé shot forward with swiftly rising speed, and struck the high-speed lane.

But the black sedan was wide open, its powerful multicylinder engine roaring gently through the muffler. It flashed rapidly faster.

"Lord, this boat can move. I could scarcely believe you when you told me about it," said Wainwright, watching the speedometer move steadily across. Eighty—one hundred—

"Still rising," said Kennedy smiling and watching the road ahead. The speed lane was practically deserted, though the slow lanes were fairly well traveled.

A whistling roar mounted suddenly from behind them and a great black shadow moved up beside them and passed them with a speed a full twenty miles an hour greater. But as it drew alongside, a dull popping, like a whole carload of champagne bottles, a burst of dull red flame, and a metallic rapping burst out suddenly.

Three machine guns were discharging high-velocity lead at the driver of the little coupé! The car suddenly fell off, a whine changed to a hum as motors suddenly became dragging generators, and the car wavered in the road. With an added burst the black car with the New York plates drove ahead!

Kennedy's face was white, his hands clasped on the wheel with an intensity that made them as white as his face. Wainwright's eyes were opened wide, and staring. Donovan looked slightly sick.

"I—I didn't guess that. Good God, how did they miss us?" he asked weakly.

"They didn't," replied Kennedy, a slow grim smile touching his lips. "Look." His groping hand found a heavy wrench on the floor of the car, and wielded it heavily against the clear plate of the windshield. The massive wrench was nearly torn from his hand, as the windshield bounced it back—the glass unharmed!

"I built for accidents. Experimental, you know—reinforced the frame and the body to protect me, used an accident-proof, and incidentally bullet-proof, window I discovered, but forgot in the discovery of the fuel battery." The grim smile of tight lips persisted. He turned to the slow lane, maneuvered over to the right, and cut into the circle.

"Wait—where are you going?" demanded Donovan, his face relaxing rapidly.

"Back, brethren, back, where they can't try again. They'll use a truck next time, and I can't guarantee the resistance of the machine to that."

"That's where they'll look for you," Donovan stated sharply. "Go back to the next circle at your highest speed, now you've started, then turn, and run back on your course a second time toward Quincy. We'll do the business we started on, and they'll be looking for us somewhere else."

Kennedy nodded, and the gray car swerved over to the Boston

lanes, turned quickly to the high-speed lanes as they passed sixty miles an hour, and mounted till they were whining down the road, the motor's song a faint scream, a curious blurbing sound of air gurgling like a brook over rocks as it passed the car. Somewhere behind, and rapidly falling farther behind, a police siren warned them to slower speed as a police speedster tried vainly to reach them. The wind howled protest, and the speedometer quivered at one hundred and fifty.

They slowed rapidly, swerved into the low-speed lane, across to the circle, and turned back again on the overpass to the Quincy lanes.

"It seems Gardner has other systems as well," said Kennedy dryly.

"What will they try next?" asked Donovan wonderingly.

"Well, we don't sleep in this bullet-proof car, and even it isn't proof against a good big truck. Also, if we take that plane up they can feel sure it isn't coated with armor plate as this machine was—by accident."

"If I were you two," said Wainwright unhappily, "I'd take that plane and go so high in the sky I couldn't be seen, and I'd move out of this town, and get lost. I'd lots rather have my life and the several millions you already have than to lose the one, and have the other mean nothing to me.

"Anyway, you can leave me here with Thompson. I'll take a train back. They might try again."

Half an hour later, Donovan's plane had been relicensed, and with the necessary papers, Kennedy and his friend started back to Boston. But they circled out, swung well to one side, taking back roads and finally coming into the city from the direction of Newton. They used Donovan's thorough knowledge of the infinitely complex network of cow-path engineered streets, and twisted through the hundreds of one-way streets toward the airfield. It was midnight when they arrived, and Donovan agreed with Wainwright that Boston was not a healthy city for them.

They displayed their papers, the plane was wheeled out of the hangar, and the Field Manager gave them the take-off signal. Instantly the propeller spun into whirring, vibrationless life; the plane leaped across the ground with a startling suddenness and pulled forward with utter quietness. Its landing and running lights flared brilliantly on the ground for a moment, then almost before they knew it, the high-lift stratosphere plane was winging its way steeply aloft, the tremendously powerful motor dragging it upward. "Great guns, Bruce, this motor pulls like a rubber band. It's so smooth you can't feel it, there's no sensation of moving, only a steady pull—and this one thousand horsepower of yours is way off. It must be three thousand. I have it cut way down, and she's still ready to pull the bolts out." Donovan was ecstatic.

"One thousand *electric* horse is 'something else.' A gasoline or oil engine gives one thousand horsepower, when the cylinder is exploding, and runs on momentum for a while. This gives one thousand horse every instant."

"Another plane taking off," said Donovan, smiling. "Let's give them a race up."

As a matter of fact, the instant the two men had appeared on the field and started for their plane, a crew of five men started for a powerful two-place racer. The racer was rushed out into the open, two men took their places in the cockpit, and one at each wing-tip, while the fifth quickly wheeled an electric starting truck into place at the nose. The powerful electric motor whined as the ratchet gripped the propeller hub, and the engine spun slowly. It was a gasoline plane, faster at the lower levels without supercharger, faster at higher levels, for it was lighter. The engine caught, barked into roaring life, and the starting truck was hauled away.

But here the plane lost out. For five full minutes it rested, its wheels chocked, its wings held while the engine warmed up. The electric plane leaped into the air gracefully while they waited, and the lights shrank into the skies.

The gasoline plane was designed for a ceiling of but thirty thousand feet, and was therefore far faster than the stratosphere plane, with its enormously larger wings and far greater pitch. The gasoline plane rose from the field with a roaring engine barking occasionally in misfires, the exhaust darting back in red flames. It climbed steeply and swiftly, the slots in its wings open, as it nearly stood on its tail and let the motor drag it up by the nose.

Two men in the plane: one a pilot, skilled in the daredevil stunts of pursuit and fighting, the other a little sleek-haired man with cold, black eyes, smoking a cigarette he could not taste in the backward sweep of a biting windstream. Nestled against his shoulder was a curiously heavy rifle, with wide flanges along its barrel, and a drum-magazine built into the heavy stock. A broad plate on the stock distributed the shock of the kick across the entire right shoulder. It spit viciously a few times in trial bursts, the sound drowned in the roar of the great X-type motor, its twenty-four cylinders barking rhythmically now.

It climbed swiftly, far more swiftly than the heavy stratosphere plane with its weighty, air-tight cabin built for five. Twelve hundred horsepower flowed out the propeller shaft and fought the rapidly chilling air. The pilot waved a hand, and the gunner behind slipped a headset over his ears.

"We'll catch 'em, Mug. They got somethin' new, I hear. A Diesel doesn't take the warmin' these gas buggies do, but even they can't take off cold, the way that bird did. I heard somebody say they had a thousan'-horse motor. We got twelve hundred, and a lot lighter plane. They've got a couple minutes start—and twenty thousand feet to go before they hit our ceilin'."

The gunner nodded. He didn't realize, as the pilot did but did not mention, that the stratosphere plane would gain rapidly in climbing speed after they left the denser air below twenty thousand, while the power of the gasoline plane would be rapidly sapped by the scant air, and the wings, designed for lower altitude than the larger machine, would begin to lose the advantages they held now.

The gas plane rose swiftly, and above the electric plane drew rapidly nearer. The gravitational altimeter was rising rapidly. Presently the gunner tried a few rounds in the direction of the plane. The tremendously high-velocity bullets, moving more than two miles a second and little larger than a thick pencil lead, moved upward and sang swiftly into the night.

Donovan was concentrating all his attention on his instruments now, while Kennedy read the indicators that told the conditions within the cabin. The soft, gentle snore of the electric motor, the louder scream of the twirling propeller, alone sounded as they climbed.

"Batteries working perfectly, Bruce," said Donovan briefly.

"How's that other plane?" asked Kennedy. "The air and temperature normal?"

"Gaining on us. Low-altitude plane, I guess, and gets better speed than we can hope to."

"Try more—oww! What the—" Kennedy cried in pain and surprise and looked at his leg. A trickle of blood oozed from a tiny puncture in his calf, the muscle was exceedingly sore, and a second tiny puncture on the other side showed something had passed completely through the flesh.

Quickly his eyes sought the metal wall, and he saw two minute holes in the sheet duraluminum. "Bob, I've been shot! That plane is shooting at us! A pencil-bullet went through my leg clean, and passed right through the plane! Use all the power!"

"What!" Donovan looked quickly down and saw the sudden intermittent flashes from the machine below. "Right—machine gun. I'm afraid of this power here—but I'll have to!" He pulled the rheostat control back smoothly, and the gentle hum of the motor mounted swiftly to a driving, tearing whine as the controller reached its limit. The heavy plane tugged forward with a sudden acceleration, and the entire fabric of the all-metal plane creaked under the strain of the great power.

"A thousand electric isn't a thousand gas, or Diesel either, Bruce. She's pulling," said Donovan. Bruce Kennedy was busy already with an iodine solution bottle and a bandage. The minute punctures caused by the clean, swift-moving bullet had closed up already, and the bleeding had stopped.

The plane below was falling behind now, as the larger plane pulled viciously under the great motor. The speed was still rising, though the power from the batteries remained the same; the hum rose to a scream as the motor ran swifter.

Kennedy listened critically. "Bob—that propeller! It's all right for one thousand gas or internal combustion power, but remember an electric motor can, like a man or a steam engine, dig in its toes and heave, so to speak. A gas engine, like any explosive power, works the first time or not at all. That thing's going too fast. One can exert enormous power for a few seconds—the other has no such reserve."

It was, and Donovan cut the power slightly; still the pitch rose, and more rapidly now. Suddenly it seemed to shoot swiftly up the scale; the shriek of the propeller became a terrible roar, an ear-shattering, threshing blast.

"Shut it off!" roared Kennedy—uselessly, for his voice could not be heard. Donovan had already done it, and yet the mad propeller continued to shriek.

With the suddenness of a brake, the thing stopped whirling madly, and an instant later the white-faced Donovan threw on the motor again.

"Too much—reached the speed of sound, and simply went faster than the air could flow in. The plane below gained a sort of caritation."

The dark silhouette of the other machine stood out nearer against the lights of the city. Pulling with all the power the metal blades could handle, the other machine still gained.

"Fast—and light. About twenty-five- to thirty-five-thousand ceiling. We're at fifteen thousand now; when we reach twenty we should be able to pull up," said Donovan.

Kennedy merely reached over and pulled the master light switch. The lights of the machine died, and a starry sky, moonless, alone shed light on them. "Let's not advertise. The bullets have no ceiling."

The plane shot on, riding higher, while the dark mass below circled more blindly now. There were occasional very high clouds, and it was hard for the pilot to keep track now.

His hand waved again, and the gunner took up his headset. "Fool! You hit and warned them. I can't follow them easily now till we get above 'em, and can see 'em against the city lights. They can spot us, though."

"Aww—maybe I punctured their tanks. If they lose the engine juice they won't climb high. Anyway, I mighta got one of 'em."

They continued silently fighting for altitude, while the pilot wondered vainly what had happened. For a moment the heavy plane had pulled away from him readily, then there came a terrific roar such as he had heard only once before, when somebody put gasoline in the fuel oil tanks of a Diesel plane, and the engine exploded. Yet after a moment the roar stopped, and the machine continued unharmed, faster than before, but still slower than he climbed.

Now he was following blindly, for only occasionally could he make out the form against the skies.

He looked anxiously at the luminous altimeter dial. Eighteen thousand. The heaters in their suits and gloves were on now, and the engine was losing power. A dribble of oxygen kept his head clearer. He had to catch them soon—or not at all. He had never seen such a plane as this. It took off cold, flew perfectly, and without trouble. The high-altitude propeller handicapped its power here, and the high-altitude wings didn't help. Yet the power of the other had not diminished a whit. The engine of even the stratosphere plane should have lost somewhat. But it hadn't.

And the noise! What had that been?

Suddenly he saw the plane again, five hundred feet above and climbing easily, faster now. The pilot saw he would never gain now. The plane was entering its own element, and he was approaching his ceiling. The altimeter quivered at twenty-one thousand.

His hand went up three times quickly. The plane vibrated sharply, and the wings stood out suddenly in reddish light. The roar of the engine drowned the crackle of the machine gun, but he knew it was working. The dark shape above did not falter, and through the headset he heard a thin crackle of curses. The light on the wings flickered steadily for a long time, and the pilot himself cursed softly and started down. The fool gunner had gotten himself thoroughly drunk on oxygen. His first trip so high, and when he should have used a mere trickle to steady his nerves and muscles, he was using it straight. No normal man would have held the fire steady, for no man could hold down the barrel of that viciously kicking little rifle.

He glanced around, and saw the barrel of the gun pointing and wavering widely. It walked up steadily as the thing kicked, and the gunner jerked it down savagely, then it walked up again—.

The pilot cursed softly to himself, cut the engine, and circled slowly toward lower levels. The fool!

CHAPTER VIII

"It looks like they gave up, Bruce," said Donovan, as he watched the plane circling downward. Their machine steadily wound itself higher and higher, above the clouds, out and up till the stars began to shine in steady flame, and the twinkling of the atmosphere was cut off. There was scarcely any atmosphere at these altitudes.

"Yes, that plane had to go back, but that doesn't mean that friend Gardner will give up. We're up out of his reach now, but we have to come down again, remember. And he will probably be looking for us."

"How about coming down up at Happy Days? The island is well out into that lonely little lake up in Maine, and it would be some time before even gangspies could locate us up there. The nearest town is Makeaho, and they don't even have a telephone in the town."

"Good idea. Stay way up, and they won't be able to see us. We can come down almost straight, and land on the island itself," agreed Kennedy. "The big field has a few stones, but I think this boat can land safely. At sea level the landing speed is most remarkably low."

The ship was still climbing steadily, and was nearly up to the fifty-thousand-foot level. Donovan was now keenly watching the instruments and Kennedy with equal fascination. "Still going strong, Bob," he said softly.

"I turned on a little more power, cut out some resistance. The propeller seems to take a heavier pull in thinner air. The batteries haven't shown signs of weakening yet."

But finally, at an altitude of seventy thousand feet the batteries did show they could work no further.

The plane skimmed along northward now, and the speed mounted swiftly to well over three hundred and fifty miles an hour. In far less time than they had spent climbing, they were over the spot on which they had intended to land, and the machine began circling noiselessly down.

With slight bumps it came to rest under a row of giant trees at the lower end of a slightly sloping field. Years before, some frugal, hard-working New Englander had pulled most of the rocks from this field, but now the winter frosts were shoving them up again, and the surface was bumpy. The great, soft airwheels rode them easily through, and they stopped safely. A low hum of the motor, the rustle of air, and the machine wheeled steadily about the locked left wheel and came into position at the proper place.

"We can move right into the cabin," said Donovan in a low voice. "I was up here in July for a while, and was called away in a hurry. The boat's in the shed, below, and there's food stored in the larders for several weeks. Remember those trick storehouses we built?" He smiled faintly, stretching stiff legs on the grassy meadow land. "Come in handy; even the bread will be fresh."

"Yes, old hermit, you may think you can isolate yourself in this lonely backwoods place, but all the same, said telegraph at Makeaho is going to be used by the Fuel Battery Company, much as we disapprove of the fact. We've got to tell Montgomery where we are."

"I think we'd best give up this whole game till we settle with Gardner somehow, sometime," said Donovan mournfully. "I think we ought to fight back the way he fights us."

Donovan produced a key as he spoke and unlocked the door of the cabin. An oil lamp stood on the table, its reservoir still full. A moment later the little cabin was brightly lit as the mantle glowed white.

Kennedy seemed to be thinking seriously. Finally he spoke again. "Bob, Montgomery's got your power of attorney, and he knows in general what our plans are. With the boat we can call down shore at Makeaho easily enough, but they know us there. That plane is conspicuous. Let's get a good secondhand Ford and park it somewhere near the lake shore. We can call at some town where we aren't known, reaching the car by the boat. Then at least they'll have some trouble finding us, and in the meantime I think I can prepare a warm welcome."

"Can Montgomery handle the stuff, and get the things you need—the right machines?"

"He merely has to tell certain companies that already have plans to go ahead and make the machines. I have already got plants to give me estimates on the cost of making the machines and have left plans with them."

"We'll do it," nodded Donovan. "Only one thing I don't like. I have plenty of money to get that Ford, all right. Too much. I'm still carrying sixty-five thousand I got and didn't have time to reinvest."

"Stick it in the flour barrel, and come to sleep," Kennedy advised with a grin.

CHAPTER IX

Gardner was looking angrily at the sleek, black-haired Cazoni, and Cazoni looked surly and uncomfortable.

"And so first he runs away from you in a bullet-proof automobile, and then escapes in a bullet-proof airplane?" Gardner smiled, a grimace. "I've heard of bullet-proof automobiles, and bullet-proof glass, but no bullet-proof glass I ever heard of failed to show the cracks! And I never heard of a bullet-proof airplane. You know as well as I that an airplane, to be proof against even the bullets of a revolver, would be so heavy with its metal plates that it couldn't lift off. And to be proof against the bullets from that little machine rifle, it would need one-inch armor plate, as you know perfectly well. No plane could fly with that. Did you use the same gun on the automobile?"

"Naw, they used an old Tommy. You can't silence a Weemar gun. Too damn many cars can make one hundred and thirty now to get away, so we used a silenced Tommy."

"Well, they *might* armor a car against Tommy bullets, but you know and I know they simply shot all over the lot as usual. You said those windows didn't even crack!"

"Chief, I shot some myself, and I *know* I hit that window, but it didn't phase it. That bird's clever, an' I'll bet he's got somethin' new. "An' I told you Gunner was the best man we could get in Boston. That damn town never was no good, they haven't any organization there. Just a lot o' squabblin' kid gangs. But Gunner is there because he ain't feelin' happy in Chi. He's good, but the damn nut don't know nothin' about goin' up. Charlie flew him, and he said Gunner got drunk. He said he got drunk on ox-eye or somethin' like that, an' I asked him what that was and he says air. How the hell can a guy get drunk on air?

"Anyway, Charlie said he was so plastered he couldn't see straight, but when he came down he was cold sober and didn't have any breath at all. He swore up an' down he hadn't had a drop, only Charlie says he got ahold of some of this ox-eye somewhere."

Gardner cursed softly. "Oxygen, Cazoni, oxygen. It is in air, and you can get drunker on oxygen than on a gallon of white mule. But you sober right away, and you have no breath, of course.

"So he got drunk. No wonder they didn't hit that plane. Well, trace him, Cazoni. And here's a hint. They've gotten scared and left Boston, their business is in the hands of that lawyer they visited, and they'll have to communicate. See if you can't grease a few palms and find out where they are."

Three days later Kennedy was busily working with a peculiar batch of apparatus. There were two large tubs, one filled with a peculiar, clear viscid fluid, a second with a slightly muddied waterlike liquid. Kennedy was drawing a long thin copper ribbon through first one tub and then through the second, moving it slowly and steadily, and finally draping it artistically over the limbs of a young oak nearby. The clear, clean copper came out of its bath with a slightly greenish, glassy look, and rapidly dried on the tree. The ribbons, each about one hundred feet long, when dry were laid on the grass of the meadow.

He worked all morning at this, and finally had several thousand feet of half-inch-wide ribbons of copper, coated with a thin, exceedingly tough insulating layer of a special cellulose closely allied to rayon and cellophane. He stopped when his copper was exhausted, and went into the cabin, returning with a powerful pair of glasses, with which he inspected the lake. Then he went in, and presently smoke began to rise from the chimney. By the time Donovan came up in the small motorboat and began unloading the materials he had brought, Kennedy leaned out of the door with a cheerful "Come an' get us!"

"I have got the things you wanted, Bruce," returned Donovan, "but I'll be hanged if I see what connection two enameled tubs, five thousand feet of copper ribbon, fifty pounds of absorbent cotton, a complicated nonperm alloy tube, and the various other things have."

"Ah, you got the three tubes?"

"I did. Will you kindly dissolve the mystery as I dissolve this fodder?"

"Not till I'm sure of myself. Did you also get a package by express?"

"One package, express. Weight three hundred pounds, I'll have you know. You son of a gun, you said there was a 'little box for you.' How did you expect me to get that into the boat from the car?"

"That was somethin' I hadn't been able to figure out. How did you do it? I was darned interested to see if you could figure out a way," said Kennedy, looking up.

"Why you— Well, anyway, I used the tow rope, and the car for power, with a handy tree as the derrick mast."

"Well, that's fine. And now, Bob, I hope we have given them enough clues."

"Enough clues—enough for what?" demanded Donovan in surprise.

"To find us, of course. Did you send that last message to Monty?"

"Yes, and now please explain."

"I promised I would. And thanks for your faith in me, Bob. That was in a code Monty can get, but no one else can, because the thing is based on a sentence that he memorized, and it is not written anywhere. I told him to lift the secrecy somewhat, just give hints."

"We can't fight Gardner openly." Kennedy's face took on a cold grimness. "And so we are fighting the murdering crook in his own way. I have some more work, and you're going to help. Then you'll see what I mean. The clues I mentioned Gardner could follow back to us. I'm afraid we can't hide, and do any work."

"So we have to leave again?"

"No, that's just the point, Bob, we aren't leaving." Kennedy looked long and steadily at his friend. A slow smile of understanding came over Donovan's face.

"And now, perhaps, I see the connection between copper ribbons and the magnetically inactive nonperm tubes," he said at last, softly.

CHAPTER X

The heavy, pounding beat of the powerful engine shook the plane, even though the sound of it had been muffled and hushed to practical silence. Beside it two much smaller planes flew. It was dusk now, and darkening rapidly on the earth, far below, but here in the high strata, the sun still shone.

"You—you're sure they have no weapons?" demanded Gardner.

"Hell, no. They'd a used 'em before if they did," grunted Cazoni. Cazoni was unhappy. He was airsick. "An' they didn't get any in either. They got a lot o' junk, some stuff on their machine, I guess. Lotta cotton an' some chemicals, an' a big box full of somethin' heavy, but it came from the Framingham Iron and Steel Company, and it wasn't a gun. That came yesterday morning, and nothin' came since."

"Are you sure they haven't left?"

"Their car's still there, an' the boat. They were there this morning."

Gardner smiled to himself. "Cazoni, you certainly have done a fine job. And they have helped a lot. I'll give you this paper, which Kennedy must sign. If he doesn't—why—eh—leave this other one as I suggested."

"Wanta burn the plane an' so forth or not?"

"Why—I'm afraid it wouldn't have anything to burn. You see it doesn't use fuel, and it's an all-metal structure."

"O.K." Cazoni pocketed the two papers and listened miserably to the pounding and creaking of the plane, and he felt miserable as it heaved in the air pockets.

The coast fell rapidly behind, and the sun set below them. Maine lay beneath them now, and under the bright light of a full moon a silvery dot, like a luminous comma with a slight defect, appeared on the dark surface, sprinkled here and there with lights. A tiny clump of lights on one side of the luminous comma marked Makeaho; a spot of light on the black defect in the shining surface marked

Happy Days camp. Tonight, Gardner thought, it would not be so happy for him. He felt he would like this Happy Days himself, but thought a good Indian name much better. The tiny log cabin must be replaced by a real house that he could bring his friends to—

The light below winked out.

"Gone to bed, I guess," said Cazoni.

But they had not gone to bed. They had gone up. Since darkness had begun to fall, Kennedy and Donovan had been taking turns at a small amplifier set. A huge inverted cone of canvas reached upward, and at its bottom was a tiny thing no larger than a wrist watch. But it had heard the peculiar shriek of the air about the airplanes while they were still many miles off. Since then the two men had been very busy. They left the cabin now, and went down to the plane, changed since it landed, for now it was coated with a dull, lusterless black, a black like an eggshell dipped in india ink.

Noiselessly the plane rose into the air, rising almost instantly as the tremendous power whirled the propeller, a new. larger propeller, and the wide wings gripped the dense surface air. A faint hum carried the plane swiftly up at a steep angle. At a thousand feet it leveled off and darted across a narrow neck of water to the mainland's black background. It continued to climb.

"Think they saw us?" asked Kennedy quietly, braced behind a thing that resembled a long black telescope, mounted rigidly into the plane's structure, poking its nose through a hole in the roof of the machine.

"No can tell," replied Donovan. "They did," he added a minute later. "They're diving."

The plane pulled sharply, and the fabric creaked as Donovan threw an overload on the super-powerful motor. The great propeller bit and tugged. The machine rose steeply.

A black form came sharply down beside them, and something like a flickering red lightning snapped from its side. Kennedy swung to a second telescopelike machine that pointed downward. Suddenly it rattled viciously on its heavy frame, and a shrill whine came from it.

A terrible rending crack, a stifled scream of agony from the black shadow, and two black shadows appeared, each smaller than the first. Something tumbled from the one, and an instant later a parachute glistened in the moonlight.

"My God! They've got a gun!" gasped Gardner.

"I don't think so. No gun shoots without some light, and it ain't a gun that cuts a machine in two," said Cazoni.

"Let's go home," wailed Gardner. The plane turned upward and rapidly started back to the south under his orders. The second small plane was flashing down at the climbing black thing, barely visible now against the forest. He lost it for a time, and when he found it again, it was above him; it crossed the moon. He himself was a shining, glistening thing now in the trim plane. His machine gunner stuttered out a few rounds of ammunition. Then something screamed through the night, a glistening sheet that moved across and swept toward their plane. Like a shimmering knife of silver light it passed resistlessly through one wing, angled forward and pelted on the heavy motor. With a roar the motor blew up and fell from the plane. The machine twisted and fell over as the wing fell off, hanging by a few guy wires.

Two shining silken umbrellas fell free.

The black machine of death swept south in swift pursuit of the fleeing plane. Rapidly it overtook it, and as they came nearer, a machine gun chattered from the larger transport.

"The black paint's working, Bob," said Kennedy calmly. "They can't see us well enough to shoot straight in this moonlight." He pulled down a lever and aimed one of the telescope tubes toward the plane slightly ahead and above. A meter flopped over on the scale before him, and the mechanism, the whole plane, jarred under a heavy hammering. A silvery sleet flew out and caught the larger plane just ahead of the tail and ran its length, finally tearing out the motor. The fuel tanks burst into flame, and with a peculiar puff the plane flew into a thousand blazing parts.

"That's the end, I think," said Kennedy. Then he began to tremble, and his face went white. "God forgive me, there were men on that plane," he muttered.

CHAPTER XI

M. C. GARDNER DEAD IN AIR CRASH
FINANCIAL HEAD KILLED WITH COMPANIONS
AS PLANE MYSTERIOUSLY EXPLODES

Makeaho, Me. Late last night the people of this town were startled by the appearance of a battered, scratched man in an aviation suit, who told the story of Mr. Chas. Gardner's death. Gardner, in a five-passenger gasoline-powered plane, was flying north on business, when for some undiscovered reason his large plane exploded in midair, dropping burning parts at the two smaller, speedier planes accompanying him. The man who brought the news was James K. Terrence, pilot of one of the smaller planes, which was destroyed by the explosion of the greater. Terrence escaped by parachute. Several others also escaped from the smaller planes, but none were able to live through the explosion of the "flying office," as Gardner entitled his large plane.

Kennedy looked up at Donovan, and rested back in his comfortable chair. They were in Boston now, for they felt the danger was gone. "Convenient account, wasn't it?"

"Very," agreed Donovan. "What are we going to do, rush the fuel battery plant now?"

Kennedy looked very thoughtful as he answered slowly, "No, Bob, I don't think so.

"Do you realize what would happen if we did? If even a substantial rumor got out, American Power, all the big oils, the big motor stocks too, would be pressed down to nothing. How many millions of people would be ruined by that? Would it be worth it to the world?"

Donovan looked at his friend steadily for some moments. "But—how can you help it? Unless you suppress the invention?"

"I own the patents outright. Can't I lease the household power-battery rights to the American Power Company, let them scrap their plant gradually as they build and sell these batteries? Their investments in power-generating equipment will immediately be written off as worthless—but even the big traders will see that the power-battery rights they have are fully as valuable. The stock will fluctuate madly—and gradually reach a steady valuation.

"The oil companies can buy the rights to manufacture smaller batteries, for automobiles, airplanes, trains perhaps. It will have to be worked out, but, Donovan, think of the misery it would inflict on the world to sell those things through a brand new company. Would it be fair?"

"It would not. I agree absolutely."

"Now there's just one more question I want to ask. What was the thing you cut up those planes with? I thought you were making a sort of machine gun."

Kennedy chuckled. "It was, Bob, it was. It was simply a long solenoid that threw little steel bullets, but it didn't use powder, it used electric power. Remember, there was practically no mechanical apparatus about it, only electrical contacts made by the bullet itself, as it was drawn through the tube by the magnetic force. The lack of mechanism meant it could fire as fast as bullets could go through the barrel; no waiting while the thing was cocked and the used cartridge removed. When the bullet reached the muzzle, it automatically turned on the current that started the next one. The bullet was then traveling about twelve thousand feet a second. The result was that the machine gun shot something like thirty thousand times a minute. It acted like a huge bandsaw, each bullet being a tooth that moved better than two miles a second.

"Any wonder it cut through the ships, motor and all?" Kennedy smiled and rose from his chair. "And now, Bob, I think we'd better see Montgomery and tell the news." He smiled dryly. "I'll do my talking to the engineers of the companies. Financial geniuses seem to be disbelieving folk."

We were acting in true self-defense. It was they or we. But it is a sad load to carry—the loss of a human life.

THE MIDDLE PERIOD

Under evolutionary pressure, the science fiction magazines changed radically in the mid-thirties. In 1933 Clayton had gone under and had sold *Astounding* to Street & Smith, the oldest and best-established publisher of pulp magazines. After another bout of horror and the occult (the first thought of an inexperienced editor taking over a science fiction magazine), the new editor, F. Orlin Tremaine, began a vigorous effort to make *Astounding* the leader in the field. He experimented with new illustrators. He solicited and got important new work from E. E. Smith, John Campbell and Jack Williamson.

Well printed on rough pulp paper with untrimmed edges, the Street & Smith *Astounding* used a distinctive bold upper-and-lower-case type for titles and by-lines, which together with its illustrations presently gave it an appearance unlike that of any other s.f. magazine. The readers' response, as shown in the letter column, was enthusiastic. In March of the following year Tremaine increased the number of pages from 144 to 160, still at the old price of 20¢.

Gernsback's response was typically bold and visionary. In April he announced the formation of the Science Fiction League, an association devoted to the advancement of science fiction, and in the following months he built up an elaborate system of local chapters and national directors (Forrest J Ackerman, Eando Binder, Jack Darrow, Edmond Hamilton, David H. Keller, P. Schuyler Miller, Clark Ashton Smith and R. F. Starzl), with club pins, stationery, etc. Meanwhile Charles D. Hornig, a young fan whom Gernsback had appointed managing editor in 1932, was beginning to introduce a note of sadomasochism into the magazine with such stories as "Death Between the Planets," by James D. Perry, in which beetles torture a space-traveler on Mars, and "Moon Plague," by Raymond Z. Gallun, in which a loathsome gray fungus attacks spacemen on the moon.

The quality of the fiction in *Wonder Stories* remained poor. The brightest new writer of the thirties, Stanley G. Weinbaum, made his debut in *Wonder* and published two stories there; then *Astounding* lured him away with its better rates and growing prestige.

Sources of ideas that later became famous in other stories are to be found in this period. Don A. Stuart's "The Machine" (*Astounding*, February 1935) introduced the idea of a computer programmed to design a better computer. Murray Leinster's "Proxima Centauri" (*Astounding*, March 1935) is a forerunner of Heinlein's "Universe," with its generation ship and conflict between the officers and the "Muts" (ex-mutineers). "Cardiaca Vera," by Dr. Arch Carr, in the same issue, is about artificial hearts and heart transplants. "Infinity Zero," by Donald Wandrei (*Astounding*, October 1936) has the U.S., Great Britain and the U.S.S.R. aligned in a war against Germany, Italy and Japan.

The formation of the Science Fiction League had far-reaching effects, not all of them favorable to *Wonder Stories*. It encouraged the creation of local fan groups and laid a foundation for the widespread growth of organized fandom in the late thirties, but it also got Gernsback involved in the politics of fan clubs. In July he announced the "reorganization" of the New York chapter, hinting at wrecking by the former director, William S. Sykora, because Sykora's chapter had only five members and he was director of "a 'competing' club." Later, for similar reasons, he expelled Donald A. Wollheim, Frederik Pohl, and John C. Michel.

Amazing, which, like *Wonder*, had changed to the pulp format in late 1933, was visibly sliding downhill. Its letter columns were full of complaints about the fiction and the magazine's drab personality. Sloane accepted these brickbats with unfailing patience, but would not or could not change.

In 1934 *Astounding*'s transformation was complete. Early in this year Tremaine had introduced the work of the illustrator Elliott Dold, brother of Douglas Dold, who had been a consulting editor of *Astounding* under Clayton, and his work dominated the magazine for the next few years. Dold, like Marchioni, who also appeared at about this time, was a science fiction enthusiast and a primitive, in contrast to the professional artists from other fields who had done most of the illustrations in *Astounding* until now. He specialized in intricate, finely detailed designs in which alien figures, spaceships, complex machines all contributed to the pattern. His human figures were awkward, but his mechanisms (including his spaceship interiors) had a lovingly applied brushed-aluminum sheen; he gave his work an aura of convincing strangeness which went beyond even Paul's.

With Weinbaum, Campbell, Gallun and Frank Belknap Long as regular contributors, Tremaine had accomplished something not achieved or even attempted by previous editors: he had shown that science fiction could be not just a trivial pastime, as Sloane thought it, or a vehicle for futurist speculation, as it was to Gernsback, or a degraded commercial form, as it had been under Clayton, but an exciting and viable branch of fiction.

Invisible, but unbreakable, it stood far
up in the air, with men helpless!

Illustrated by Paul Orban

The Wall

By Howard W. Graham, Ph.D.

ONE EYE blackening, his clothing disheveled, and his necktie
jerked into a permanent knot, Jasper watched the scene with
amazement and incredulity. He had fought his way out of that
incredible chaos inch by inch and had at last gained a point of
vantage on the top steps of the public library.

This was no mere traffic stoppage. There was something else, an
element of terrible surprise and the suggestion that something more
was involved than the wreckage of a few fine cars. But 42nd Street
was a chaos past belief, wherein men and women fought like animals
in a kind of nightmare in broad daylight.

A short, doglike man came running around the corner of the
library and accosted Jasper as though he had found the man
responsible for the whole business. He was breathless, and soggy
with perspiration.

"Well!" he ejaculated.

"What?" said Jasper.

"They got a jam like this on Sixth, and another one, only a damn
sight worse, on Broadway!"

"What are you talking about?" Jasper shrank away from the
fellow, appalled and a little angry.

"You don't haff to believe me," said the stranger, "only the
subways is all smashed up all across town, and all the L's is spilling
off the tracks. What I seen, you wouldn't believe it. Listen! I been
tryin' for more than an hour to get uptown, and there's no place you
can get past 42nd Street, not even through the buildings. I simply got
to see a man! What is this all about, hah?" He seized Jasper's coat
and began weeping.

Jasper looked down at the man as though he had not heard a word
he said. A truck down there had overturned, and something in it was
screaming above the whole uproar. The pedestrian crowd, entering
the spirit of the occasion, swarmed over the jam of cars and fought

159

with each other wholeheartedly. It was not the accident itself, but this ugly aftermath of mob violence that caused so many injuries and deaths.

It was then that Jasper saw the pigeons. There was a heavy beat of wings that came from an uncommonly large flight of these birds that frequented the library courts. They wheeled in a wide, frightened arc over the street, high over the scene of the accident, where they piled up in the air in a flurried mass. They seemed to have struck an invisible wall in midair; their fuddled wings thrashed, and numbers of them showered down on the wreckage below with broken wings and necks.

At this same time there was another aerial disaster far worse. A scout plane cruising over the metropolitan area had taken interest in the unaccountable state of affairs below. It dropped as low as it dared, hurtling down in a fatal power dive, and met that invisible dividing line, thenceforth to be known as the "42nd Street Wall." It was actually about thirty feet from the building line toward 43rd Street. The plane exploded with the impact, and before that unlucky land crew of motorists and pedestrians knew what had occurred, the flaming ship was down on them.

Where the 42nd Street Wall crossed the North River, the liner *Bergen* was to account for a badly damaged hull by having struck the wall obliquely. A number of small boats were totally wrecked, but no lives were lost on the water. Ashore and inland the damage was more serious. Commerce north and south ceased completely, and minor accidents of the most bewildering nature had an appalling frequency.

As one might expect of them, the columnists took it up as a kind of grim jest. If you read such columns you saw: "Now that the most salient feature of the New Yorker is his broken nose—" This because of those scores of persons who charged unwittingly into the Gotham Wall.

Worse, the Hudson River quickly inundated the land once it was dammed by this obstacle. Aside from incalculable property damage, numbers were marooned in the taller buildings as the waters of Flushing Bay were enormously augmented and the Hudson found a new course to the sea.

However confounding this state of affairs was, two persons knew where the trouble lay and were the entirely innocent cause of it.

While picked corps of engineers were attacking thin air—the wall had no measurable thickness—with every tool at the command of science, Harold Jasper and Professor Maxim Gorsch stared at each other in an experimental laboratory on Lexington Avenue in a cold sweat of fear.

Jasper arrived at the office in midafternoon on the seventeenth, looking as though he had spent the day at rough-and-tumble sports. He made no apology for his absence, but for that matter Professor Gorsch did not turn around when he entered the room. Gorsch kept his position in the arena of experimental crucibles, retorts, and what-not, and rocked complacently on his heels. A swiveled power drill, of the sort using tanganim-metal bits, was mounted on the floor. It was turned on a one-sixteenth-inch sheet of steel that had just received a coat of an iridescent green lacquer. This plate was securely mounted between concrete pillars. The professor was pleased because sixty tons and a needle drill were making no headway whatever on what was little more than a tin can rolled flat.

At last he did turn around. He did not notice Jasper's battered face nor his dishevelment.

"It works. You see? It works," he said, rather smugly.

Jasper glared at him, speechless. All he could think of was the uproar in the streets. Along that wall New York was a madhouse. Upper Manhattan was like some idiotic aquarium, with men and women thrashing about in the muddy waters of the Hudson and random fish leaping between their legs. Mud and muck were suspended in sheets against the transparent wall, like some juggler's hideous trick. And simple Gorsch was engrossed in his labors all this while, with no thought or knowledge of anything that might occur outside this laboratory.

"The armor plate there," the professor explained, frowning. "I haff broken three of the smaller drills on it, and still it is only one-sixteenth of an inch in thickness. My boy, no projectile in the world will pierce it. That drill hass been going since ten-thirty, and yet not a mark. My boy, we are both of us millionaires, easily. I will give you half."

He rubbed his hands with satisfaction.

Jasper thought of a number of things, both his job and the chaos in the streets calling his attention at once. The plate was about thirty feet north of the building line. That was coincidence. It was true they had expected marvelous things of the new paint. The plate was mounted perpendicularly, parallel with 42nd Street. And Gorsch had turned his trick at about the time Jasper had had his eye blackened. More coincidence!

"What have you put on that plate?" he asked suspiciously.

"Why, the lacquer," said Gorsch.

He pointed to a jar full of green stuff on the desk. It was so, then; he had already used the paint. This material was Gorsch's new development, prepared, of course, with a few of Jasper's own ideas. This particular paint was the byproduct of high-power discharges which they had filtered through a "perfect occurrence" mixture of the inert gases—these gases proportioned as they occur in the atmosphere.

Both men were retained by the Greater American Products Corporation as "engineering counsel in new construction methods." They had perfected the company's synthetic wood and stone and various paints of remarkable permanence, not to speak of a superior brand of flexible glass. The power discharge through the inert gases, under a pressure of from thirteen to fifteen atmospheres, produced a brilliant green powder, for which Jasper had found a solvent. In solution the stuff made magnificent paint. In Jasper's absence the professor took unto himself, as usual, the prerogative of doing a little fiddling on his own. He had already named the product "Beetle Lacquer" and was thinking about retirement.

"When did you put it on?" barked Jasper.

The professor was startled. He looked at Jasper with considerable resentment. "Ten o'clock sharp," he said. "I painted the plate at ten this morning. What is the matter with you? Did you have an accident?"

"An accident!" Jasper ejaculated. "Have you been outside at all today, you old fool?"

"When I begin a test," said Gorsch, bristling, "I bring my lunch. I do not leave anything half done."

Jasper strode past him, ignoring the insinuation, and hastily went over Gorsch's apparatus. The drill was turning at high speed but making no impression whatever on the steel plate. Jasper started around it and ran into the invisible wall. He swore. There it was, coinciding exactly with the plane of green lacquer on the plate. He flattened his hands against it and followed it to the lacquer itself; he was ready to assume then that the great Gotham Wall was of the identical thickness of the coat of paint, and no more.

Gorsch watched him, dumfounded, as he cranked the drill off to one side and turned the point into this impassable barrier. The motor snarled, and the oily tanganim point began to smoke with heat. There was no drilling through that substanceless plane.

He rightly suspected that some similar phenomenon must be connected with the original jar of lacquer itself. Turning to the desk, he tried to pass his hand over this jar and met solid resistance. He was totally flabbergasted. Once before this they had concocted a paint that would turn a drill, but this was quite something else. This paint, some disastrous allotropic form of the inert gases, so changed in hardening, a freak accountable to the vast, unlucky store of power in the laboratory, that the air around it was rendered solid and immovable.

Gorsch, of course, had smeared the edge of the jar somewhat when he painted the plate. Wet, the enamel was unremarkable save for its intense color, for Jasper had handled it carelessly enough the night before. But as a dry coat it became a singularly impenetrable substance which exhibited the further property of extending a plane of resistance outside itself, in a ratio yet to be discovered. Thus, by encircling the invisible column above the jar with his hands, Jasper found that its diameter was that of the jar, measuring from the rim of dried lacquer around the cover. How high this column extended he could only guess.

Jasper rapped the air above the jar smartly with his knuckles and caused a clear, faint, bell-like ringing. This column of air, subtly changed by the influence of the lacquer, had the rigidity of metal. Outside, there were so many crashes of all kinds with the wall itself, that it sounded over Manhattan and over the sea like an everlasting gong.

Jasper turned on Gorsch and said, "Beautiful! Millionaires, eh? Gorsch, though it's no fault of yours, you'll have us on the penal island as public menaces for this. Do you know what you've done?"

Gorsch listened to Jasper's account with glassy eyes. The wall, Jasper figured, was only of the thickness of the coat of lacquer. It ran across town, through all structures crossing a point about thirty feet north of the building line on 42nd Street. What its length was he did not yet know.

There was something that must be found out, and that quickly. The plane, the Gotham Wall itself, could not be moved in the slightest. Though it had the transparency of the air itself, it had a greater inertia than any mass of stone or metal. It had stopped a plane and motor trucks driven into it at high speed. But, possibly, the plate could be taken off its supports and destroyed.

Gorsch watched Jasper free the armor plate from the binding posts. He took a deep breath, then, with a common suction cup from the toilet, he pulled the plate outward, the faintest shadow of a degree off the perpendicular. The concrete floor cracked briskly across the room. A bit of plaster fell. Jasper shuddered and screwed the plate back into position.

"Professor Gorsch," said he, his voice quavering, "you put that thing up—now you can take it down again!"

Gorsch was alarmed. He chewed at his white mustache in perplexity.

"We could bring the plate to the horizontal," he suggested timidly.

"I just tried that," said Jasper. "If you move that plate you'll shovel up half the buildings in New York and throw them into the Atlantic Ocean. For all I know"—he shuddered again as he thought of this—"you'll scoop a hole in the bottom of the ocean itself. And then where will Manhattan be?"

It was the absolute inertia of the lacquer which they could not cope with. The invisible wall which extended outside the film of paint was impassable, an immovable object. But the fact of such a wall's existence was not so disastrous, after all, as the fact that the object which had been painted *could be moved,* and moved easily. For, in motion, its extended and transparent plane moved with it; and in moving was irresistible.

On the third day of the tie-up New York was declared under martial law. These extreme measures were found necessary when the mob of rioting, bewildered citizens had caused immeasurable property damage and when organized crime began to avail itself of the opportunities offered by this unprecedented confusion.

All cross streets were rerouted for policing; Governor Harris stationed a sixty-mile double cordon of militia to the limits of the wall on the mainland. North of the wall there was a brisk trade in small boats. These carried the police and the overflow of citizens from the elevateds. The subways, of course, were flooded, with Manhattan somewhat more than a fathom under muck and water.

At the end of the second week, on the thirtieth, the city itself had split into two main governments. The old political machine enjoyed a brief renaissance under an emergency board on its cwn side of the wall, with its own mayor, and having its own special officials by appointment. Mayor Russel, casting aside the minor financial troubles of the moment, set up a "Commission for Inquiring into the Nature of the 42nd Street Wall." Mayor Byam followed suit, creating a great deal of unnecessary confusion. There seemed to be small logic in any extensive underwater inquiries when the south of the wall was not so obstructed, but a step of some kind had to be taken since the fire departments and Red Cross had already relieved most of the victims from their distress with scaling ladders.

The Russel Commission gave Jasper and Gorsch one sleepless night after another. While Gorsch stood guard, Jasper bathed the plate with every acid in the laboratory and treated the lacquer with every chemical that might have an effect on it. The solvent he had discovered for the powder would not dissolve the lacquer once it had dried. Heat affected it not at all, and it was unsafe to apply more pressure than had been used in the drill. Jasper could have knocked down the two supporting concrete pillars with comparative ease, but that was just what he was afraid of doing. If the plate moved at all, the building would have been split from top to bottom.

Like a leash of ferrets, the Russel Commission's engineers went over the wall from beginning to end. When anyone came in sight in the halls, Gorsch would make a sign to Jasper, who would slide a bureau that was innocent enough against the plate. This bureau, with two cots, made the laboratory into very satisfactory living quarters. Many had done the same, making their offices their homes when they could not conveniently get back uptown.

There was nothing extraordinary about the room, but Russel's men were a suspicious lot and looked upon every man along the wall as a potential criminal. They held powers of arrest and would brook no interference even of the most casual nature. They were uncomfortably inquisitive.

"Where did that come from?" asked one of them narrowly, pointing at the drill.

"Why, it belongs here," said Jasper. "We're engineering counsels for the American Products Corporation."

"Counsels hell!" snapped the inquisitor. "What's it for?"

"We're trying to get through the wall ourselves," said Gorsch meekly. "I haven't seen my wife for three weeks."

"You leave that to us," said the engineer menacingly. "If there's a way of getting through, *we'll* do it!"

He passed on an order or two, and that morning the power drill was dismantled and confiscated by authority of Mayor Russel. The engineer in charge of the work—he was Francis Herder, soon to become a great name in engineering—came dangerously near the jar of lacquer. Jasper's heart was in his throat. If that jar had been moved, the building would have been down about their ears, knocked to pieces by the pillar of rigid air that extended above and below it. The plate would have gone down with the building, and the city of New York down with the plate, into the sea.

Both sat down weakly on the cots when the commission had gone.

"Did you hear what they said?" asked Jasper.

"About Lexington Avenue?"

"Yes. They've measured the wall from end to end. Even the meteorologists are in on it. They've measured rainfall and say that the wall is a hundred and twenty miles long and approximately sixty miles high. Lexington runs through the middle of it. If they're right about its going sixty miles deep into the earth, that damned plate has made a wall that's a perfect square. Gorsch, this is the end of everything. They say they'll find the reason for all this somewhere near Lexington Avenue."

"We have got to run away," said the professor.

"We have got to do nothing of the sort," Jasper retorted. "Don't you feel any responsibility for all this? If that bungling commission starts poking around in this room, all they'll have to do is upset that blasted jar of lacquer. It would be wholesale murder. Tell me how you'd feel, Maxim Gorsch, with thousands of deaths on your soul! If you've got one," he added bitterly.

"But you are unjust—I can do nothing!" the professor wailed. "I am going to the commission and tell them what I have done. I am sorry for it!"

"You're not going to tell anyone anything!" shouted Jasper. "There'd be an investigation that would smell to high heaven. And how about the formula of that lacquer? Would you keep your mouth closed, eh? Let any unscrupulous agent get hold of it, and you know what would happen as well as I do. Absolute inertia. It's a perfect weapon for offensive or defensive war. Think, Gorsch! Think of what a long-range club you could make out of—out of a pencil! Why, with one of these plates the size of a penny at your back, you could plow up a navy! With a pencil! I don't suppose you'd care about that, though, would you? Oh, no, Maxim Gorsch, you won't tell. We have got to destroy that stuff somehow, and no one but ourselves is ever going to know what happened."

It was easily said, but time was getting terribly short. Something had to be done in a hurry, because the Russel Commission was definitely concentrating at Lexington Avenue. Buildings there were infested with them. The Lexington area became their headquarters, and you could not come or go without running into someone who was an engineer and a secret agent in one. There was a war scare that year, and there was reason enough in eyeing even the most innocent citizen twice when this thing might easily be an alien government's first surprise move.

The commission evacuated subways and made tests below ground. They agreed that the wall extended deep into the earth and were satisfied that the distance was roughly sixty miles.

The wall would not pass anything solid. It would filter water very slowly, however, and air circulated through it to some slight extent. Electric cables that were laid north and south functioned as well as ever, but all radio broadcasting was cut with a terrific field of static. It was only the fact that all parts of the wall caused equal disturbance that had prevented the radio finders from locating the dead center of the wall.

One engineer wanted to run diagonals from corner to corner and thus find that dead center. Other engineers wanted to know what diagonals running from what corners to what corners. Jasper told Professor Gorsch it was a damned lucky thing he hadn't used a two-yard plate instead of a two-foot one, or he might, if the area of the wall did answer to the area of the plate, have cut the whole country in two and very likely sunk the continent before he enjoyed the honors of discovery.

The jar of lacquer was rapidly assuming importance of the grandest kind. There was dust on the desk that neither counsel—Gorsch and Jasper were bitterly sorry they had ever heard that title—dared to disturb. The slightest tremors of the building, the merest vibration at all, filled them with anguish.

At last Gorsch opened a container of one of their own incomparable glass binders and tenderly applied it to the base of the jar. Sweat pumped out of his old frame in a steady flow. He catfooted nervously back and forth, perfectly well aware of the possibility of unequal hardening, until the binder was thoroughly set. Then, and not until he tried a needle on it, he breathed a gasp of relief, and Jasper and he set about fixing the legs of the desk to the floor.

As they were so occupied, the building superintendent, a fat, harassed, but soft-footed individual of fifty-five, puffed into the room. The two counsels were completely surprised and rose shakily to their feet. The superintendent announced pathetically that the commission was evacuating, one by one, all occupied offices on the line. No notice was to be served other than verbal. When the commission arrived, an office was expected to be unoccupied. Apologizing, the superintendent puffed out again.

"Well," said Jasper, somewhat relieved, "at least they can't get this outfit loose without using an ax." He meant the desk and jar. Once set, the glass binder made them an integral part of the floor.

But Professor Gorsch sank back to his cot and groaned. He was a proud man and could see nothing for himself any longer in this affair but ruin. Jasper stamped back and forth, his brow wrinkled, and abruptly vanished through the door. He was going down himself to see the commission.

Herder was in charge.

Jasper walked up to him and said, "I understand you're cleaning us out."

Herder didn't answer. He simply nodded his head at Jasper and kept on nodding, as though he never tired of agreeing with someone. Underneath he was still a politician, the one-time proprietor of a cigar store in Brooklyn.

Jasper said, "We *can't* move. All our crucibles came through the elevator window in the north end."

"Leave them behind," said Herder softly. There was something essentially vicious in his manner.

"We're in the G suite on fourteen," said Jasper. "What's the deadline?"

"We may be up there tomorrow," said Herder, "and maybe not for six weeks. Take your pick. But don't let us find you there when we call."

Jasper hurried out, feeling outraged, as though he had been caught in some act of counterfeiting. When he arrived at the laboratory he was panting like a dog.

"The game's up," he said. "If you can think of something, let's have it. Gorsch, I never had to come into this thing with you, and now we're both in to the neck. I'm not sorry. I've seen that louse Herder, and he's got a bad eye. Think of something, Gorsch."

"I was thinking," said Gorsch, "that maybe lacquer would dissolve lacquer."

Jasper swiveled around in his chair and stared at the jar of green paint anchored to the desk.

"Maybe it would," he said, "but how are you going to get at it? You can't get to the cover any more, because the column starts with the dried lacquer on the rim and the cover is inside it. There's no time to make any more of the stuff, either, because our apparatus is on the other side of the wall."

"There is acid," suggested Gorsch, "to eat the glass away."

Jasper shook his head. It was too dangerous. Paint would spill out of the jar—some of it was bound to—and they would be in a worse predicament than before. It would mean immediate discovery; at this moment someone might have run into that fourth-dimensional column that extended upward from the jar of lacquer, and downward from it also, through the floors below, through the very headquarters of the Russel Commission.

Jasper rose and examined the jar again, effectually sealed against the most determined safe-cracking by an invisible barrier. His knife slipped off this column like a pencil on glass. If only he had the time to inquire into the nature of the phenomenon, and how the paint in drying effected this absolute inertia in the air extended from it! It would have been valuable to know whether the same freak took place in a vacuum; whether this column in particular stood only as high as the Gotham Wall, or, indeed, mounted above the earth's atmosphere into open space.

The column was not a perfect cylinder, its contours following the conformation of the dried lacquer on the rim of the jar. At one point, where areas of paint touched but did not overlap, the knife blade caught in, but did not enter, a crack.

With a glass trained on that crack, Jasper called the professor and told him he thought they could get in, or at least find out whether it would do them any good to get in. Gorsch hunted up a tray of platinum filaments in graduated sizes and tendered them to Jasper as though he were handing over his soul. Jasper took them and fished with one wire after another.

Gorsch hung on his shoulder and said, "Does it go? Does it go?"

"Get away, I can't see!" exclaimed Jasper irritably.

He set himself to the brain-racking task of twisting an almost-invisible corkscrew of platinum through a quite invisible crack in the air, down through the brush hole in the lid of the jar, and into the lacquer. He managed it. A few glistening green beads of paint came up on the wire and scraped off in the crack. Jasper fished again, and once more the beads scraped off. One small drop collected. The two men stood there, fidgeting and waiting.

Jasper tried his knife in the crack. It had widened; the new paint had softened the dried film on the jar.

"It works, Gorsch!" said Jasper in a hoarse whisper.

He tried a pencil. The pencil passed through the crack, and shortly he was able to reach the brush Gorsch had left in the jar. In a few minutes he had applied lacquer to the circumference of the rim.

Meanwhile Gorsch had started a crucible, and by the time it had reached white heat Jasper had penetrated the whole column above the jar and wiped off the excess lacquer with waste. He threw waste, pencil, wire, and cover into the crucible, instantly. All were consumed, with a sharp, clear report like the explosion of a shell. The glass cover melted at once and danced and blistered in the trough of the open furnace.

Jasper worked desperately, polishing the jar with waste soaked in the chemical solvent of the lacquer powder. He kept throwing these pieces of waste into the crucible while the reports diminished and finally ceased. Then he poured a quantity of the solvent into the jar to ensure Gorsch's "Beetle Lacquer" against any quick drying, slid a glass panel over it, and rested, mopping his brow.

A trio from the Russel gang downstairs burst through the doorway and shouted as one man: "What was that?"

"What was what?"

The whole thing seemed very silly, now that success seemed to be on the way; Jasper eyed these intruders with irritation and contempt.

"Those explosions. What's going on here?" It was the cursed voice of authority speaking again.

"Nothing!" snapped Jasper enigmatically. "Get along, you! We're moving out of here."

That was his sole explanation, but he stood against Russel's men so belligerently that they shuffled their feet like a group of small boys. They hesitated, then moved on together to find the cause of the disturbance elsewhere, as though no one of them had a mind of his own.

Gorsch returned to the crucible at once, extracting every last calorie out of his machine. The glass cover had blistered out of sight. There was no time to find out whether the air above the crucible had been affected or not, but they rightly assumed that the lacquer had been broken down into its essential gases.

Gorsch worked as though he had only one purpose in life. He had rigged up a "booster" line for additional current and nursed this power supply until he came within a hair of reaching the fusing point of the crucible. There was smoke in the air. When he looked at Jasper there was impatience, but still something boyish and eager in his manner, as though he realized he had done something well.

"Ready?" asked Jasper.

"Ready!" Gorsch croaked.

Jasper painstakingly inserted a ball of waste into the jar, removed it and managed not to spill a drop. He applied this evenly to the armor plate, covering every pin point of lacquer, and tossed the waste into the furnace. There was an eruption of green flame; the vertical explosion which followed dropped a perfectly cylindrical piece of the ceiling, a disk of beryl steel and concrete, into the crucible, where it quickly melted and puddled like a mass of hot quicksilver. Jasper and Gorsch stood on their toes and cracked their jaws, momentarily deafened.

The whole commission would be in on them in no time at all. Jasper kept his knife blade against the plate until he could scrape through to bare metal. He waited a second or two before he hazarded everything, then clipped the screws holding the plate and to   it—plate, knife, clippers, and screw heads—into the crucible. Another column of green flame struck up from it.

Gorsch and Jasper plugged their ears and watched fragments of concrete shower down from the floors above. Molten stone splashed out of the furnace and peppered them with miniature showers of sand as particles exploded in the air. There were pin-pricks of blood on Gorsch's head.

"The jar!" Jasper shouted.

Gorsch pointed to a bottle on the shelf. Jasper and Gorsch never prepared a perfect binder without a perfect solvent for it. Jasper unstoppered the bottle and poured its contents liberally around the jar of lacquer. Gorsch left the crucible and stationed himself in the doorway. The empty halls were still reverberating with a long chain of echoes, but he thought he could hear an uproar of voices below.

"Here they come, Jasper!" he shouted.

Jasper tugged at the jar.

It gave.

"Ready!" he screamed, with all the power in his lungs.

Gorsch nodded and covered his face with his long, bony fingers. Jasper tossed the jar gently and carefully into the exact middle of the furnace and sprinted for the doorway. He was a fairly powerful man, and picked up Gorsch as though he were a scarecrow. He guessed right, and leaped into the air with Gorsch in his arms as the lacquer went off.

The crucible plunged down into earth, missing, as luck would have it, every last engineer in the Russel Commission below. Jasper and Gorsch had stopped their ears and felt rather than heard that cataclysm of sound as they sprawled along the corridor. It was a fortunate thing, for a long section of the wall of the building caved in following the tremendous suction, and eardrums burst with it.

The report was heard, or so it was claimed, in Ireland. But what reached widespread fame was the pole of solid green fire that flagstaffed far out into space. It was an unforgettable sight, like a connecting bar between earth and the shell of stars.

The Hudson River, undammed, returned to its channel at once and tossed stranded boats into wreckage. The uptown subways emptied, and for hours the whole underground system ran like a network of sewers. Uptown New York lay stinking under the sun, blanketed with the muck that the diverted Hudson had left behind.

There were earth temblors that year, running east and west. Out to sea the bed of the ocean boiled, and a certain area in the Atlantic was unpleasantly warm.

As one consequence of the affair, a source of everlasting joy to Jasper and Gorsch, Francis Herder, Russel's chief engineer, came in for considerable attention. He had been working below with a machine using centrifugal explosives of a perfectly ordinary patent and had fired at about the time Jasper threw the jar of green paint into Gorsch's crucible.

Jasper and Gorsch, totally helpless in the matter, had managed to advance the man, the engineer in charge at the time the Gotham

Wall was broken down, into being the most-sought-after engineer anywhere in the world. Neither counsel cared very much about that. They were free.

A day later, sixty men from every part of the world assembled in a room with perfect acoustics.

Illustrated by Morey

The Lost Language

By David H. Keller, M.D.

DAVID PHILLIPS 3rd was a beautiful child.
He was a baby any parent would be proud of.
His father, David Phillips, Jr., and his grandfather, David Phillips, were proud of him; also his mother and all his sisters. They bragged about his sturdy body and his bright eyes and his crop of black hair. They talked about the fortune of the family in finally having a male heir after three daughters. But when the boy reached the age of two they talked less, and when he was four years old they ceased to talk.

There was nothing wrong with the boy's body.

But he would not talk.

That is the way they put it. He would not talk.

Even when he was four they would not admit that he could not—because all of his relatives, even some of the physicians they consulted, were sure that he could talk *if he wanted to.*

He did not even vocalize.

As a baby he had cried. As he grew older, he outgrew the infantile noises of displeasure. It almost seemed as though he were training himself to accept the vicissitudes of life from the standpoint of a stoic—perhaps even of a philosopher.

There did not seem to be much mental deficiency. He learned to take care of himself, to adjust himself to his environment, to dress, feed, and amuse himself. He was really a bright, adorable, loving child. Accepting life as he found it, he lived in the home and with his family without in any way being a burden. At five years he was a little man, but he did not talk.

By this time the child's family was decidedly interested in the problem. Being a wealthy family, it was able to secure the services of specialists in speech-training, who also became personally interested.

But just being interested did not help. Even when he became a national problem, even when learned men devoted some days of their vacations to a visit to the Phillips home, even when psychologists and brain experts offered their services and advice *gratis,* there was no improvement.

Every effort was made to arouse his interest in language as a medium of communicating thought. He was studied, bribed, and even punished in the endeavor to make him utter a sound. He simply accepted any treatment with a certain degree of patience and kept on living his silent life.

He played with the playthings of children of his age. He worked, ate, slept, loved, had pets, took trips with the family, grew into sturdy seven-year boyhood, in every way a nice, adaptable, lovable youngster, the pride of his family and their despair.

He was a silent boy.

At that he was never out of communication with the world. He learned what was expected of him, but he learned by imitation. Not that he was deaf; in fact, all the tests showed him to be peculiarly sensitive to sounds. When a snail crawled out of the aquarium at night and dropped to the carpeted floor, he heard it fall and went to its rescue. He liked to hear the birds sing, the radio play, the family talk; there was no doubt he could hear noises unheard by the older members of the family, but words, just plain words, the sound of letters conjoined, left him cold and uninterested. Thus he grew up learning what people expected of him and making his wants known, but never through the medium of language.

From the age of two he had one outstanding habit, scribbling on paper with a pencil; later he used crayon, or pen and ink. At first it was just plain baby scrawls, the kind of marks any child would make, given white paper and a pencil; marks like this:

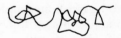

But later on he developed a rather systematized series of marks which, while they varied from day to day, had a certain uniformity and a definite sequence, like this:

$$M o \sim \sim \wedge \square \vee \text{M} \mathbin{-} \cdot \wedge$$

"That is writing!" exclaimed a specialist who had come a

thousand miles to study the child. "That is writing, and the child is trying to communicate with the world."

It was all well enough to say that it was writing; in fact everyone knew that it was writing. What else could it be called? But what kind of writing? And what did it mean? Even when they found out by the boy's actions that

V ⌣ O ⋀⋀ · · ⌣

meant he would like grapefruit for breakfast, how much better off was he, and his family and the world?

The specialist continued: "The child knows what he wants to express, and is expressing it in his own way. The marks he makes have no relation to any other known writing. An intensive study of these marks would ultimately bring him into communication with a selected few. He happens to belong to a wealthy family who could hire a few educated persons to learn some of the signs. If he were a child of a poor family he would end in a school for the feebleminded. The state would not, could not, afford to bother with him."

"But he is not a case of mental deficiency," protested the mother.

"That is purely an academic question," argued the specialist. "For centuries the human race has communicated with one another, first by sounds, and later by writing. Writing is simply a mode of sound. I admit that people learn to read silently, but even then they transpose the typed symbols into sounds subconsciously and thus obtain the meaning of the printed line and page. The dot and dash of the Morse code simply replace letters which, in proper combination, have definite sounds, and those sounds for centuries have had definite meaning. This boy forms his own symbols. There is no doubt they mean definite things to him. You have shown me that, and my experiments with him have convinced me that you are right. But his refusal to adopt the symbols of the herd, to learn the alphabet, to follow the lines of communication used by his ancestors and his associates, stamps him at once as abnormal."

"But not feebleminded!" cried the father. "I have visited the schools where imbeciles are cared for. I have talked with the physicians who care for them. I have placed my son in every possible relation with them, made every possible comparison. I am not a neuropsychiatrist, don't pretend to be a psychologist, but if my son is mentally deficient, then I am a white elephant."

The scientist smiled the smile of despair as he replied, "Have it your own way. After all, he is your son. You have a right to have a familial pride. I admit that he is a nice boy, but that is all he will be, all he ever will be, just a nice boy, just a healthy animal. He will grow to be a man, and when he does, he will be just what he is today, only larger. The herd will not like him; they will shun him as they do everyone who does not conform to the pattern, who does not run in the common groove of life. He is an abnormal, and he will stay an abnormal unless he learns to adopt the means of communication used by the rest of the human race. A deaf-mute can be taught to write, he can even be taught to talk, but this boy is a psychic rebel. He refuses to learn."

"Perhaps he cannot learn. Is that refusing?" asked an interested sister, a college graduate who had majored in psychology, speech, and habit training because she loved her little brother and wanted to be of service to him.

"You are right and I was wrong," admitted the psychologist, "but after all I am wrong merely in the words used and not in the idea. The child is so bright in every other way that he creates the impression of willful resistance. Let me explain. I was working with him yesterday. Take his symbol for an egg; you know what it is, but let me draw it as he does:

$$\lambda \; o \; -\; \backslash \cdot$$

By that he means an egg. Now I write it the way we do in English:

$$EGG$$

I show it to him. I hand him an egg. I show him his symbol. In every way that I can, I try to explain to him that his symbol and my symbol and the actual egg are all the same. Then I take away his symbol and give him another piece of paper and show him that I want him to copy my symbol for an egg. He simply shakes his head and draws his symbol. Now I know any number of children three years old who would copy my symbol and understand that it meant an egg, but he refuses to do it. He thinks that I am wrong. That shows his rebel mind. He refuses to accept instruction. He thinks his symbol for an egg is right and mine is wrong. You cannot teach a child like him. He wants us to learn his language, while refusing to learn ours. From a purely academic viewpoint it is possible to do so, but here is the difficulty. His language is not a sound language. It never can be spoken."

"Certainly it can!" exclaimed the sister. "He makes a sign for an egg. I understand the sign. I translate it into sound and say the word '*Egg.*' What do you mean by saying that it cannot be spoken?"

The man shook his head.

"I insist that there can be no language without sound."

"How about the finger talk of the deaf-mutes?" asked the father.

"What is it? They form signs with their fingers, and those signs are words or letters; and the letters make words, and the words are the words everybody uses and knows the signs and sounds of. Even the Maya symbols are meaningless till we translate them into words, and then we have to speak the words. If your son would only learn the finger language of the deaf-mute, it would at once change the entire picture. What I am trying to say is that he refuses to accept the modes of communication used by any group of the human race. To that extent he has a rebel mind."

"I have been close to the lad," the father retorted. "I have been with him a lot recently. We have gone fishing together and camping out and all that sort of thing. He may have a rebel mind, though it is my opinion that he is the way he is because he cannot help it. But there is one thing I do believe. He is perfectly satisfied with his written language, and it means something to him. He is very much pleased when the family uses it. Somehow it makes him feel we are interested in him and love him. His writing means a lot to him, and he is proud of it. I think that at times he is sad because we are not intelligent enough to understand it."

"You find someone to translate it into sound, and then I will accept it as a bona-fide language, and that is my last word," said the scientist, and with that he left.

The father, the following year, took David Phillips 3rd to London. There was a man there, Henry Jordon, who had gained international renown by his work with vibrations. He was the inventor of the vibrowriter, the new typewriter that could be talked to, and which transposed the spoken sound into typed words, a contrivance which made perfect spelling possible, provided the words were perfectly pronounced. The father had an idea and was willing to travel four thousand miles and spend any amount of money to find out whether he was right or wrong. His letters of introduction opened the door to the scientist's workshop; his story opened the door to the man's heart; the adorable, healthy boy at once won the inventor's interest and love.

"I may be asking the impossible," explained David Phillips, Jr., "but the boy is my son, and perhaps the impossible can be made possible. You have a machine that can turn sound into a written language. Can you make a machine that can do the reverse? Can you make some kind of apparatus we could run this lad's writing through and change it into sound?"

"What kind of sound?"

"Any kind. Take this symbol for egg to start with."

"But you know what the sound is for that. It is E G—*EGG*—just *egg*. You do not need a machine to do that."

"Yes, but that is our sound, the English sound. His sound may be entirely different."

"How can it be? You have just told me that he never talks, never even vocalizes."

"That is true, but the experts in America tell me that there can be no language without a foundation of sound, so there must be some corresponding sounds to his symbols even if he does not make them. But here are his papers. You may not believe it, but on the way over from New York, he was writing all the time, having the best kind of a time, and I think he was writing a story. At least he was happy doing it. And here is something else. He wants a typewriter."

"Why not buy him one?"

"I would, but he does not want our kind. He keeps on showing me his writing, and then points to my portable machine."

"In other words, you mean that he is telling you he wants a machine of his own, with his own symbols?"

"That must be it."

"I will make it for him," declared Henry Jordon. "You leave his papers here. I will have them analyzed and broken up into units and have a typewriter made that he can write with, just as well as he can write with a pen or pencil. You take him to see the Tower of London and Trafalgar Square. Come back in three days, and I will have a present for him."

On the third day father and son returned to the workshop of Henry Jordon. The inventor took them into a room that had only a chair and a table, but on the table was a typewriter, and in it was a sheet of white paper. Jordon touched five keys, took the paper out and showed it to the boy. He had written the symbols for egg,

$$\not\times \, ♢ \, ⌐\big\backslash \text{\Large .}$$

David Phillips 3rd looked at it, then at the machine, and then he took the paper and showed that he wanted it put back into the machine. Then he looked at the keyboard, and slowly, painfully slowly, he started to write his symbols for eggs. Then he started to cry, great tears of happiness, and he kissed his father, and went and hugged the inventor, and all the rest of that day he wrote on the machine while the two men watched him and compared the writing with his papers and experimented, handing him simple objects, and urging him to write their names on the machine.

That night, in the hotel, he would not go to sleep till the machine was securely placed on the bed where he could hold it while he slept.

"All you have to do now," said the father, "is to take his typed manuscripts and translate them into sound."

"That is all," replied Jordon, "but that may not be so easy as you think. Come back in a week."

That night the father could not sleep. He sat most of the night by the boy's bed, looking at him, the pride and hope, the last hope of the family. The boy slept peacefully, but in his sleep he never lost contact with the typewriter. Early in the morning the father arrived at a decision. He sent a radiogram to his daughter, the one who had majored in psychology, speech and habit training, because she loved her little brother. He said:

Anna Phillips;
57 Park Place;
New York City, N. Y.
Come to London on next boat. We need you. Father.

Because of this there were three of the family who called on Henry Jordon at the expiration of a week. They found the inventor tired and hollow eyed, but happy.

"I have done it," he said simply, "and you do not owe me a cent. I can use the same principle with any type. In a month's time, tired people will be placing pages of a book in their machine and hear it read to them. Suppose we try it. Have the lad write something on his machine."

By signs they explained to David Phillips 3rd what they wanted. He wrote three lines double spaced. Then the inventor took the paper, placed it in another machine, and pressed a button. Sounds came from the machine, sounds that seemed to be speech, but that were unintelligible to the audience. But the boy was spellbound. He looked from his father to his sister and then to Jordon and by signs asked that it all be done over again. Jordon wrote his signs for the word egg and showed it to him. When he put it in the second machine and pressed the button, a single sound was heard.

"And that," commented Jordon, "is the sound that means 'egg' to him. It is the sound that corresponds to his symbol. Suppose we learn to make that sound. I will get twenty different objects and place them on the table. Then his sister can make that sound and we will see what he does."

Again and again they had the machine sound the word for egg, till the sister learned to say it. Then a watch, keys, matches, money, pins, and an egg were placed on the table. The sister took the lad over and made the sound, just once, pointing to the table. The lad listened and without hesitation picked up the egg and handed it to his sister.

"That tells the story," commented the father. "My boy can hear. We always knew that. He can hear but cannot talk, but he can write. What he writes can be transposed into sound, and when that sound is reproduced he can understand it, and the rest is just training."

"It is a track," frowned Jordon, "on which the trains run only one way."

"At least it is a track," insisted the father. "Suppose you put a whole page of his type in and see how it sounds."

"It is gibberish to me," commented the inventor.

"That is because you are not a linguist," retorted the sister sharply. "Perhaps someone else could understand it."

"Let us put it to the test," said the inventor, smiling. "At this very time there is a meeting in London of scientists from all over the world. Perhaps fifty different languages are represented. We will go there and have them listen to it. Someone there may recognize some of the sounds."

A day later, sixty men from every part of the world assembled in a room with perfect acoustics. The problem was explained to them. A hundred questions were asked and answered, so they would have a clear understanding of the situation. Then an entire page of the lad's typing was run through the sound-transposing machine, purposely slowed so that the sounds could be differentiated.

And then silence, followed by a mixture of speech, but no one seemed to be sure. One by one the lingual experts rose and, saying that they could not understand it, left the room. At last only one man was left. He came up to the disappointed experimenters.

"I am not sure of what I am going to say, but it may help," he began, in a rather apologetic tone. "I am from Wales, and I know a few of the Welsh dialects but not all. I believe that these words are Welsh, but it is not any dialect I am familiar with. But there was a little corner of Wales where they had an odd language years ago, something different from the other dialects. I went there five years ago to investigate it, and there was just one old woman there— Granny Lanarch, they called her—who could talk it, but no one could understand her. She talked it for me, and as I remember it, it sounded a little like this language you have had us listen to. So the best I can say is that it may be an old Welsh dialect and Granny Lanarch can talk it. I will give you her address. She talks fairly good English in addition to her dialect, so you could have her listen to it and even make some phonographic records of her old speech."

"We will go there," said David Phillips.

"But it cannot be Welsh," commented the inventor. "You are from New York."

"My family came from that town in 1765," announced the New Yorker, "so we certainly were Welsh at that time."

"And it may be a case of inherited memory," added the daughter. "At least the psychologists think that there may be such a thing."

They went to Wales, and at last they came to the little town by the Irish Sea where Granny Lanarch had lived. Had lived, for she had been dead these two years. They went into her little cottage, they sat on her old chairs, they looked out on the waves through windows she had looked out of, but Granny Lanarch was dead.

The inventor beat a restless tattoo on the table with his fingers, not knowing what to say or how to say it. The father sat unstrung and nerve-broken. The boy, interested in new sights, smiled happily. The sister sat with white face and closed eyes. At last the father shook himself, as though waking from a dream.

"We have come to the end of the trail," he whispered. "My son knows something, but it is a lost language. He will have to live his life alone."

The sister opened her eyes, opened her arms and pulled her brother to her lap. She turned fiercely to her father.

"What do you mean?" she demanded. "What do you mean by saying that he will be alone? He can write what he thinks, and when I put it in the machine I can hear it and learn to understand it; and if I can understand it I can learn to talk it, and when I talk it, he can hear me and answer me on his typewriter. What do you mean by saying that he will be alone when he has me?"

"You cannot do that," whispered her father gently, almost with a caress in his tone. "You cannot do that, Anna. It would mean a life of sacrifice, a life of solitary devotion. You could not do anything else. Why should you sacrifice everything for him?"

She simply held her brother the tighter as she replied, "Because I love him."

It spread its gigantic lacy wings and soared swiftly into the sky. The swiftness of its flight choked Maljoc, and his eyes were blinded by motes of dust.

Illustrated by Howard V. Brown

The Last Men

By Frank Belknap Long, Jr.

MALJOC had come of age. On a bright, cold evening in the fall of the year, fifty million years after the last perishing remnant of his race had surrendered its sovereignty to the swarming masters, he awoke proud and happy and not ashamed of his heritage. He knew, and the masters knew, that his kind had once held undisputed sway over the planet. Down through dim eons the tradition—it was more than a legend—had persisted, and not all the humiliations of the intervening millenniums could erase its splendor.

Maljoc awoke and gazed up at the great moon. It shone down resplendently through the health-prism at the summit of the homorium. Its rays, passing through the prism, strengthened his muscles, his internal organs, and the soft parts of his body.

Arising from his bed, he stood proudly erect in the silver light and beat a rhythmic tattoo with his fists on his naked chest. He was of age, and among the clustering homoriums of the females of his race which hung suspended in the maturing nurseries of Agrahan was a woman who would share his pride of race and rejoice with him under the moon.

As the massive metallic portals of the homorium swung inward, a great happiness came upon him. The swarming masters had instructed him wisely as he lay maturing under the modified lunar rays in the nursery homorium.

He knew that he was a man and that the swarming masters were the descendants of the chitin-armored, segmented creatures called insects, which his ancestors had once ruthlessly despised and trampled under foot. At the front of his mind was this primary awareness of origins; at the back a storehouse of geologic data.

He knew when and why his race had succumbed to the swarming masters. In imagination he had frequently returned across the wide wastes of the years, visualizing with scientific accuracy the post-

Pleistocene glacial inundations as they streamed equatorward from the poles.

He knew that four of the earth's remaining continents had once lain beneath ice sheets a half mile thick, and that the last pitiful and cold-weakened remnants of his race had succumbed to the superior sense-endowments of the swarming masters in the central core of a great land mass called Africa, now submerged beneath the waters of the southern ocean.

The swarming masters were almost godlike in their endowments. With their complex and prodigious brains, which seemed to Maljoc as all-embracing as the unfathomable forces which governed the constellations, they instructed their servitors in the rudiments of earth history.

In hanging nursery homoriums thousands of men and women were yearly grown and instructed. The process of growth was unbelievably rapid. The growth-span of the human race had once embraced a number of years, but the swarming masters could transform a tiny infant into a gangling youth in six months, and into a bearded adult, strong-limbed and robust, in twelve or fourteen. Gland injections and prism-ray baths were the chief causal agents of this extraordinary metamorphosis, but the growth process was further speeded up by the judicious administration of a carefully selected diet.

The swarming masters were both benevolent and merciless. They despised men, but they wished them to be reasonably happy. With a kind of grim, sardonic toleration they even allowed them to choose their own mates, and it was the novelty and splendor of that great privilege which caused Maljoc's little body to vibrate with intense happiness.

The great metallic portal swung open, and Maljoc emerged into the starlight and looked up at the swinging constellations. Five hundred feet below, the massive domed dwellings of Agrahan glistened resplendently in the silvery radiance, but only the white, glittering immensity of the Milky Way was in harmony with his mood.

A droning assailed his ears as he walked along the narrow metal terrace toward the swinging nurseries of the women of his race. Several of the swarming masters were hovering in the air above him, but he smiled up at them without fear, for his heart was warm with the splendor of his mission.

The homoriums, sky promenades, and air terraces were suspended above the dwellings of Agrahan by great swinging cables attached to gas-inflated, billowing air floats perpetually at anchor. As Maljoc trod the terrace, one of the swarming masters flew swiftly between the cables and swooped down upon him.

Maljoc recoiled in terror. The swarming masters obeyed a strange, inhuman ethic. They reared their servitors with care, but they believed also that the life of a servitor was simply a little puff of useful energy. Sometimes, when in sportive mood, they crushed the little puffs out between their claws.

A chitin-clad extremity gripped Maljoc about his middle and lifted him into the air. Calmly then, and without reversing its direction, the swarming master flew with him toward the clouds.

Up and up they went, till the air grew rarefied. Then the swarming master laid the cool tips of its antennae on Maljoc's forehead and conversed with him in a friendly tone.

"Your nuptial night, my little friend?" it asked.

"Yes," replied Maljoc. "Yes—yes—it is."

He was so relieved that he stammered. The master was pleased. The warmth of its pleasure communicated itself to Maljoc through the vibrations of its antennae.

"It is well," it said. "Even you little ones are born to be happy. Only a cruel and thoughtless insect would crush a man under its claw in wanton pleasure."

Maljoc knew, then, that he was to be spared. He smiled up into the great luminous compound eyes of his benefactor.

"It amused me to lift you into the air," conveyed the master. "I could see that you wanted to soar above the earth; that your little wingless body was vibrant with happiness and desire for·expansion."

"That is true," said Maljoc.

He was grateful and—awed. He had never before been carried so high. The immense soaring wings of the master almost brushed the stratosphere.

For a moment the benevolent creature winged its way above the clouds, in rhythmic glee. Then, slowly, its body tilted, and it swept downward in a slow curve toward the sky terrace.

"You must not pick a too-beautiful mate," cautioned the master. "You know what happens sometimes to the too beautiful."

Maljoc knew. He knew that his own ancestors had once pierced the ancestors of the swarming masters with cruel blades of steel and had set them in decorative rows in square boxes because they were too beautiful. His instructors had not neglected to dwell with fervor on the grim expiation which the swarming masters were in the habit of exacting. He knew that certain men and women who were too beautiful were frequently lifted from the little slave world of routine duties in the dwellings of the masters and anesthetized, embalmed, and preserved under glass in the museum mausoleums of Agrahan.

The master set Maljoc gently down on the edge of the sky terrace and patted him benevolently on the shoulder with the tip of its hindermost leg. Then it soared swiftly upward and vanished from sight.

Maljoc began to chant again. The Galaxy glimmered majestically in the heavens above him, and as he progressed along the sky promenade he feasted his gaze on the glowing misty fringes of stupendous island universes lying far beyond the milky nebulae to which his little race and the swarming masters belonged.

Nearer at hand, as though loosely enmeshed in the supporting cables, the pole star winked and glittered ruddily, while Sirius vied with Betelgeuse in outshining the giant, cloud-obscured Antares, and the wheeling fire chariot of the planet Mars.

Above him great wings droned, and careening shapes usurped his vision. He quickened his stride and drew nearer, and ever nearer, to the object of his desire.

The nursery homorium of the women of his race was a towering vault of copper on the edge of the cable-suspended walk. As he came abreast of it he began to tremble, and the color ebbed from his face. The women of his race were unfathomable, dark enigmas to him—bewildering shapes of loveliness that utterly eluded his comprehension.

He had glimpsed them evanescently in pictures—the swarming masters had shown him animated pictures in colors—but why the pictures enraptured and disturbed him so he did not know.

For a moment he stood gazing fearfully up at the massive metal portal of the homorium. Awe and a kind of panicky terror contended with exultation in his bosom. Then, resolutely, he threw out his chest and began to sing.

The door of the homorium swung slowly open, and a dim blue light engirded him as he stood limned in the aperture. The illumination came from deep within the homorium. Maljoc did not hesitate. Shouting and singing exultantly, he passed quickly through the luminous portal, down a long, dim corridor, and into a vast, rectangular chamber.

The women of his race were standing about in little groups. Having reached maturity, they were discussing such grave and solemn topics as the past history of their kind and their future duties as obedient servants of the swarming masters. Without hesitation, Maljoc moved into the center of the chamber.

The women uttered little gasping cries of delight when they beheld him. Clustering boldly about him, they ran their slim white hands over his glistening tunic and caressed with fervor his beard and hair. They even gazed exultantly into his boyish gray eyes, and when he flushed they tittered.

Maljoc was disturbed and frightened. Ceasing to sing, he backed away precipitously toward the rear of the chamber.

"Do not be afraid," said a tall, flaxen-haired virago at his elbow. "We will not harm you."

Maljoc looked at her. She was attractive in a bold, flamboyant way, but he did not like her. He tried to move away from her, but she linked her arm in his and pulled him back toward the center of the chamber.

He cried out in protest. "I do not like you!" he exclaimed. "You are not the kind of woman—"

The amazon's lips set in hard lines. "You are far too young to know your own mind," she said. "I will be a good wife to you."

As she spoke, she thrust out a powerful right arm and sent three of her rivals sprawling.

Maljoc was panic-stricken. He pleaded and struggled. The woman was pulling him toward the center of the chamber, and two of the other women were contending with her.

The struggle terminated suddenly. Maljoc reeled, lost his balance, and went down with a thud on the hard metallic floor. The metal bruised his skull, stunning him.

For several seconds a wavering twilight engulfed Maljoc's faculties. Needles pierced his temples, and the relentless eyes of the amazon burned into his brain. Then, slowly and painfully, his senses cleared, and his eyelids flickered open in confused bewilderment.

Two compassionate blue eyes were gazing steadily down at him. Dazedly, Maljoc became aware of a lithely slim form, and a clear, lovely face. As he stared up in wonderment, the apparition moved closer and spoke in accents of assurance.

"I will not let them harm you," she said.

Maljoc groaned, and his hand went out in helpless appeal. Slim, firm fingers encircled his palm, and a gentle caress eased the pain in his forehead.

Gently he drew his comforter close and whispered, "Let us escape from these devils."

The woman beside him hesitated. She seemed both frightened and eager. "I am only eight months old," she told him in a furtive whisper. "I am really too young to go forth. They say, too, that it would be dangerous, for I am—" A blush suffused her cheeks.

"She is dangerously beautiful," said a harsh voice behind her. "The instructors here are indifferent to beauty, but when she goes forth she will be seized and impaled. You had better take me."

Maljoc raised himself defiantly on his elbow. "It is my privilege to choose," he said. "And I take this woman. Will you go forth with me, my little one?"

The woman's eyes opened widely. She looked slowly up at the amazon, who was standing in the shadows behind her, and said in a voice which did not tremble, "I will take this man. I will go forth with him."

The amazon's features were convulsed with wrath. But she was powerless to intervene. Maljoc was privileged to choose, and the woman was privileged to accept. With an infuriated shrug she retreated farther into the shadows.

Maljoc arose from the floor and gazed rapturously at his chosen mate. She did not evade his scrutiny. As Maljoc continued to stare at her, the strained look vanished from his face and mighty energies were released within him.

He stepped to her and lifted her with impassioned chantings into the air. Her long hair descended and enmeshed his shoulders, and as he pressed her to his heart, her arms tightened clingingly about him.

The other women clustered quickly about the exultant couple. Laughing and nudging one another, they examined the strong biceps of the bridegroom and ran their fingers enviously through the woman's dark hair.

Maljoc ignored them. Holding his precious burden very firmly in his muscular arms, he walked across the chamber, down the long outer corridor, and out through the massive door. Above him in another moment the Cyclopean luminous cables loomed beneath far-glimmering stars. He walked joyfully along the sky promenade, chanting, singing, unquenchably happy in his little hour of triumph and rapture.

The woman in his arms was unbelievably beautiful. She lay limply and calmly in his embrace, her eyes luminous with tenderness. Orion gleamed more brightly now, and the great horned moon was a silver fire weaving fantastically in and out of the nebulae-laced firmament.

As Maljoc sang and chanted, the enormous droning shapes above him seemed mere alien intruders in a world of imperishable loveliness. He thought of himself now as lord of the earth and the sky, and the burden in his arms was more important in his sight than his destiny as a servitor and the benefits which the swarming masters had promised to bestow upon him if he served them diligently and well.

He no longer coveted slave joys and gratifications. He wished to be forever his own master under the stars. It was a daring and impious wish, and as if aware of his insurgent yearnings a great form came sweeping down upon him out of the sky. For an instant it hovered with sonorously vibrating wings in the air above him. But Maljoc was so obsessed with joy that he ignored the chill menace of its presence. He walked on, and the woman in his arms shared his momentary forgetfulness.

The end of their pathetic and insane dream came with a sickening abruptness. A great claw descended and gripped the woman's slim body, tearing her with brutal violence from Maljoc's clasp.

The woman screamed twice shrilly. With a harsh cry, Maljoc leaped back. As he shook with horror, a quivering feeler brushed his forehead and spoke to him in accents of contempt: "She is too beautiful for you, little one. Return to the homorium and choose another mate."

Fear and awe of the swarming masters were instinctive in all men, but as the words vibrated through Maljoc's brain he experienced a blind agony which transcended instinct. With a scream he leaped into the air and entwined his little hands about the enormous bulbous hairs on the master's abdomen.

The master made no attempt to brush him off. It spread its gigantic lacy wings and soared swiftly into the sky. Maljoc tore and pulled at the hairs in a fury of defiance. The swiftness of the flight choked the breath in his lungs, and his eyes were blinded by swirling motes of dust. But though his vision was obscured, he could still glimpse dimly the figure of the woman as she swung limply in the clasp of the great claw a few yards above him.

Grimly, he pulled himself along the master's abdomen toward the claw. He pulled himself forward by transferring his fingers from hair to hair. The master's flat, broad stinger swung slowly toward him in a menacing arc, but he was sustained in his struggle by a sacrificial courage which transcended fear.

Yet the stinger moved so swiftly that it thwarted his daring purpose. In a fraction of time his brain grew poignantly aware that the stinger would sear his flesh before he could get to his dear one, and the realization was like a knife in his vitals. In despair and rage, he thrust out his puny jaw and sank his teeth deep into the soft flesh beneath him. The flesh quivered.

At the same instant the master swooped and turned over. Maljoc bit again. It screeched with pain and turned over and over, and suddenly, as it careened in pain, a white shape fell from its claw.

Maljoc caught the shape as it fell. With one hand clinging to the hair of the master's palpitating abdomen, and the other supporting the woman of his choice, he gazed downward into the abyss.

A mile below him the unfriendly earth loomed obscurely through riven tiers of cirrus clouds. But Maljoc did not hesitate. With a proud, exultant cry he tightened his hold on the woman and released his fingers from the hair.

The two lovers fell swiftly to the earth. But in that moment of swooning flight that could end only in destruction, Maljoc knew that he was mightier than the masters, and having recaptured for an imperishable instant the lost glory of his race, he went without fear into darkness.

Illustrated by Elliot Dold

He seized the reporter, shook him like a rat.

The Other

By Howard W. Graham, Ph.D.

B ASIL SASH was a feature writer on the *Metropolitan* and a
damned good one. He knew that he was on the trail of
something hot. As he skipped up the steps of Captain Björn
Ingvaldssen's Manhattan residence that morning he had no doubt
that he was going to cash in on a feature second to none. That was
saying a great deal.

He jabbed the bell. He gave the knocker a boost for good measure
and was pretty cocky about it. Then he yawned and blinked his eyes
dopily, for it was morning, and Basil Sash's nights generally reeled.
Sash was dead sober and wide-awake all the same.

The door opened like a shutter. The man who confronted him was
exactly the man Sash was looking for, but Sash was sleepily
nonplused. It was the explorer and scientist himself. He eyed the
reporter with such fishy, icy fury that Sash was speechless. Ingvaldssen stood six feet two and carried the brawn that goes with it; he had
something decidedly beefy in his appearance.

"Captain Ingvaldssen?" inquired Sash at last. He was uncommonly polite and even raised his hat.

"What the devil do you want, mister?" barked the captain.

"Let's have the story on that stiff, captain," he suggested. He
adopted his easiest, most persuasive and placating manner. Sash had
a lot of English on the ball. He had handled some pretty knotty
customers. "You know, captain, that swell little cadaver you've got
in the ice box."

Ingvaldssen slammed the door violently with volcanic dispatch.
This door was massive. The architect had used up four hundred and
fifty pounds of logwood when it was hung, but it clapped very
briskly indeed. Sash had scarcely time enough to blink and open his
mouth. Then the door banged in again just as quickly as it had shut.
A hand shot out, grasped him fiercely by the throat, yanked him
inside.

He swung his feet helplessly in the air. He plucked at an enormous hand which he found collaring his throat more and more tightly. Ingvaldssen had him off the floor and pinned to the door like one of his damned trophies. Sash's eyes bulged and darkened with blood. All at once the elephantine Ingvaldssen changed his mind. He gave the reporter a violent shake that came near disarticulating the vertebræ and dropped him.

"For a minute," Sash choked out, "I thought you were going to throttle me. Now, was that nice?"

"I was!" exploded the captain grimly. He rocked on his heels, keeping his hands behind his back. "That's just what I planned to do, but I felt that perhaps someone might know you had come here, had seen you enter. Murder is a serious thing when there are witnesses, but it is all meddlers deserve."

The reporter shivered. The "Norski Cow," the name by which Ingvaldssen was known back of the city desk, had changed a lot since his last expedition. Whence this ferocity?

"Let's skip it, captain." Sash essayed a sickly grin. "All I want is the feature. The story about that lady corpse you've been keeping on ice. Give it to Basil Sash and we'll be buddies all over again."

The Norwegian's eyes narrowed. He seemed to be thinking about mayhem.

"Maybe," he said at last, to Sash's relief.

He jerked his head, indicating that the reporter should follow him. Sash trailed the big fellow into a long work chamber opening off the hall, a room packed with an explorer's impedimenta and trophies. Skins and small beasts mounted as in life. A great deal of stuff was still crated as it had come from the ship, the *Petrel*.

The two men went through into a spacious back room, a laboratory in the proper sense. Here Ingvaldssen folded hairy bear's arms on his chest and stared at the reporter without speaking. Sash's eyes flickered craftily from the captain's ominous face to an object near the back wall. He got a full view of that which he had only peeked at as it was trucked off from the pier the day before.

That peek had been enough, enough to tell him that the captain had been up to something. While Ingvaldssen turned off a handful of reporters with his stock, technical report, Sash had been peering through a rent in a tarpaulin-wrapped block which a crane was planting on a waiting motor van. Something that had come on the *Petrel* from the high latitudes, via Stockholm! Here it was.

"Sweet Heaven!" gasped the reporter.

The thing really was a body, and it was a queer one. It was the body of a woman, sealed in some special kind of refrigerator. It was sheathed in an icicle, a watery stalagmite. Some specimen!

Bjöern Ingvaldssen, Sc.D. by his own simple choice, stood well up in the services of the American Technological Survey and had gone to the Arctic with an elaborate machine fabricated by his sponsors. He had explored polar territories previously under his own government and was acquainted with the field.

The machinery he took along was one of seven outfits being tested in various quarters of the globe by other men, all field workers in the survey. The problem confronting these men was to set up the apparatus entrusted to them in certain strategic places, notably mountain peaks and other high altitudes, in order to check on the mysterious and elusive cosmic-ray drift at various latitudes. It was a mechanical problem with vast implications.

The field workers, however, had merely to operate their sensitive instruments a given length of time, seal them, return them intact to the survey to be clocked and compared. Ingvaldssen drew the polar territory. He was the most reliable man available for what was considered the most hazardous piece of work. The polar-gray vortex, too, was of the utmost importance in the survey's calculations. The captain had got some queer facts of ray distortion—cosmic bends, as it were—down on his recorders.

He did his job thoroughly with characteristic precision and shipped all his instruments to his sponsors. But he had brought something else back with him from the arctic wastes. Distance and seasonal hazards alone were not what had made him the last man in. He anchored the *Petrel* in at Stockholm first, ostensibly for repairs. There was nothing in his reports about the real reason for delay— this precious cake of ice.

When the *Petrel* nosed at last into the North River, the only newsy information the Norwegian had to give out was the fact that he had picked up the frozen rear quarters of what was supposed to be a mastodon, preserved in an arctic glacier. His men had eaten some of it.

Sash crossed to the refrigerator. This was a plate-glass box, specially constructed so as to accommodate the body within to the best advantage. A drain at the lower side of the case conducted melted ice into a small reservoir. The case stood on a pedestal or dais and could be viewed from all four sides.

Refrigerating machinery was inclosed in the pedestal and more of it spilled out, connected by cables to a mass of apparatus at one side. Dials and gauges were piped up from the pedestal alongside the glass, and more of them stood in nests on the control machinery.

Nothing else in the laboratory really mattered—the usual stock of jars and retorts, a few electrical devices. Sash had seen many shops like it. But the refrigerator! He had a story here worth a whole front page, and it would have his name on it. Boy, what a feature! By Sash.

He circled the refrigerator. The girl inside was five feet nine or ten in height and not a type he had ever seen before. She was of no known race. Her hair was molten bronze, her skin reddish, coppery. Her eyes were open. They were sidelong, but not Mongoloid, and sooty green in color. Her lips, a natural scarlet, were parted in derision, and on her face was an expression of the most ferocious cruelty. She stood at half turn, her right arm partly raised. In her hand was a thing like a steel cigar, a metal plug with fluted sides and a button on the end.

She wore a fabulously wrought ring with a white stone on her left middle finger. Her fingernails, winking as though they had life, had dirt under the tips. That interested Sash.

But what filled him with consternation was the insolence and arrogance that went with her beauty. Even when dead she had the assurance of some immeasurable power. This was no garden variety of beauty he was looking at. She was superior to anything one might imagine on earth, any type or any race, ancient or modern. She was a thing exalted, a creation of unimaginable splendor. And she was frozen stiff.

Sash was crouching, candidly gloating on the inaccessible contours of her naked thighs, when Ingvaldssen jerked him to his feet by the coat collar. Sash faced the explorer and scientist, surprised. The man's eyes were heated and frantic. He seized the reporter by the lapels and began shaking him helpless, shook him until his teeth chattered and his sight blurred.

"You don't have to look at her like that!" shouted the captain. He bared his teeth. "She does not concern you! Who found her, eh? Answer me that! I did! She belongs to me!"

Sash was afraid the man was going mad. In the opinion of the reporter, a stiff was a stiff, even if it was a woman, and even if the woman was as unspeakably beautiful as this one. Captain Ingvaldssen brought his face close to Sash's. He began to rage. Sash thought he would choke on the explorer's heavy breath.

He snarled in self-defense and struck out futilely at Ingvaldssen's heavy face. He kicked. Sash was no coward, but he wasn't strong enough. Ingvaldssen's jaws bulged till they looked like ripe apples. His lips flattened, hardened. He shook Sash still more angrily.

"You know where I found her, eh? I'll tell you, you land rat. An old Eskimo showed me the place. I gave him three boxes of cigars. I bought that girl for three boxes of cigars!"

He gave a bellow of satisfaction and jammed the reporter into a chair, dazed. Ingvaldssen stood back, still threatening. He was calmer, but his eyes glittered as though they had been crystallized.

"She was ten feet deep in the side of a glacier, an ice pack that had slipped all the way down to the sea from the pole, maybe. Who knows? We took three kayaks, and Waller and I chopped her out with hatchets."

James Waller, thought Sash. And where was James Waller now? Waller had been Ingvaldssen's chief assistant, the man who had been lost overboard in a North Atlantic storm on the return trip from Stockholm. Ingvaldssen's voice deepened to a rasping whisper. The somber, brutal passion in it shocked Sash.

"Have you ever seen anything so beautiful?" muttered the explorer. He glared as though he had lost his reason.

"She's clever-looking, all right," admitted Sash shakily, "for an Eskimo."

"Eskimo!" yelled Ingvaldssen. "Do you think I would trouble with a damn Eskimo? No! My friend," he went on in a low, intense voice, "she is not an Eskimo. She is not Asiatic, not Mongolian at all. Let me tell you something. Waller was a geologist, and he was much better at it than I am. He was a very clever man, but meddlesome. That girl is not a hundred years old, nor three hundred. My friend, Waller told me that this girl whom we found incased in ice in that terrible polar desert was thirty or forty thousand years old. That is a fact. There were no such regal types on earth then. There aren't now, for that matter. Don't you know anything at all about anthropology, you blind fool? Look at the shape of her head!"

"Guff! You're nuts, Ingvaldssen!" Sash felt like arguing. One might find things out that way. "How would Waller know?"

"I will not give you a technical lecture," Ingvaldssen snorted. "Even I could tell that after examining the terrain. That glacier came down from the roof of the world, the immemorial icecaps. Even I could tell that. If she is not as old as Waller said, then all the scientific teachings in the world are poppycock. They are nuts, as you say. Good Heaven, man! Look at her closely—do you sit there and tell me a creature like that was ever born on earth?"

Sash got out of the chair sidewise. He backed cagily to the refrigerator. The old duffer meant well, apparently, but his invitations were two-edged. He looked again, furtively. Not of earth? It was hard to believe, when he could hear the sound of motor traffic outside the window and see ugly facades and ordinary people walking outside.

The girl was dressed in leather shorts. Tawny leather sustained with a needlessly broad, sturdy belt, the buckle of which was jeweled. She was a museum piece. She belonged in the big building in the park. He noted small items—the socket or holster in the belt, the loose jacket of scaled leather, the like of which no one had ever seen before.

He noticed that her forefingers were as long as the middle finger, and that the thumbs were twice the average length, nearly as long as any finger on her hands—shapely hands, though some might call them deformed. Her leather garb was blown hard against her as though by wind, revealing the contours of her body. Her inescapable perfection disturbed Sash enormously, and he could see how Ingvaldssen had been affected to the point of insanity. It would take a rare vision like this to wreck the great Norwegian's equilibrium. That rock-visaged, incorruptible misogynist!

"Maybe you would like to know something," Ingvaldssen rumbled. "I said she is not earthborn, and that must be so. That means I believe, of course, that other planets are inhabited. It is possible, probable, even. Maybe you can do a feature on it later, Mr. Sash, on this: if men are going to explore outer space personally in some kind of ship, they have got to take into account the cosmic rays which we have been measuring. The drift. Direction is everything. Later I will give you specifications of the machine which must be built.

"The ray drift is a constant and is also the source of necessary power. Of inexhaustible power. When it is trapped we can forget about gravity. I will tell you about sensitized plates which will absorb ray particles, a battery which no one has dreamed of. Ha, ha, Sash, no one can get off the earth in a rocket without bursting himself open! I know a good man who is going to kill himself trying, and I am going to let him do it because he would not listen to me.

"Yesterday I told you boys that the ray drift bends to the pole. The region above the pole is a cosmic funnel, a vortex of power, and I can tap it. I have already made a model. At the pole is where any spaceship has got to start. Someday there will be an airport at the pole. It is the only possible place to take off because of the direction of the ray drift, and it is the only place anyone can land. I think that girl's people knew all this. She used the drift to get here, and she had to land at the pole. Maybe I am crazy, but I don't think so."

True, she was not of earth, save only in form. She was an exotic, not mundane in the slightest. Sash lost himself for a moment in hypnotized speculation. She had traveled out of some crypt of antiquity into today, by accident. Come from where, and how? Maybe Ingvaldssen had found the answer. Sash wished he could hear this girl's voice and what she had to say. A voice from time's dawn. She was dead.

Her pose indicated something elusive. It interested Sash profoundly. She had been raising her arm when something attracted her scorn. What was it? He gave it up and looked at Ingvaldssen.

"O.K., captain." He grinned. "She doesn't belong on this little old green apple at all. If you found her at the pole, she must have come from somewhere to get there, what? Well? What are you going to do with this—this Other?"

"I am going to bring her back to life, make her tell us what happened. And about herself." Ingvaldssen's eyes glinted. "And I am going to marry her. If you laugh, my friend, I am going to kill you now with my hands."

Sash had been thinking about ways of buzzing Jennings, the staff photographer. Photographs! He had to have them, and he cursed himself for not carrying a camera, though that was not his job. He had to get to a phone. And he wanted to get at his own end of this incomparable feature. By Basil Sash. He swallowed Ingvaldssen's bait, though. He did not laugh, but blinked incredulously.

"Why, she's dead, captain, dead as a cold-storage egg! What kind of guff are you handing me?"

Ingvaldssen walked over to his refrigerating machinery and moved the pointer of a dial a fraction of a degree with his thumb nail. Sash was aware that the ice sheath was gradually diminishing, melting away from the corpse. Certainly it was a corpse—forty thousand years dead. The Norski Cow's mind was affected by the arctic cold. Ingvaldssen turned slowly and said with enormous precision, "I swore Waller to secrecy, and we got this Other aboard the *Petrel* by ourselves. No one in the crew suspected. I told Waller what I was going to do, and why I should succeed. My friend, after I had got my apparatus assembled, he was convinced that I was going to be successful, and he wanted to steal her. He was a very meddlesome man and a passionate one. He wanted to buy her.

"He was crazy to promise me anything I would listen to. I would not listen. Then I could see he was going to kill me, so I murdered him. I took the knife away from him and strangled him with my bare hands. It was at night, on the bridge. Then I threw him overboard. Do you see? Nothing is going to stand in my way. People do not necessarily die from cold. I am going to prove it. Maybe you would like to stay and see it done."

"Ing, old boy," Sash grinned, "you couldn't throw me out now."

"If I do not succeed," Ingvaldssen promised, "you will get a picture. Maybe you get one, anyhow, and the story. But hands off of her! You had better keep your lips shut about Waller. It was his fault. I am going to succeed. What I set out to do, I do. Once I thought no woman was good enough for me. Isn't it a crazy thing? Now I want this Other."

"The Other." Sash remained in his chair and examined her at a respectable distance while Ingvaldssen did business in an adjoining room. There were sounds of kitchen utensils, the crackle of frying. Ingvaldssen came back with a piece of leather which he dropped in Sash's lap. It was a yard square and close to an inch in thickness, like a rug, very heavy, but soft and pliable at the same time. Sash fingered it.

"From the mastodon's rump," said Ingvaldssen with a frosty smile. "That story was true, and one of the crew tanned it for me. Very shortly we are going to have lunch—rump steak from the same animal. It is still good to eat." He scratched his head, perplexed. "I cannot understand what happened to the front quarters of that animal, nor how it happened to be there in the first place. It was cut in two, literally broken in half. We found the right front foot."

The two men ate generous portions of the meat. It was well cooked, but remained somewhat tough. What it lacked in texture, however, it made up for in its succulent, gamy flavor. Ingvaldssen talked about his refrigerating plant while he picked shreds of meat fiber from his teeth with his fingernails.

The scientist was an ox of a man with long, blunt fingers, but he was as high-strung as a hummingbird all the same. Having had a sample of Ingvaldssen's anger, Sash wondered just what the Norski Cow would be like if he chanced to run amok. The explorer was as much beast as man, a drinker of blood by choice and addicted to a meat diet. A dog with a hungry, restless brain. The refrigerator, it seemed, was no inconsiderable achievement.

"Chiefly I am an engineer," said Ingvaldssen modestly. "I stood in at Stockholm because I knew this Other would not keep on the ocean voyage. She would spoil the way some of the mastodon did. I have friends there who furnish me with materials. Every day I poured water on the cake of ice the girl was in to keep up the size of the block. Because no matter how cold it is, ice evaporates. In the meantime I was inventing a refrigerator.

"Sash, my boy, you would not realize how difficult it was, that ice box. Do you see why? The ice would still melt. I didn't dare to expose an inch of that girl's skin. How do I know what the world was like when she came into it? Maybe there are factors other than evolution which created present animal forms. I put it badly. Perhaps it is something in the air, which would be part of evolution. If she was constituted to endure conditions then, maybe conditions today are worse for her, however we may think. Exposure to the air might kill her, rot her before I had my way."

"But she didn't survive, Ing," Sash pointed out. "She's frozen. I say she's dead. All I want is to see the proof of it and get my feature. I've got to hold down my job, you know."

Ingvaldssen paid no attention.

"What if her nervous system is different," he pondered, "and she froze like this without feeling anything? That would explain a great deal. Anyhow, I was not taking chances. This ice box had to have not only elaborate temperature control, but a system of sprayers to keep the size of the ice cake constant. I had to ensure the formation of ice on all sides of the block.

"Look at them. Those crossbars at the bottom of the case travel up the sides. They contain a solution of water and a volatile salt at two degrees below zero, centigrade. When the sprayers are working, the salt volatilizes and passes off through the ventilator, and only the water strikes the ice cake. It freezes at once. It would be a simple matter to fill the refrigerator with ice and burst it in three minutes."

"But there's scarcely any ice on the girl's body at all."

"I don't need ice anymore. I am trying to revive her, this Other. The de-refrigerating element has been working at slow speed since yesterday morning when I landed, and the temperature inside the case is now close to one degree above zero. Pretty soon we shall see."

A chip of ice fell from the girl's body now and then. Sash could hear the small sounds issuing through the ventilator of the case. It was rather eerie. He had no real faith whatever in Ingvaldssen's experiment, then. He was ready to go down on record believing that explorers as well as artists and writers—even including Basil Sash—were dotty. A curved shell of ice slipped from the Other's shoulder and shattered delicately at her feet. The reservoir on the side of the case was filled. There was no longer any ice in the case save on the girl's leather garments and in the fist that held the metal instrument.

The shadowed green eyes were clear now, the face moist. The girl's expression was intensified. She must have been a person of naive, if high, intelligence. She had seen something that aroused her contempt. Her expression was scornful. Sash wondered again what she had been looking at and what that thing in her hand could be. He noticed that her gaze was fixed on the back of Ingvaldssen's head.

So suddenly that Sash jumped a little, Ingvaldssen rose and returned the dial on the case to zero. His circulation motor whined under the pedestal. He stood facing the Other. The ice had melted down evenly, planting the girl on her feet on an even balance. That was lucky, thought Sash. If she had fallen she might have crashed through the glass wall.

"Lose your nerve?" he asked.

"Of course not!" snapped Ingvaldssen. "Remember, she is still all ice. The temperature of her skin is zero. She is colder than that inside. Being a newspaper fellow, you should have some odd bits of information. Do you know what happens to flesh that has been frozen and then is warmed?"

"I know that it is fatal."

"But you surely know what is done to bring back circulation to a frozen member? For example, if you were to freeze a hand or an ear?"

"Oh, yes. Rub it with snow. Warm it gradually, in other words."

"That is correct. You suggest that ice flays the fine system of blood vessels in the body, literally. Capillaries burst. It does something like that. You know, water expands when it freezes. It is one of the few substances that does. The water in a man's body wrecks him accordingly as his temperature is raised or lowered. Water is a great catalytic agent in the life chemistry.

"I have not lost my nerve. I am waiting until temperature is equalized throughout the refrigerator, till the temperature of the girl's flesh is zero. Then you will see something. She has to be brought just to the verge of melting, do you see? I think I have been given what you would call a lucky break. I will oxygenize her with my outfit here, otherwise. But do you notice anything especially peculiar about this Other?"

"She is a damned lovely kid, and then she has a gadget in her hand that she was going to do something with."

"You don't see the point at all. Look at her breast. It is expanded fully. You can see the conformation of her ribs. How beautifully muscled she is! She is as handsome as a wild cat."

Sash thought that was a fly remark. "What difference does her breast make? Its expansion, I mean?"

"You will see," said Ingvaldssen irritably. "But you should have some imagination. I want your opinion. What is she so scornful about?"

"She saw something, naturally. If you really want the opinion of a city columnist, I should say it was something big, but that where she comes from they aren't afraid of size alone. Maybe she saw that mastodon, or weren't they running around at that time? Maybe she did hop in from another planet, and she got the notion the earth wasn't worth a barrel of apples.

"Look here, Ingvaldssen, don't you think it's mighty odd that a corpse should have any expression on its face at all? They don't, do they, unless they've been drugged?"

"You're smarter than I thought, Sash," grunted Ingvaldssen. "I've been thinking. She was frozen just like that!" He snapped his fingers briskly. "It was quick, and it kept the expression on her face. The cold must have fallen instantly. That's my lucky break number two. It gives me a chance, a much better chance than if it had happened slowly."

Basil Sash had scarcely removed his eyes from the Other in the glass case all this while. There was something magical in the mere appearance of the girl, something that got you a swift one in the ribs.

He did not know what chasm this divine girl had bridged by accident, but he was getting the creeps. He had a terrible feeling that something disastrous was about to happen.

Ingvaldssen spoke, consulting a watch. "I should say the temperature of her flesh was at zero all through. Now!" He pulled a small double switch that regulated an electric timing device. This device advanced the needle of the temperature gauge by infinitely slow degrees, not a full degree an hour. "You are going to see something happen, my friend."

"Listen, captain," said Sash hurriedly. "Did you ever read a magazine called *Astounding Stories*? No? I wish you had! Listen! I'm afraid of that gadget she has in her paw-paw!"

"Paw-paw?"

"Hand. Listen. I read a story in this magazine about a gun that uses a ray, a gadget just like that one she has. What if it should go off when she melts and blow us both to hell? I wouldn't like that!"

"A gun? How could it be a gun when this Other has been in the ice forty thousand years? Are you crazy? It looks solid, doesn't it? More likely it is a tool of some kind which she keeps in that socket in her belt."

"Ing, I tell you I'm scared! I don't like this a little bit! This gun I read about used atoms instead of bullets and powder. Atomic disintegration. It cut a hole in three-inch-alloy steel like paper, and the gun wasn't any bigger than that. Anyhow, I don't like the look on her face. She's up to something even if she is stiff. Remember now, I warned you. If you get hurt, I'll swear on a million Bibles that you kept me here against my will, and you can't back out of it. You kidnaped me."

"Can that be possible?" wondered Ingvaldssen reluctantly. "I never saw a gun shaped like that!"

He frowned stolidly and closed another switch. The temperature needle swung to forty degrees, somewhat above blood heat, and stayed there. This action of the scientist's was quite deliberate, and it solved a number of problems with one stroke.

Against what followed, Sash recollected several major points. Chief among these was the fact that the Other had been arrested in some mysterious action. One day forty thousand years ago the temperature had fallen deep and suddenly, stopping her hand half raised. Then, in his heart, Sash knew that the Other really had come from some place outside the earth, some alien planet in the sky, by some unknown means. This explanation offered itself most readily since no other logic would serve.

Also, and this was something he had not dared mention to Ingvaldssen, the Other was a mighty superior being, taken at face value alone. Sash had one brief moment to wonder about her antecedents, some age-old tradition of beauty and culture from which she had sprung, a superior race of another world. It was not impossible. He had read stories of such things and half believed them. If all this was true, that she had indeed come from far abroad in space, if the singing beauty, the thrilling and somewhat terrible intelligence apparent in her face, was to live again, then Ingvaldssen was something like a stupid ox for supposing he could marry her. Marry the earth to the stars! Basil Sash wanted to get out of there in a hurry. The fact that Ingvaldssen had brought back any creature at all in the ice was a feature in itself. It had heaps of human interest. He jumped up.

The Other's hand trembled. Sash hesitated, thunderstruck. He saw her abnormally long thumb tighten on the metal tool she held. Her lungs collapsed with an audible gust; she folded forward, caught her balance again. Then she looked at both men glancingly with a kind of bitter amusement.

Perhaps her flesh was more resistant than ours, resistant to the fate of death by freezing. At any rate, Ingvaldssen's hope was clear now. In collapsing, the lungs stimulated the heart, which beat heavily once with such force as to raise purple veins in her broad, coppery forehead. Her little breasts rose and fell with her quick breathing. If she had seen something that she was derisive of when the world was much younger, what she saw of earth now deepened her expression tenfold. A small line appeared between her brows, and her fine lips curled. Her hand rose, and something came from it, a blinding cone.

"Ah!" roared Ingvaldssen. He opened his arms. "Ah, my love! Come to me! Co—"

Ingvaldssen disappeared. That is, nothing was left of his heroic body from the thighs upward. His stumps banged on the floor and fingertips dropped from midair. Once, the Other had started to do something. Shocked terrifically by the irony of the thing, Sash realized that the Other had simply completed the movement she had begun forty thousand years ago, this time with a new target.

Suddenly Sash knew what had happened to the mastodonic remains of the beast Ingvaldssen found. The girl had shot and obliterated half of it.

A hole appeared in the glass in front of the girl's hand. Sash turned mechanically and saw that Ingvaldssen had vanished save for the terrible relics on the floor. The cone projecting from the girl's gun had knocked out a piece of the front chamber big enough to walk through. Sash caught a glimpse of traffic on Fifth Avenue, and the start of a colossal uproar across the street, where the gun had wrought vast and incomprehensible destruction. He saw a shelving, curved swath cut into the earth for the distance of a mile and a quarter and saw the boiling waters of the Hudson leap into the end of it.

Then Sash turned and shrieked, his face contorted beyond human likeness. He clawed himself, gouged his eyes as though he could not bear to look quietly in the girl's time-forgotten, fresh face. He heard an agonizing sound. It was the fluid tinkle of the Other's disdainful silver laughter.

"Get out! Beat it! Scram!"
he shouted at the giggling,
gibbering creatures—

Illustrated by Thompson

The Mad Moon

BY STANLEY G. WEINBAUM

The great, idiotic heads, the silly grins, and giggles—those giggles would drive him crazy.

I

"IDIOTS!" howled Grant Calthorpe. "Fools—nitwits—imbeciles!" He sought wildly for some more expressive terms, failed, and vented his exasperation in a vicious kick at the pile of rubbish on the ground.

Too vicious a kick, in fact; he had again forgotten the one-third normal gravitation of Io, and his whole body followed his kick in a long, twelve-foot arc.

As he struck the ground the four loonies giggled. Their great, idiotic heads, looking like nothing so much as the comic faces painted on Sunday balloons for children, swayed in unison on their five-foot necks, as thin as Grant's wrist.

"Get out!" he blazed, scrambling erect. "Beat it, skiddoo, scram! No chocolate. No candy. Not until you learn that I want ferva leaves, and not any junk you happen to grab. Clear out!"

The loonies—*Lunae Jovis Magnicapites,* or literally, Bigheads of Jupiter's Moon—backed away, giggling plaintively. Beyond doubt, they considered Grant fully as idiotic as he considered them and were quite unable to understand the reasons for his anger. But they certainly realized that no candy was to be forthcoming, and their giggles took on a note of keen disappointment.

So keen, indeed, that the leader, after twisting his ridiculous blue face in an imbecilic grin at Grant, voiced a last wild giggle and dashed his head against a glittering stone-bark tree. His companions casually picked up his body and moved off, with his head dragging behind them on its neck like a prisoner's ball on a chain.

Grant brushed his hand across his forehead and turned wearily toward his stone-bark log shack. A pair of tiny, glittering red eyes caught his attention, and a slinker—*Mus Sapiens*—skipped his six-inch form across the threshold, bearing under his tiny, skinny arm what looked very much like Grant's clinical thermometer.

Grant yelled angrily at the creature, seized a stone, and flung it vainly. At the edge of the brush, the slinker turned its ratlike, semihuman face toward him, squeaked its thin gibberish, shook a microscopic fist in manlike wrath, and vanished, its batlike cowl of skin fluttering like a cape. It looked, indeed, very much like a black rat wearing a cape.

It had been a mistake, Grant knew, to throw the stone at it. Now the tiny fiends would never permit him any peace, and their diminutive size and pseudo-human intelligence made them infernally troublesome as enemies. Yet, neither that reflection nor the loony's suicide troubled him particularly; he had witnessed instances like the latter too often, and besides, his head felt as if he were in for another siege of white fever.

He entered the shack, closed the door, and stared down at his pet parcat. "Oliver," he growled, "you're a fine one. Why the devil don't you watch out for slinkers? What are you here for?"

The parcat rose on its single, powerful hind leg, clawing at his knees with its two forelegs. "The red jack on the black queen," it observed placidly. "Ten loonies make one halfwit."

Grant placed both statements easily. The first was, of course, an echo of his preceding evening's solitaire game, and the second of yesterday's session with the loonies. He grunted abstractedly and rubbed his aching head. White fever again, beyond doubt.

He swallowed two ferverin tablets and sank listlessly to the edge of his bunk, wondering whether this attack of *blancha* would culminate in delirium.

He cursed himself for a fool for ever taking this job on Jupiter's third habitable moon, Io. The tiny world was a planet of madness, good for nothing except the production of ferva leaves, out of which Earthly chemists made as many potent alkaloids as they once had made from opium.

Invaluable to medical science, of course, but what difference did that make to him? What difference, even, did the munificent salary make, if he got back to Earth a raving maniac after a year in the equatorial regions of Io? He swore bitterly that when the plane from Junopolis landed next month for his ferva, he'd go back to the polar city with it, even though his contract with Neilan Drug called for a full year, and he'd get no pay if he broke it. What good was money to a lunatic?

II

The whole little planet was mad—loonies, parcats, slinkers and Grant Calthorpe—all crazy. At least, anybody who ever ventured outside either of the two polar cities, Junopolis on the north and Herapolis on the south, was crazy. One could live there in safety from white fever, but anywhere below the twentieth parallel it was worse than the Cambodian jungles on Earth.

He amused himself by dreaming of Earth. Just two years ago he had been happy there, known as a wealthy, popular sportsman. He had been just that, too; before he was twenty-one he had hunted knife-kite and threadworm on Titan, and triops and uniped on Venus.

That had been before the gold crisis of 2110 had wiped out his fortune. And—well, if he had to work, it had seemed logical to use his interplanetary experience as a means of livelihood. He had really been enthusiastic at the chance to associate himself with Neilan Drug.

He had never been on Io before. This wild little world was no sportsman's paradise, with its idiotic loonies and wicked, intelligent, tiny slinkers. There wasn't anything worth hunting on the feverish little moon, bathed in warmth by the giant Jupiter only a quarter million miles away.

If he *had* happened to visit it, he told himself ruefully, he'd never have taken the job; he had visualized Io as something like Titan, cold but clean.

Instead it was as hot as the Venus Hotlands because of its glowing primary, and subject to half a dozen different forms of steamy daylight—sun day, Jovian day, Jovian and sun day, Europa light, and occasionally actual and dismal night. And most of these came in the course of Io's forty-two-hour revolution, too—a mad succession of changing lights. He hated the dizzy days, the jungle, and Idiots' Hills stretching behind his shack.

It was Jovian and solar day at the present moment, and that was the worst of all, because the distant sun added its modicum of heat to that of Jupiter. And to complete Grant's discomfort now was the prospect of a white fever attack. He swore as his head gave an additional twinge, and then he swallowed another ferverin tablet. His supply of these was diminishing, he noticed; he'd have to remember to ask for some when the plane called—no, he was going back with it.

Oliver rubbed against his leg. "Idiots, fools, nitwits, imbeciles," remarked the parcat affectionately. "Why did I have to go to that damn dance?"

"Huh?" said Grant. He couldn't remember having said anything about a dance. It must, he decided, have been said during his last fever madness.

Oliver creaked like the door, then giggled like a loony. "It'll be all right," he assured Grant. "Father is bound to come soon."

"Father!" echoed the man. His father had died fifteen years before. "Where'd you get that from, Oliver?"

"It must be the fever," observed Oliver placidly. "You're a nice kitty, but I wish you had sense enough to know what you're saying. And I wish father would come." He finished with a suppressed gurgle that might have been a sob.

Grant stared dizzily at him. He hadn't said any of those things; he was positive. The parcat must have heard them from somebody else— Somebody else? Where within five hundred miles was there anybody else?

"Oliver!" he bellowed. "Where'd you hear that? Where'd you hear it?"

The parcat backed away, startled. "Father is idiots, fools, nitwits, imbeciles," he said anxiously. "The red jack on the nice kitty."

"Come here!" roared Grant. "Whose father? Where have you— Come here, you imp!"

He lunged at the creature. Oliver flexed his single hind leg and flung himself frantically to the cowl of the wood stove. "It must be the fever!" he squalled. "No chocolate!"

He leaped like a three-legged flash for the flue opening. There came a sound of claws grating on metal, and then he had scrambled through.

Grant followed him. His head ached from the effort, and with the still sane part of his mind he knew that the whole episode was doubtless white fever delirium, but he plowed on.

His progress was a nightmare. Loonies kept bobbing their long necks above the tall bleeding-grass, their idiotic giggles and imbecilic faces adding to the general atmosphere of madness.

Wisps of fetid, fever-bearing vapors spouted up at every step on the spongy soil. Somewhere to his right a slinker squeaked and gibbered; he knew that a tiny slinker village was over in that direction, for once he had glimpsed the neat little buildings, constructed of small, perfectly fitted stones like a miniature medieval town, complete to towers and battlements. It was said that there were even slinker wars.

His head buzzed and whirled from the combined effects of ferverin and fever. It was an attack of *blancha,* right enough, and he realized that he was an imbecile, a loony, to wander thus away from his shack. He should be lying on his bunk; the fever was not serious, but more than one man had died on Io in the delirium, with its attendant hallucinations.

He was delirious now. He knew it as soon as he saw Oliver, for Oliver was placidly regarding an attractive young lady in perfect evening dress of the style of the second decade of the twenty-second century. Very obviously that was a hallucination, since girls had no business in the Ionian tropics, and if by some wild chance one should appear there, she would certainly not choose formal garb.

The hallucination had fever, apparently, for her face was pale with the whiteness that gave *blancha* its name. Her gray eyes regarded him without surprise as he wound his way through the bleeding-grass to her.

"Good afternoon, evening, or morning," he remarked, giving a puzzled glance at Jupiter, which was rising, and the sun, which was setting. "Or perhaps merely good day, Miss Lee Neilan."

She gazed seriously at him. "Do you know," she said, "you're the first one of the illusions that I haven't recognized? All my friends have been around, but you're the first stranger. Or are you a stranger? You know my name—but you ought to, of course, being my own hallucination."

"We won't argue about which of us is the hallucination," he suggested. "Let's do it this way. The one of us that disappears first is the illusion. Bet you five dollars you do."

"How could I collect?" she said. "I can't very well collect from my own dream."

"That is a problem." He frowned. "My problem, of course, not yours. I know I'm real."

"How do you know my name?" she demanded.

"Ah!" he said. "From intensive reading of the society sections of the newspapers brought by my supply plane. As a matter of fact, I have one of your pictures cut out and pasted next to my bunk. That probably accounts for my seeing you now. I'd like to really meet you sometime."

"What a gallant remark for an apparition!" she exclaimed. "And who are you supposed to be?"

"Why, I'm Grant Calthorpe. In fact, I work for your father, trading with the loonies for ferva."

"Grant Calthorpe," she echoed. She narrowed her fever-dulled eyes as if to bring him into better focus. "Why, you are!"

Her voice wavered for a moment, and she brushed her hand across her pale brow. "Why should you pop up out of my memories? It's strange. Three or four years ago, when I was a romantic schoolgirl and you the famous sportsman, I was madly in love with you. I had a whole book filled with your pictures—Grant Calthorpe dressed in parka for hunting threadworm on Titan—Grant Calthorpe beside the giant uniped he killed near the Mountains of Eternity. You're—you're really the pleasantest hallucination I've had so far. Delirium would be—fun"—she pressed her hand to her brow again—"if one's head—didn't ache so!"

"Gee!" thought Grant, "I wish that were true, that about the book. This is what psychology calls a wish-fulfillment dream." A drop of warm rain plopped on his neck. "Got to get to bed," he said aloud. "Rain's bad for *blancha*. Hope to see you next time I'm feverish."

"Thank you," said Lee Neilan with dignity. "It's quite mutual."

He nodded, sending a twinge through his head. "Here, Oliver," he said to the drowsing parcat. "Come on."

"That isn't Oliver," said Lee. "It's Polly. It's kept me company for two days, and I've named it Polly."

"Wrong gender," muttered Grant. "Anyway, it's my parcat, Oliver. Aren't you, Oliver?"

"Hope to see you," said Oliver sleepily.

"It's Polly. Aren't you, Polly?"

"Bet you five dollars," said the parcat. He rose, stretched and loped off into the underbrush. "It must be the fever," he observed as he vanished.

"It must be," agreed Grant. He turned away. "Good-by, Miss—or I might as well call you Lee, since you're not real. Good-by, Lee."

"Good-by, Grant. But don't go that way. There's a slinker village over in the grass."

"No. It's over there."

"It's *there*," she insisted. "I've been watching them build it. But they can't hurt you anyway, can they? Not even a slinker could hurt an apparition. Good-by, Grant." She closed her eyes wearily.

III

It was raining harder now. Grant pushed his way through the bleeding-grass, whose red sap collected in bloody drops on his boots. He had to get back to his shack quickly, before the white fever and its attendant delirium set him wandering utterly astray. He needed ferverin.

Suddenly he stopped short. Directly before him the grass had been cleared away, and in the little clearing were the shoulder-high towers and battlements of a slinker village—a new one, for half-finished houses stood among the others, and hooded six-inch forms toiled over the stones.

There was an outcry of squeaks and gibberish. He backed away, but a dozen tiny darts whizzed about him. One stuck like a toothpick in his boot, but none, luckily, scratched his skin, for they were undoubtedly poisoned. He moved more quickly, but all around in the thick, fleshy grasses were rustlings, squeakings, and incomprehensible imprecations.

He circled away. Loonies kept popping their balloon heads over the vegetation, and now and again one giggled in pain as a slinker bit or stabbed it. Grant cut toward a group of the creatures, hoping to distract the tiny fiends in the grass, and a tall, purple-faced loony curved its long neck above him, giggling and gesturing with its skinny fingers at a bundle under its arm.

He ignored the thing and veered toward his shack. He seemed to have eluded the slinkers, so he trudged doggedly on, for he needed a ferverin tablet badly. Yet, suddenly he came to a frowning halt, turned, and began to retrace his steps.

"It can't be so," he muttered. "But she told me the truth about the slinker village. I didn't know it was there. Yet how could a hallucination tell me something I didn't know?"

Lee Neilan was sitting on the stone-bark log exactly as he had left her, with Oliver again at her side. Her eyes were closed, and two slinkers were cutting at the long skirt of her gown with tiny, glittering knives.

Grant knew that they were always attracted by Terrestrial textiles; apparently they were unable to duplicate the fascinating sheen of satin, though the fiends were infernally clever with their tiny hands. As he approached, they tore a strip from thigh to ankle, but the girl made no move. Grant shouted, and the vicious little creatures mouthed unutterable curses at him as they skittered away with their silken plunder.

Lee Neilan opened her eyes. "You again," she murmured vaguely. "A moment ago it was father. Now it's you." Her pallor had increased; the white fever was running its course in her body.

"Your father! Then that's where Oliver heard— Listen, Lee. I found the slinker village. I didn't know it was there, but I found it just as you said. Do you see what that means? We're both real!"

"Real?" she said dully. "There's a purple loony grinning over your shoulder. Make him go away. He makes me feel—sick."

He glanced around; true enough, the purple-faced loony was behind him. "Look here," he said, seizing her arm. The feel of her smooth skin was added proof. "You're coming to the shack for ferverin." He pulled her to her feet. "Don't you understand? I'm *real!*"

"No, you're not," she said dazedly.

"Listen, Lee. I don't know how in the devil you got here or why, but I know Io hasn't driven me that crazy yet. You're real and I'm real." He shook her violently. "I'm *real!*" he shouted.

Faint comprehension showed in her dazed eyes. "Real?" she whispered. "Real! Oh, Lord! Then take—me out of—this mad place!" She swayed, made a stubborn effort to control herself, then pitched forward against him.

Of course on Io her weight was negligible, less than a third Earth normal. He swung her into his arms and set off toward the shack, keeping well away from both slinker settlements. Around him bobbed excited loonies, and now and again the purple-faced one, or another exactly like him, giggled and pointed and gestured.

The rain had increased, and warm rivulets flowed down his neck, and to add to the madness, he blundered near a copse of stinging palms, and their barbed lashes stung painfully through his shirt. Those stings were virulent too, if one failed to disinfect them; indeed, it was largely the stinging palms that kept traders from gathering their own ferva instead of depending on the loonies.

Behind the low rain clouds, the sun had set, and it was ruddy Jupiter daylight, which lent a false flush to the cheeks of the unconscious Lee Neilan, making her still features very lovely.

Perhaps he kept his eyes too steadily on her face, for suddenly Grant was among slinkers again; they were squeaking and sputtering, and the purple loony leaped in pain as teeth and darts pricked his legs. But, of course, loonies were immune to the poison.

The tiny devils were around his feet now. He swore in a low voice and kicked vigorously, sending a ratlike form spinning fifty feet in the air. He had both automatic and flame pistol at his hip, but he could not use them for several reasons.

First, using an automatic against the tiny hordes was much like firing into a swarm of mosquitoes; if the bullet killed one or two or a dozen, it made no appreciable impression on the remaining thousands. And as for the flame pistol, that was like using a Big Bertha to swat a fly. Its vast belch of fire would certainly incinerate all the slinkers in its immediate path, along with grass, trees, and loonies, but that again would make but little impress on the surviving hordes, and it meant laboriously recharging the pistol with another black diamond and another barrel.

He had gas bulbs in the shack, but they were not available at the moment, and besides, he had no spare mask, and no chemist has yet succeeded in devising a gas that would kill slinkers without being also deadly to humans. And, finally, he couldn't use any weapon whatsoever right now, because he dared not drop Lee Neilan to free his hands.

Ahead was the clearing around the shack. The space was full of slinkers, but the shack itself was supposed to be slinkerproof, at least for reasonable lengths of time, since stone-bark logs were very resistant to their tiny tools.

But Grant perceived that a group of the diminutive devils were around the door, and suddenly he realized their intent. They had looped a cord of some sort over the knob, and were engaged now in twisting it!

Grant yelled and broke into a run. While he was yet half a hundred feet distant, the door swung inward and the rabble of slinkers flowed into the shack.

He dashed through the entrance. Within was turmoil. Little hooded shapes were cutting at the blankets on his bunk, his extra clothing, the sacks he hoped to fill with ferva leaves, and were pulling at the cooking utensils, or at any and all loose objects.

He bellowed and kicked at the swarm. A wild chorus of squeaks and gibberish arose as the creatures skipped and dodged about him. The fiends were intelligent enough to realize that he could do nothing with his arms occupied by Lee Neilan. They skittered out of the way of his kicks, and while he threatened a group at the stove, another rabble tore at his blankets.

In desperation he charged at the bunk. He swept the girl's body across it to clear it, dropped her on it, and seized a grass broom he had made to facilitate his housekeeping. With wide strokes of its handle he attacked the slinkers, and the squeals were checkered by cries and whimpers of pain.

A few broke for the door, dragging whatever loot they had. He spun around in time to see half a dozen swarming around Lee Neilan, tearing at her clothing, at the wristwatch on her arm, at the satin evening pumps on her small feet. He roared a curse at them and battered them away, hoping that none had pricked her skin with virulent dagger or poisonous tooth.

He began to win the skirmish. More of the creatures drew their black capes close about them and scurried over the threshold with their plunder. At last, with a burst of squeaks, the remainder, laden and empty-handed alike, broke and ran for safety, leaving a dozen furry, impish bodies slain or wounded.

Grant swept these after the others with his erstwhile weapon, closed the door in the face of a loony that bobbed in the opening, latched it against any repetition of the slinker's trick, and stared in dismay about the plundered dwelling.

Cans had been rolled or dragged away. Every loose object had been pawed by the slinkers' foul little hands, and Grant's clothes hung in ruins on their hooks against the wall. But the tiny robbers had not succeeded in opening the cabinet nor the table drawer, and there was food left.

Six months of Ionian life had left him philosophical; he swore heartily, shrugged resignedly, and pulled his bottle of ferverin from the cabinet.

His own spell of fever had vanished as suddenly and completely as *blancha* always does when treated, but the girl, lacking ferverin, was paper-white and still. Grant glanced at the bottle; eight tablets remained.

"Well, I can always chew ferva leaves," he muttered. That was less effective than the alkaloid itself, but it would serve, and Lee Neilan needed the tablets. He dissolved two of them in a glass of water, and lifted her head.

She was not too inert to swallow, and he poured the solution between her pale lips, then arranged her as comfortably as he could. Her dress was a tattered silken ruin, and he covered her with a blanket that was no less a ruin. Then he disinfected his palm stings, pulled two chairs together, and sprawled across them to sleep.

He started up at the sound of claws on the roof, but it was only Oliver, gingerly testing the flue to see if it was hot. In a moment the parcat scrambled through, stretched himself, and remarked, "I'm real and you're real."

"Imagine that!" grunted Grant sleepily.

IV

When he awoke it was Jupiter and Europa light, which meant he had slept about seven hours, since the brilliant little third moon was just rising. He rose and gazed at Lee Neilan, who was sleeping soundly with a tinge of color in her face that was not entirely due to the ruddy daylight. The *blancha* was passing.

He dissolved two more tablets in water, then shook the girl's shoulder. Instantly her gray eyes opened, quite clear now, and she looked up at him without surprise.

"Hello, Grant," she murmured. "So it's you again. Fever isn't so bad, after all."

"Maybe I ought to let you stay feverish." He grinned. "You say such nice things. Wake up and drink this, Lee."

She became suddenly aware of the shack's interior. "Why— Where is this? It looks—real!"

"It is. Drink this ferverin."

She obeyed, then lay back and stared at him perplexedly. "Real?" she said. "And you're real?"

"I think I am."

A rush of tears clouded her eyes. "Then—I'm out of that place? That horrible place?"

"You certainly are." He saw signs of her relief becoming hysteria, and hastened to distract her. "Would you mind telling me how you happened to be there—and dressed for a party, too?"

She controlled herself. "I was dressed for a party. A party in Herapolis. But I was in Junopolis, you see."

"I don't see. In the first place, what are you doing on Io, anyway? Every time I ever heard of you, it was in connection with New York or Paris society."

She smiled. "Then it wasn't all delirium, was it? You did say that you had one of my pictures— Oh, that one!" She frowned at the print on the wall. "Next time a news photographer wants to snap my picture, I'll remember not to grin like—like a loony. But as to how I happen to be on Io, I came with father, who's looking over the possibilities of raising ferva on plantations instead of having to depend on traders and loonies. We've been here three months, and I've been terribly bored. I thought Io would be exciting, but it wasn't—until recently."

"But what about that dance? How'd you manage to get here, a thousand miles from Junopolis?"

"Well," she said slowly, "it was terribly tiresome in Junopolis. No shows, no sport, nothing but an occasional dance. I got restless. When there were dances in Herapolis, I formed the habit of flying over there. It's only four or five hours in a fast plane, you know. And last week—or whenever it was—I'd planned on flying down, and Harvey—that's father's secretary—was to take me. But at the last minute father needed him and forbade my flying alone."

Grant felt a strong dislike for Harvey. "Well?" he asked.

"So I flew alone," she finished demurely.

"And cracked up, eh?"

"I can fly as well as anybody," she retorted. "It was just that I followed a different route, and suddenly there were mountains ahead."

He nodded. "The Idiots' Hills," he said. "My supply plane detours five hundred miles to avoid them. They're not high, but they stick right out above the atmosphere of this crazy planet. The air here is dense but shallow."

"I know that. I knew I couldn't fly above them, but I thought I could hurdle them. Work up full speed, you know, and then throw the plane upward. I had a closed plane, and gravitation is so weak here. And besides, I've seen it done several times, especially with rocket-driven craft. The jets help to support the plane even after the wings are useless for lack of air."

"What a damn-fool stunt!" exclaimed Grant. "Sure it can be done, but you have to be an expert to pull out of it when you hit the air on the other side. You hit fast, and there isn't much falling room."

"So I found out," said Lee ruefully. "I almost pulled out, but not quite, and I hit in the middle of some stinging palms. I guess the crash dazed them, because I managed to get out before they started lashing around. But I couldn't reach my plane again, and it was—I only remember two days of it—but it was horrible!"

"It must have been," he said gently.

"I knew that if I didn't eat or drink, I had a chance of avoiding white fever. The not eating wasn't so bad, but the not drinking— well, I finally gave up and drank out of a brook. I didn't care what happened if I could have a few moments that weren't thirst-tortured. And after that it's all confused and vague."

"You should have chewed ferva leaves."

"I didn't know that. I wouldn't have even known what they looked like, and besides, I kept expecting father to appear. He must be having a search made by now."

"He probably is," rejoined Grant ironically. "Has it occurred to you that there are thirteen million square miles of surface on little Io? And that for all he knows, you might have crashed on any square mile of it? When you're flying from North Pole to South Pole, there *isn't* any shortest route. You can cross any point on the planet."

Her gray eyes started wide. "But I—"

"Furthermore," said Grant, "this is probably the *last* place a searching party would look. They wouldn't think any one but a loony would try to hurdle Idiots' Hills, in which thesis I quite agree. So it looks very much, Lee Neilan, as if you're marooned here until my supply plane gets here next month!"

"But father will be crazy! He'll think I'm dead!"

"He thinks that now, no doubt."

"But we can't—" She broke off, staring around the tiny shack's single room. After a moment she sighed resignedly, smiled, and said softly, "Well, it might have been worse, Grant. I'll try to earn my keep."

"Good. How do you feel, Lee?"

"Quite normal. I'll start right to work." She flung off the tattered blanket, sat up, and dropped her feet to the floor. "I'll fix dinn— Good night! My dress!" She snatched the blanket about her again.

He grinned. "We had a little run-in with the slinkers after you had passed out. They did for my spare wardrobe too."

"It's ruined!" she wailed.

"Would needle and thread help? They left that, at least, because it was in the table drawer."

"Why, I couldn't make a good swimming suit out of this!" she retorted. "Let me try one of yours."

By dint of cutting, patching, and mending, she at last managed to piece one of Grant's suits to respectable proportions. She looked very lovely in shirt and trousers, but he was troubled to note that a sudden pallor had overtaken her.

It was the *riblancha*, the second spell of fever that usually followed a severe or prolonged attack. His face was serious as he cupped two of his last four ferverin tablets in his hand.

"Take these," he ordered. "And we've got to get some ferva leaves somewhere. The plane took my supply away last week, and I've had bad luck with my loonies ever since. They haven't brought me anything but weeds and rubbish."

Lee puckered her lips at the bitterness of the drug, then closed her eyes against its momentary dizziness and nausea. "Where can you find ferva?" she asked.

He shook his head perplexedly, glancing out at the setting mass of Jupiter, with its bands glowing creamy and brown, and the Red Spot boiling near the western edge. Close above it was the brilliant little disk of Europa. He frowned suddenly, glanced at his watch and then at the almanac on the inside of the cabinet door.

"It'll be Europa light in fifteen minutes," he muttered, "and true night in twenty-five—the first true night in half a month. I wonder—"

He gazed thoughtfully at Lee's face. He knew where ferva grew. One dared not penetrate the jungle itself, where stinging palms and arrow vines and the deadly worms called toothers made such a venture sheer suicide for any creatures but loonies and slinkers. But he knew where ferva grew—

In Io's rare true night even the clearing might be dangerous. Not merely from slinkers, either; he knew well enough that in the darkness creatures crept out of the jungle who otherwise remained in the eternal shadows of its depths—toothers, bullet-head frogs, and doubtless many unknown slimy, venomous, mysterious beings never seen by man. One heard stories in Herapolis and—

But he had to get ferva, and he knew where it grew. Not even a loony would try to gather it there, but in the little gardens or farms around the tiny slinker towns, there was ferva growing.

He switched on a light in the gathering dusk. "I'm going outside a moment," he told Lee Neilan. "If the *blancha* starts coming back, take the other two tablets. Wouldn't hurt you to take 'em anyway. The slinkers got away with my thermometer, but if you get dizzy again, you take 'em."

"Grant! Where—"

"I'll be back," he called, closing the door behind him.

A loony, purple in the bluish Europa light, bobbed up with a long giggle. He waved the creature aside and set off on a cautious approach to the neighborhood of the slinker village—the old one, for the other could hardly have had time to cultivate its surrounding ground. He crept warily through the bleeding-grass, but he knew his stealth was pure optimism. He was in exactly the position of a hundred-foot giant trying to approach a human city in secrecy—a difficult matter even in the utter darkness of night.

He reached the edge of the slinker clearing. Behind him, Europa, moving as fast as the second hand on his watch, plummeted toward the horizon. He paused in momentary surprise at the sight of the exquisite little town, a hundred feet away across the tiny square fields, with lights flickering in its hand-wide windows. He had not known that slinker culture included the use of lights, but there they were, tiny candles, or perhaps diminutive oil lamps.

He blinked in the darkness. The second of the ten-foot fields looked like—it was—ferva. He stooped low, crept out, and reached his hand for the fleshy white leaves. And at that moment came a shrill giggle and the crackle of grass behind him. The loony! The idiotic purple loony!

Squeaking shrieks sounded. He snatched a double handful of

ferva, rose, and dashed toward the lighted window of his shack. He had no wish to face poisoned barbs or disease-bearing teeth, and the slinkers were certainly aroused. Their gibbering sounded in chorus; the ground looked black with them.

He reached the shack, burst in, slammed and latched the door. "Got it!" He grinned. "Let 'em rave outside now."

They were raving. Their gibberish sounded like the creaking of worn machinery. Even Oliver opened his drowsy eyes to listen. "It must be the fever," observed the parcat placidly.

Lee was certainly no paler; the *riblancha* was passing safely. "Ugh!" she said, listening to the tumult without. "I've always hated rats, but slinkers are worse. All the shrewdness and viciousness of rats plus the intelligence of devils."

"Well," said Grant thoughtfully, "I don't see what they can do. They've had it in for me anyway."

"It sounds as if they're going off," said the girl, listening. "The noise is fading."

Grant peered out of the window. "They're still around. They've just passed from swearing to planning, and I wish I knew what. Someday, if this crazy little planet ever becomes worth human occupation, there's going to be a showdown between humans and slinkers."

"Well? They're not civilized enough to be really a serious obstacle, and they're so small, besides."

"But they learn," he said. "They learn so quickly, and they breed like flies. Suppose they pick up the use of gas, or suppose they develop little rifles for their poisonous darts. That's possible, because they work in metals right now, and they know fire. That would put them practically on a par with man as far as offense goes, for what good are our giant cannons and rocket planes against six-inch slinkers? And to be just on even terms would be fatal; one slinker for one man would be a hell of a trade."

Lee yawned. "Well, it's not our problem. I'm hungry, Grant."

"Good. That's a sign the *blancha's* through with you. We'll eat and then sleep a while, for there's five hours of darkness."

"But the slinkers?"

"I don't see what they can do. They couldn't cut through stone-bark walls in five hours, and anyway, Oliver would warn us if one managed to slip in somewhere."

V

It was light when Grant awoke, and he stretched his cramped limbs painfully across his two chairs. Something had wakened him, but he didn't know just what. Oliver was pacing nervously beside him, and now looked anxiously up at him.

"I've had bad luck with my loonies," announced the parcat plaintively. "You're a nice kitty."

"So are you," said Grant. Something had wakened him, but what? Then he knew, for it came again—the merest trembling of the stone-bark floor. He frowned in puzzlement. Earthquakes? Not on Io, for the tiny sphere had lost its internal heat untold ages ago. Then what?

Comprehension dawned suddenly. He sprang to his feet with so wild a yell that Oliver scrambled sideways with an infernal babble. The startled parcat leaped to the stove and vanished up the flue. His squall drifted faintly back: "It must be the fever!"

Lee had started to a sitting position on the bunk, her gray eyes blinking sleepily.

"Outside!" he roared, pulling her to her feet. "Get out! Quickly!"

"Wh-what—why—"

"Get out!" He thrust her through the door, then spun to seize his belt and weapons, the bag of ferva leaves, a package of chocolate. The floor trembled again, and he burst out of the door with a frantic leap to the side of the dazed girl.

"They've undermined it!" he choked. "The devils undermined the—"

He had no time to say more. A corner of the shack suddenly subsided; the stone-bark logs grated, and the whole structure collapsed like a child's house of blocks. The crash died into silence, and there was no motion save a lazy wisp of vapor, a few black, ratlike forms scurrying toward the grass, and a purple loony bobbing beyond the ruins.

"The dirty devils!" he swore bitterly. "The damn little black rats! The—"

A dart whistled so close that it grazed his ear and then twitched a lock of Lee's tousled brown hair. A chorus of squeaking sounded in the bleeding-grass.

"Come on!" he cried. "They're out to exterminate us this time. No—this way. Toward the hills. There's less jungle this way."

They could outrun the tiny slinkers easily enough. In a few moments they had lost the sound of squeaking voices, and they stopped to gaze ruefully back on the fallen dwelling.

"Now," he said miserably, "we're both where you were to start with."

"Oh, no." Lee looked up at him. "We're together now, Grant. I'm not afraid."

"We'll manage," he said with a show of assurance. "We'll put up a temporary shack somehow. We'll—"

A dart struck his boot with a sharp *blup*. The slinkers had caught up to them.

Again they ran toward Idiots' Hills. When at last they stopped, they could look down a long slope and far over the Ionian jungles. There was the ruined shack, and there, neatly checkered, the fields and towers of the nearer slinker town. But they had scarcely caught their breath when gibbering and squeaking came out of the brush.

They were being driven into Idiots' Hills, a region as unknown to man as the icy wastes of Pluto. It was as if the tiny fiends behind them had determined that this time their enemy, the giant trampler and despoiler of their fields, should be pursued to extinction.

Weapons were useless. Grant could not even glimpse their pursuers, slipping like hooded rats through the vegetation. A bullet, even if chance sped it through a slinker's body, was futile, and his flame pistol, though its lightning stroke should incinerate tons of brush and bleeding-grass, could no more than cut a narrow path through their horde of tormentors. The only weapons that might have availed, the gas bulbs, were lost in the ruins of the shack.

Grant and Lee were forced upward. They had risen a thousand feet above the plain, and the air was thinning. There was no jungle here, but only great stretches of bleeding-grass, across which a few loonies were visible, bobbing their heads on their long necks.

"Toward—the peaks!" gasped Grant, now painfully short of breath. "Perhaps we can stand rarer air than they."

Lee was beyond answer. She panted doggedly along beside him as they plodded now over patches of bare rock. Before them were two low peaks, like the pillars of a gate. Glancing back, Grant caught a glimpse of tiny black forms on a clear area, and in sheer anger he fired a shot. A single slinker leaped convulsively, its cape flapping, but the rest flowed on. There must have been thousands of them.

The peaks were closer, no more than a few hundred yards away. They were sheer, smooth, unscalable.

"Between them," muttered Grant.

The passage that separated them was bare and narrow. The twin peaks had been one in ages past; some forgotten volcanic convulsion had split them, leaving this slender canyon between.

He slipped an arm about Lee, whose breath, from effort and altitude, was a series of rasping gasps. A bright dart tinkled on the rocks as they reached the opening, but looking back, Grant could see only a purple loony plodding upward, and a few more to his right.

They raced down a straight fifty-foot passage that debouched suddenly into a sizable valley—and there, thunderstruck for a moment, they paused.

A city lay there. For a brief instant Grant thought they had burst upon a vast slinker metropolis, but the merest glance showed otherwise. This was no city of medieval blocks, but a poem in marble, classical in beauty, and of human or near-human proportions. White columns, glorious arches, pure curving domes, an architectural loveliness that might have been born on the Acropolis. It took a second look to discern that the city was dead, deserted, in ruins.

Even in her exhaustion, Lee felt its beauty. "How—how exquisite!" she panted. "One could almost forgive them—for being—slinkers!"

"They won't forgive us for being human," he muttered. "We'll have to make a stand somewhere. We'd better pick a building."

But before they could move more than a few feet from the canyon mouth, a wild disturbance halted them. Grant whirled, and for a moment found himself actually paralyzed by amazement. The narrow canyon was filled with a gibbering horde of slinkers, like a nauseous, heaving black carpet. But they came no farther than the valley end, for grinning, giggling, and bobbing, blocking the opening with tramping three-toed feet, were four loonies!

It was a battle. The slinkers were biting and stabbing at the miserable defenders, whose shrill keenings of pain were less giggles than shrieks. But with a determination and purpose utterly foreign to loonies, their clawed feet tramped methodically up and down, up and down.

Grant exploded, "I'll be damned!" Then an idea struck him. "Lee! They're packed in the canyon, the whole devil's brood of 'em!"

He rushed toward the opening. He thrust his flame pistol between the skinny legs of a loony, aimed it straight along the canyon, and fired.

VI

Inferno burst. The tiny diamond, giving up all its energy in one terrific blast, shot a jagged stream of fire that filled the canyon from wall to wall and vomited out beyond to cut a fan of fire through the bleeding-grass of the slope.

Idiots' Hills reverberated to the roar, and when the rain of debris settled, there was nothing in the canyon save a few bits of flesh and the head of an unfortunate loony, still bouncing and rolling.

Three of the loonies survived. A purple-faced one was pulling his arm, grinning and giggling in imbecilic glee. He waved the thing aside and returned to the girl.

"Thank goodness!" he said. "We're out of that, anyway."

"I wasn't afraid, Grant. Not with you."

He smiled. "Perhaps we can find a place here," he suggested. "The fever ought to be less troublesome at this altitude. But—say, this must have been the capital city of the whole slinker race in ancient times. I can scarcely imagine those fiends creating an architecture as beautiful as this—or as large. Why these buildings are as colossal in proportion to slinker size as the skyscrapers of New York to us!"

"But so beautiful," said Lee softly, sweeping her eyes over the glory of the ruins. "One might almost forgive— Grant! Look at those!"

He followed the gesture. On the inner side of the canyon's portals were gigantic carvings. But the thing that set him staring in amazement was the subject of the portrayal. There, towering far up the cliff sides, were the figures, not of slinkers, but of—loonies! Exquisitely carved, smiling rather than grinning, and smiling somehow sadly, regretfully, pityingly—yet beyond doubt, loonies!

"Good night!" he whispered. "Do you see, Lee? This must once have been a loony city. The steps, the doors, the buildings, all are on their scale of size. Somehow, some time, they must have achieved civilization, and the loonies we know are the degenerate residue of a great race."

"And," put in Lee, "the reason those four blocked the way when the slinkers tried to come through is that they still remember. Or probably they don't actually remember, but they have a tradition of past glories, or more likely still, just a superstitious feeling that this place is in some way sacred. They let us pass because, after all, we look more like loonies than like slinkers. But the amazing thing is that they still possess even that dim memory, because this city must have been in ruins for centuries. Or perhaps even for thousands of years."

"But to think that loonies could ever have had the intelligence to create a culture of their own," said Grant, waving away the purple one bobbing and giggling at his side. Suddenly he paused, turning a gaze of new respect on the creature. "This one's been following me for days. All right, old chap, what is it?"

The purple one extended a sorely bedraggled bundle of bleeding-grass and twigs, giggling idiotically. His ridiculous mouth twisted; his eyes popped in an agony of effort at mental concentration.

"Canny!" he giggled triumphantly.

"The imbecile!" flared Grant. "Nitwit! Idiot!" He broke off, then laughed. "Never mind. I guess you deserve it." He tossed his package of chocolate to the three delighted loonies. "Here's your candy."

A scream from Lee startled him. She was waving her arms wildly, and over the crest of Idiots' Hills a rocket plane roared, circled, and nosed its way into the valley.

The door opened. Oliver stalked gravely out, remarking casually, "I'm real and you're real." A man followed the parcat—two men.

"Father!" screamed Lee.

It was some time later that Gustavus Neilan turned to Grant. "I can't thank you," he said. "If there's ever any way I can show my appreciation for—"

"There is. You can cancel my contract."

"Oh, you work for me?"

"I'm Grant Calthorpe, one of your traders, and I'm about sick of this crazy planet."

"Of course, if you wish," said Neilan. "If it's a question of pay—"

"You can pay me for the six months I've worked."

"If you'd care to stay," said the older man, "there won't be trading much longer. We've been able to grow ferva near the polar cities, and I prefer plantations to the uncertainties of relying on loonies. If you'd work out your year, we might be able to put you in charge of a plantation by the end of that time."

Grant met Lee Neilan's gray eyes, and hesitated. "Thanks," he said slowly, "but I'm sick of it." He smiled at the girl, then turned back to her father. "Would you mind telling me how you happened to find us? This is the most unlikely place on the planet."

"That's just the reason," said Neilan. "When Lee didn't get back, I thought things over pretty carefully. At last I decided, knowing her as I did, to search the least likely places first. We tried the shores of the Fever Sea, and then the White Desert, and finally Idiots' Hills. We spotted the ruins of a shack, and on the debris was this chap"—he indicated Oliver—"remarking that 'Ten loonies make one halfwit.' Well, the halfwit part sounded very much like a reference to my daughter, and we cruised about until the roar of your flame pistol attracted our attention."

Lee pouted, then turned her serious gray eyes on Grant, "Do you remember," she said softly, "what I told you there in the jungle?"

"I wouldn't even have mentioned that," he replied. "I knew you were delirious."

"But—perhaps I wasn't. Would companionship make it any easier to work out your year? I mean if—for instance—you were to fly back with us to Junopolis and return with a wife?"

"Lee," he said huskily, "you know what a difference that would make, though I can't understand why you'd ever dream of it."

"It must," suggested Oliver, "be the fever."

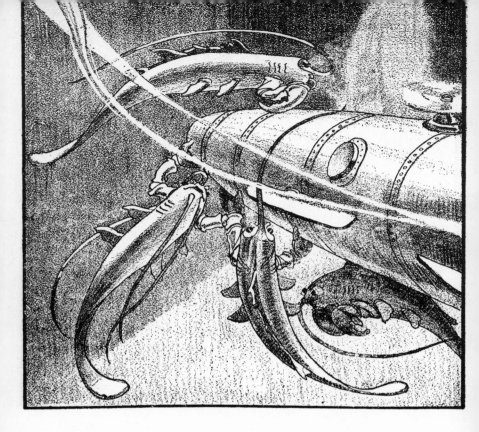

Davey Jones' Ambassador

By Raymond Z. Gallun

I

I<small>T DIDN'T</small> look like a jet of water at all. It seemed too rigid, like a rod of glass; and it spattered over the instruments with a brittle, jingling sound, for such was the effect of the pressure behind it: more than four thousand pounds per square inch—the weight of nearly two and a half miles of black ocean.

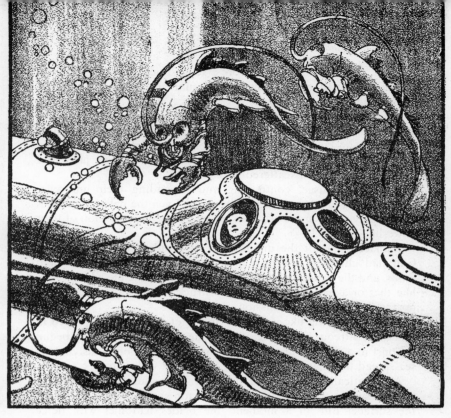

Cliff's blood ran cold as he watched the fleshy beak closing in nearer, nearer—

Cliff Rodney, hunched in the pilot seat, stared at the widening stream. It made him see how good a thing life was, and how empty and drab the alternative was going to be. Cliff Rodney was young; he did not wish to die.

A few seconds ago all had been normal aboard the bathyspheric submarine. The velvet darkness of the depths, visible beyond the massive ports of the craft, had inspired awe in him, as it always would in human hearts; but to Cliff it had become familiar. The same was true of the schools of phosphorescent fish shining foggily through the gloom, and of the swarms of nether-world horrors that had darted in the bright golden path of the search beam.

Clifford Rodney, during his explorations, had grown accustomed to these elements of the deep-sea environment, until they had assumed an aspect that was almost friendly.

But the illusion that it was safe here had been abruptly broken.

Sinuous, rusty shadows which bore a suggestion of menace that was new to him had surged toward the submarine from out of the surrounding murk and ooze.

Attenuated, spidery crustaceans with long feelers had burrowed into the shelter of the mud beneath them. Little fish, some of them equipped with lamplike organs, some blind and lightless, all of them at once dreadful and comic with their needle-fanged jaws and grotesque heads, had scattered in terror.

Bulbous medusae, contracting and expanding their umbrella-shaped bodies, had swum hurriedly away. Even the pallid anemones had displayed defensive attitudes in the guarded contraction of their flowerlike crowns.

With canny craft the unknowns had avoided the search beam. Cliff had glimpsed only the swift motion of monstrous, armored limbs, and the baneful glitter of great eyes. Then the blow had fallen, like that of a battering ram. It had struck the forward observation port with a grinding concussion.

A crack, looking like a twisted ribbon of silver, had appeared in the thick, vitreous substance of the pane. From it, water had begun to spurt in a slender, unstanchable shaft that grew ominously as the sea spread the edges of the crevice wider and wider apart.

Automatically Cliff had done what he could. He had set the vertical screws of his craft churning at top speed to raise it toward the surface. But, in a moment, the blades had met with fierce resistance, as though clutched and held. The motors had refused to turn. The submarine had sunk back into the muck of the Atlantic's bed. An S.O.S. was the last resort.

Cliff had sent it out quickly, knowing that though it would be picked up by the *Etruria*, the surface ship that served as his base of operations, nothing could be done to help him. He had reached the end of his resources.

Now there was a breathless pause. The blackness without was inky. Cliff continued to gaze impotently at that slim cylinder of water. Ricocheting bits of it struck him, stinging fiercely, but he did not heed. It fascinated him, making him forget, almost, how it had all happened. His mind was blurred so that it conceived odd notions.

Pretty, the way that jet of water broke apart when it hit the bright metal of the instruments. You wouldn't think that it was dangerous. Flying droplets scattered here and there like jewels, each of them glinting in the shaded glow of the light bulbs. And the sounds they made resembled the chucklings of elves and fairies.

A small creature of the depths, sucked through the breach, burst with a dull plop as the pressure of its normal habitat was removed. He and that creature had much in common, Rodney thought. Both were pawns which chance had elected to annihilate. Only he was a man; men boasted of their control over natural forces. And he himself was a blatant and ironic symbol of that boast: They had sent him here in the belief that even the bed of the Atlantic might soon yield to human dominance!

The submarine gave a gentle lurch. The youth's eyes sharpened to a keener focus. A yard beyond the fractured port a pair of orbs hung suspended. Beneath them was a fleshy beak that opened and closed as the creature sucked water through its gills. Black, whiplike tentacles swarmed around it like the hairs of a Gorgon beard. And the flesh of the monster was transparent. Cliff could see the throbbing outlines of its vital organs.

Nothing unusual here—just another devil of the depths. So Cliff Rodney would have thought had it not been for certain suggestive impressions that touched lightly on his blurred faculties. That beaked mouth was vacuously empty of expression, but the great limpid orbs were keen. The tentacles clutched a little rod, pointed at one end as a goad would be. The impression was fleeting. With a ripple of finny members the horror disappeared from view.

"That rod," Cliff muttered aloud. "I wonder if that thing made it!"

He felt a cold twinge, which was an expression of many emotions, ripple over his flesh. He moved quickly, his booted feet sloshing in the water that was now six inches deep within the stout hull of the submarine. He turned a switch; the lights winked out. It was best to be concealed in darkness.

Once more the bathyspheric submarine rocked. Then it was whirled completely over. Cliff Rodney tumbled from the pilot chair. Icy fluid cascaded around him as his body struck the hard steel of the craft's interior.

He managed to protect his head with his arms, but contact with the metal sent a numbing, aching shock through his flesh. Electricity; it could not have been anything else. He tried to curse, but the result was only a ragged gasp. Clinging desperately to the sunset edge of oblivion, he fell back among his instruments.

Impressions were very dim after that. The submarine was being towed somewhere by something. Water continued to pour into the hull, making a confused babble of sound. Rodney lay in the growing pool, the briny stuff bitter on his lips. Too near stunned to master his limbs, he rolled about the inundated floor.

With each eccentric motion of the craft, churning water slapped viciously against his face. He choked and coughed. If only he could keep his nose above the flood and breathe!

In some foggy recess of his mind he wondered why he was fighting for life, when the broken port alone was enough to doom him. Was instinct, or some deeper, more reasoned urge responsible? Cliff did not know, but for a fleeting instant the blank look of pain on his face was punctuated by a grim smile.

He was not the mythical iron man; he was a median of strengths and weaknesses as are most humans. And, among humans, courage is almost as cheap as it is glorious.

Cliff could still hear the swish of great flippers shearing the sea beyond the eighteen-inch shell of the submarine. Harsh to his submerged ears, it was the last impression he received when consciousness faded out.

II

Reawakening was slow agony. He had been half-drowned. When his brain was clear enough for him to take stock of his surroundings he did not immediately note any remarkable change.

He was still within the stout little undersea boat that had brought him to the depths. The vessel was nearly two-thirds full of brine, but by luck his body had been thrown over a metal brace, and for part of the time his head had been supported above the flood.

No more water was entering the hull through the eroded crevice in the window. In fact there was no motion at all, and, except for a distant, pulsating hiss, the stillness was tomblike.

The air was heavy and oppressive. It reeked with a fetid stench that was almost unbearable. Mingled with the odor was a faint pungence of chlorine, doubtless brought about by the electrolysis of sea water where it had penetrated some minor fault in the insulation of the submarine's electrical equipment. A gray luminescence seeped through the ports, lighting up the interior of the vessel dimly.

Soaked, dazed, battered, and chilled to the bone, Cliff struggled to the fractured window. There was air beyond it, not water. He had not extinguished the searchlight, and it still burned, for the storage cells that supplied current had been well protected against mishap.

There was no need to waste power to produce light here. A faint but adequate radiance seemed to come from the curving walls of the chamber in which the submarine had been docked. Cliff switched off the beam.

Groping down under the water, he found a lever and tugged at it. A valve opened, and the brine began to drain out of the submarine. The gurgling sound it made was harsh to his ears. Evidently the atmospheric pressure here was far above normal.

Next, he unfastened the hatch above his head and hoisted its ponderous weight. Wearily he clambered through the opening and dropped down beside his craft.

The room was elliptical, domed, and bare of any furnishings. Its largest diameter was perhaps thirty-five feet, twice the length of the submarine. Puddles dotted the floor, and the walls were beaded with moisture which showed plainly that the place had been flooded recently. At opposite points there had been circular openings in the walls, one much larger than the other. Both were blocked now by great plugs of a translucent, amorphous material.

Cliff had two immediate urges: One was to get a better idea of where he was; the other was to find, if possible, a means of allaying his discomfort.

He started his investigations with the larger of the two plugs. It was held in place by a tough, glutinous cement, still sticky to the touch. From beyond it came a distant murmur of the sea. This, then, was the way by which the submarine had entered the chamber.

After the entrance had been sealed the water had been drawn off by some means through the several drains in the floor. The stream from the valve in the side of the submarine still gurgled into them, pumped away, perhaps, by some hidden mechanism. So much was clear.

Cliff's attention wandered to the walls, in quest of some explanation of the phosphorescence that came from them. Their surface was hard and smooth like that of glass, but the substance that composed them was not glass. It had a peculiar, milky opalescent sheen, like mother-of-pearl. Squinting, he tried to peer through the cloudy, semitransparent material.

At a depth of a few inches little specks of fire flitted. They were tiny, self-luminous marine animals. Beyond the swarming myriads of them was another shell, white and opaque. He understood. The chamber was double-walled. There was water between the walls, and in it those minute light-giving organisms were imprisoned for the purpose of supplying illumination.

It was a simple bit of inventive ingenuity, but not one which men would be likely to make use of. In fact there was nothing about his new surroundings that was not at least subtly different from any similar thing that human beings would produce.

The glass of the domed chamber was not glass. It seemed to be nearer to the substance that composes the inner portion of a mollusk's shell, and yet it had apparently been made in one piece, for there was no visible evidence of joints where separate parts of the dome might have been fastened together. The blocks that sealed the openings in the walls were almost equally strange. Among men they would surely have been made of metal.

Clifford Rodney became more and more aware of the fact that he had come in contact with a civilization and science more fantastic than that of Mars or Venus could ever be. Those planets were worlds of air, as was the Earth he knew, while this was a world of water. Environment here presented handicaps and possibly offered advantages which might well have turned the sea folk's path of advancement in a direction utterly different from that followed by mankind.

Continuing his investigations, Cliff discovered that the air under the dome was admitted through four pipelike tubes which penetrated the double walls of his prison; but, of course, he could not discover where they originated. The air came through those tubes in rhythmic, hissing puffs, and escaped, he supposed, down the drains through which the water had been drawn, since there was no other outlet in evidence.

He wondered how the rancid stuff had been produced, and how his hosts had even known that he needed gaseous oxygen to breathe. He wondered whether they could have any conception of the place whence he had come. To them a land of sunshine must be as ungraspable as a region of the fourth dimension!

He remembered the electric shock that had almost stunned him at the time of his capture. Electricity was produced here then. But how? As yet he had not so much as glimpsed a scrap of metal in his new surroundings.

Cliff shuddered, nor was the dank, bitter cold alone responsible.

He could realize clearer than before that beyond the barriers that protected him was a realm of pressure and darkness and water with which his own normal environment had few things in common.

Belatedly it occurred to him that he was being watched by the curious of Submarinia. Standing now in the center of the slippery floor, he scanned the dome above him for evidence that his logic was correct. It was. Spaced evenly around the arching roof, more than halfway toward its central axis, was a ring of circular areas more transparent than the surrounding texture of the double walls.

Though not easily discernible at a casual glance, they were plain enough to him now. Through each, a pair of huge, glowing eyes and a Gorgon mass of black tentacles was visible. The ovoid bodies of the creatures were silhouetted against a nebulous luminescence originating from some unknown source beyond them.

The gaze of those monsters seemed cool and interested and intense, though Clifford Rodney felt that one could never be sure of what emotions, if any, their vacuous, beaked lips and limpid eyes betrayed. It would be difficult indeed to forget that they were completely inhuman.

Cliff's reaction was a kind of terror; though the only outward evidences of it were the strained hollows that came suddenly into his cheeks; still, the realization of his position thudded with ghastly weight into his mind. To those sea beings he was doubtless like a simple ameba beneath a microscope, a specimen to be observed and studied!

Then his sense of humor rescued him. He chuckled half-heartedly through chattering teeth. At least no man had ever before been in a situation quite as novel as this. It was one which a scientist, eager to learn new things, should appreciate. Besides, perhaps now he could bring the adventure to a head.

He waved his arms toward the pairs of eyes that gazed steadily at him. "Hello!" he shouted. "What in the name of good manners are you trying to do to me? Get me out of here!"

They couldn't understand him, but anyway they could see by his gestures that he had discovered them, and that he was insisting on some sort of attention. Cliff Rodney was cold, and half-choked by the rancid air.

Things had to happen soon, or his stamina would be worn down and he would no longer be in a position to see them happen. The dank, frigid chill was the worst. The air would not have been so bad if it had not been for the retch-provoking stench that impregnated it. If only he had a dry cigarette and a match, it would help a lot.

That was a funny thought—a cigarette and a match! Had he expected these ovoid beings to supply him with such luxuries?

However, since there was no one else to whom he might appeal for help, he continued to shout epithets and pleas, and to flail his arms until he was nearly spent with the effort.

Yet, the sea people gave no evidence of special response. The vital organs throbbed within their transparent bodies, tympanic membranes beneath their beaked mouths vibrated, perhaps transmitting to the water around them signals of a kind of vocal speech, inaudible to him, of course; and their tentacles scurried over the outer surfaces of the spy windows, producing a noise such as a mouse scampering inside a box might make, but Cliff saw no promise in their evident interest.

Every few moments, one pair of eyes would turn away from a window, and another pair would take its place. The ovoids were managing the scrutiny of him just as humans would manage a show featuring a freak. He could imagine them out there waiting in line for a chance to see him. It was funny, but it was ghastly too.

Exhausted, he gave up. Probably they couldn't help him anyway. If he only had something dry to keep the chill away from his shivering flesh!

Hopefully he scrambled up the side of the submarine and lowered himself through the hatch. There was a little electric heater there, but a brief examination of it confirmed his well-founded suspicions. Soaked with brine, its coils were shorted and it refused to work. He had no means of drying it out sufficiently, and so he turned on the search beam. If he crouched against the lamp, he might capture a little heat.

He climbed out of the dripping, disordered interior. Before dropping to the floor of the domed chamber he stood on tiptoe on the curved back of the submarine and attempted to peer through one of the spy windows in the rotunda over his head.

Even now the mystery of what lay beyond the glowing walls of the room beneath the sea could fascinate him. But his vantage point was not quite high enough, nor was there any easy means to make it higher. He saw only a flicker of soft, greenish light beyond the motionless, ovoid shape that occupied the window.

He slid weakly off the submarine and pressed his body against the lens of the searchlight. The rays warmed him a little—a very little—enough to tantalize him with the thought that such a thing as warmth really existed.

He thought of exercise as a means to start his sluggish blood circulating faster; he even made an effort to put the thought into execution by shaking his arms and stamping his feet. But he felt too far gone to keep up the exertion. His head slumped against the mounting of the searchlight.

Some minutes later, a throbbing radiance caused him to look up. At one of the spy windows was a creature different from the sea people. Its body was flat, and as pallid as a mushroom.

It was shaped curiously like an oak leaf with curled edges. Its mouth was a slit at the anterior extremity of its queer form. On either side of it were pulsing gill openings, and above were beady eyes supported on stalky members. From the thin edges of the creature's body, long, slender filaments projected, glinting like new-drawn copper wire. And the flesh of the thing glowed intermittently like a firefly.

After several seconds this phenomenon ceased, and another far more startling one took its place. The creature turned its dorsal surface toward the window.

Then it was as though some invisible hand and brush were printing a message in letters of fire on the pallid hide of the monster. They were old, familiar letters spelling out English words. One by one they appeared, traced with swift and practiced accuracy until the message was complete:

I am far away, man; but I am coming. I wish to write with you. Do not die yet. Wait until I arrive.

The Student.

If Clifford Rodney had been himself, his consternation at this odd note and the outlandish means of its transmission would have been greater, and his analysis of the phenomena involved would have been more keen. As matters were, he was still able to discern the shadows of the causes underlying the enigma.

This was the subsea version of wireless. He was too tired to construct a theory of its principle; he only glanced at the fine filaments projecting from the body of the creature that had served as an agent of the miracle, and dismissed the vague germ of an idea that had oozed unbidden into his sluggish mind.

Even though this was a science completely inhuman, still it was self-evident that there were logical explanations. At present Cliff didn't care particularly whether he ever learned them. Nor did he ponder for long the riddle of how this distant spokesman of the ovoids was able to write English. Somewhere there must be a simple answer.

However, the wording of the message, strikingly demonstrating the broad physical and psychological differences between his kind and the unknowns, won somewhat more attention from him. It was "I wish to write with you," instead of "I wish to speak with you." The ovoid tympanums, vibrating in water, could not produce or convey to him the sounds of human speech.

"Do not die yet. Wait until I arrive." Did those two simple commands express naive brutality or— Cliff scarcely knew how to think the thought. No human being would have expressed an idea of that sort with such guileless frankness. The meaning, of course, was perfectly clear; and Cliff knew that he had been afforded a glimpse into a mind differing radically from those of men.

"The Student." That at least had a familiar aspect. Because of the way the message was signed, the anger and depression which it aroused in him subsided.

The lettering vanished from the flat back of the creature which had been the means of conveying to Cliff Rodney the first expression of subsea thought. Another fire-traced message appeared, letter by letter:

We have waited long for the arrival of one of you, man. We must learn more about your kind before you die. All in our power has been done for you. If you require more, perhaps it is beyond the small sealed exit. Unseal it. Live until I come.

The Student.

Rodney cursed and shook his fist feebly at the messenger. Nevertheless, hope gave him fresh energy. He proceeded to obey the suggestion. Returning to the submarine he procured a heavy knife, extinguished the search beam for economy, and came forth again to attack the smaller door.

The cement here was thoroughly hard, glassy; but tough and elastic rather than brittle. Cliff worked at it fiercely, digging out the gummy stuff with the point of his knife. For a time it seemed that the stubborn block would never yield; but at length, when his expiring energies were all but burned up, and little specks of blackness flitted before his vision, success came.

The plug of amorphous material toppled from the opening and thudded resoundingly to the floor. For a minute young Rodney lay exhausted beside it, a rustle in his ears that he knew was not the distant whisper of the ocean.

Then, rested a bit, he crept through the opening. He was too dazed to be very conscious of the things around him. The character of the chamber was much the same as that of the one he had just quitted, except that it was larger, and the floor was a much more elongated oval. It had the same kind of pearly, phosphorescent dome equipped with spy windows.

Even now the windows were being occupied by the grotesque forms of the sea people, eager to observe the fresh reactions of their strange captive. The air, though, was drier, for the place had not recently been flooded, and it was musty with the odor of ancient decay, like that of a tomb.

The floor was piled high with a numerous assortment of things— every one of them of human origin. Cliff let his eyes wander over the array. There was a generator, part of a ship's turbine, several life preservers, a fire extinguisher, books, tattered and pulped by sea water and pressure, rugs, and so forth. There were even two human figures.

They were propped on a dilapidated divan, and were fully clothed. Whoever had placed them there had apparently made some attempt to arrange them naturally.

Cliff Rodney came closer to examine them. One had been a man, the other a woman. Their flesh was gone, their faces only skeleton masks. The woman's dress had once been white and beautiful, but now it was just a mottled, gray rag. Yet, the diamond pendant at her throat still gleamed as brightly as ever. The pair clutched each other with a fierceness that was still apparent. Perhaps they had died in each other's arms like that long ago. A grim tragedy of the Atlantic—

Rodney's reactions were not quite normal. He felt sick. "Damn museum!" he grumbled in a sort of inane disgust. "Damn stinky museum of Davey Jones!" He choked and sneezed.

The haze of his numbed faculties was not so dense that it obscured the animal urge to seek comfort, however. He picked up a heavy rug which, though rotted and odorous, was fairly dry.

He stripped off his soaked garments and wrapped himself in the rug. Tearing up a book and heaping the fragments into a pile with the intention of making a fire was quite natural and automatic. So was locating his cigarette lighter and attempting to make it work. Here, though, he struck a snag. Sparks flew, but the wick was too wet to burn.

Out of his angry chagrin an inspiration was born. He unscrewed the cap from the fuel container, poured a few drops of benzine onto the paper, and applied the sparks direct. The tinder flared up merrily, and grotesque shadows leaped about the walls of the eerie chamber. Delighted, Cliff huddled down beside the blaze, absorbing its welcome heat.

Only once did he glance at the ovoids watching him. He could not have guessed what wonder his activities provoked in the minds of those strange people of the depths.

"Go to hell!" he called to them in dismissal.

The air didn't smell so bad with the smoke in it. As the embers began to die, Clifford Rodney drew the carpet tighter about him and sprawled on the pavement. Worn out, he was quickly asleep.

III

Through the gloom of the bottoms, seven slim shapes were speeding. They were neither crustaceans nor sharklike elasmobranchs; they bore some of the characteristics of both.

Their bodies were protected by horny armor and were tapered in such a manner as to suggest the lines of a torpedo, a comparison that was heightened by the waspish air of concentrated power about them. Rows of flippers along their flanks churned the dark water, sending them swiftly on their way. Folded carefully against their bellies were pairs of huge claws resembling the pinchers of a crawfish, though much larger. Projecting like swollen cheeks on either side of their heads were protuberances of modified muscle— their most effective weapons.

These monstrous creations were not entirely the product of nature. The knowledge of a gifted people working on their kind for ages had achieved a miracle, making of them efficient, dependable fighting machines.

They swam in a military formation. The largest individual of the group formed its center. Above, below, ahead, behind, and on either side—one in each position—the others swam. There was a reason. Every now and then schools of small, devil-fanged fish would glide out of the darkness to attack the cavalcade. The nearest members of the escort would leap to meet them.

For an instant, many fierce little teeth would try to penetrate the tough shells of the fighters. Then the latter would strike back, invisibly, except for a momentary flicker of lavender sparks around their snouts. The attacking fish would stiffen and go drifting limply into the darkness again, dead or stunned.

The fighters were protecting their master, he who had named himself "The Student." He rode the central individual of the formation, suckerlike cups on the ventral surface of his body, clinging to its back. He had flattened himself against his mount to minimize the surge of water that swept past him. His eyes peered ahead with an expectant glitter.

He changed position only to trace queer symbols, with a goad of glassy material, on the flesh of the fragile messenger that clung beside him, and to scan the phosphorescent replies to his queries that came in return. But within him, dread and eagerness were mingled. He had received the call that he had both hoped for and feared. And he was responding.

Out of the murk and ooze that blanketed the sea floor ahead, an emerald glow arose like some infernal dawn. The cavalcade continued to speed on its way, and the radiance brightened.

A broad depression in the bottoms emerged from the fog of suspended mud, gray like tarnished silver. Above it swarmed myriads of minute luminous animals, forming an immense canopy of green light, limned against the blackness of the depths. That canopy looked as though it had been placed there for a purpose.

To paint the scene beneath would have challenged the genius of Gustave Doré. It was as abhorrent as the visions of a mad demon; still it possessed elements of majesty and beauty.

A city was there in the hollow—a city or a colony. The seven fighters were moving close above it now. The valley was pitted by countless small openings, arranged edge to edge after the fashion of the cells of a honeycomb. Into them and from them, ovoids swam, going about whatever business was theirs. Here and there, queer structures of a pearly translucent material reared twisted spires that seemed to wriggle with the motion of the water.

Monsters were everywhere, vague in the shifting shadows. Scores of types were represented, each type seemingly stranger than its associates. All of the monsters were busy, guided in their activities by alert ovoids that hung in the water, goads poised, flippers stirring idly.

Some of the monsters wallowed in the muck, digging with broad, spatulate members. Wormlike in form, pallid and smooth, one knew that their purpose in life was to dig, and nothing else.

Others kneaded their bloated, shapeless bodies, forming elfin creations around them, seemingly from their own substance. Some fanned the water with long, flattened limbs, perhaps performing a function akin to ventilation. Others—they were fighters like The Student's escort—guarded the colony, swimming steadily back and forth.

And so it went. Each of the horrors followed the vocation for which it was intended. Each was a robot, a machine of living flesh, capable of some special function.

A man would have been held spellbound by this teeming, alien activity; but The Student scarcely noticed it at all. Everything—the lights, the motion, the whispering, slithering sounds that found their way to his auditory organs—held the familiarity of life-long experience, of home.

His gaze, though, wandered intently across the valley to the place where the gutted hull of an ocean liner sprawled half over on its side, its form almost obscured by the dusty murk of the depths.

Slim ribbons that had the appearance of vegetation streamed up from it, waving like banners. They were not vegetation, though they were alive. There were no plants here, away from the sunshine; and the fauna of this world was dependent for its sustenance upon organic debris settling from above, where there was sunlight, where chlorophyll could act, and where both fauna and flora could exist.

Always the wrecks of upper-world ships had interested The Student, as something from another planet would interest us. He had rummaged through their slimy interiors, examining and exploring this and that.

Of all their wondrous contents, books had fascinated him the most. With a zeal and care and love that an archaeologist would understand, he had made copies of those fragile, water-soaked storehouses of knowledge, tracing the still legible parts of them on a parchment that could withstand the action of the sea.

He had studied the queer symbol groups they bore; he had discovered the value of the dictionary. And as the Rosetta Stone had been the key to Egyptian hieroglyphics, so the dictionary had been his means of solving the riddle of mankind's literature.

There was another thing that won a brief glance from The Student, as he guided his mount and escort toward the concourse of ovoids that had collected around the structures which housed the reason for his coming.

On a low rise a circular vat, filled with living protoplasm, squatted. Above it two crudely hammered bars of iron converged. Between their adjacent ends blue sparks purred. The apparatus was a recent development which would have startled the wise inventors who had contributed so much to another culture.

With a thrusting motion The Student hurled himself from the back of the fighter. The flippers along his sides took hold of the water with powerful sweeps. The crowd made a lane for him as he approached. Tympanic voices buzzed around him, questioning, demanding; yet, he paid no heed.

IV

The Student reached a spy window in the dome, looked down. The man was there, sprawled motionless amid the relics of his civilization. A piece of ragged fabric wrapped his pallid body.

Revulsion, fear, hope, and anxiety were not beyond The Student's understanding, and he felt them all now.

Was the prisoner dead? Was all that had been promised to end in disappointment? Paradoxically The Student would have been more at ease if such were the case. There is no harm in an enemy whose vital functions have stopped. Yet The Student himself did not live for peace and security alone. The boom of existence has many meanings.

He moved to a window in the smaller dome and surveyed the bathyspheric submarine, marveling at the smooth metal hull and the precise perfection of each detail. No ovoid could fabricate such wonders.

Patiently he waited until the buzzing tympanic voice of the throng about him impinged on his sense organs, telling him that the time had arrived.

Coolly The Student returned to the window of the museum chamber. The man was awake. He stood unsteadily in the center of the floor, the rug still wrapped around him and his eyes turned upward.

Two peoples, two cultures, two backgrounds, two histories, and two points of view were face to face at last, ready for whatever might come of the meeting. The bizarre stood versus the bizarre from opposite angles. Between them the abyss was wide. Was there— could there be—any sympathy to bridge it?

It was up to The Student to open negotiations, and he did not hesitate, for he had planned well. From a pouch that was a natural part of him he removed a stylus of chalky material. Then, concentrating on what he had learned during his years of study, he printed a command on the pane of the window: "You made fire, man. Make it again."

He traced the letters in reverse, so that they would appear normally to the being inside the dome.

The prisoner seemed uncertain for a brief spell; then he obeyed. Paper, a daub of liquid from what appeared to be a tiny black box, a swift movement, sparks, and finally—flame! The man held up the blazing paper for his visitor to see.

The Student watched the phenomenon of rapid oxidation, drinking in the marvel of it until the flame was burned out. The water had washed the chalky letters from the window. He traced another message: "Fire gives you metals, machines, power—everything you have?"

If, before it had happened, Clifford Rodney had had an opportunity to construct a mental picture of what this meeting would be like, he would no doubt have expected to be amazed. But he could not have conceived beforehand an adequate idea of his own wonder. Tangible truth was so much more startling than a bare thought could be.

Here was a thing which bore many of the outward characteristics of the marine animals with which he was acquainted—pulsing gills, stirring flippers—organs used in a medium which must ever be foreign to those forms of life that live in air and sunshine.

There was even in the visage of the thing—if visage it might be called—a deceptive look of vacuity which only the cool glitter of the great eyes denied. And yet, clutched in the being's tentacles was a crayon, with which it was writing in English, words that displayed a considerable knowledge of human attainments!

Cliff almost forgot that he himself was a delver after hidden facts. Then his own calm purpose conquered. His sleep had refreshed him; and though he felt stiff, sore, and uncomfortable, he could still respond to the appeal of an enigma.

He looked about for some means to answer. His attention was drawn to a small area of unencumbered floor, on which a thin layer of sea sand had been deposited. With a finger he traced words in it: "Yes. Fire brought us out of the Stone Age and has kept us going since. You got it right, friend. How?"

And the swift-moving tentacles traced a reply: "I have translated books—men's books. I have read of fire. But we have never produced fire. We might produce fire from electric sparks—soon."

Rodney looked with quizzical awe at the gleaming orbs of the ovoid. Behind them, he knew, was a brilliant brain, whose brilliance had perhaps been augmented by the very handicaps which it had faced and overcome. The truth concealed behind this intriguing statement was already dimly formulated in his mind. Now he might clear up the matter completely.

He smoothed out the sand and printed another message: "You have electricity, glass, and a kind of wireless—still, no fire. It is too wet here for fire; but how did you do it all? And you write like a man—how?"

The Student chose to answer the last question first. "I mimic the writing of men," he printed. "I must—so men understand. Glass, electricity, wireless, and other things, come from animals. Nearly everything comes from animals. We have made the animals so. We have developed the useful characteristics of the animals—great care, selection, breeding, crossbreeding—a long time—ages."

It was a confirmation of the vague theory that Cliff had formulated. Handicapped by the impossibility of fire in their normal environment, the sea folk's advancement had followed another path. Controlled evolution was what it amounted to.

Cliff remembered what miracles men such as Luther Burbank had achieved with plants—changing them, improving them. And to a lesser extent, similar marvels had been achieved with animals. Here in the depths of the Atlantic the same science had been used for ages!

Without visible excitement Cliff traced another note in the sand: "Electricity from living flesh, from modified muscle as in the electric eel or the torpedo? Glass from— Tell me!"

And on the spy window the answer appeared: "Yes. Glass from animal—from mollusk—deposited and grown as a mollusk's shell is deposited and grown. And it is formed as we wish. Electricity from modified muscle, as in the electric eel or the torpedo. I have read of them. We have animals like them—but larger. The animals fight for us, kill with electricity. And we have—electric batteries—metal from the ships. Rods—protoplasm—"

The Student's black tentacles switched and hesitated uncertainly as he groped for words that would express his thoughts to this strange monstrosity of another realm.

But Clifford Rodney had captured enough of his meaning to make a guess. "You mean," he wrote, "that you have developed a way of producing a steady current of electricity from a form of living protoplasm? A sort of isolated electric organ with metal details and grids to draw off the power?"

"Yes."

Cliff thought it over, briefly but intensely. Such protoplasm would need only food to keep it active, and it could probably obtain food from the organic dust in the sea water around it.

"Splendid!" he printed. "And the wireless, the radio beast—tell me about it!"

The Student concentrated all his powers on the task of formulating an adequate response. Slowly, hesitantly, now, he began to trace it out; for he was thinking almost in an alien plane, working with words and ideas subtly different from his own. To make the man understand, he had to choose phrases and expressions from the books he had read.

"It is the same," he inscribed. "A characteristic developed to usefulness. Long ago we studied these animals. We discovered that they could—communicate—through—over great distances. We increased—improved this power by—by—"

"By choosing those individuals in which the power was strongest, for breeding purposes, and in turn selecting those of their offspring and the descendants of their offspring in which the characteristics

you desired to emphasize were most prominent," Cliff prompted.
"Thus the abilities of these messenger creatures were gradually
improved. Right?"

"Yes. Right," The Student printed. "Now, we make marks on the
flesh of a messenger creature. The irritation produces stimuli—a
sequence of stimuli through nerves of skin, through brain, through—
communicating organs. Other creatures, far off, pick up the impulses.
Again there is a sequence of stimuli—communicating organs, nerves
of skin, luminous cells of skin. The luminous cells which—which—"

Cliff had followed the strange explanation keenly, and now his
own quick analytical powers grasped the idea which The Student
was trying to express.

"The result is that the luminous cells in the skin of the receiving
animals, corresponding in position to the luminous cells in the skin
of the transmitting animal, are stimulated so that they emit light.
Thus the symbols are made visible on the hide of the receiving
messenger, just as they were originally traced. Is that correct?"

"Correct," the ovoid printed.

"There are entomologists who have suggested that certain insects
have the power to communicate over distances like that," Cliff
answered, "the cockroach, for instance. Their antennae are supposed
to be miniature wireless sets, or something."

The Student did not offer to reply to this immediately, and so
Rodney scratched one word in the sand. It was "Wait." For a minute
or two he was busy piling odds and ends of wreckage beneath the
spy window. Then, equipped with a piece of board, and a pencil
taken from his discarded clothing, he scrambled to the top.

V

For the first time, he viewed the colony of the ovoids, the green
canopy of luminous organisms, the hordes of sea people, the welter
of infernal activity, the protoplasmic battery sparking on its isolated
knoll, the moving shadows of robot beings, and the alert fighters that
patrolled the outskirts of the city, where light and darkness met, like
enemies holding each other in deadlock.

And the greatest of these miracles was this devil who called
himself The Student, and who had now backed off in revulsion at
Cliff's approach.

But there were matters still to be investigated more closely. Dimly visible against the outer walls of the dome was a great shapeless mass that expanded and contracted as if it were breathing. Above the thing, and projecting from the dome like a canopy, was a curious curved shell of pearly, vitreous material.

His deductive faculties keyed up, Cliff was almost certain that he understood the function of the arrangement. With his pencil he traced two questions on the board he held: "You know chemistry, physics, what oxygen and nitrogen are?"

"Yes. I have learned from research. I have learned from men's books," The Student replied, conquering his revulsion.

"You know that the air bladders of fish are filled with a mixture of oxygen and nitrogen?" Cliff asked. "You know that these gases are derived from the blood through the capillaries that line the air bladders, and that this oxygen and nitrogen are drawn originally from the oxygen and nitrogen dissolved in sea water, by means of the gills?"

"Yes."

"Then," Rodney went on, "the air in this place comes from animals too! That creature out there under that roof arrangement— it has gills which take the gases from the sea water and deliver them into the blood stream.

"Part of the oxygen is used to keep the creature alive, of course; but another part of it, together with the nitrogen, is discharged through the walls of capillaries as an actual, free gas, just as a portion of the oxygen and nitrogen in the blood of a fish is discharged into its hydrostatic organ or air bladder! The roof arrangement probably collects it in some way, and delivers it here to me!"

"That is correct," The Student printed. "Several animals work to give you air. Something new—ages to produce."

"Ages, all right." Cliff breathed fervently. "I can well believe it!" He had spoken aloud.

But he was not finished yet. His face was flushed with eagerness, and his pulses were pounding. He had another question to print: "How is the water kept out of here? Nothing of flesh could prevent it from entering when the pressure is so great."

"There our skill failed," The Student responded. "We used the skill of men. We made pumps from parts of ships and from materials which were our own. Air is pumped into the domes and from the domes—and water, when necessary."

The black tendrils withdrew from the window. Transparent lids flickered over the ovoid's great eyes. The transparent body swayed languorously, reminding Cliff of the first sting ray he had seen in an aquarium when he was a child.

It was clear at last, this alien science. Low down beyond the window, and against the shell of the dome, he glimpsed vague motion, where a monster toiled, swinging the lever of a rusty mechanism back and forth. The machine was a pump. Its operator was forcing to him the air which those other monsters produced. And beyond extended the murky, unbelievable reality of this submarine world.

"It is all glorious," Cliff printed in tribute, "even beautiful, almost—your achievements, your ways of doing things!"

The Student's tentacles stirred uneasily, but he made no reply.

A climax had been reached and passed. Rodney's enthusiasm began to cool a little, leaving him to become more cognizant of his own position. He thought of people and friends that he had known and experiences he had enjoyed. The thoughts made him feel very cold and lonely.

His pencil scratched in the silence. "What are you going to do with me?" he was demanding.

"Keep you," was the response.

"Until I rot?"

"Until you rot."

It was a simple statement, devoid of either malice or compassion. Yet it was loaded with a dread significance. It meant staying here in this awful place, dying of starvation, perhaps, if the icy dankness didn't get him.

It meant death in any event; probably it meant madness. There would be ovoid eyes watching him, studying him; there would be ovoid beaks opening and closing vacuously—crazy, wonderful things everywhere, but only his submarine, and the depressing relics in the museum, familiar!

They had conversed, The Student and he. They had been almost friends. But beneath their apparently amicable attitudes toward each other had lain mistrust, broadened and deepened by the fact that they had so very little in common. Cliff saw it now.

Fury smoldered within him, but he held it in check.

He tossed aside the board, which was too covered with messages to be of any further use, and selected in its stead the pulped remnants of a book from the stack of things which supported him close to the spy window.

On one of the illegible pages he printed a note and held it up for the ovoid to see: "I know a better way for you to learn about my kind. Why not establish friendly relations with the world above? Certainly we have many things that you could use. And you have many things that we could use."

"No!" The Student's slender, boneless limbs seemed to jerk with emphasis as they traced the word and repeated it. "No!"

"It will happen anyway," Cliff promised. "Soon my people will come in machines of steel. They will make you understand what is best."

"Men coming here will not return," The Student answered.

And Clifford Rodney, remembering his own capture and seeing now the waspish fighters patrolling the city of the ovoids, had no reason to doubt the weight of the statement. The sea people could protect themselves in their native element.

"You fear us? You mistrust us?" Cliff wanted to know.

The response was frank: "Yes."

"There is no reason."

To this The Student offered nothing.

Cliff tried a new angle, printing swiftly: "What do you know of the place we live in, really—sun, stars, planets, day, night? You have read of such things, no doubt. Wouldn't you like to see them? They are beautiful!"

"Beautiful?" The Student questioned. "Beautiful to you. To me—to us—horrible. The sun, the great dazzling light—it is horrible —and the heat, and the emptiness of air. They make me afraid. But they are wonderful—interesting, very interesting."

Some emotion seemed to stir the nameless soul of the ovoid, making him hesitant and uncertain.

Clifford Rodney thought he glimpsed a shadow of hope. He scarcely understood why he argued; whether he had some dim idea that he might save himself, or whether he was trying to advance the cause of mankind in its demand for expansion into alien realms.

Perhaps he was urging this queer intelligence of the deeps only because it is in the nature of any strong, healthy-minded youth to fight even the most adverse circumstance.

"You are interested, but you are afraid," he wrote. "Why don't you give your interest the chance it deserves? Why don't you—" He hesitated, not knowing quite what he wished to say. "Why don't you try to make contact with my people?"

For a flickering instant The Student paused, in a way that betrayed some hidden process within him. Then his decision seemed to come. "The world of men is the world of men," he printed. "The world of the sea is our world."

Further urgings on Cliff's part met only with flat refusal. He desisted at last, feeling oddly like a salesman who, through a slip in technique, has lost a sale. But that comparison could not be true either. He felt that The Student's obstinacy was too deep-seated to be overcome by mere salesmanship.

Dejectedly he watched the chalky words of the ovoid's last rebuff being washed from the window by the ocean.

Then those black tendrils holding the crayon went to work once more. "You wish to escape," they printed. "It would be interesting, man, to watch you trying to escape."

Startled, Cliff wondered what bizarre mental process had given birth to these statements. Hope was resurrected.

"I cannot escape," he printed warily. "A glass port of my submarine needs repairing, for one thing. I have no materials."

"We will give you materials," was the astounding assertion.

"Eh?" the man said aloud, before he remembered that the ovoid could not hear his words, or understand them if he had been able to hear. "I could not get out of these domes anyway," he wrote. "It is useless."

Cliff Rodney was trying to make a subtle suggestion, in the hope that his unfathomable jailer would offer him a chance for freedom.

"Men have many tricks," The Student responded. "Watching you make use of tricks will be very interesting. We will learn much. Men have powerful explosives."

"I have no explosives!" Cliff insisted truthfully. A feeling of exasperation was rising within him.

"Men have many tricks," the ovoid repeated.

It was a tribute, nothing less; a tribute of mingled awe and mistrust, which the people of the depths felt for the people of the upper air. It was an example of other-world minds at work.

"You expect me to escape?" Cliff demanded.

"You will not escape," was the answer. "This is a test of your powers—a test of men's powers—an experiment. If you escape from the domes you shall be recaptured. We understand caution, man."

Thus Rodney's hopes were broken. But before this message had faded from the spy window, he wrote on a page of the tattered book an acceptance of the challenge: "Good! Get materials you promised, and go to the devil!"

"Materials shall come," was the reply. "Go to the devil."

Breaking off the conversation thus, The Student wheeled in the water. His silvery fins flashed, and he vanished amid the throng of nightmare watchers.

Cliff wondered in a detached way what emotion, if any, had prompted the ovoid to repeat his angry epithet. Was it fury, amusement, some feeling beyond human conception, or just another bit of mimicry? Cliff didn't know; and because he didn't, the skin at the back of his neck tightened unpleasantly.

VI

The Student was out there among his fellows, giving orders in buzzing, tympanic tones and preparing for the test. None could see the turmoil inside his brain—fear pitted against intense eagerness and interest.

He had made no decisions yet, nor would the decision he had in mind be sanctioned by his people. And it is certain, too, that he had no sympathy for the man who had fallen into his clutches, nor any desire to help him win his way to freedom.

Clifford Rodney did not immediately climb down from his position atop the wreckage he had piled up. Instead he remained by the window, looking out, for no particular reason. The only sound, the gentle, pulsing hiss of air being forced into his prison, had a monotonous effect that was more oppressive than absolute silence.

The weird colony wasn't so very different, though, from the cities at home, if you allowed your eyes to sort of blur out of focus; if you didn't see that sunken liner with the wispy ribbons trailing up from it, or the twisted architecture, or the inhabitants. The moving lights made you think of gay places and of gay music and people. One corner of his mouth drew back thoughtfully.

He could see that his chance of getting out of this mess was practically nil: In the first place, he had not the ghost of an idea how he might escape from the two domes. And if he did manage to break free from them, those armored fighters would bar his way. Their great claws would grip the submarine while they discharged their bolts of electric force. The metal hull would protect him to some extent, but not sufficiently, as he knew from experience.

More conscious than ever of the aches in his body, his loneliness and dejection, he looked down at his feet absently. Under them were books. He toed one. Its gilt title was almost obliterated, but he still could make it out—Kipling's "Barrack Room Ballads."

There was a friendliness in those dim, familiar words, and he chuckled a bit. Funny to think of an ovoid intellect trying to read and understand the poems in that volume—"Danny Deever," "Mandalay"! "If" was one of Kipling's works too: "If you can keep your head—"

Cliff smiled ruefully. Anyway he couldn't go wrong by attempting to improve matters a little.

He cast a final glance through the spy window. The ovoid crowd was growing thicker, anticipating activity. Behind them the fighters were gathering in the dusky shadows. In their claws some of them clutched massive bars of some material—rams, no doubt. Probably it had been one of those rams that had broken the port of his submarine.

Still garmented in the tattered carpet, he started in by setting his craft in order as best he could; straightening a warped propeller blade, draining water out of machines and instruments, and repairing those that were broken, whenever it was possible. At least, he had cloth and paper from the museum to help him mop up the wetness of everything.

The radio was a tangle, but he had hope of fixing it some way so that, by means of its beam, he could get a word up to the boys aboard the *Etruria*, on the surface. They couldn't help him, of course; they could only watch and wait.

Several hours must have passed without incident. While he worked, Cliff kept a close lookout for some sign of The Student. When it came, it was not delivered by the wizard of the deeps in person, but through the proxy of a messenger beast. The oak-leaf body of the creature wavered before a window, and on its hide luminous words appeared: "Food is coming through an air tube. Eat."

Cliff waited. From one of the air passages that entered the

chamber, a mass of albuminous substance was blown, and it plopped to the floor. It looked like white of egg. Cliff touched a finger to it, and tasted the adhering dab.

No doubt it was from the body of some specialized marine animal. Probably it was very nourishing, and though it hardly excited Cliff's appetite, he realized that a man might train himself to relish such fare. At present, however, he preferred the brine-soaked chocolate and other food articles that he had brought with him on his adventure.

The messenger now exhibited another message: "Cement for port of the submarine, through same tube."

Its manner of arrival was similar to that of the food. A great lump of clear, firm jelly, probably also the product of a subsea creature.

Rodney gathered it up. As he carried it, a thin film of the substance hardened to glassy consistency on his hands, as collodion would do. He applied the jelly to the submarine's fractured port, inside and out, pressing it as firmly as he could. It would take some time for the cement to set.

He returned his attention to the radio transmitter, but only for a moment. Out of some inner well of his consciousness, the faint shadow of an idea had appeared.

He clambered from the submarine, and with a knife proceeded to dig the cement from around the huge, glassy plug that kept out the sea, just as he had done before with the smaller plug that had sealed the entrance dome from the museum.

He worked entirely around the circular mass, loosening the adhesive substance as deeply as he could probe with his blade. No seepage of sea water appeared. The great block was intended to open outwardly. It was very thick, and beyond it, holding it shut, was the weight of the Atlantic.

But Clifford Rodney's plan was maturing. His efforts were not entirely useless. Undoubtedly that external door was not as firmly placed as it had previously been.

Cliff felt that he might yet demonstrate his ability to get out of the domes, though once beyond them, he could find no glimmer of reason to expect that he could elude the circle of horror that awaited him, even for a few seconds. He could only try to do his best, not so much in the expectation of escape, but to keep his energies busy.

Conscious that his every move was watched with absorbing

interest by the ovoid audience at the spy windows, he rummaged in the museum, finding there some wire and strips of metal. These he brought back beside the submarine.

The drinking-water container of his craft was glass-lined. He unfastened it from its mounting, bashed in the top, and added to its contents a small amount of acid from his batteries. Then he carried it up through the hatch and set it on the floor of the chamber.

Into the water, at opposite sides of the container, he placed upright strips of metal to act as electrodes. To each of these he fastened wires, and attached their opposite ends to the powerful storage batteries of the submarine.

Next, with paper and other refuse, he plugged the air tubes and drains of the two domes. Then he closed the switch, sending current through the apparatus he had just constructed.

There was a hiss as of a caldron boiling as the electricity went through the water in the container, splitting it up into the elemental gases that composed it. Free oxygen and hydrogen bubbled away from the electrodes, mixing with the air of the domes.

This crude process of electrolysis was only the beginning. From the museum Cliff collected all the combustible materials he could find and carried them into the chamber of the submarine—books, wood, a few scraps of celluloid, hard rubber, and so forth. Then, with a little of the glassy cement that remained, he sealed the block that had separated the two domes back into place.

There was another matter. For a few seconds it puzzled him, but finally a solution came. With wrenches he unbolted the heavy glass lens of the submarine's searchlight. Carefully he tapped the incandescent bulb beneath, breaking it, but leaving the delicate tungsten filaments undamaged. Against them he placed a wad of paper, daubed with the remaining benzine of his cigarette lighter.

So far, so good. He investigated the electrolysis apparatus again, shutting off the current for a moment while he scraped away the interfering bubbles that had collected on the crude electrodes.

Satisfied that his preparations were as complete as they could be made for the present, he shut himself inside the submarine and continued to work on the radio. After perhaps an hour of fussing and tampering, he believed that he might get a code message up to the *Etruria.*

He was almost ready, but there was one thing more. Aboard the craft there were ten flasks of compressed oxygen. Opening the valves of nine of these, he tossed them through the hatch, retaining only one for breathing purposes.

While their contents soughed away he disconnected the electrolysis wires and closed the heavy steel door over his head. Working the key of the radio, he flashed out his appeal:

Rodney calling S. S. *Etruria*. . . . Rodney calling S. S. *Etruria*. . . . Captured by deep-sea creatures. . . . Trying to escape. . . . Get position and stand by to help. . . ."

He repeated the communication several times. If it were received, it would be simple for his confreres to calculate his position from the direction the waves came in. They'd be waiting to pick him up. He even chuckled ruefully at the thought.

Through the ports he could see that the ovoids had moved back from the spy windows of the dome, anticipating danger; but their forms, and the forms of their fighters, still hovered tensely in the luminescent haze of the ocean bed. He could not see many from his unfavorable position, but doubtless they were above and all around the dome, waiting for him to make a move!

VII

Cliff forced himself to forget these unnerving thoughts. His hand touched the searchlight switch. His face was grim as he directed his gaze through another port toward the great, circular block that kept out the sea.

"Any one of three things can happen," he muttered. "The force can be insufficient, in which case what I have done won't accomplish anything at all—I'll still be locked in this dome. Or it can be too great, forcing out that plug all at once and letting the water in here all at once, to smash this steel coffin—all at once. Or it can be just right, admitting the ocean gradually enough so that this old tub can stand the strain."

Even the stout steel hull couldn't withstand the sudden thrust of the pressure of the deeps, he knew. Its position would be something like that of a nut under the blow of a hammer.

Cliff didn't want to give himself time to think. He closed the switch. Almost immediately there was a flash of red, as the hot filaments of the searchlight ignited the benzine-soaked paper that was in contact with them.

The flame spread through the dome in a wave of orange, as the hydrogen in the air burned. The sound which penetrated the thick shell of the craft was not the concussion of an explosion. Rather, it was a whispering, soughing roar; for the weight of the sea without was too vast for this feeble beginning of chemical forces to combat.

However, the reserves now came into action. Immersed in a highly oxygenated atmosphere under pressure, the paraphernalia from the museum took fire and, though damp, rapidly became an inferno of incandescence that threw off enormous volumes of gas, expanding irresistibly with heat.

His heart thumping, Rodney kept his eyes glued to the great block which he hoped to dislodge. Stubbornly it continued to stand its ground, unmoved. He gritted his teeth as if, by sheer force of will, he sought to move the insensate thing that barred his way.

Moments passed. There was a snap like a muffled rifle shot. The block jerked, shuddered. Around its rim a curtain of glass appeared —no—not glass—water, screaming like a concourse of mad devils. The flood rolled over the floor, found the fire, and burst into steam, the pressure of which added to the titanic forces combating the titanic weight of the deeps.

More moments—the chamber was half full of water. Then, with a sort of majestic resignation, the plug yielded, folding outward like a dying colossus. The ocean was in then, swiftly—so swiftly that a living eye could not capture its movements. The thud of it was heavier than a clap of thunder.

The submarine bobbed in the maelstrom like a bit of flotsam. But its hull held, even though it was flung repeatedly against the walls of the dome.

A minute went by before Clifford Rodney was able to do anything. He picked himself up from the place where he had been hurled, and scrambled to the controls. He could see the opening which led from his prison. The motors throbbed and the submarine turned, heading through the still surging water.

It did get clear of the dome. Cliff almost thought he had a chance. Maybe the confusion produced in the vicinity by the suction when the sea had entered the dome, had unnerved the ovoids momentarily.

He set the vertical screws spinning. Their lift wasn't very good.

They had been damaged again. It was hardly remarkable after the way the little ship had been bounced around.

Cliff looked up through a ceiling port. Six fighters were pouncing down upon him, their hinged claws spread wide, their long, armored forms ghostly in the shadows. Others were approaching from all directions, accompanied by a horde of ovoids.

A seventh had joined the six now. Rodney had not seen it dart up from the deep muck of the bottoms, where it had lain, hidden even to the people of the depths. It bore a strange, glassy object of considerable size. Without much attention the man wondered what it might be.

"All right," he muttered, "you win! I hope you enjoyed the show!"

The fighters were upon him. He could hear the scrape of their claws against metal. Clouds of black stuff, like the ink of a squid, surrounded the submarine, hiding everything from view. He was still rising, though—rather rapidly, he thought. In a moment the electric bolts would stun him.

Upward and upward he went. Cliff began to be puzzled. He detected scraping noises that he could not interpret. He must have advanced half a mile toward the surface since the start. It was all very odd.

There was a jolt. The climb became halting and erratic. The motors labored doggedly.

The water cleared. Cliff could make out schools of phosphorescent fish, hanging in the darkness like scattered galaxies. He was alone, far above the bottoms. There were no fighters around him, though he thought he glimpsed dim shapes vanishing beneath. They could not endure the reduced pressure that existed here.

Matters were better, far better, than he had dared to expect—mysteriously so. Now if the vertical screws continued to function at all— The submarine appeared to be badly damaged. It seemed clumsy, heavy.

Cliff came into a region of deep bluish light, beautiful as some fairy-peopled realm of infinity. Not long thereafter the bathyspheric craft broke through the sunlighted surface of the Atlantic. Cliff opened the valves of a pressure tank, inflating the bellows like water wings which supported the heavy submarine when it was on the surface.

How had this all happened? There was still the mystery. He almost forgot that he must gradually reduce the pressure around him, to avoid the "bends."

At length he opened the hatch and crawled out onto the rounded top of the undersea boat. An egg-shaped object was fastened to the metal shell just behind the hatch. Rodney approached it, unable yet to fathom its nature. Glassy cement, like that with which he had recently become acquainted, held the thing in place.

It was a massive object, six feet through at its greatest diameter. It was made of the same material as the domes, except that this substance was darker, perhaps to shield what it covered from the fierce sun.

Rodney peered into the semitransparent depths of the object, discerning there a huddled form enveloped in a milky, semiliquid film. The form was delicate; vital organs pulsed visibly beneath its skin. It had flippers, and masses of black tendrils. Its beaked mouth opened and closed, giving it an air of vacuous solemnity, but its eyes were keen. Its tentacles clutched a white crayon. It was The Student!

Clifford Rodney's mind was a whirl as he sought to solve the riddle. Then, since no other means of printing a message was available, he traced words with a finger on the wet surface of the oval object:

"You helped me—how?"

The Student's tendrils trembled as he printed the answer on the inside of his protecting shell: "I helped you. The six fighters, and the seventh, were mine. They did not attack you. Concealed by the liquid that darkens the sea, they raised your submarine upward.

"They attached me to the submarine. They raised it as far as they could climb. It was a trick to outwit my people. They forbid traffic with the upper world. They are afraid. I was afraid, but at last I chose. While you prepared for the test an idea came. I used it, outwitting my people. I am afraid. But I am glad."

Rodney was lost in the fantastic wonder of it all. "Thank you, my friend!" he printed.

The Student plied his crayon again: "Friend? No. I am not your friend. What I did, I did for myself."

"Then why in reason's name are you here?" Cliff printed. "Men will put you in an aquarium, and stare at and study you!"

"Good," was the response, "I am glad. Men study me. I study them. Good. That is why I came: to see the accomplishments of men, to see the stars, to see the planets. Now I see the sun and sky—dreadful but interesting—very interesting. Good."

"Good if you don't smother before you can be transferred to a suitable aquarium," Rodney traced.

"I am safe here," the ovoid answered with a nervous flurry of tendrils. "The pressure is normal. There is much oxygen in the fluid which surrounds me. But do what you must, man. I am waiting."

Cliff was accustomed enough to the situation by now to grin down at the great dark egg. Mixed with his awe there was a curious inner warmth. Man and ovoid were different in form and mind; perhaps real sympathy between them was impossible. But Cliff had found a tangible similarity.

In this sullen devil of the depths, eagerness to know the unknown had battled fear, and had won. The Student had placed himself, without defense, in the power of the unknown. It took guts to do that, courage—

Young Rodney thought of many things as he looked out over the water in search of signs of rescue. A ship was approaching. It was near enough so that he could recognize it as the *Etruria*.

"The boys'll probably call you Davey Jones' ambassador or something," he said banteringly, addressing the ovoid. "I hope you're sport enough to take it, old socks!"

But The Student wouldn't have listened even if he were able. His eyes were drinking in the miracle of the approaching ship.

"Why should he move?" she asked. That stopped me for a little.

Illustrated by Elliot Dold

Alas, All Thinking

By Harry Bates

I

STRICTLY CONFIDENTIAL. (This is dynamite! Be careful who sees it!)
From: Charles Wayland.

To: Harold C. Pendleton, Chairman of the Human Salvage
Section of the National Lunacy Commission.

Subject: Report on the conversations and actions of Harlan T.
Frick on the night of June 7, 1963.

Method: I used the silent pocket dictograph you gave me; and my
report is a literal transcription of the record obtained, with only such
additions of my own as are needed to make it fully intelligible.

Special Notes: (a) The report, backed by the dictograph record,
may be considered as one-third of the proof that your "amateur
neurosis detective" Wayland is not himself a subject for psychopathic observation, since this fantastic report can be corroborated in
all its details by Miles Matson, who was with us that night, and
would be, I think, by Frick himself.

(b) Pending any action by you, I have cautioned both Matson and
Frick to maintain absolute silence with regard to the conversation
and events covered. They may be trusted to comply.

(c) So that you may follow the report more intelligently, I feel that
it is necessary to say here, in advance, that Frick will be proved to be
wholly sane, but that never again may his tremendous talents be
utilized for the advancement of science. As his friend, I have to
recommend that you give up all hope of salvaging him, and leave
him to go his prodigal, pleasure-seeking way alone. You might think
of him as a great scientist who has died. He is reasonable, but
human, and I see his waste of his life as humanly reasonable. You
will see, too.

Report: The amazing events of the evening started in a manner commonplace enough at the Lotus Gardens, where I had made a dinner engagement with Frick and our old mutual friend, Miles Matson, chemist and recent author of an amusing mathematical theory of inverse variables as applied to feminine curves, which Frick had expressed a desire to hear. I should have preferred to observe Frick alone, but was not sure that alone I would be able to hold the interest of his restless, vigorous mind for a third time within two weeks. Ten minutes of boredom and my psychological observations would come to a sudden end, and you would have to find and impress someone else to do your psychological sleuthing.

I got to our reserved table fifteen minutes early to get settled, set up the dictograph in my pocket, and review for the last time my plans. I had three valuable leads. I had discovered (see my reports of May 26th and May 30th) peculiar, invariable, marked emotional reactions in him when the words "brains," "human progress," and "love" were mentioned. I was sure that this was symptomatic. And I hoped to get nearer the roots of his altered behavior pattern by the common method of using a prepared and memorized list of words, remarks, and questions, which I would spring on him from time to time.

I could only trust that Frick was not too familiar with psychoanalysis, and so would not notice what I was doing.

I confess that for a moment while waiting I was swept with the feeling that it was hopeless, but I soon roused from that. One can do no more than try, and I was going to try my hardest. With another I might have been tempted to renege, but never with Frick. For he was my old friend of college days, and so eminently worth saving! He was still so young; had so much to give to mankind!

I guessed once more at the things that might have altered his pattern so. A physicist, perhaps the most brilliant and certainly the most promising in the world, enters his laboratory after his graduation from college and for eleven years hardly so much as sticks his nose outside its door. All the while he sends from it a stream of discoveries, new theories, and integrations of old laws the like of which has never before been equaled; and then this same physicist walks out of his laboratory, locks the door, shuns the place, and for two years devotes himself with casual abandon to such trivialisms of the modern idler as golfing, clothes, travel, fishing, nightclubs, and so on. Astounding is a weak word for this spectacle. I could think of nothing that would remotely suit.

Miles Matson arrived a minute early—which was, for him, a phenomenon, and showed how the anticipation of dining with Frick had affected him. Miles is forty-five, short, solid, bald—but then I needn't describe him.

"He'll come?" were his first words, before seating himself on the other side of the table.

"I think so," I assured him, smiling a little at his apparent anxiety. He looked a little relieved, and fished from the jacket of his dinner clothes that abominable pipe he smokes whenever and wherever he pleases, and be damned to frowning head waiters. He lighted it, took a few quick puffs, then leaned back, smiled, and volunteered frankly, "Charles, I feel like a little boy about to have dinner with the principal of his school."

I could understand that, for most scientists would feel that way where Frick was concerned. I smiled, too, and chaffed him.

"What—you and that pipe intimidated by a mere playboy?"

"No—by the mystery behind the playboy," was his serious rejoinder. "What's your guess at the solution? Quick, before he comes," he asked earnestly.

I shrugged my shoulders. Miles, of course, was not in my confidence.

"Could it be a woman?" he went on. "I haven't heard of any one woman. A disappointment in his work? Some spoiled-child reaction? Is he crazy? What's made the change?"

If I only knew!

"Frick, further than any man alive, has touched out to the infinite unknowable," he continued almost grumbling, "and I want to know how such a man can trade his tremendous future for a suit of evening clothes!"

"Perhaps he is just relaxing a little," I suggested with a smile.

"Ah, of course—relaxing," he answered sarcastically. "For two years!"

I knew at once Frick had heard what we had been saying, for at that moment I looked up and around just in time to see him, lean and graceful in his dinner clothes, his mouth twisted with amusement, stepping past the head waiter to his place at the table. Miles and I rose; and we must have shown our confusion, for one simply did not mention that topic in Frick's hearing. But he showed no offense—indeed, he seemed in unusually good spirits—for he lightly acknowledged our greeting, waved us back in our places, and, seating himself, added to our dialogue.

"Yes, for two years. And will for forty-two more!"

This opening of the conversation threw me unexpectedly off stride, but I remembered to switch on the dictograph, and then seized the opportunity to ask what otherwise I would never have dared.

"Why?"

Still he showed no offense, but instead, surprisingly, indulged in a long, low chuckle that seemed to swell up as from a spring of inexhaustible deliciousness. He answered cryptically, bubblingly, enjoying our puzzlement with every word.

"Because Humpty Dumpty had a great fall. Because thought is withering, and sensation sweet. Because I've recovered my sense of humor. Because 'why' is a dangerous word, and makes people unhappy. Because I have had a glimpse of the most horrible cerebral future. Yes!" He laughed, paused for a moment, then said in a lower voice with dramatic impressiveness, "Would you believe it? I have terminated the genus Homo Sapiens."

II

He was not drunk, and, as you will see, not crazy—though I would not have bet any money on it just then. His mood was only one of extraordinary good humor. Vastly amused at our reaction to his wild words, he allowed himself to shock us, and did it again and again. I might say here that it is my opinion that all the revelations of the night were, in the main, the result of Frick's sudden notion to shock us, and that no credit whatever is due me and my intended plan of psychological attack.

Miles' face showed blank dismay. Frick ceased chuckling and, his gray eyes gleaming, enjoyed our discomfiture in quiet for a moment. Then he added, "No. Strictly speaking, there is one piece of unfinished business. A matter of one murder. I was sort of dallying with the idea of committing it tonight, and finishing off the whole affair. Would you two like to be in on it?"

Miles looked as if he would like to excuse himself. He coughed, smiled unhappily, glanced doubtfully at me. I at once decided that if

Frick was going to attempt murder, I was going to be on hand to prevent it. I suppose that the desperate resolution showed in my face, for Frick, looking at me, laughed outright. Miles then revived enough to smile wanly at Frick and suggest he was joking. He added, "I'm surprised that anyone with the brains you have should make so feeble a joke!"

At the word "brains" Frick almost exploded.

"Brains!" he exclaimed. "Not me! I'm dumb! Dumb as the greasy-haired saxophone player over there! I understand that I used to have brains, but that's all over; it's horrible; let's not think about it. I tell you I'm dumb, now—normally, contentedly dumb!"

Miles did not know how to understand Frick any more than did I. He reminded him, "You used to have an I.Q. of 248—"

"I've changed!" Frick interrupted. He was still vehement, but I could see that he was full of internal amusement.

"But no healthy person's intelligence can drop much in the course of a few years," Miles objected strongly.

"Yes—I'm dumb!" Frick reiterated.

My opportunities lay in keeping him on the subject. I asked him, "Why have you come to consider the possession of brains such an awful thing?"

" 'Ah, to have seen what I have seen, know what I know'!" he quoted.

Miles showed irritation. "Well, then, let's call him dumb!" he said, looking at me. "To insist on such a stupid jest!"

I took another turn at arousing Frick. "You are, of course, speaking ironically out of some cryptic notion that exists only in your own head; but whatever this notion, it is absurd. Brains in quantity are the exclusive possession of the human race. They have inspired all human progress; they have made us what we are today, masters of the whole animal kingdom, lords of creation. Two other things have helped—the human hand and human love; but even above these ranks the human brain. You are only ridiculous when you scoff at its value."

"Oh, love and human progress!" Frick exclaimed, laughing. "Charles, I tell you brains will be the ruination of the human race," he answered with great delight.

"Brains will be the salvation of the human race!" Miles contradicted with heat.

"You make a mistake, a very common mistake, Miles," Frick

declared, more seriously. "Charles is of course right in placing man at the top of creation, but you're very wrong in assuming he will always remain there. Consider. Nature made the cell, and after a time the cell became a fish; and that fish was the lord of creation. The very top. For a while. For just a few million years. Because one day a fish crawled out of the sea and set about becoming a reptile. He became a magnificent one. Tyrannosaurus Rex was fifty feet long, twenty high; he had teeth half a foot long, and feet armed with claws that were terrible. No other creature could stand against him; he had speed, size, power and ferocity; *he* became the lord of creation.

"What happened to the fish? He had been the lord of creation, but, well, he never got anywhere. What of Tyrannosaurus Rex? He, too, was the lord of creation, but he, alas, is quite, quite extinct.

"Nature tried speed with the fish, then size with the saurians. Neither worked; the fish got stuck, the saurian died off. But did she quit experimenting at that? Not at all—she tried mobility, and we got the monkey. The first monkey swung from limb to limb screeching, 'I am the lord of creation!' and, by Jove, he was! But he could not know that one day, after a few millions of years, one of his poor relations would go down on the ground, find fire, invent writing, assume clothing, devise modern inconveniences, discover he had lost his tail, and crow, 'Behold, I am the lord of creation!'

"Why did this tailless monkey have his turn? Because his makeup featured brains? You will bellow yes—but I hear Mother Nature laughing at you. For you are only her *latest* experiment! The lord of creation! That you are—but only for a little while! Only for a few million years!"

Frick paused, his eyes flashed, his nostrils distended contemptuously. "How dare man be so impertinent as to assume nature has stopped experimenting!" he exclaimed at length.

In the quiet which followed this surprising outburst I could see Miles putting two and two together. But he took his time before speaking. He relighted his pipe and gave it a good, fiery start before removing it from his mouth and saying, almost in a drawl, "It amounts to this, then. Anticipating that nature is about to scrap brains and try again along new lines, you choose to attempt immortality by denying your own undoubted brains and trying to be the first to jump in the new direction."

Frick only laughed. "Wrong again, Miles," he said. "I'm just standing pat."

"To go back a little," I said to Frick; "it seems to me you're assuming far too much when you tell us that the human race is not the last, but only the most recent of nature's experiments."

The man acted almost shocked. "But have you forgotten what I told you just a little while ago? I said I have *terminated* the genus Homo Sapiens!"

Miles snorted with disgust. I was alarmed. Miles tried sarcasm.

"Have you and Mother Nature already decided, then, what the next lord of creation is to be?"

"I myself have nothing to say about it," Frick replied with assumed naiveté, "nor do I know what it will be. I could find out, but I doubt if I ever shall. It's much more fun not to know—don't you think? Though, if I had to guess," he added, "I should say she will feature instinct."

This was too much for Miles. He started to rise, saying, as he pushed his chair back, "This is enough. You're either crazy or else you're a conceited fool! Personally, I think it's both!"

But Frick held him with a gesture, and in a voice wholly sincere said, "Sit down, Miles; keep your shirt on. You know very well I neither lie nor boast. I promise to prove everything I have said."

Miles resumed his seat and looked at Frick almost sneeringly as he went on.

"You're quite right about my being a fool, though. I was one; oh, a most gorgeous fool! But I am not conceited. I am so little conceited that I offer to show you myself in what must surely be the most ridiculous situation that a jackass or a monkey without a tail has ever been in. I'll exchange my dignity for your good opinion; you'll see that I'm not crazy; and then we'll have the most intelligent good laugh possible to Genus Homo. Yes? Shall we?"

Miles gave me a look which clearly expressed his doubt of Frick's sanity. Frick, seeing, chuckled and offered another inducement.

"And I'll throw in, incidentally, a most interesting murder!"

Our friend was completely disgusted. "We came here to eat," he said. "Let's get it over with." And with the words he picked up the menu which had been lying in front of him all this time. Frick looked at me.

"I'm not hungry," he said. "Are you?"

I wasn't. I shook my head.

"Shall we two go, then?"

I hesitated. I was not overanxious to accompany, alone, a madman on a mission of murder. But I caught Miles' eye, and like the noble he is, he said he'd come too. Frick smiled softly.

III

Ten minutes later we had made the short flight along the north shore to Glen Cove, where Frick has his estate, and were escorted by him into a small, bare room on the second floor of the laboratory building which adjoins his beautiful home.

While we stood there wondering, Frick went into an adjoining room and returned with two chairs, and then, in two more trips, with a third chair and a tray on which rested a large thermos bottle and a tea service for three. The chairs he arranged facing each other in an intimate group, and the tray he set on the floor by the chair he was to take himself.

"First I have to tell a rather long story," he explained. "The house would be more comfortable, but this room will be more convenient."

Frick was now a changed man. His levity of before was gone; tense, serious lines appeared on his rugged face; his great head lowered with the struggle to arrange thoughts that were difficult, and perhaps painful, to him. When he spoke, it was softly, in a voice likewise changed.

My dictograph was still turned on.

"Charles, Miles," Frick began, "forgive me for my conduct back in the Gardens. I had so much on my mind, and you were so smugly skeptical, that the inclination to overpower you with what I know was irresistible. I had not expected to make any of these revelations to you. I offered to on impulse; but do not fear, I shall not regret it. I think—I see now that I have been carrying a very heavy load—

"What I have to say would fill a large book, but I will make it as short as I can. You will not believe me at first, but please be patient, for proof will eventually be forthcoming. Every single thing I said to you is true, even to the murder I must commit—"

He paused, and seemed to relax, as if tired. Unknown black shadows closed over my heart. Miles watched him closely, quite motionless. We waited. Frick rubbed the flat of his hand slowly over his eyes and forehead, then let it drop.

"No," he said at length, "I have never been conceited. I don't think so. But there was a time when I was very proud of my intelligence. I worked; I accomplished things that seemed to be important; I felt myself a leader in the rush of events. Work was enough, I thought; brain was the prime tool of life; and with my brain I dared try anything. Anything! I dared try to assemble the equation of a device that would enable me to peer into the future! And when I thought I had it, I started the construction of that device! I never finished it, and I never shall, now; but the attempt brought Pearl to me—

"Yes," he added, as if necessary that he convince himself, "I am certain that had I not attempted that, Pearl would not have come. Back through the ages she had somehow felt me out—don't ask me how, for I don't know—and through me chose to enter for a brief space this, our time.

"I was as surprised as you would have been. I was working in this very room, though then it was twice as large and fairly cluttered with clumsy apparatus I have since had removed. I had been working feverishly for months; I was unshaven, red-eyed and dirty—and there, suddenly, she was. Over there, beyond that door at which I'm pointing. She was in a golden-glowing cylinder whose bottom hung two feet off the floor. For a moment she stood suspended there; and then the glow disappeared and she stepped through to the floor.

"You do not believe me? Well, of course, I don't expect you to. But there will be proof. There will be proof.

"I was surprised, but somehow I wasn't much frightened. The person of my visitor was not intimidating. She was just a barefooted young woman, very slender, of average height, clad in a shiny black shift which reached her knees. I cannot say she was well formed. Her body was too thin, her hips too narrow, her head too large. And she was miles from being pretty. Her hair and eyes were all right; they were brown; but her face was plain and flat, with an extraordinary and forbidding expression of dry intellectuality. The whole effect of her was not normal, yet certainly not weird; she was just peculiar, different—baroque.

"She spoke to me in English! In nonidiomatic English with the words run together and an accent that was atrocious! She asked severely, 'Do you mind too much this intrusion of mine?'

" 'Why—why no!' I said when I had recovered from the shock of the sound of her speech. 'But are you real, or just an illusion?'

" 'I do not know,' she replied. 'That is a tremendous problem. It has occupied the attention of our greatest minds for ages. Excuse me, sir.' And with these last words she calmly sat herself down on the floor, right where she was, and appeared to go off into deep thought!

"You can imagine my astonishment! She sat there for a full two minutes, while I gaped at her in wonder. When she rose again to her feet she finished with, 'I do not know. It is a tremendous problem.'

"I began to suspect that a trick was being played on me, for all this was done with the greatest seriousness.

" 'Perhaps there is a magician outside,' I suggested.

" 'I am the magician,' she informed me.

" 'Oh!' I said ironically. 'I understand everything now.'

" 'Or no, fate is the magician,' she went on as if in doubt. 'Or no, I am—a very deep problem—' Whereupon she sat down on the floor and again went off into meditation!

"I stepped around her, examining her from all angles, and, since she was oblivious to everything outside of herself, I made a cursory examination of the thing she had come in on. It looked simple enough—a flat, plain, circular box, maybe four feet in diameter and six inches deep, made of some sort of dull-green metal. Fixed to its center, and sticking vertically upward, was a post of the same stuff capped with a plate containing a number of dials and levers. Around the edge of the upper surface of the box was a two-inch bevel of what seemed to be yellow glass. And that was all—except that the thing continued to remain fixed in the air two feet off the floor!

"I began to get a little scared. I turned back to the girl and again looked her over from all sides. She was so deep in her thoughts that I dared to touch her. She was real, all right!

"My touch brought her to her feet again.

" 'You have a larger head than most men,' she informed me.

" 'Who are you, anyway?' I asked with increasing amazement. She gave me a name that it took me two days to memorize, so horrible was its jumble of sounds. I'll just say here that I soon gave her another—Pearl—because she was such a baroque—and by that name I always think of her.

" 'How did you get in?' I demanded.

"She pointed to the box.

" 'But what is it?' I wanted to know.

" 'You have no name for it,' she replied. 'It goes to yesterday, to last year, to the last thousand years—like that.'

" 'You mean it's a time traveler?' I asked, astounded. 'That you can go back and forth in time?'

" 'Yes,' she answered. 'I stopped to see you, for you are something like me.'

" 'You wouldn't misinform me?' I asked sarcastically, feeling I must surely be the victim of some colossal practical joke.

" 'Oh, no, I would not misinform you,' she replied aridly.

"I was very skeptical. 'What do you want here?' I asked.

" 'I should like you to show me the New York of your time. Will you, a little?'

" 'If you'll take me for a ride on that thing, and it works, I'll show you anything you want,' I answered, still more skeptical.

"She was glad to do it.

" 'Come,' she commanded. I stepped gingerly up on the box. 'Stand here, and hold on to this,' she went on, indicating the rod in the center. I did so, and she stepped up to position just opposite me, and very close. I was conscious of how vulnerable I was if a joke was intended.

" 'You must not move,' she warned me. I assured her I would not. 'Then, when do you want to go?'

" 'A week back,' I said at random, with, in spite of everything, a creeping sensation going up and down my spine.

" 'That will do,' she decided; and again she warned me not to move. Then her hands went to the controls.

"A golden veil sprang up around us and the room grew dim through it, then disappeared. A peculiar silence came over me, a silence that seemed not so much outside of me as within. There was just a second of this, and then I was again looking into the room through the golden veil. Though it dimmed the light I could clearly make out the figure of a man stretched full length on the floor working on the under part of a piece of apparatus there.

" 'It's I!' I exclaimed, and every cell in my body leaped at the miracle of it. That this could be! That I could be standing outside of myself looking at myself! That last week had come back, and that I, who already belonged to a later time, could be back there again in it! As I peered, thoughts and emotions all out of control, I saw happen a thing that stilled the last thin voice of inward doubt.

"The man on the floor rolled over, sat up, turned his face—*my* face—toward us, and, deep in thought, gently fingered a sore place on his head—from a bump that no one, positively, knew anything about. Trickery seemed excluded.

"But a contradictory thing occurred to me. I asked Pearl, 'Why doesn't he see us, since he's looking right this way? I never saw anything at the time.'

" 'It is only in the next stage toward arriving that we can be seen,' she explained with her hands still on the controls. 'At this moment I'm keeping us unmaterialized. This stage is extremely important. If we tried to materialize within some solid, and not in free space, we should explode.

" 'Now, let us return,' she said. 'Hold still.'

"The room disappeared; the peculiar silence returned; then I saw the room again, dim through the golden veil. Abruptly the veil vanished and the room came clear; and we stepped down on the floor on the day we had left.

"My legs were trembling so as to be unreliable. I leaned against a table, and my amazing visitor, as it seemed her habit, sat down on the floor.

"That was my introduction to Pearl."

IV

Frick rose and walked to the far corner of the room and back. The thoughts in his mind were causing some internal disturbance, that was obvious.

I prayed that my dictograph was working properly!

When Frick sat down again he was calmer. Not for long could any emotion sweep out of control his fine mind and dominating will. With a faint smile and an outflung gesture of his arm he said, "That was the beginning!"

Again he paused, and ended it with one of his old chuckles. "I showed Pearl New York. I showed her!

"Charles, Miles, there is just too much," he resumed at a tangent, shaking his head. "There is the tendency to go off into details, but I'll try to avoid it. Maybe some other time. I want to be brief, just now.

"Well, I got her some clothes and showed her New York City. It was a major experience. For she was not your ordinary out-of-towner, but a baroque out of far future time. She had learned our language and many of our customs; she was most amazingly mental;

and yet, under the difficult task of orienting herself to what she called our crudeness, she exhibited a most delicious naiveté.

"I showed her my laboratory and explained the things I had done. She was not much interested in that. I showed her my house, others too, and explained how we of the twentieth century live.

" 'Why do you waste your time acquiring and operating gadgets?' she would ask. She liked that word 'gadgets'; it became her favorite. By it she meant electricity, changes of clothing, flying, meals in courses, cigarettes, variety of furniture, even the number of rooms in our homes. She'd say, 'You are a superior man for this time; why don't you throw out all your material luxuries so as to live more completely in the realms of the mind?'

"I would ask her what standard she judged our civilization against; but whenever I did that she'd always go obscure, and say she guessed we were too primitive to appreciate the higher values. She consistently refused to describe the sort of civilization she had come from; though, toward the end, she began promising me that if I were a good guide, and answered all her questions, she might—only might—take me there to see it. You can imagine I was a good guide!

"But meanwhile, I got nothing but my own inferences; and what an extraordinary set I acquired from her questions and reactions! You make your own set as I go along!

"I showed her New York. She'd say, 'But why do the people hurry so? Is it really necessary for all those automobiles to keep going and coming? Do the people *like* to live in layers? If the United States is as big as you say it is, why do you build such high buildings? What is your reason for having so few people rich, so many people poor?' It was like that. And endless.

"I took her to restaurants. 'Why does everybody take a whole hour just to eat?' I told her that people enjoyed eating; it seemed not to have occurred to her. 'But if they spent only a few minutes at it they'd have that much more time for meditation!' I couldn't but agree.

"I took her to a nightclub. 'Why do all those men do all the carrying, and those others all the eating?' I explained that the first were waiters, the latter guests. 'Will the guests have a turn at carrying?' I told her I thought so, some day.

" 'Is that man a singing waiter?'

" 'No, only a crooner.'

" 'Why do those men with the things make such an awful noise?'

" 'Because dance bands get paid for making it.'

" 'It must be awfully hard on them.' I told her I hoped so. 'Are those people doing what you call dancing?'

" 'Yes.'

" 'Do they like to do it?'

" 'Yes.'

" 'The old ones, too?'

" 'I doubt it.'

" 'Then why do they do it?' I didn't know. At the end she asked me almost poignantly, 'Don't they *ever* spend any time in meditation?' and I had to express my doubts.

"In our little jaunts it became increasingly clear to her that there was very little meditation being done in New York. It was the biggest surprise that our civilization gave her.

"However, she continued to indulge her peculiar habit of going off into meditation when something profound, or interesting, or puzzling came to her attention; and the most extraordinary thing about it was that she had to sit down at it, no matter where she was. If there was a chair handy, all right, but if not, she would plunk right down on the floor, or, outside, even in the street! This was not so bad when we were alone, but once it happened under Murphy's flagpole in Union Square as we stood observing the bellowings of a soap-box orator, and once again in Macy's, where we lingered a moment listening to a demonstrator with the last word possible in beauty preparations. It was quite embarrassing! Toward the end I grew adept in detecting signs of the coming descent and was fairly successful in holding her up!

"In all the six days I spent showing Pearl New York, not once did she show any emotion other than that of intellectual curiosity; not once did she smile; not once did she so much as alter the dry expression on her face. And *this*, my friends, was the creature who became a student and an exponent of love!

"It bears on my main theme, so I will tell you in some detail about her experiences with love, or what she thought was love.

"During the first three days she did not mention the word; and from what I know of her now, I can say with surety that she was holding herself back. During those three days she had seen one performance of *Romeo and Juliet*, had read two romantic novels containing overwhelming love themes, had observed everywhere the instinct for young people to seek each other out, had seen two couples kiss while dancing, had seen the fleet come in and the sailors make for Riverside Drive, and had heard I don't know how many hours of crooning on radio broadcasts.

"After all this, one day in my drawing room, she suddenly asked me, 'What is this love that everyone is always talking about?'

"Never dreaming of the part love was to play between us, I answered simply that it was nature's device to make mature humans attractive to each other and ensure the arrival of offspring and the maintenance of the race. That, it seems, is what she thought it was, but what she couldn't understand was why everybody made such a to-do about it. Take kissing, for instance. That was when a male and a female pushed each other on the lips. Did they like that? I assured her they did. Was it, since they held it so long, a kind of meditation? Well, no, not exactly. Would I try it with her?

"Don't smile yet, you two—that's nothing! Wait! Anyway, you wouldn't want me to spoil my chances of being taken for a visit to her own time, would you?

"Well, we kissed. She stood on tiptoe, her dry face looking up at mine, her arms stiffly at her sides, while I bent down, my sober face looking down at hers, and my arms stiffly at my sides. We both pushed; our lips met; and we stayed that way a little. Then, almost maintaining contact, Pearl asked me, 'Is it supposed to sort of scrape?' I assured her it was—something like a scrape. After a moment she said, 'Then there's a great mystery here, somewhere—' And damned if she didn't squat right down on the floor and go off into a think! I couldn't keep a straight face, so I bounced out of the room; and when I returned several minutes later there she was still meditating on her kiss. *O tempora!*

"That kiss happened on the third day, and she stayed six, and for the remainder of her visit in our time she said not one thing more about this thing called love—which told me it was a mystery always on her mind, for she asked questions by the score about every other conceivable thing.

"But I also knew from another thing. For the three days following that kiss she went innumerable times to my radio and tuned in dance and vocal programs whose songs would, of course, inevitably be about love. She fairly saturated herself with love's and above's, star's and are's, blue's and you's, June's and moon's. What a horrible flock of mangy clichés must have come to flap around in her mental—all too mental—mind! What peculiar notions about love they must have given her!

"But enough of that phase. You have an idea. You have seen Pearl in New York, tasting of love. Six nights to the very hour after she first appeared to me I stood again on the round base of the time traveler, and this time I accompanied her forward to her time. I do not know how far in the future that was, but I estimate it to be around three million years."

V

Frick paused, rose, and, without asking us if we wanted any, served some cold tea from the thermos bottle by his chair. This time we were glad to have it.

By then I was as close to fully believing as was, I think, Miles. We wasted little time over the tea, but, considerably refreshed and extremely eager with anticipations of what would follow, leaned forward and were again lost in Frick's extraordinary story.

"The trip forward took what seemed to be only half a minute, and I believe it might have been instantaneous but for the time needed to bring the machine to a stop on exactly the right day. As before, the passage was a period of ineffable silence; but I was aware that all the time Pearl fingered the controls. Very suddenly I saw we were in a dimly lighted room; with equal suddenness the golden screen vanished and normal daylight took its place. We had arrived.

"I stepped off the traveler and looked curiously about. We were in a small place, the walls of which were partitions which projected perhaps ten feet up toward a very high ceiling. Everything I could see was made of an ugly, mud-yellow metallic substance, and everything seemed to be built on the square. Light entered from large windows on all sides. The section of the great room in which we had arrived was bare of everything but our traveler. I saw that this time it rested firmly on the floor—a very dirty floor.

"I suppose it would be superfluous to paint the tremendous state of excitement and curiosity I was in. To be the only man of our time to have voyaged forward! To be the only one allowed to see the human race in marvelous maturity! What honor, glory, luck, that such an unmerited distinction should fall upon me! Every atom of my body was living and tingling at that moment. I was going to drink in and remember everything that crossed my senses.

"I was full of questions at once, but Pearl had warned me not to talk. She had told me that there were several caretakers from whose sight I was to remain hidden; and now the first thing she did was to put her finger to her lips and peer down the corridor outside. She listened a moment, then stepped out and beckoned me to follow.

"I did—and all but exclaimed out loud to see that the corridor was carpeted with fine dust fully an inch deep!

"How could this be in an important building of so advanced an age? For surely that building was important, to house, as it did, so marvelous a device as the traveler!

"But I had no time for wonderment, for Pearl led me rapidly toward the far side of the great room. At our every step clouds of dust billowed out on each side, so that a hasty glance behind showed such diffusion of it that all there was hidden. The corridor was quite wide, and ran lengthwise of the building on one side of the center. At varying distances we passed doorways, all of them closed, and at the end we turned to the left, to come quickly to a high, wide door. It was open, and golden sunlight was shining through. For a second Pearl held me back while she peered around the edge, then, taking me by the hand, she led me out into our world of the future.

"What would you have expected to see, Charles? You, Miles? Towering buildings, perhaps, transversed on their higher levels by aerial traffic ways? And crowds of people strangely mannered and curiously dressed? And mysterious-powered aerial carriers? And parks? And flowers? And much use of metal and synthetic marble? Well, of these there was nothing. My eyes looked out over a common, ordinary, flat, 1963 field. In the distance were some patches of trees; nearby were some wild grass, low bushes, and millions of daisies; and that was all!

"My first thought was that Pearl had made some mistake in our time of destination, and when I sought her face, and saw that this was only what she expected, I grew alarmed. She misread my thoughts, though, and saying 'Don't be afraid' led me along a wide walk to a corner of the building, where she peeped around the edge, and, apparently satisfied with what she found, stepped forth and motioned me to follow. Then she spoke:

" 'Here we are,' she said.

"Before me stretched the same sort of landscape as on the other quarter, except that here the immediate field was tenanted with a square block of large metallic boxes, six on a side, and each separated by about ten yards from its neighbors.

"I suppose I stood there and gaped. I didn't understand, and I told Pearl as much. Her tone in replying came as near surprise as I ever heard it.

" 'Not understand?' she asked. 'What do you mean? Isn't this just about what you expected?'

"Eventually I found words. 'But where is your city?' I asked.

" 'There,' she answered, with a gesture of her arm toward the boxes.

" 'But the people!' I exclaimed.

" 'They are inside.'

" 'But I—I—there's something wrong!' I stammered. 'Those things are no city, and they couldn't hold ten people apiece!'

" 'They hold only one apiece,' she informed me with dignity.

"I was completely flabbergasted. 'Then—then your total population is—'

" 'Just thirty-six, out here; or, rather, thirty-five, for one of us has just died.'

"I thought I saw the catch. 'But how many have you that aren't out here?'

" 'Just us younger ones—four, including myself,' she answered simply. She added, 'And, of course, the two who are not yet born.'

"All before this had turned my head; her last statement came near turning my stomach. Clutching at straws, I blurted out, 'But this is just a small community; the chief centers of your population lie elsewhere?'

" 'No,' she corrected levelly, 'this is the only center of our civilization. All human beings are gathered here.' She fixed me with her dry gaze. 'How primitive you are!' she said, as a zoologist might, looking at a threadworm. 'I see that you expected numbers, mere numbers. But I suppose that a comparative savage like you might be expected to prefer quantity of life to quality of life.

" 'We have here quality,' she went on with noble utterance, 'the finest of the finest, for ten thousand generations. Nature has need of quantity in her lower orders, but in allowing the perfection of such towering supermen as are my friends out here she has indulged in the final luxury of quality.

" 'Nor is that all. With quality we have at last achieved simplicity;

and in the apotheosis of humanity these two things are the ultimates.'

"All I could do was mumble that simplicity was too weak a word."

Frick stopped here, laughed, and rose. "She had my mind down and its shoulders touching! And from that moment—I assure you, my friends—the whole thing began to amuse me."

He took a few steps about the room, laughing silently; then, leaning with one shoulder against the wall, he went on.

"Pearl was on an awfully high horse, there, for a moment, but she soon dismounted and considered what she might offer for my entertainment. She expressed polite regret that her civilization contained so little for me to see with my eyes. She implied that the vast quantities of intellectual activity going on would be far past my understanding.

"I asked, then, if there was any way I might have a peep at their quality group in action; and to this she replied that her countrymen never came together in groups, and neither did they indulge in actions, but that it would be easy to show me one or two of the leading citizens.

"I of course told her I did not want her to run a risk of getting in trouble, but she assured me there was no danger of that. The guardians of the place—they were the three other 'younger ones' she had just mentioned—were quiet somewhere, and as for the adults, 'They,' she said, 'will be able neither to see nor hear you.'

"Well, she showed me two. And merciful heavens!"

Frick laughed so that for a moment he could not go on. Miles by now was reflecting Frick's every mood, and would smile in anticipation when he laughed. I suppose I was doing the same. We were both completely under Frick's spell.

"She escorted me openly across the field to the nearest box, and I remember that on the way I got a bur in my ankle which I stopped to remove. I found from close up that the boxes were about ten feet square and made of the same ugly yellow metal used in the big building. The upper part of each side had a double row of narrow horizontal slits, and in the middle of each front side there was a closely fitted door. I was remembering Pearl's promise that they would be able neither to see nor to hear me, so I was alarmed when without ceremony she opened the door and half pushed me in.

"What I saw! I was so shocked that, as Pearl told me later, I gasped out an involuntary 'Oh!' and fairly jumped backward. Had she not been right behind and held me, I might have run. As it was I remained, hypnotized by sight of what met my eyes, trembling, and I think gagging.

"I saw a man; or some kind of a man. He sat right in front of me, nude from the waist up, and covered as the floor was covered from the waist down. How shall I adequately describe him!

"He was in some ways like an unwrapped mummy, except that a fallen-in mummy presents a fairly respectable appearance. And then he was something like a spider—a spider with only three legs. And again, looking quickly, he was all one gigantic head, or at least a great mass on whose parchment surface appeared a little round two-holed knoll where the nose customarily is, lidded caverns where the eyes belong, small craters where the ears commonly are, and, on the underside, a horrible, wrinkled, half-inch slit, below which more parchment backed almost horizontally to a three-inch striated and, in places, bumpy pipe.

"By not the slightest movement of any kind did the monster show he knew I was there. He sat on a high dais; his arms were only bones converging downward; his body, only half the usual thickness, showed every rib and even, I think, the front side of some of his vertebrae; and his pipe of a neck, unable alone to support his head, gave most of that job to two curved metal pieces that came out of the wall.

"He had a musty smell.

"And, final horror, the stuff that covered him to the waist was dust; and there were two inches of dust on the top of his head and lesser piles of it on every little upper surface!

VI

"It was horrible; but I swear that as I stood there goggling at him he began to strike me funny. It grew on me, until I think I should have laughed in the old gent's face had I not been restrained by a slight fear that he might in some way be dangerous.

"Goodness knows what all I thought of as I stood there. I know I eventually asked Pearl, for caution's sake:

" 'You're sure he can't see or hear me?'

"She told me he could not.

"I was not surprised; he looked too old for such strenuous

activities. I scrutinized him, inch by inch. After a little I announced with conviction, 'He's dead! I'm sure of it!'

"She assured me he was not.

" 'But look at the dust! He can't have moved for years!'

" 'Why should he move?' she asked.

"That stopped me for a little.

" 'But—but,' I stammered eventually, 'he's as good as dead! He's not doing anything!'

" 'He certainly is doing something,' was her dignified correction. 'He's meditating.'

"All I could think to say was 'Good night!'

"At that, Pearl turned on me reproachfully. 'Your attitude is bestial,' she said. 'I have done you the honor of bringing you to witness the highest flowering of the human race, and you act like a pig. Life can hold nothing more beautiful than this man you see here; he is the ultimate in human progress, one who is in truth perfection, whose every taint of animal desire has been cleaned away, who is the very limit in the simplicity of his life and the purity of his thoughts and intentions.'

"Not to miss anything, she added, 'He embodies the extension of every quality that makes for civilization; he's reached the logical end of man's ambitious climb up from the monkey.'

" 'My Lord!' I said. 'Here's a dead end!'

" 'For myself, I sum it all in five words,' she went on nobly: 'He leads the mental life.'

"After a little my emotions suddenly got out of control. 'Does—does he *like* it?' I blurted out. But that was a mistake. I tried, 'Do you mean to imply he spends his life sitting here and thinking?'

" 'Pure living and high thinking,' she put it.

" 'No living, I'm thinking!' I retorted. 'What does he think of?'

" 'He is probably our greatest aesthetician,' she answered proudly. 'It's a pity you can't know the trueness and beauty of his formulations.'

" 'How do you know they are beautiful?' I asked with my primitive skepticism.

" 'I can hear his thoughts, of course,' was the answer.

"This surprising statement started me on another string of questions, and when I got through I had learned the following: This old bird and the others could not hear me think because my intellectual wave length was too short for their receivers; that Pearl, when talking and thinking with me, was for the same reason below their range; and that Pearl shared with the old guys the power of tuning in or out of such private meditations or general conversations as might be going on.

"'We utilize this telepathic faculty,' Pearl added, 'in the education of our young. Especially the babies, while they are still unborn. The adults take turns in tutoring them for their cells. I, it happens, was a premature baby—only eleven months—so I missed most of my prenatal instruction. That's why I'm different from the others here, and inferior. Though they say I was bad material all the way back from conception.'

"Her words made my stomach turn over, and the sight of that disproportioned cadaver didn't help it any, either. Still I stood my ground and did my best to absorb every single detail.

"While so engaged I saw one of the most fantastic things yet. The nasty little slit of a mouth under our host's head slowly separated until it revealed a dark and gummy opening; and as it reached its maximum I heard a click behind my back and jumped to one side just in time to see a small gray object shoot from a box fastened to the wall, and, after a wide arc through the air, make a perfect landing in the old gentleman's mouth!

"'He felt the need for some sustenance,' Pearl explained. 'Those pellets contain his food and water. Naturally he needs very little. They are ejected by a mechanism sensitive to the force of his mind waves.'

"'Let me out,' I said.

"We went out into the clean, warm sunshine. How sweet that homely field looked! I sat down on the grass and picked a daisy. It was not one whit different from those of my own time, at home.

"Pearl sat down beside me.

"'We now have an empty cell,' she said, 'but one of our younger men is ready to fill it. He has been waiting until we installed a new and larger food receptacle—one that will hold enough for seventy-five years without refilling. We've just finished. It is, of course, the young of our community who take care of the elders by preparing the food pellets and doing what other few chores are necessary. They do this until they outgrow the strength of their bodies and can no longer get around—when they have the honor of maturity and may take their place in one of the cells.'

" 'But how in the devil do creatures like—like that in there, manage to have children?' I had to ask.

" 'Oh, I know what you mean, but you've got the wrong idea,' came her instant explanation. 'That matter is attended to while they are still comparatively young. From the very beginning the young are raised in incubators.'

"I have always had a quick stomach—and she insisted on trying to prove it!

" 'With us, it takes fifteen months,' she went along. 'We have two underway at present. Would you like to see them?'

"I told her that I would see them, but that I would not like it. 'But first,' I asked, 'if you don't mind, show me one other of these adults of yours. I—I—I can't get over it. I still can't quite believe it.'

"She said she would. A woman. And at that we got up and she led me to the next cell.

"I did not go in. I stood outside and took one look at the inmate through the door. Horrible! Female that she was, it was at that moment I first thought what a decent thing it would be—yes, and how pleasant—to hold each one of the necks of those cartoons of humankind in the ring of my two strong hands for a moment—

"But I was a trusted visitor, and such thoughts were not to be encouraged. I asked Pearl to lead on to the incubators.

"We had left the block of cells and were rounding the corner of the building when Pearl stopped and pulled me back. Apparently she had gotten some thought warning just in time, for in a moment three outlandish figures filed out of the very door of the big building that we had been making for. All wore black shiny shifts like Pearl's, and they were, very obviously, young flowers of Genus Homo in full perfection.

"The first was the size, but had not nearly the emaciated proportions, of the old aesthetician, and his great bald head wabbled precariously on his outrageous neck as he made his uncertain way along. The second—a girl, I think—was smaller, younger, stronger, but she followed her elder at a respectful distance in the same awful manner. The third in the procession was a male, little more than a baby, and he half stumbled after the others in his own version of their caricature of a walk.

"They walked straight out into the field; and do you know, that little fellow, pure monster in appearance, ugly as ultimate sin, did a thing that brought tears to my eyes. As he came to the edge of the walk and stepped off into the grass, he bent laboriously over and plucked a daisy—and looked at it in preoccupied fashion as he toddled on after the others!

"I was much relieved that they had not discovered us, and so was Pearl. As soon as they were a safe distance away, she whispered to me, 'I had to be careful. They all can see, and the two younger ones still can hear.'

" 'What are they going to do out there?' I asked.

" 'Take a lesson in metaphysics,' she answered, and almost with her words the first one sat down thoughtfully out in the middle of the field—to be followed in turn by the second and even the little fellow!

" 'The tallest one,' Pearl informed me, 'is the one who is to take a place in the vacant cell. He had better do it soon. It's becoming dangerous for him to walk about. His neck's too weak.'

"With care we edged our way up and into the building, but this time Pearl conducted me along the corridor on the other side. The dust there was as thick as in the first, except along the middle, where many footprints testified to much use. We came to the incubators.

"There I saw them. I saw them; I made myself look at them; but I tell you it was an effort! I—I think, if you don't mind, I won't describe them. You know—my personal peculiarity. They were wonderful. Curvings of glass and tubes. Two, in them. Different stages. I left right away; went back to the front door; and in a few minutes felt better.

"Pearl, of course, had to come after me and try to take me back; and I noticed an amusing thing. The sight of those coming babies had had a sort of maternal effect on her! I swear it! For she *would* talk about them; and before long she timidly—ah, but as dryly as ever!—suggested that we attempt a kiss!—only she forgot the word and called it a scrape. Ye gods! Well, we scraped—exactly as before—and that, my friends, was the incident which led straight and terribly to the termination of the genus Homo Sapiens!

"You could never imagine what happened. It was this, like one-two-three: Pearl and I touched lips; I heard a soft, weird cry behind me; I wheeled; saw, in the entrance, side by side, the three creatures I had thought were safely out in the field getting tutored; saw the eldest's face contort, his head wabble; heard a sharp snap; and then in a twinkling he had fallen over on the other two; and when the dust had settled we saw the young flowers of perfect humanity in an ugly pile, and they lay still, quite still, with, each one, a broken neck!

"They represented the total stock of the race, and they were dead, and I had been the innocent cause!

"I was scared; but how do you think their death affected Pearl? Do you think she showed any sign of emotion? She did not. She ratiocinated. She was sorry of course—so her words said—the tallest guy had been such a beautiful soul!—a born philosopher!—but it had happened; there was nothing to do about it except remove the bodies, and now it was up to her alone to look after the incubators and that cemetery of thinkers.

" 'But first,' she said, 'I'd better take you back to your time.'

" 'But no!' I said, and I invented lots of reasons why I'd better stay a little. Now that there was no one to discover my presence I more than ever did not want to go. There were a hundred things I wanted to study—the old men, how they functioned, the conditions of the outside world, and so on—but particularly, I confess, I wanted to examine the contents of that building. If it could produce a time traveler, it must contain other marvels, the secrets of which I might be able to learn and take back home with me.

"We went out into the sun and argued, and my guide did a lot of squatting and meditating, and in the end I won out. I could stay three days.

"On the afternoon of the first day something went wrong with the incubators, and Pearl came hurrying to tell me in her abstracted fashion that the two occupants, the last hopes of the human race, were dead.

"She did not know it, but I had done things to the mechanisms of the incubators.

"I had murdered those unborn monsters—

"Charles, Miles, let's have some more tea."

VII

Frick went over to the thermos bottle, poured for us, returned it to the floor, and resumed his chair. We rested for several minutes, and my dictograph shows that again not a word was spoken. I will not try to describe my thoughts except to say that the break in the tension had found me in need of the stimulation I was given.

When Frick resumed, it was suddenly, with unexpected bitterness and vehemence.

"Homo Sapiens had become a caricature and an abomination!" he exclaimed. "I did not murder those unborn babies on impulse, nor did I commit my later murders on impulse. My actions were considered; my decisions were reached after hours of the calmest, clearest thinking I have ever done; I accepted full responsibility, and I still accept it!

"I want now to make a statement which above all I want you to believe. It is this. At the time I made up my mind to destroy those little monsters, and so terminate Genus Homo, I expected to bring Pearl back to live out her years in our time. That was the disposition I had planned for her. Her future did not work out that way. To put it baldly, Mother Nature made the most ridiculous ass of all time out of me; but remember, in justice to me, that the current of events got changed *after* my decision.

"I have said that Pearl took the death of the race's only young stock in her usual arid manner. She certainly did; but, as I think back over those days, it seems to me she did show a tiny bit, oh, a most infinitesimal amount, of feeling. That feeling was directed wholly toward me. You may ask how she could differ temperamentally—and physically—from those others, but I can only suggest that the enigma of her personal equation was bound up in the unique conditions of her birth. As she said, she may have been 'bad material' to start with. Then, something had gone wrong with an incubator; she was born after only eleven months; was four months premature; had received remote prenatal tutoring for that much less time; and had functioned in a different and far more physical manner much earlier, and with fewer built-in restraints, than the others.

"It was this difference in her, this independence and initiative, that caused her to find the time traveler, the unused and forgotten achievement of a far previous age. It was this difference that allowed her to dare use it in the way we know. And it was this difference— now I am speaking chiefly of her *physical* difference—that gave rise in me to the cosmic ambitions which took me from farce to horror, and which I will now try to describe.

"Toward the evening of the second day we sat out on the wold grass before that corroboree of static philosophers and discussed the remaining future of the human race.

"I argued, since there was no one else to look after them now, and since they could live only as long as she lived, it was clear that the best thing—and, in the event of accident to her, the most humane thing—would be for me to kill them all as painlessly as possible and take her back to my time to live.

"I need not mention the impossibility of there being any more descendants from them.

"But for the only time during all the period I knew her she refused to face the facts. She wouldn't admit a single thing; I got nowhere; argue and plead as I would, all she would say, over and over, was that it was a pity that the human race had to come to an end. I see now that I was dense to take so long to get what she was driving at. When I did finally get it I nearly fell over backward in the grass.

"My friends, she was delicately hinting that I was acceptable to her as the father of a future race!

"Oh, that was gorgeous! I simply couldn't restrain my laughter; I had to turn my back; and I had a devil of a time explaining what I was doing, and why my shoulders shook so. To let her down easily, I told her I would think it over that night and give her my decision in the morning. And that was all there was to it at the time.

"Now comes the joke; now comes the beginning of my elevation to the supreme heights of asshood, and you are at liberty to laugh as much as you please. That night, under the low-hung stars of that far future world, I *did* decide to become the father of a future race! Yes—the single father of ultimate humanity!

"That night was perhaps the most tremendous experience of my life. The wide thinking I did! The abandoned planning! What were not the possibilities of my union with Pearl! She, on her side, had superb intellectuality, was the product of millions of years' culture; while I had emotion, vitality, the physicalness that she and the withered remains of her people so lacked! Who might guess what renaissance of degenerated humanity our posterity might bring! I walked, that night; I shouted; I laughed; I cried. I was to become a latter-day god! I spent emotion terrifically; it could not last till dawn; morning found Pearl waking me, quite wet with dew, far out in the hills.

"I had settled everything in my mind. Pearl and I would mate, and nature would take her course; but there was one prime condition. There would have to be a house-cleaning, first. Those cartoons of humanity would have to be destroyed. They represented all that was absurd and decadent; they were utterly without value; they were a stench and an abomination. Death to the old, and on with the new!

"I told Pearl of my decision. She was not exactly torrid with gratitude when she heard me say I would make her my wife, but she did give some severely logical approval, and that was something. She balked, however, at my plan to exterminate her redoubtable exponents of the mental life. She was quite stubborn.

"All that day I tried to convince her. I pointed out the old folks' uselessness, but she argued they were otherwise: that usefulness gives birth to the notion of beauty; that, therefore, beauty accompanies usefulness; and that because the old gentlemen were such paragons of subjective beauty they were, therefore, paragons of usefulness. I got lost on that airy plane of reasoning. I informed her that I, too, was something of an aesthetician, and that I had proved to myself they smelled bad and were intolerable; and how easy it would be to exterminate them!—how slender their hold on life!

"Nothing doing. At one time I made the mistake of trying vile humor. Here's a splendid solution of the in-law problem! As if she could be made to smile! She made me explain what I had meant! And this seemed to give her new thinking material, and resulted in her going down into squat-thinks so often that I was almost ready to run amok.

"I suppose there must be a great unconscious loyalty to race in humans, for even in that attenuated time Pearl, unsentimental as she always was, doggedly insisted that they be allowed to live out their unnatural lives.

"I never did persuade her. I forced her. Either they had to go or I would. Late that night she gave me her permission.

"I awoke the morning of the fourth day in glorious high spirits. This was the day that was to leave me the lord of creation! I was not at all disturbed that it entailed my first assuming the office of high executioner. I went gaily to meet Pearl and asked her if she had settled her mind for the work of the day. She had. As we breakfasted on some damnable stuff like sawdust we talked over various methods of extermination.

"Oh, I was in splendid spirits! To prove to Pearl that I was a just executioner, I offered to consider the case of each philostatician separately and to spare any for whom extenuating circumstances could be found. We started on the male monster of my first day.

Standing before him in his cell I asked Pearl, 'What good can you say of this alleged aesthetician?'

" 'He has a beautiful soul,' she claimed.

" 'But look at his body!'

" 'You are no judge,' she retorted. 'And what if his body does decay?—his mind is eternal.'

" 'What's he meditating on?'

"Pearl went into a think. After a moment she said, 'A hole in the ground.'

" 'Can you interpret his thoughts for me?' I asked.

" 'It is difficult, but I'll try,' she said. After a little she began tonelessly, 'It's a hole. There is something—a certain something about it— Once caught my leg in one— I pulled. Yes, there is something—ineffable— So-called matter around—air within— Holes—depth—moisture—leaks—juice— Yes, it is the *idea* of a hole— Hole—inverse infinity—holiness—

" 'That'll do!' I said—and pulled the receptacle of all this wisdom suddenly forward. There was a sharp crack, like the breaking of a dry stick, and the receptacle hung swaying pendulously against his ribs. 'Justice!' I cried.

"The old woman was next. 'What's there good about her?' I asked.

" 'She is a mother,' Pearl replied.

" 'Enough!' I cried, and the flip of my arm was followed by another sharp crack. 'Justice to the mother who bore Homo Sapiens! Next!'

"The next was an awful-looking wreck—worse than the first. 'What good can you say of him?' I asked.

" 'He is a great scientist.'

" 'Can you interpret his thoughts?'

"Pearl sank and thought. 'Mind force,' she said tonelessly. 'How powerful—mm—yes, powerful— Basis of everything living—mm— really is everything—no living, all thinking—in direct proportion as it is not, there is nothing— Mm, yes, everything is relative, but everything together makes unity—therefore, we have a relative unit—or, since the reverse is the other half of the obverse, the two together equal another unity, and we get the equation: a relative unit equals a unit of relativity— Sounds as if it might mean something. Einstein was a primitive. I agree with Wlyxzso. He was a greater mind than Yutwlxi. And so it is proved that mind always triumphs over matter—'

" 'Proved!' I said—and crack went his neck! 'Justice!' I cried. 'Next!'

"The next, Pearl told me, was a metaphysician. 'Ye gods,' I cried, 'don't tell me that among this lot of supermetaphysicians there is a specialist and an ultra. What's he thinking?'

"But this time poor Pearl was in doubt. 'To tell the truth, we're not sure whether he thinks or not,' she said, 'or whether he is alive or dead. Sometimes we seem to get ideas so faint that we doubt if we really hear them; at others there is a pure blank.'

" 'Try,' I ordered. 'Try hard. Every last dead one must have his chance to be killed.'

"She tried. Eventually she said, 'I really think he is alive— Truth—air—truth firmly rooted high in air—ah, branching luxuriantly down toward earth—but never touching, so I cannot quite reach the branches, though I so easily grasp the roots—'

"Crack! went his neck.

"I cracked a dozen others. It got easier all the time. Then Pearl presented me to the prize of the collection. He had a head the size of a bushel basket.

" 'What good can you say of him?'

" 'He is the greatest of us all, and I do beg that you will spare him,' was her reply. 'I don't know what his specialty is, but everyone here regarded him so highly!'

" 'What is he thinking?' I asked.

" 'That's it,' she replied. 'No one knows. From birth he has never spoken; he used to drool at the mouth; no one has been able to detect any sign of cerebration. We put him in a cell very early. One of us gave an opinion that he was a congenital hydrocephalic idiot, but that was an error of judgment, for the rest of us have always been sure that his blankness is only apparent. His meditations are simply beyond our gross sensibilities. He no doubt ponders the uttermost problems of infinity.'

" 'Try,' I said. 'Even he gets his chance.'

"Pearl tried, and got nothing. Crack! went his neck.

"And so it went. One by one, with rapid dispatch, and with a gusto that still surprises me when I think of it, I rid the earth of its public enemies. By the time the sun was high in the heavens the job was complete, and I had become the next lord of creation!

VIII

"The effect of the morning's work sent Pearl into a meditation that lasted for hours. When she came out of it she seemed her usual self; but inside, as I know now, something was changed, or, let us say, accelerated; and when this acceleration had reached a certain point my goosish ambition was ignominiously cooked. Ah, and very well cooked! Humorous and serious—I was well done on both sides!

"But realization of my final humiliation came late and suddenly. My thoughts were not at all on any danger like that, but on millions of darling descendants in whose every parlor would hang my picture, when Pearl came out of her extended trance.

"I had decided to be awfully nice to her—a model father even if not the perfect lover—so it was almost like a courtier that I escorted her out on the field and handed her over to a large stone, where she promptly sat and efficiently asked what I wanted. I imagined she showed a trace of disappointment when I told her I only wished to talk over some arrangements relative to our coming civilization; but she made no remark, let me paint a glowing picture of the possibilities, and agreed with me on the outlines of the various plans I had formed.

"I was in a hurry. I asked her if she desired to slip back to my time to have the ceremony performed.

"This offer was, I thought, a delicate gesture on my part. She came back with what amounted to a terrific right to the heart. She said severely, 'Yes, Frick, I will marry you, but first, you must court me.'

"Observe, now, Miles, and you, Charles, my rapid ascent to asshood's most sublime peak. Countless other men have spent their lives trying to attain that dizzy height; a few have almost reached its summit, but it remained for me, the acting lord of creation, to achieve it. For—there was nothing else to do about it—I began to court her!

" 'Hold my hand,' she said—and I held her hand. She thought. 'Tell me that you love me,' she required. I told her that I loved her. 'But look at me when you say it,' she demanded—and I looked into her fleshless face with the thin lips that always reminded me of alum and said again that I loved her. Again she took thought, and I got the impression that she was inspecting her sensations. 'Kiss me,' she ordered; and when I did she slid to the ground in a think!

" 'There are mysteries in there somewhere,' she said when I pulled her up. 'I shall have to give a great deal of thought to them.'

"I was in a hurry! I told her—Lord forgive me!—that she was clearly falling in love with me! And within herself she found something—I can't imagine what—that encouraged the idea. I struck while the iron was—well, not at absolute zero.

" 'Oh, come on,' I urged her. 'You see how we love each other; let's get married and get it over with.'

" 'No, you'll have to court me,' she answered, and I'll swear she was being coy. 'And court me for a long time, too,' she added. 'I found out all about it, in your time. It takes months.'

"This was terrible! 'But why wait? Why? We love each other. Look at Romeo and Juliet! Remember?'

" 'I liked that young man Rudy better,' she came back at a tangent.

" 'You mean the man in the nightclub?' I asked.

" 'Yes,' she answered. 'He seemed to be singing just to me.'

" 'Not singing—crooning!' I corrected irritably.

" 'Yes, crooning,' she allowed. 'You croon to me, Frick.'

"Imagine it! Me, of all people; she, of all people; and out in the middle of that field in broad daylight!

"But did I croon? I crooned. You have not seen me at the heights yet!

" 'More,' she said abstractedly. 'I think I feel something.'

"I crooned some more.

" 'Something with love and above in it,' she ordered.

"I made up something with love and above in it.

" 'And something with you and true,' she went on.

"I did it.

" 'Now kiss me again.'

"And I did that!

"Thank Heaven she flopped into another think! I escaped to the woods while she was unconscious, and did not see her again till the next day.

"My friends, this was the ignoble pattern of my life for the two weeks that followed.

"I suffered; how I suffered! There I was, all a-burning to be the author of a new civilization, luxuriating in advance at thought of titanic tasks complete; and there she was, surely the most extraordinary block to superhuman ambition that ever was, forever chilling my ardor, ruthlessly demanding to be courted! I held hands with her all over that portion of time; I gazed into her eyes at the tomb of old Hydrocephalus himself; I crooned to her at midnight; and I'll bet that neighborhood was pitted for years in the places she suddenly sat down to meditate on in the midst of a kiss!

"She had observed closely—all too closely—the technique of love overtures here in our time; and noted particularly the effect on the woman, so she must needs always be going off into a personal huddle to see if, perhaps, she was beginning to react in the desired manner!

"Ah, there was brains! How glad I am that I'm dumb!

"I began to lose weight and go around tired. I saw that our courtship could go on forever. But she saved me with an idea she got out of one of those novels she had read. She told me one rainy morning, brightly, that it might be a good thing if we did not see each other for a couple of months. She had so very, very much to think over, and, incidentally, how sorry she was for her poor countrymen who had died without dreaming life could hold such wealth of emotional experience as she had accumulated from me!

"By then I was as much as ever in a rush to get my revised race off under their own power, but I was physically so exhausted that my protests lacked force, and I had to give in. So we made all arrangements and had our last talk. It was fully understood that I was to come back in two months and take her as my bride. She showed me how to operate the traveler. I set the controls, and in a matter of a minute I was back here in this room.

"But I tricked her. That is, in a sense. For I didn't wait two months. The idea occurred to me to straddle that period in the traveler—so in only another minute I was materializing in the time two months away that I was to call back and claim her! I was thankful for that machine, for the long ordeal had left my body weak and my nerves frazzled, and I don't know how I could have stood so long a delay. You see, I was in such a hurry!

"Ah, had I known! The catastrophe was already upon me! Note its terrible, brief acceleration!

"When I arrived, all was exactly as before. The great building was as dusty, the community as deserted, the block of cells just as morbid as when I left. Only the fields had changed. I found Pearl sitting before the tomb of Hydrocephalus, meditating.

" 'I'm surprised to find you back so soon,' were her words of greeting. 'It seemed only a week.'

" 'Did you have a good time, my Pearl-of-great-price?' I asked tenderly. (She had come to insist on that name. Once, near despair, I had used it with a different meaning, and afterward she required me to lash myself with it whenever I addressed her.)

" 'It was a period of most interesting integration,' she replied. 'In fact, it has been a precious experience. But I have come to realize that we were hasty in terminating the noble lives of my fellow men.'

"This was ominous! I made her go for a walk in the fields with me. Three times on the way out she found things I lightly mentioned to be problems requiring immediate squatting and meditating!

"I sensed that this was the crisis, and it was. I threw all my resources into an attempt to force immediate victory. I held her hands with one of mine, hooked my free arm around her waist, placed my lips to hers and crooned, 'Marry me right now, darling! I can't wait! I love you, I adore you, I am quite mad over you!'—and damn it, at the word mad she squatted!

"I picked her up and tried it again, but like clockwork, on the word mad she went down again. Oh, I was mad over her, all right!

"I was boiling! You see, I had to hurry so! She was changing right under my nose!

"I fairly flew back to the time machine. I was going to learn once and for all what my future with regard to a potential human race was to be. I set its dials one year ahead.

"This time I found Pearl in the vacant cell. She was distinctly older, dryer, thinner, and her head was larger in size. She sat on the dais as had the others; and there was a light dust on her clothing—

" 'It is strange that you should come at this moment,' she said in a rusty voice. 'I was thinking of you.'

"With the last word she closed her eyes—so she should not see me, only think of me. I saw that the food box was full. Despair in my heart. I went back to the traveler.

"For a long time I hesitated in front of it. I was close to the bottom. The change had happened so quickly! To Pearl it took a year, to me, only an hour; yet her acts were as fixed, her character as immutable, as if they had been petrified under the weight of a millennium.

"I nerved myself for what I had to do. Suddenly, recklessly, I jumped on the traveler, set it for seventy years ahead, and shot forth into time.

"I saw Pearl once more. I hardly recognized her in the monster who sat on the dais in her cell. Her body was shriveled. Her head had grown huge. Her nose had subsided. Her mouth was a nasty, crooked slit. She sat in thick dust, and there was an inch of it where there had once been brown hair, and more on every little upper surface.

"She had a musty smell!

"She had reverted to type. She had overcome the differentness of her start and was already far down the nauseating road which over-brained humanity has yet to go.

"As I stood looking at her, her eyelids trembled a little, and I felt she knew I was there. It was horrible; but worse was to come. The mouth, too, moved; it twisted; opened; and out of it came an awful creak.

" 'Tell me that you love me.'

"I fled back to my time!"

IX

Frick's long narrative had come to a close, but its end effect was of such sudden horror that Miles and I could not move from the edges of our chairs. In the silence Frick's voice still seemed to go on, exuberant, laughing, bitter, flexing with changing moods. The man himself sat slumped back in his chair, head low, drained of energy.

We sat this way long minutes, each with his thoughts, and each one's thoughts fixing terribly on the thing we knew Frick was going to do and which we would not ask him not to do. Frick raised his head and spoke, and I quivered at the implication of his words.

"The last time she had food for only five years," he said.

Out of the depths of me came a voice, answering, "It will be an act of mercy."

"For you," Frick said. "I shall do it because she is the loathsome last."

He got up; fixed us in turn with bitter eyes.

"You will come?" he asked.

We did not answer. He must have read our assent in our eyes. He smiled sardonically.

He went over to the door he had pointed out, unlocked it with a key from his pocket, pulled its heavy weight open, entered, switched on a light. I got up and followed, trembling, Miles after me.

"I had the traveler walled up," Frick said. "I have never used it since."

I saw the machine. It was as he had described it. It hung in nothingness two feet off the floor! For a moment I lacked the courage to step on, and Frick pushed me up roughly. He was beginning to show the excitement which was to gather such momentum.

Miles stepped up promptly, and then Frick himself was up, hands on the controls. "Don't move!" he cried—and then the room was dim goldenness, then nothing at all, and I felt permeated with fathomless silence.

Suddenly there was the goldenness again, and just as suddenly it left. We were in a small dark room. It was night.

I wondered if she knew we were coming.

We went to her silently, prowlers in infinity, our carpet the dust of ages. A turn, a door—and there was field land asleep under the pale wash of a gibbous moon. A walk, a turn—and there were the thirty-six sepulchers of the degenerate dead. One not quite dead.

I was as in a dream.

Through the tall grass we struck, stealthily, Frick in the van like a swiftstalking animal. Straight through the wet grass he led us, though it clung to our legs as if to restrain us from our single purpose. Straight in among those silent sepulchers we went. Nature was nodding; her earth stretched out everywhere oblivious; and the ages to come, they did not care. Nor cared the mummied tenants of each tomb around us. Not now, with their heads resting on their ribs. Only Frick did, very much. He was a young humanity's agent before an old one's degradation. Splendidly, he was judge and executioner.

He slowed down before the sepulcher where was one who was yet alive. He paused there; and I prayed. An intake of breath, and he pulled open the door and entered. Dreadfully, Miles, then I, edged in after.

The door swung closed.

The tomb was a well of ink. Unseen dust rose to finger my throat. There was a musty smell! I held my breath, but my heart pounded on furiously. Ever so faintly through the pressing silence I heard the pounding of two others.

Could it be possible that a fourth heart was weakly beating there?

Faint sounds of movement came from my left. An arm brushed my side, groping. I heard a smothered gasp; I think it was from Miles. Soon I had to have air, and breathed, in catches. I waited, straining, my eyes toward where, ahead, there might have been a deeper blackness through the incessant gloom.

Silence. Was Frick gathering courage? I could *feel* him peering beside me there, afraid of what he had to see.

I knew a moment when the suspense became intolerable, and in that moment it was all over. There was a movement, a scratch, a match sputtered into light; for one eternal second I looked through a dim haze of dust on a mummied monstrosity whose eyelids moved!—and then darkness swept over us again, and there was a sharp crack, as of a broken stick, and I was running wildly with Death itself at my heels through that graveyard of a race to the building where lay our traveler.

In minutes we were back in our own time; in a few more Frick had blown up the traveler and I was out of the laboratory making for the Sound, sharp on my mind, as I went, the never-to-be-forgotten picture of Miles as he had raced behind me blurting, "She blinked! Oh, she blinked!" and that other, striding godlike in the rear, a little out of his head at the moment, who waved his arms over that fulfilled cemetery and thundered,

"Sic transit gloria mundi!"

Illustrated by Elliot Dold

Now it seemed that he had skipped forty years! Four and forty—four was the square of two—and the universe was a union of four dimensions—

The Time Decelerator

By A. Macfadyen, Jr.

In the month of January, in the year 1935, Dr. George Kirschner said, "One of the crumbs which men have managed to extract from relativity and get into their custom-clogged heads is the idea that a moving clock runs slower than when at rest. Specific values may be computed with the Lorentz correction, and at the velocity of light a second would never end. Since time, as we know it, is really change or causality, and since a clock merely measures the rate of change, what is meant is that the rate of change is a function of the velocity of the system referred to.

"Thus a quantity of Radium A, at low velocities, has a half-life period of three minutes. At 161,000 miles per second, its period would be six minutes, and at the velocity of light the period would be infinite; the radium would never decay. Thus the speed of physical processes and events varies with the velocity of the reference system. This is true of living processes, of course. If a man were to travel at the velocity of light he would never die—"

In June he said, "The discovery, by mass spectrum analysis, that mass was a function of motion, upset the classical dictum that gravitation was a function of mass. And the view of Einstein and others that distances varied with the velocity of the observer similarly threw light on the previously unquestioned principle that gravitation varied inversely as the square of the distance.

"From these premises Einstein made the deduction that motion and gravitation are exactly and ultimately equivalent, that the phenomena each give rise to are wholly identical. Consequently, time is a function, not only of motion, but of gravitation also, and the speed of a chemical reaction, for instance, varies inversely as the intensity of the gravitational field in which the reaction takes place.

Johnny, do you remember what I said months ago? Then, under the influence of a suitable gravity field, a man would never die—"

In January 1936 he said, "The control must be independent of the G-field, or it will be subject to the lengthening of the time interval also. You'd go up, Johnny, and never come down— What's the answer?"

In February, Dr. Johnny Latimer, the one to whom all these remarks had been addressed, and the only other person now present in the big laboratory, frowned again at the strange device which had occupied their attention for thirteen months.

The rigid, welded framework of steel tubing formed a hemisphere fully ten feet across the flat top, or diameter, and, mounted into complicated mass of cross braces, struts and supporting members, was an equally complex assembly of electrical apparatus.

There had been no room for the thing on any of the benches, so a space had been cleared for it on the floor, and it rested there on its six air wheels, like the top of an inverted mushroom. He let his glance move among the coils, valves, huge condensers and transformers, and found the maze familiar, now. There was the seat in the center of the top, a nice comfortable seat with pneumatic cushions, and the complex switchboard mounted in a semicircle about it.

On the board were devices which showed the state, at any instant, of any of the dozens of separate mechanisms which combined into the entire machine. There were potentiometers, ammeters, and switches inserted into the many separate circuits; pyrometers to indicate the temperatures of the huge oscillator tubes, and, most important of all, there were the dozen or so instruments which controlled and registered the G-field.

Latimer mounted the network of steel, placed himself in the seat and smiled gently at his companion—the inventor of this device. "Shall I move it outside?"

"Yes." Kirschner moved to the wall and threw over a heavy switch. Electric motors whined into life at the other end of the big laboratory. The two huge doors separated silently and Latimer, at the controls of the machine, closed a switch and grasped a rheostat. On its six wheels the strange vehicle rolled forward, passed beneath the roof, and came out upon the cement driveway, into the warm sun of July. It turned off the driveway and moved on over the close-cut lawn, its huge tires leaving no impressions on the creeping, bent grass.

Some fifty yards from the house, Latimer stopped, close to another queer device resembling a complex searchlight, but that the huge parabolic reflector was built not from silvered metal, but from many-strand copper wire.

As Kirschner examined this other device once more, Latimer turned in his seat and stared again at the low, rambling white house to which his companion had retired three years previously, there to pursue independent research in chemistry with Latimer as his chief assistant.

Exactly why Kirschner had left the university, the engineer still was not sure. His patents brought him an enormous income; yet it barely covered his research expenses. It was true that there were no classes to take up a small fraction of his time, yet there was also no convenient board of trustees, who could be expected to grant any appropriation within reason, such was the reputation of the gray-haired scientist. But Dr. George Kirschner was colossally independent.

New York City was but twenty miles distant from this house, yet the grounds were amazingly extensive. Fifty yards away the trees began, and continued for a hundred yards to the garden wall. Beyond the garden wall was Number 9 highway. Among the trees, in cleared spaces, were several greenhouses.

He brought his attention back to his surroundings when Kirschner said, "I think we're ready." He made a minute adjustment. "Remember a hundred feet of altitude, exactly. If you get beyond the radio beam, or away from its path, no one knows what would happen."

He stepped close to the machine, reached across the maze of apparatus, and gravely shook hands with Latimer. "I think there's no danger. In fifteen minutes I'll bring you down again, and you will have known what it is like to have traveled in time."

Latimer grinned at him suddenly. There was no danger that he could see, either. He said, "O.K.," and before the older man could reply, grasped his switches.

The machine rose smoothly into the air like a silent elevator, to stop and hang motionless when the gravitational altimeter indicated that its height was a hundred feet, exactly. He looked over the side, down through warm air and sunlight, and saw the foreshortened figure of Kirschner, staring up at him.

He examined his switchboard carefully, waved an arm and called, "Here she goes!" and closed five switches, the switches which controlled the G-field, that peculiar structure of force of the same nature as gravitation, yet whose influence was locked into a closed sphere. Had the effect not been confined in this manner, the earth would have been disturbed in her orbit, such was the intolerable power generated in that relatively small mass of apparatus.

As his fingers moved the last switch between its silver contacts there flashed about that hemispherical framework and its operator what appeared to be a perfect, continuous concave mirror. It was as if the machine had been suddenly transferred to the center of a hollow sphere, whose sides were silvered with incredible perfection. It was the boundary of the G-field, forming an impenetrable barrier to all actions, and lengthening the time interval of all physical events within its radius.

An unimaginable lethargy fell over Latimer's brain. He attempted to unclasp his fingers and remove them from the last switch. From a great distance he watched his fingers, waiting for signs of the motion which should respond to the command of his brain. As he watched them they seemed to recede into infinite distance, and across a darkening void he saw the tips of them uncoil, slowly. Then his brain sped with accelerated velocity into the void, and complete darkness closed about it. The time interval of the reference system which was his body and the machine had lengthened until a second with respect to it would never end. He knew nothing more.

A hundred feet beneath the machine and its operator, Dr. George Kirschner stood, one hand grasping a stopwatch and the other the switch, whose closing would send a series of short-wave impulses to the heart of that machine poised in the sunlight, and cut off the G-field. Two minutes before he had watched the strange framework, with Latimer seated in its center, slowly fade from sight until complete invisibility shrouded it. Where it should have been, there was now merely warm air, sunlight and the blue sky.

Dr. George Kirschner frowned at his expensive stopwatch and waited—

Latimer's return to the spatial system which the earth constituted was without abnormal incident. There was simply a reversal of those events which had preceded his unconsciousness. It was a strange experience. As the physical processes of his body and of all the matter under the influence of the G-field began to speed up once more, his brain, or consciousness, headed back across that void into the depths of which it had seemed to vanish. Across a shrinking distance he watched his fingers unwrap themselves from the rubber of the switch handle, and was aware that the darkness about him was lifting.

And then, abruptly, the last darkness fled, his hand dropped away from the switch and he was sitting in the center of a strange machine immersed in warm sunlight and air, beneath a blue sky. He finished the drawing in of a breath he had begun, as he thought, some fifteen minutes before, and looked over the side of the machine, down toward where he should see Kirschner.

But he saw no Kirschner, no lawn, no house, no short-wave directional antenna.

He saw only a low hill covered with low verdure, several trees and some long, untended, ripe, green grass. About the hill, stretching to the distant horizon haze, was a calm countryside, with verdure, trees, and ripe grass, untended. It all had a strange appearance of intentional disarray, as though planned by those who desired pleasant disorder.

Latimer slapped his face so violently that tears came from his eyes. He was not dreaming, then, or was in a dream so veridical that he could never hope to get out of it. He said, "What the blue Sam Hill—" and stared and stared—

He turned back to the control board and began adjusting voltages and making connections. The machine, at its altitude of a hundred feet, sped off across the calm landscape, the air-speed indicator moved over to the thirty-mile-an-hour mark. It was possible that, somehow, the machine had moved of its own accord away from the house, and that Dr. Kirschner waited in perplexity at no great distance. In which event, how in Heaven's name had he come back to earth time?

He stared at the earth speeding past beneath him. Such a country as this he had never seen in any part of the United States. It was like a colossal, endless, abandoned garden. Over on the left something white kicked up and fled away; it was a cottontail. Latimer had never seen a wild rabbit before, in thirty years. He twisted in his seat, surveyed the rolling, tumbling green and brown, the occasional flashing white of scattered birch and spruce.

As the machine sped silently over the green hills and flats, Latimer understood what a remarkable device it was, which could not only leave time behind, but could also travel with ultimate convenience in space. The propulsion he understood; the G-field, at reduced power, interacted with earth's own gravity field, and the resulting reaction supported the craft in the atmosphere. Forward motion was obtained by allowing the craft to fall "downhill" in a straight line, like rolling on an inclined plane without the plane.

He passed over a tiny lake set like a jewel among the hills and was nearing the slopes which swelled away from its farther edge when interruption came. There was a strange high whine from behind him, and a second air machine drew up by the side of his speeding craft, keeping pace easily.

In a glance he saw that it resembled an autogiro. Spinning rotors supported it; there was an air screw on each stubby wing, invisible in strangely silent speed.

A hard-faced man with black-clad, wide shoulders put his head through an open window and yelled, "Pull up, guy! Where the hell do you think you're going?"

Latimer stopped his forward velocity, and the plane slowed with him, a dozen feet away. Both machines hung there in the air, one motionless, the other hovering easily. Latimer called, "What do you want?"

The hard-faced man spoke to an invisible companion in the cabin. "He wants to know what we want. The lug!" He spoke across the gap. "What's the name, brother? What's that thing you're riding in?"

Latimer was not unwilling. "I'm John Latimer. What's the date?"

"May fifth. Toss across your iden."

"What year is this?"

"1940. What the hell's the matter with you? Let's see your iden. Snap it up!"

1940! Latimer stopped thinking for a moment. 1940! What had happened? Kirschner should have brought him back, yet Kirschner had not. Then, how had he come back at all? What had awakened him?

The fellow in the plane whispered something and his shoulders moved. "Last chance, brother, where's your iden?"

"What's that?"

The hard-faced man jerked back from the window, and Latimer had a brief flash of a stubby thing with a ridged barrel in his hands. It kicked and roared violently, and the air about him was suddenly filled with crackling, sputtering streams of visible smoke.

Without thinking, Latimer huddled in his seat, and his hand

moved on the forward switch, which it had never left. The machine leaped away, and sped with rising speed over the green earth. There was a yell behind him, and he glimpsed lightning smoke trails in the air to his left. He slued away, and advanced the rheostat to its limit, wondering how long his batteries would last.

He looked back and saw not one, but five planes whining in his wake. They would soon be within accurate range again, for his own speed was limited by the weight of his machine, since it functioned with the aid of earth's gravity. He cursed violently.

In a few minutes the leading plane was smoking the air about him with invisible, miniature shells, which came ever closer to their mark. There was absolutely nothing he could do about it. To land was impossible, simply suicide. Nothing he could do— There was one thing! He had come back to earth time once, with the assistance of some power at present wholly beyond his comprehension. He might do it again; even so, possible eternity was preferable to certain death.

Smoke streams were spitting and crackling about the machine as he carefully closed the switches that controlled the G-field. That concave mirror flashed about him again, then lethargy fell and darkness closed in. Great fingers, slow and heavy and deadening, shut over all his movements, and there was a weight upon his brain. Then there was only an eternal void of darkness—

His consciousness struggled against a slowly lifting haze which obscured his thinking, and his eyes fought a thinning darkness which hid his surroundings. His body seemed immeasurably heavy, but its normal lightness returned after a long time; it seemed long, at least. Finally, though, he conquered the incubus, and haze and darkness lifted. Again, miraculously, he had come back from the limbo of eternal, infinite time. Some outside agency had interfered with his machine, which he and Kirschner had thought inviolate, and had brought him back to the spatial system of earth.

There was only time for this brief thought to flicker in his brain before, with a faint sense of anticipation, he looked about him.

This time he hung above a vast and endless area of small, white, flat-roofed buildings, set among streets and roads which seemed to have been laid out by a geometrician, in rectangles, squares and triangles—curves having been ignored entirely. The buildings— dwellings by their appearance—were as unvarying as the streets; all were identical within the limits of his vision; they were merely embellished cubes.

The treeless roads were bordered with the green of close-sheared grass, and there were figures walking about on the glaring white under the powerful sun and the faint blue sky. It was like an exaggerated suburb, and the eternal order and discipline had something unpleasant and distasteful about it. Definitely, he did not like it.

He twisted in his seat and stared from his height in all directions; but the city persisted to all four horizons. He turned back in time to see an air machine bearing down upon him, and caution caused his hand to tighten on the first switch of the G-field bank.

The plane sped up and stopped on invisible rotors, little changed from the machine of his other experience, save that a certain refinement was apparent, a smoother molding of the motor fairings, even stubbier wings. He felt a sense of duplication, when a window slid back and a head frowned at him.

Latimer stared back, across the few feet of intervening air, and saw that the eyes of this man had weariness in them, that there was a looseness, as of fatigue, in the muscles of the face. He spoke first. "What year is this?"

"Lost your memory?" The inquiry was slow-spoken, as though the fellow would not be surprised at almost anything. "This is 1980, friend, and I want to see your token. Flash it, will you?"

It was 1980! Latimer, little surprised now, was struck with a new thought. He had slept, the first time, for four years. Now, it seemed that he had skipped forty years. Four and forty. Four was the square of two, and the universe was a union of four dimensions.

"All right, brother." The sad-faced man was mild and patient. "Come out of the fog and flash your token. I've other things to do, and I don't want to get tough."

"I haven't got a token," Latimer said. "I don't know what it is, and I want time to explain. Who are you?"

"He hasn't got a token," the fellow said quietly to a companion in the cabin. "Flash a call, will you?" He turned back and said to Latimer, "Last time, friend. Will you show your token?"

"I haven't got one."

The weariness left the slack features, and the fellow snapped, "You damn fool, do you know what you're saying?" Abruptly his head withdrew and there was a gun there instead.

But Latimer was prepared, now. He threw his body flat and pulled at the switch. The machine leaped away from the plane and the smoky streamers which now spurted from it in jetty ribbons of death. Even the gun was the same, and Latimer wondered, as the machine sped away above the changeless and endless dwellings, if the fellow had been lying about the year, lying reasonlessly. It seemed unlikely.

He looked back and saw not one plane, nor five, but eight machines speeding with rapidly rising velocity after him. He cursed again and considered landing, hunting refuge among the buildings, and decided against the attempt, for it was an unfavorable world to be stranded in.

And so, as the machines were almost within range once more, he closed the circuits of the G-field, and gave himself up to darkness and heavy, lethargic oblivion—

He awoke, for the third time, to hard sunlight and a blue sky, and was dimly puzzled, for in three attempts the laws of chance indicated that he should have returned to darkness and night at least once. That he should have come back to sunshine and a cloudless sky, three times— He looked down and about the machine.

The strange white buildings no longer spread in duplicate over the land; instead there seemed to have been a reversal to the scene of his first returning, in 1940. There were rolling hills and flats, strewn with the thick green grass, currant bushes, scattered trees and a small lake in the distance. The cycle had moved again.

He had skipped four years, then forty. It would now be the height of perplexity if, this last journey, he had been away for four hundred years of earth time. There was obviously a factor which neither he nor Kirschner had foreseen, a recurring variable like the displacement of the perihelion of a planet, which in some manner was able to cut the field of force which they had called the G-field. Yet why should this factor move in obedience to the decimal system?

He closed a switch, and the machine started forward smoothly, picked up speed and fled over the green land fifty feet beneath. After a while he came upon an incredibly wide road, white-surfaced, and altered his course to follow it into the east. Speeding above its amazing width, fully a quarter of a mile, he examined its length ahead until it was lost in the blue horizon shimmer, eager to see signs of movement upon it, signs of anything.

He increased his speed until the wind whined through the struts of the machine, tore at his hair and whipped the laboratory smock which he still wore. After a few minutes he picked out a speck on the road ahead. At closer distance the speck become double. It was a small vehicle, mounted on two huge wheels, and there was a figure pulling it.

He set the machine down upon the white road and got out.

The figure stopped and looked up as he came across and smiled cheerfully at him. It was, he saw, a girl dressed in a light cloak and a cross between shorts and his conception of a Scottish kilt. She was tall, with wind-blown black hair, and possessed a certain beauty which he could not define.

Latimer said, succinctly, "Stuck? Want any help?"

She said, "No, thanks," and looked calmly past him, at the machine resting on the wide road. He watched her eyes scan it swiftly and intently, then swing back to him, and saw that they were puzzled and surprised.

"A field machine!" she said. "And so old that it must be the grandfather of all field machines. Did you come in that? Where did you get it?"

"I helped to build it," Latimer told her, "and I think I've come farther than I intended. What year is this?"

"Don't you know?" The girl was surprised. "This is 2380. How far have you come?"

There it was—twenty-three eighty. It was the cycle again; four, forty, four hundred. The machine, he thought, must have a screw loose; there must be a fault in it. Perhaps the radio waves which should have shut off the G-field after fifteen minutes of operation, earth time, had been twisted by some warped freak of time and space, something that built up to a potential, like the rising charge of a condenser, and periodically interfered with the mechanism.

"I have come exactly," he said, "four hundred and forty-four years—"

"Four forty-four!" the girl exclaimed. "1936— But that's impossible, you must be mistaken. The curve field wasn't developed until 2060, and the field machine is even more recent—2210, I think. It's impossible."

"That machine," he said firmly, pointing to it, "was developed in 1936, by Dr. George Kirschner and Dr. Johnny Latimer. I am Latimer, and I have come in it against my will. If this is 2380 I have skipped four hundred and forty-four years, and I would like to get back if only to find out what happened to Kirschner, who was a friend of mine."

"You can't go back." Slowly she shook her head. "The curve field operates in one direction only, as you probably know. The interval can be lengthened, but it cannot be shortened or reversed. We have had it for a hundred and seventy years, but few have ever dared to skip more than a dozen years, or less, for it is difficult to control at higher velocities. What are you going to do?"

What could he do? Latimer reflected that another leap forward beyond time might be embarrassing—it would be four thousand years this time, if his reasoning was correct.

"The G-field," he began, "or the curve field, as you call it—do you know all about it? Are you certain that it works one way only?"

She was almost certain. "Although Veblen recently has said otherwise, I think. But I don't know all about it that my brother Lenar does. He might be able to help you. Would you like to come with me and meet him?"

Latimer was willing. He directed her to the seat of the machine and perched himself on the framework, within reach of the controls. She gave him the direction. He started the machine again, and as they fled over the green land he discovered that she was Mora Kessel, university student, living with her brother, who was an instructor somewhere.

He told her more about the enigmatically accidental—he had assumed that some mishap had occurred to Dr. Kirschner—manner in which his life had been transposed across the centuries, and discovered that there was a record, to which one resorted in such matters, but which had not been begun until 2010. Yet it might contain data regarding Kirschner, since he had been quite famous. The record contained the fingerprints and other material concerning all persons born since 2010—

He discovered, in turn, that she had been pulling the vehicle, no great effort since it was almost frictionless, purely for reasons of exercise. It was not self-propelling, being a sort of training shell. She was training for something or other, some type of racing, where it was necessary to possess sufficient physical strength to withstand sudden accelerations. Sport was violent and almost wholly mechanized—

He decided suddenly to visit and inspect the record of which she spoke before interviewing her brother Lenar. He was troubled with an intense and consuming curiosity regarding the fate of Kirschner. He was bothered with a faint sorrow. Accordingly, he questioned Mora Kessel and then altered his course, heading for the nearest branch of the record, speeding across a wide river which he failed to recognize, but which she said was the Hudson.

The branch which housed that colossal monument to organization, the record, was an enormous white, flat, low building, with dozens of huge portals. They landed on the green turf surrounding, made their way past banks of enormous flowers, passed along wide walks sparsely occupied by men and women dressed much the same—in the manner of Mora Kessel—and walked under one of the arched portals, into the cool of the building.

Sunshine flooded the place from heavy electron tubes girding the walls, and they traversed corridor after corridor. Moving floors and escalators, it seemed, had been turned down for reasons of health. Health and science were the dominant factors of this year and age of 2380. Latimer saw hundreds of sections where enigmatic shelves and cabinets bore the numbers of years and months, and at last they entered a large room and headed for a distant shelf.

After careful scanning, Mora Kessel found the volume. Latimer took it, found the index and flipped the opaque, tough, metallic pages rapidly. And there it was—

George Sachse Kirschner—doctor of this and that—born 1885 A.D.—and so on. Latimer read on eagerly. Kirschner had died in bed! He had died in 1970, at the comfortable age of eighty-five, from "natural causes"! The mystery was thicker than ever. If Kirschner had been stricken during their experiment, only death would have sealed his lips regarding Latimer, still presumably hanging there in midair, in the sky. Latimer studied the ample account, in the small, clear print.

Kirschner had been educated at Munich and Princeton, was the discoverer of the proton method for curing leukemia, by killing the excess white corpuscles, inventor of the direct-vision ultraviolet microscope and the infrared device for examining the state of the moving blood in the veins and arteries three inches beneath the skin—and so on. Latimer had helped on the last two. There were others, some developed after 1937, about which Latimer knew nothing.

Puzzled, he flipped the page—and his heart skipped. There he was, *himself!* Under "Associates" there was the name, John Hervey Latimer, born 1905, educated Massachusetts Institute and so on—doctor of science in chemistry—chief assistant to Kirschner; it was all there. All but the date of his death—and the length of his term as chief assistant. In fact, the data was meager. Evidently he had not made much of a mark on the world—evidently he had never returned.

He sighed and let Mora Kessel read it, then together they walked out of the building, and set off once more for home and brother Lenar.

Once they passed over a colossal manufacturing center, stretching for miles beneath the flashing machine, a great mass of white buildings constructed largely from tempered, bubbled glass, sprawling for hundreds of acres along the bank of a convenient river. He learned that those buildings were jammed with eternally moving machines, molding and processing raw materials into synthetic food, machines which functioned in inscrutable silence, wholly automatic.

As Latimer stared down at this monument to science, he suffered a peculiar hallucination, enigmatic and disturbing. While the machine sped on over the distant hills and grassed plains, he thought he saw the sunlight visibly dim and darken, and became aware of a subdued roaring, like the mutter of far thunder. For an instant it seemed that his brain was receding from his body into an endless void; he tried to unclasp his fingers from the switch and could not—

The sensation lasted for but an instant, yet time seemed to lengthen out, and just before the hallucination lifted he caught a momentary flash of his body, as though his eyes were outside it. His body was standing with wide-spread feet and head thrown back, and there were two spheres of radiance somewhere. It was like a nightmare; nothing was substantial. He had a foot in each, and the spheres were colossal things. Blood drummed in his ears, and he seemed to be standing between two worlds—

Then, suddenly, he was back on the machine, standing erect against the thrust of the wind. He was standing there in the sunshine and Mora Kessel was there also, her strong fingers holding his right arm tightly, and staring at him with perplexed black eyes.

"Are you ill?" she asked gravely. "You stood up and seemed to be going to faint. What happened?"

"I'm all right," he said. "It was something like fainting, but I'm not ill. I'm all right."

But as he spoke he felt the stirrings of warning somewhere in his brain, and was tormented by doubt. His own time was separated from him now, by many millions of miles of airless, heatless space. There was no such thing as time. Many things had happened while he had been gone, locked into eternity, and, for convenience, men had fixed the order of their occurrence by means of a device called the year. That was all.

But there seemed to be another factor; several times he almost grasped it but the thing eluded him. It seemed to evolve somehow from the thinking of Ouspensky, the conception of time as a static space dimension, with past, present and future existing simultaneously, but perceived in succession due to the limitations imposed by the senses of the observer. The machine had been based on the effect of motion on time according to another conception—that time was simply the causal form of events: Kirschner had named it change, which amounted to the same thing.

His brain struggled with this for a minute. If time was static it was simple to conceive of traveling in both directions; if it was dynamic, merely the name applied to continuous causality, then it was difficult to imagine traveling in any direction but forward—into the future. He had simply skipped time, that was all, and had arrived at the future in a very rational manner. It was as if he had simply slept through it all.

The remainder of the journey was without incident, and finally they came to her home, a low green structure, squarish and flat-roofed. It seemed that the roof was the accepted place for landing, being braced and strengthened for the purpose. And then, as they were about to land, the haziness of Latimer's dread took on shape.

Again, darkness settled with slow wings about him, and there was a distant mutter, faint as though heard from behind a barrier. Latimer threw all his will against the lethargy which tried to stifle his actions, and his hands on the switches moved frantically. They thumped down upon the white roof with such violence that Mora was thrown flat on the framework of the machine, and Latimer heard his voice yelling, "Get off, Mora! Get off the damned thing!"

But the girl lay still, and Latimer, struggling against that darkness which threatened to engulf his senses, slipped an arm under her shoulders and picked her up. His brain was fleeing again, and across a distance he saw her cloak catch on a projecting switch handle, and come away from her shoulders. His legs moved slowly; as he leaped down from the machine, onto the white roof, he seemed to float gently through the air. But when his feet touched the yielding surface, his legs seemed to die and to be of no more use than twigs.

They could not support his body at all. He collapsed on the roof, his grip loosened, and Mora Kessel slid and rolled away from him. The darkness was almost complete and the roaring violence was like a colossal, sounding voice. Through a dark haze he saw Mora come to her feet and leap toward him, with sudden, shocked realization in her eyes.

Too late!

As he half crouched there on the roof, fighting to get up and away from the machine, there was a gigantic tugging at his body, and instantly it seemed to snatch him back on the framework of that strange device. Then darkness closed in, and even the roaring voice was stilled—

He returned to consciousness as he had done before, but slowly and familiarly now. His eyes pierced a lifting, thinning darkness, and saw that his body was sprawled half out of the seat of the machine, and that there was a well-known scene around him. The last wisps cleared, and he was able to look over the edge of the machine, down through a hundred feet of air and sunshine, and see the foreshortened figure of Dr. George Kirschner staring up at him.

The gray-haired man yelled, in a cracked wheeze, "Come down, come down, for Heaven's sake!" Then his voice broke.

Without thinking very much, Latimer manipulated his switches carefully and brought the machine to a gentle rest on the green turf, close to the short-wave transmitter. Kirschner ran up and, as Latimer stepped from the machine, gripped his arm powerfully and yelled, needlessly, "In Heaven's name, what happened? You've been away forty minutes, not fifteen! I've been yelling myself hoarse for a dozen minutes! Where the devil were you? What happened?"

Latimer said slowly, "There is a missing factor, doctor, in your conception of time, for causality does not explain the—"

And there was a driving voice within him saying, "I must get back.

I must get back—" as he held out to the startled gaze of Kirschner an object which he had brought from the seat of the machine—a cloak cut strangely from a cloth of peculiar texture and shade of color, such a thing as no earth girl wore in 1937 A.D.

But, Masoul, the intelligence we possess is to our liking, and we find that we do not wish to be considered lazy individuals with no aim in life.

Illustrated by Morey

The Council of Drones

By W. K. Sonnemann

CHAPTER I

THE FULL magnitude of the genius of Newton Ware had never dawned on me. I was aware of the fact that he was a most brilliant engineer-physicist, but I had always had a tendency to consider him more theoretical than practical. During his discourse on and demonstration of his new invention, which he had named "Cross-Rays, with Lifex Modulation," I concluded that he was not only a genius but also intensely practical.

"I can understand the 'Cross-Rays' term," I said, "because I see that you focus two rays of light upon a spot where they cross, but wherein do you derive the term 'Lifex'?"

Newton looked at me in the manner of an old friend about to divulge a confidence.

"Do you know what life is?" he asked, very seriously.

"No, not exactly." My answer was ready enough, even though I was somewhat surprised, for we had talked on the subject before.

"Neither do I, but I believe I am on the track of it. I mean in terms of something you can define with scientific accuracy, like vibrations of a given frequency in a given medium. So far, I have learned more about the frequency of vibration and its relation to electrical frequencies than I have about the medium. Because I cannot yet define life definitely, I have chosen the term 'lifex' rather than 'life.' "

Newton was like that. Even in the face of his great invention, his unselfishness and modesty made him careful lest he should overrate its value even by suggestion in the name. At once his other sturdy characteristics flashed through my mind and gave me a deeper insight into the probable import of his invention.

"Life rays, eh?" I mused, aloud. "Not death rays, and so not an instrument of war. But how does it work? Does it affect life in some tangible way?"

"I called you over to witness an experiment of the largest magnitude I have yet attempted, if you would care to see it," he replied.

"If I would care to? Proceed at once. I am all eyes."

Newton produced from a cabinet a live mouse in a cage.

"I have studied this mouse through that." He indicated a detached part of his equipment consisting of a maze of lights, light filters, screens transparent and opaque, graphs, and something that resembled a pair of binoculars made over.

"I have also studied the family cat, Puss," he continued, "who now sleeps so unsuspectingly on yonder chair. Watch both of them closely."

Newton placed the mouse on a pedestal where the modulated rays of light were made to cross when the apparatus was in operation. He then sat down before his equipment and closed a number of switches starting current to two very large lamps, an X-ray machine, an ultraviolet lamp, and a battery of radio tubes and coils. Following this, he manipulated a number of dials on a panel. Occasionally he paused for a consultation of his notes, which were mostly in the form of logographs. In a moment or two his adjustments were satisfactory, I presumed, for he grasped an electrode in his left hand and pressed a key momentarily with his right, a look of expectation on his face. The mouse immediately began to behave queerly, whereupon Newton released it from the cage.

It was a matter of several seconds before the answer to the peculiar behavior of the mouse and the cat dawned upon my mind. The life of the cat and the life of the mouse had exchanged bodies! As extraordinary as this revelation was, there was no other explanation to a cat trying to squeeze through a small hole in the wall while a mouse cuffed at it, jumped on it, and bit it. I wanted to laugh, but sheer amazement prevented me, and Newton later told me that I merely sat with my jaw dropped and my eyes popping. Finally, when the mouse began to lacerate one of Puss's ears, Newton called a halt. He captured the mouse as easily as he would a pet cat and returned it to the cage.

"Would you call the experiment a success?" he asked gleefully.

I was still too amazed to reply.

"Never mind," he continued. "Let's reverse the process first, changing the cat back to a cat, and then we shall discuss the matter."

For all I could tell, he went through exactly the same proceedings

as before, but with different adjustments. It was over in a few seconds. The mouse quivered in the cage, frightened, while Puss ceased trying to escape from the room. When the mouse was again released, Puss made short work of it.

"Now," he continued, "tell me how you liked that."

"How did I like it?" I queried. "It was most interesting. I enjoyed the experience thoroughly, I think. But I am still nonplused. And if this is really the machine that you have been so secretive about the last six months, how in the world did you get thus far along in so short a time?"

"Oh, things just seemed to work out right. The cat-mouse episode was merely the final experiment to confirm my equations in their final form. I am now ready for larger subjects."

"Such as man?" I asked, almost fearfully.

"No less a subject than a man himself, Fred," he replied, quite seriously. "I am hopeful that you might give me an idea as to just what a man might care to exchange bodies with for a short while in order to—well, say, to increase his knowledge. I need some valuable idea so that the first subject could be persuaded."

I thought this over for a while before replying. A great many thoughts raced through my mind, and I was highly suspicious that Newton Ware had already conceived the idea that was forming in my own mind.

My mind turned quickly to thoughts of life itself. Sometimes, when things go awry and there is nothing but discouragement on every side, the pattern seems haphazard and purposeless. Then some peculiar coincidence, accident, or happening turns up that seems to have such definite bearing on the case as to unify the whole of what has gone before, and one wonders whether it be coincidence or a part of an unknown plan. This was one such incident, if I interpreted it correctly.

It had been ten years since Newton and I were college classmates in engineering. Our lives had separated at graduation as we reported to different employers, and now they had been thrown together again in the small Texas town, from which we both hailed, through the operation of economic disturbances. Newton had lost his position when his employer became insolvent, and, after a fruitless search for other work, he had returned, single, to his father's home to play around with his own ideas on his own time until times got better.

As for myself, I had brought my family to my father's farm as a temporary measure to make my savings last longer while I determined what was to be the next move. I had not been long in finding it. During my absence, my father had acquired a few colonies of bees to manage as a sideline and a hobby, and I was more or less amazed myself at how quickly I, an electrical engineer by training, had become so deeply interested in those marvelous insects. In my consuming desire to find another way to make a living, I found it easy to learn that the country was full of flowers, understocked with bees, and to come to the conclusion that scientific methods and mass production could be applied to beekeeping in such a way as to make it a profitable vocation. I had determined to embark on the venture wholeheartedly the following spring.

And now this had occurred. If a man could really *know* his bees—know everything that goes on inside of the hive and its relationship to instinct and outside conditions—how much better could he manage them? Newton was now offering me such a means of really studying my bees as no other man before had ever been able to apply. Was this a mere coincidence, or—?

"I have a very definite idea," I said, somewhat warily.

Newton Ware was all attention.

"Bees. The ordinary honey bee."

"Just what would you expect to learn?" he asked. The peculiar light in his eyes betrayed a subdued satisfaction, and I knew that I had guessed the truth.

"Several things," I replied. "For instance, no one knows exactly why bees swarm, except that it is an instinct designed for the preservation of the species through the establishment of new colonies to replace those that die from one cause or another, or are destroyed. We know that we can keep swarming down to a minimum by giving bees plenty of hive room when they need it, by leaving them plenty of honey and pollen for their own use as food, and by keeping the colony supplied with a young queen so that the bees are contented with their home. Bees will sometimes cast a swarm in spite of these precautions, however, and swarms are a plague to the commercial honey producer who already has as many colonies as he needs. From his standpoint, Dame Nature's method of making two colonies out of one by swarming is merely a division of the working forces resulting in a decreased honey crop. If we could know more about the conditions or influences that cause the swarming instinct to become dominant, we might be able to devise additional means to entirely prevent it. There are several other things concerning colony life that could be learned to advantage, too."

"Would you care to attempt the experiment as a subject?" he asked, barely able to control his excitement.

"Not today, thank you. I shall have to think about it some. I have a wife and kids at home, you know. It would not be so good if anything went wrong."

"Yes, I know." Newton's manner evidenced both relief and patience.

"Now, if you are interested, let's go into some of the scientific details of this thing."

I spent four solid hours with him and learned very little. It would have been foolish, of course, to expect to learn in four hours all that Newton Ware's brilliant and imaginative mind had developed in six months of diligent effort. I could see that he had several equations representing as many different forms of life, all of them derived by complicated mathematics from one master equation. The variables were the same in each equation, although sometimes with different exponents, but the constants were different for different forms of life. Nature's constant, the natural logarithm, $e = 2.71828$, appeared at least once in each. A constant appeared in the human equation which did not occur in any of the other equations. He called it the immortality constant. In deriving and setting up the various sub-equations, Newton had had to develop the elements of a new branch of mathematics that was very difficult for me to follow, and, ten years ago, I had made A's and B's in calculus. I became convinced that his particular inspiration for the conception and interpretation of all the equations and the principles involved was peculiar to himself alone, and I rather doubted if anyone else would fully understand his work for many years to come. I gave up at last and took my leave, fatigued, and with a touch of headache.

CHAPTER II

I spent a troubled night, alternating between periods of doubt and periods of confidence. I did not consult my wife, of course. To have done so would have been to put an end to all further deliberation. Her vote would have been a most emphatic *no!*, and I could not have blamed her. I am open to criticism for not having treated her squarely in the matter, but let that drop. My eyes were turned toward the glorious prize involved. Newton had offered me the opportunity of becoming the greatest living authority on the subject of beekeeping, through intimate first-hand experience, and my ambitions were far from being dead. It was not that I particularly cared for the fame that would come to me, but that I did particularly care with all my soul for the means of making a substantial living for my family in a vocation that interested me tremendously. To emerge from the experiment successfully would, without the shadow of a doubt, contribute greatly to my success in my new vocation, for I should know what to do for my bees in their management, how to do it, when to do it, and why it should be done. I would be equipped to become the nation's leading honey producer and, quite possibly, the nation's most successful breeder of high-quality queen bees. But how about the risk involved? I was confident that Newton was a genius and that, in all probability, the experiment would go through without a hitch. But suppose it did not? Suppose I should die in the experiment, leaving my wife a widow and my children fatherless? I wondered what the percentage was, and what percentage risk of dying I should take without consulting my wife. Perhaps I should have erased the whole thing from my mind, but I could not. Ambition urged me on.

It was not until I visited the post office the following day to obtain the mail that I made up my mind definitely. An item I had been expecting was in the box, and again the coincidence factor occupied the foreground of my thoughts. I could not get away from the subtle suggestion that, once again, the means of making the experiment had been thrust into my life. The item in the mail was a queen bee in a mailing cage. I made up my mind definitely, once and for all, win or lose. A few minutes later I was ushered into Newton's laboratory.

I handed him the queen bee mailing cage that had arrived in the morning mail. It consisted of a small block of wood about one and one-quarter inches by three and a half inches by five-eighths inches. On one flat side three holes of about one inch diameter had been drilled nearly through, these holes overlapping so that there was passage between them, and the cavity thus formed in the block was covered by a piece of wire screen secured by tacks. In this cavity there were one dozen worker bees and one queen bee. The space they occupied, however, was restricted to two of the one-inch holes; the other, on one end, being filled with a special candy prepared by kneading together a mixture of honey and powdered sugar. This candy-filled hole connected with the outside world through a smaller exit hole drilled into it through the end of the block and which was also filled with candy. A similar hole in the other end of the block connecting with the open space that the bees occupied was closed with a piece of metal. It was through this latter hole that the bees had been forced to enter the cage.

"Inspect the future abode of my soul," I said lightly.

"Do tell! Just which one of these devilish bugs do you wish to be?"

I pointed out the queen.

"Tell me about her," he said.

"I intended to. I bought this young queen from a well-known queen bee breeder, because I wanted to give his strain of Italian bees a trial. Dad and I have a colony in which the queen is old and failing and we wish to replace her. Left to themselves, the bees would ultimately raise a new queen themselves, but there is no reason why we should wait on their fancies. We shall open the hive, seek out the old queen, and destroy her. We shall then place this queen in the hive, cage and all, and close it up. The hive bees will eat away at the candy from the outside and the caged bees will continue to use it for food. In three to four days the candy will be eaten away to a point where the new queen can emerge from the cage. By this time she will have acquired the colony odor, and, in all probability, will be accepted as the new queen of the colony."

"Accepted?" he queried.

"Yes. If I released this queen in a normal colony of bees she would meet her death. Bees, as a rule, will not tolerate but one queen at a time.* They would recognize the stranger as such by her different odor and would put her to death by a means known as 'balling,' in which a tight cluster of bees about the size of your fist surrounds her and literally hugs her to death. Even if she escaped this fate, as soon as the new queen met the old one there would be a fight to the death between them. But, in using the method I outlined, the bees become acquainted with the fact that they are queenless in a few minutes after the old one is killed and are ready to 'be reasonable' when the

---

* When bees raise a new queen to supersede an old one they will sometimes permit the old queen to live for a while after the new queen begins to function before they kill the old queen. Thus two queens may sometimes be found in the same hive at the same time. A queen will ordinarily live three, four, or five years if unmolested, but she does her best work in her first two years.

new one walks out of her cage. The proposition of her acquiring the colony odor is in accordance with the best beekeeping texts. Anyway, the method works, and it is perhaps the simplest one of several."

"Very interesting," he commented.

"Very. Now, if you are still interested, focus your binoculars and graphically strained light rays on her majesty and measure the pulse of her life frequencies."

Newton took up the task with an exclamation of delight.

"You're next," he said, when finished.

"Oh, no! Not yet," I countered. "Wait until she is successfully introduced to the colony. I want to be a queen bee in a normal colony and not a queen bee in a cage."

One week later I reported to Newton, rather nervously, that the new queen was safely introduced.

"Now, listen," I exclaimed. "You understand, I only want to make this exchange for a period of five minutes, and no longer. If I get back to humanity without difficulty, I shall consider a longer period of time for the next trip, but I can't learn much this time and be worrying about whether I am going to get back or not."

"Your wishes shall be respected. Five minutes—no longer."

I felt kind of dizzy as Newton turned those crazy looking binoculars on me. I didn't know for sure but what I would have a little rather undergone a major operation. At least, in major operations, there were records to show what percentage of cases for different ailments survived. In my particular case, there was absolutely no human precedent. Even granting that Newton was the wizard I gave him credit for being, I knew that the business of tampering with my mind was risky. I might come out of the experiment alive but without any mind. Good Lord! I would rather be dead! In the latter case, I at least had the present consolation that my life insurance was paid up.

My thoughts grew hazy. I wondered if I was half-hypnotized by Newton's eyes and those ungodly binoculars. Five minutes, then back to humanity, safe, sane and sound. Newton was able to manage it.

"All ready now," he announced. "If you will just step over here under the cross-rays."

I did, numbly. The intense light hurt my eyes, but, through half-closed lids, I watched him make the adjustments. Then—

I might as well have been hit by a bolt of lightning. The staggering, man-killing, terrifying jolt that I received can never be adequately described. I might say that, in a way, it felt as if my life had been taken apart, resolved into as many parts as he had terms in his equations, and each part separately treated to hell's fire and brimstone. It was over in an instant, however, and the pain was gone.

CHAPTER III

Things seemed so strange. I was different. I struggled to place myself—to raise my hands to my face to see if I was still here, or somewhere else, and I found that there was no physical response to my will. Then, suddenly, I realized that that which I had expected to happen had actually occurred. My own single unit of human intelligence, that which I call I, was now bound up in the physical confines of a queen bee! In spite of the fact that I had expected it, it was a staggering thought to find that I actually was an insect. I had no hands, and no face to raise them to. Merciful heavens!

These thoughts occupied but a moment before the physical senses of the queen bee's body that I now occupied began to make themselves more manifest. There was a sense of hearing that I recognized as such, and a sense of feeling. Struggling to forget the turmoil in my consciousness, I concentrated on these senses to more thoroughly interpret the impulses to my brain.

There was a slight buzz about me. I had thought so at first, half-consciously, and now I was sure of it. And—why, yes, there were a number of worker bees massaging my body with their mandibles. One was even offering me food.

Here, indeed, was a real problem. How was I to take that food? The human impulse to open my mouth failed entirely, for I had no human mouth to open. It was at once apparent that I must endeavor to establish controlling contact with the nervous system of my new body in order to govern it. How could I? While debating the problem, I attempted to shift my position slightly, much as a human does when he is uncomfortable, or fidgety, and I found to my delight that four of my legs moved. The return impulses that told me that I had moved by means of my legs seemed to reveal the key to the situation in a manner very difficult to describe. It seemed that I must first become cognizant of the parts to be moved, and realize a sense of possession. In a moment, I had fluttered my wings. With the greatest delight in this success and an incomparable spirit of adventure, I concentrated on my mouth parts. In a moment I was fully aware of them and what they felt like, and I had extended my proboscis to sip up the food offered me.

At the same time that I was assuming control of my physical attributes I was also unconsciously becoming more closely attuned with instincts that seemed inseparably bound up in the queen bee's body. Even though I was already aware of the functions of a queen bee in the colony as a matter of human knowledge, I now became aware of these functions and duties from the standpoint of the bee. It dawned upon me that I had entered the body of the queen during a normal rest period during which she takes food and rests, and that the rest period was about over. The offering of food that I had received had been the last of several, and, now that it was consumed, I was expected very shortly to be up and about the business of laying eggs for the maintenance of the colony population. Holy, jumping Jehosophat! I, a man, expected to lay eggs! Oh, well, it was a part of the bargain, and it would perhaps be instructive to me at that.

With what was now an almost perfect control over my physical equipment, I set about my duties. Forgetting human will, I gave myself over to queen bee instinct and progressed over the combs, laying eggs in cells prepared to receive them as the urge came. It was rather an easy job, with no hurry, no fretting, and everywhere a circle of worker bees to pay me homage as I passed them on the combs. I paused once in my labors to observe the pollen dance of a worker bee, and again to observe the nectar* dance of another, those peculiar dances they perform to announce the finding of a new supply in the field. After all, the whole experiment was full of romance and adventure.

It seemed to me that I had been engaged in laying eggs for only a very short period of time when the next rest period occurred. I felt a faint foreboding, but I was tired and felt the need of nourishment,

---

* Nectar is the raw material from which honey is made. It is the secretion of nectaries on honey plants, these nectaries not necessarily being located only in the blooms. As gathered, it is highly diluted with water. The bees evaporate the excess water from the nectar by thorough ventilation of the hive as a part of the ripening process. When thoroughly ripened into honey, the cells containing it are sealed with a capping of wax.

and paid it no heed. The rest period was about half over when, as I was becoming refreshed, the truth of the matter shot through me in its sickening entirety. The working periods of the queen bee cover a span of about twenty-five minutes! Good Lord! What had happened to Newton and his apparatus? I was to be here only five minutes! I knew that nothing in the world that he was capable of controlling would have prevented him from carrying out his pledged word to me; consequently I was certain that some dire catastrophe had overtaken him, and he was unable to return me to my own body. My wife and children—everything that I held dear upon the earth that I had, to all practical purposes, departed from—passed in instant review before my mind. The awful realization that some terrible mishap had prevented the successful completion of the experiment sapped my strength away.

CHAPTER IV

It was the following day before I could gather the remnants of my horror-stricken mind together to do any ordered thinking. I knew then that it was a day later—the night period having come and gone—and I furthermore knew that any ordinary accident that could have happened to Newton's apparatus, save possibly the breakage of the X-ray tube, could have been repaired by this time and I would have been returned. Some kind of premonition told me that I would never escape from the hive alive, and yet my saner reason told me that it was possible that the X-ray tube had broken, and that in a matter of a few days it could be replaced. I pinned my faith to this hope and set about making the best of the conditions in which I found myself.

It seemed logical to me to begin with a study of my own capabilities and my place and powers in the life of the colony. Almost immediately, in this more relaxed mental state, I discovered that a sense, granted me in my new physical equipment, was of considerable importance, and somewhat of a nature that humanity would call a sixth sense. The organs located in my antennae, those delicate little "feelers" that emanate from the head, were the means by which this sense was manifest. I relaxed still more, giving myself over as much as possible to the full play of this sense, and was delighted. It seemed double in nature, although I could never be sure whether this was the case, or if there were two distinct senses. At any rate, there was a sense of location. (I recalled having observed, when still in human form, that I had almost never seen a bee leave the hive for a flight in the fields without first stroking her antennae with her first pair of legs. At the time I had assumed that she was getting her "homing instinct" into play—"oiling up the direction finder," as I was wont to put it. This sense of location appeared to be very efficient, and I realized that the defective sense of sight granted me was of small importance by comparison. Without being aware of it, I had been utilizing this sense in making my way about the combs as well as if I had been guided by my human eyes and the broad light of day.

My admiration of this phase of sixth sense, which I shall hereafter speak of as "location," was suddenly interrupted by the manifestation of the second phase, which was a means of communication between individuals. Without sound, of producing which a bee is capable, and without hearing, of which a bee is capable, I was being addressed through this phase of my sixth sense. I was not being *spoken* to, and yet I know of no better way to describe the transference of thought from one individual to another than to speak of it in this narrative as though so many words had been spoken.

"The nectar is good, Masoul. The nectar is bounteous, Masoul. There is plentiful pollen. Let the life of the city wax strong, Masoul. Let us raise brood to raise more brood."

Sixth sense told me that I was being addressed by two workers, one an older bee with not many more days to live, and another younger bee. And, I reflected instantly, my name must be "Masoul." Probably I interpreted the meaning of the thought sense as such because I was the soul of the colony, being the mother of all.

"More eggs you would have, Owo?" I said.

"More eggs in the empty cells. It is good to fill all empty cells with eggs of the Owo. But, O Masoul, be sparing of the eggs for the drone.* Just a few of the drones. Our city is now beautiful with many drones. O Masoul, is it good?"

"It is good, Owo," I replied.

Something about it all seemed so droll that I would have laughed if I could, and yet it was utterly serious. I resolved upon an experiment.

"There will be more food for me if I lay more eggs, Owo?" I asked.

* The male bee.

"The food will be good. It will be plenteous, Masoul."

"That is good. But, Owo, please instruct my nurse bees that, while I find the nectar from the mesquite and the pollen from the goldenrod go to make a delightful food, I would like a dessert of royal jelly." *

The experiment was successful from the standpoint of demonstrating a point. I knew, without question, that the thought had emanated from me through sixth sense. I also knew that it had not properly registered in the consciousness of the worker bees. They were creatures of some intelligence, but which intelligence was dominated by the binding chains of instinct. Instinct told them to feed the queen a predigested food of pollen and honey and they could do no other way. They could not vary the proportions, nor could they produce royal jelly for my consumption. Royal jelly would never be produced except under the stimulus of a developing queen cell in the hive.

"There will be plenteous food for Masoul," was the reply, and that settled that. I had learned that any attempt to change the routine of life in the colony would be beset with difficulties.

The days began to pass in dreary succession. The only diversion granted to me was to think, and because that process was usually far from being pleasant, there were long periods when I was practically nothing but a machine. I laid the eggs the colony demanded, and it is doubtful in my mind if ever a natural queen laid eggs in such symmetrical patterns, or skipped so few cells as she progressed over the combs.

Occasionally, however, I found myself thinking fast and furiously, usually raging against my fate and the loss of all connection with those I held dear on earth. Self-abasement was often a prominent note in these mental sprees, and each left me a bit more discouraged and dejected. There seemed to be no hope of improving my condition. Even my greater intelligence apparently would not allow me to speed up to any appreciable degree the processes of evolution so that I might effect any changes. As a matter of fact, I was not able

---

* A white, jellylike substance secreted by nurse bees, which is used to feed those larvae which are intended to develop into queen bees. Chemical analyses of the foods given to queen larvae, worker larvae, and drone larvae show that they differ materially in the relative percentages of proteid, fat, and sugar. The nurse bees must have a diet of both honey and pollen in order to produce these foods.

to conceive any changes that I would like to make, that would in any wise alter the fact that, after all, I was queen bee, doomed to exhaust the vitality of my body in the laying of eggs, until age overtook me and death came. Furthermore, I was unable to conceive any means of my own by which I might be returned to humanity. I did not blame Newton for his failure to return me to my own body, but I would desperately have liked to know what had happened. In my discouragement and despair, I relaxed into a state of tired, dull, half-conscious dreaming, allowing queen bee instinct full control in governing my actions.

Then came the havoc. What kind of mental reaction, if any, is produced in the brain of a normal bee by the smell of pungent smoke I did not know or care. With me, it wreaked destruction. The first blast of smoke welled up through the hive and strangled me. The fact that I knew what the smoke was for was no consolation. I knew that a man was about, and there was no doubt in my mind but that the man was my own father. I remembered instantly that he always smoked the bees far more than I did, and I despised him for it on the instant. He knew that smoke takes the fight out of bees that would have stung him, and that these bees, instead of stinging, become demoralized, and start gorging themselves on honey from uncapped cells. Another blast of smoke surged up through the hive to deal me misery, and I fretted and fumed and swore. Forgetting for the moment that the smoke at the entrance was only preparatory to opening the hive, I dashed madly for the top, only to be greeted by the full benefits of a hot, strangling blast as the cover was lifted. Memory returned, and I sought fresh air at the bottom and near the entrance, where fanning bees were laboring to clear the hive of smoke.

It seemed to me that the examination of the colony must have lasted for fifteen minutes. There was no robbing of the hive. It seemed that my father was merely looking things over to see how the colony was getting along. One by one, the frames of comb were lifted from the hive, examined, and replaced. I recalled that in days gone by, when we had worked together in these examinations, we always kept a sharp look-out for the queen to see that she had not been accidentally killed on the last examination, and I knew that he was looking for me. I did not wish tc be seen, for I was in no mood for any closer contact with a human and his terrible smoke than could be avoided. I managed to avoid the frames that were lifted for examination, and to lose myself always in the largest group of bees that could be found. If my father wanted to know that the queen was still alive and healthy, he could determine that by looking for eggs. At the end, the hive was closed, and I breathed a sigh of relief.

The excited activity of the worker bees in clearing the hive of the last vestiges of smoke was efficient and orderly, and accomplished results in a remarkably short time. It was an hour or so, however, before the usual colony activities were resumed, for, on the first blast of smoke, instinct had caused vast numbers of the bees within the hive to gorge themselves on honey from the uncapped cells. Instinct had told them that there was trouble; that they might lose the last drop of the sweet fluid; and that they would need all they could hold, a supply sufficient to last for several days with which to make a fresh start. Time was required for the scare to pass away and for these bees to disgorge themselves. During this time I was left to my own devices.

It was perhaps best that little attention was paid to me, for I was experiencing the utmost in mental turmoil and agitation. I am quite unable to explain just how those strangling fumes worked the change in me that they did, but the fact remains that my outlook on my life in its present conditions was considerably changed. Previously, I had been human in a different form; now, I found that I was neither human in mind nor yet entirely bee. I might say that my mentality was brought more in accord with the self-preservation instincts that are typical of the bee, and that my human intelligence went through a change which did not erase its ability to reason, but which threw its sympathies with the bees more than with humanity. The terrible discomfort I had suffered had removed from me in some way the last vestiges of human emotion, and I can say now, though with regret, that love for my family did not exist. Memory of my previous emotional life was vague, and any recollection that I cared for my wife and children, or any other human, was of no consequence. It mattered only to me that I knew that I was an unusual queen; that I had reasoning powers that were now diabolically cunning and that such reasoning powers could operate to their fullest extent without losing in any way the connection between them and the natural senses and capabilities of the queen bee body that I possessed. Along with this introspection that revealed my powers, I was conscious of the fact that seeds of hate for the robbing, smoking humans had been sown, and that I expected to use my reasoning powers to fight humanity and its meddling with our colony life to the fullest extent.

There were signs that the orderly work of the colony was about to be resumed, and I prepared for a round of egg-laying. I had made the rounds of the combs since my stay in the hive, and it was now time to begin over again, where I had originally started, where I knew that bees would be crawling out and vacating cells. With a firm step and a directness of purpose, I made my way to this section, only to find that I was a bit early. I had done good work in the last twenty-one days, and had filled all available empty cells in just slightly less time than is required for the original eggs to hatch, pass through the larval stage and pupal stage and emerge. There was nothing to do but wait, and I was suddenly grateful for the rest. I had some hard thinking to do. For the moment, I began a review of the things I knew about colony organization.

When nectar is plentiful and there is much work to do in the fields, the average life of the worker bee is about six weeks. The first two or three weeks are spent within the hive, where the worker does such inside duties as comb building with the wax secreted from her wax glands, ventilation, cleaning, standing guard, and feeding the young larvae. The remainder of her life is spent in field work bringing in loads of nectar and pollen for use in the colony. At night, when more nectar is being brought in than is required to meet the daily needs of the colony, these older bees assume the additional duty of augmenting the force of bees that ventilate the hive in order to hasten the process of ripening the nectar into honey. Thus, when the season is good, they work themselves to death. Hundreds of them fail to return each day, probably because worn-out wings are unable to carry the load.[*]

As far as I was able to determine, there was no social organization nor duly constituted authority established to administer colony affairs. The younger bees did the inside work because it came natural to them and because there was inside work to do. The older bees gathered nectar and pollen because instinct bade them do so. Instinct was the same in them all and governed their actions. The same instinct caused them to feed me greater quantities of food as more food was available in the field, and the natural result was that I laid more eggs to replenish the population. If the flow of nectar

[*] During the height of the season the population of a strong colony of bees will run about 60 to 70,000 individuals.

diminished I was given shorter rations, laid fewer eggs, and the field bees lived longer. They regarded me as a necessary item, of course, but only as an egg-laying machine. If there was any vested authority within the hive, it rested solely with the middle-aged worker bees in the prime of their lives as a group, and as instinct affected them.

It was time to make a change. I expected to take up the reins of supervision myself and control the destinies of the colony. There was no time better than the present in which to begin. Several of the middle-aged bees passed close to me and I halted them with the sixth sense.

"Owo," I said, "I have long been your faithful servant and have done well in filling the cells with eggs. Is it not so?"

"It is well, Masoul."

"I have followed your orders to lay more eggs for more brood under your able direction," I continued.

"It is well, O Masoul," was the reply. "We of the Owos know best how to direct you."

"You lack a whole lot of knowing what is best for you, for me, or for our beautiful city, Owo," I retorted. "I, Masoul, know best. From now on I am chief supervisor of all activities. You understand?"

Prior to that change which was effected in me by my terrible ordeal at the hands of my father and his ill-smelling smoke, I would not have been able to get this idea across. Now, however, I was in more closely adjusted tune with my bee instincts and senses, and the thought registered perfectly. I was delighted, even though the results were not satisfactory. The immediate reply showed this:

"It is not according to the age-old plan, Masoul. We die soon, to be followed by others who die soon. We have age. The life of the ages back is in tune with us, and we know from the ages. You must serve us as Masoul has always served us."

I knew that what they meant was that instinct was stronger in them than in me, therefore, according to instinct, they should direct. The queen of the colony, preceding me and from ages back, had been a creature of less intelligence than even the workers, and she had always followed the direction of the workers in whom instinct was strongest. They did not know that I was different.

"Owo," I replied, "the ages are dead. My Masoul mother is dead, and I am different from her. I have the ages in me, but I also have the future. I am different. I am stronger than you as no Masoul has ever been. I know best. You will follow my direction."

I had made a distinct impression, possibly because my will was strong, but I did not take time to rejoice over it. I was surging forward.

"What would you have us do, Masoul?"

"I would have you prepare yourselves to fight away the smoke and the man. You enjoyed them?"

"We did not!"

"I will deliver you from them. We will gather nectar for our own use, and not for the use of man. We will have no more smoke after a while. We will have no more robbing after a while. We will conquer man. But it will take planning and organization."

"O Masoul, if you can deliver us from man and his smoke, we shall have even a more beautiful city."

I properly understood this to mean that life would be more pleasant.

"Very well, Owo, we shall begin. You have six legs. You can count to six?"

"We can number for our legs, Masoul."

"Then I direct you to form a guard of seventy-two bees, and yet another guard of like number, and yet another guard. You do not comprehend seventy-two, but I shall teach you. Choose you from among the aged field bees the number of six, one for each of your legs, and number one leg for these six bees. Do this again for another leg, and again until you have six bees for each leg. You will then have thirty-six bees. Choose another thirty-six bees, and then you shall have the seventy-two bees which I charged you to get. We shall call this the number one company, and the first six bees shall be leaders. I want three companies."

By dint of much effort and repetition, I got the idea across so that these workers knew just how to choose three companies of seventy-two bees each. I would rather have had companies of an even hundred, but this, I felt, would require too much effort.

"We shall choose the guard from among the old field bees, Masoul."

"It is good, Owo. And I have fair reasons to choose the guard from the older bees, as you shall see. You remember the smoke today?"

"We were present, and we suffered much."

"How many of my bees stung the man? How many of my bees died?"

"But one of us stung the man. She lost her stinger and died. Two bees were crushed by his clumsy hands as he went through our beautiful city."

"Were they old?"

"The two crushed bees were young, Masoul. The stinging bee was old."

"The stinging bee was old," I replied. "She would have died soon. She lost not many days of useful life in gathering the nectar by stinging the man. It is better so. If young bees sting the man, then we lose many days of life, and our city loses. Let not young bees form the guard to lose many days of life. Let always the guard be formed of old bees who have not many days to live. Are my thoughts not wisest, Owo?"

"O Masoul, you have more than the ages in you."

"Then be about your task. When you have organized the three companies come again to me, and I shall further direct."

"We go."

CHAPTER V

It occurred to me when they were gone that I had taken a tremendous responsibility upon myself. From now on I had to perform in order to warrant the confidence I had just gained. If it required only the skill and patience necessary to keep a military organization on duty and suitably directed, I had little to worry about, for I felt completely capable of that feat. On the other hand, I was not sure that a military organization such as I planned would accomplish the results that I had promised. I had promised to free the colony from the meddling of man. If the first step failed, I must think of something else. If I failed altogether, then what? To tell the truth, I was suddenly a little afraid.

My newly found worries were short-lived. Underneath my feet a young bee was gnawing away at the capping covering her cell as she prepared to emerge. I moved away to give her room, and began to reflect upon the subject of how difficult it was going to be to persuade a company of seventy-two bees to attempt to sting a man all at once. I did not reflect on this subject long.

The emerging bee completed her task, stood for a moment drying her wings and massaging her antennae, and then became aware of my presence.

To put into words of the English language the thought that

emanated from the young bee is an extremely difficult task. In English, it almost sounds ridiculous, yet, from the standpoint of its startling effect, she might as well have spoken the following: "Why, hello, Mom, old girl. What the Sam Hill are you doing here? What am I doing here?"

Having finished approximately this thought emanation through sixth sense, the newly emerged worker was quite evidently as surprised as I, and incapable of further communication at the moment. To say that I was surprised would be putting it mildly. Paralyzed, I clung to the combs, my mind alternately racing in thought and frozen in consternation. At length I recovered sufficiently to "speak."

"What did you say, Owo?" I might say I gasped.

"I hardly know, Masoul. What is this? What is it all about? I find myself a newly emerged bee. Instinct pictures my life plan before me, and yet it does not seem quite right. Why should I be a bee?"

There could be only one possible explanation of this most unusual situation wherein a worker bee seemed to exhibit an intelligence akin to my own, and I conceived it. In haste, I proceeded to explain to this new worker my theory of how it came about with the intention of enlisting her aid in explaining to the other thousands of workers that would be emerging from now on.

I told the new worker that mentally I was human, and physically a queen bee. Passing briefly over the fact that my intelligence had exchanged bodies with an insect as the result of an unfortunate experiment that had been only half completed, I next informed her that she was the first offspring from eggs laid by my body after the change. As such, through the operation of hereditary laws, she had been endowed in half with human intelligence, doubtlessly of limited capabilities by virtue of the fact that half of her hereditary gifts came from the drone father, which had mated with my queen bee body before my occupancy, and which drone was, of course, merely a normal male bee. I told her that I could expect much more from her in the matter of cooperation, and from her new sisters than I ever could from those workers which had developed from eggs laid before that fateful experiment twenty-one days ago. Still more briefly, I explained that I had assumed control in the colony for the betterment of our lives, and that I expected her and her sisters to fall readily in line. The reason for my haste in this explanation was good, for all about me young bees were gnawing away the cappings of their cells. I dispatched the new worker to the nearest with definite instructions to repeat this story to the emerging bees as quickly as possible.

I repeated my story to a half-dozen surprised new workers, organized them into a corps of instructors, and then obtained respite. My instructors worked fast and each new bee became a recruit so that my services were no longer needed. My prediction had been correct, for each new bee was found to be half human in intelligence.

I was glad at the cessation of my labors, for I wanted to think. Certainly I must be right, but how? Another bee with intelligence derived from me! It seemed preposterous, but it was so. I had dismissed the problem as solved in my first haste by assuming that hereditary laws were responsible without knowing exactly how. Now that I had more time to think, the complete explanation gradually worked itself out in my mind.

I had entered the insect body and had taken complete control of its functions. The body muscles responded to my will, thus indicating that my mentality was in controlling contact with the nervous system. If this be so, and it certainly was, then why should not the bodily processes, through which chromosomes are formed, also be in tune with my life through the nervous system equally as well as it was in tune with the former queen? The results proved the point. Then again, I thought, the capacity for intelligence must certainly be a dominant factor as treated in the Mendelian law of inheritance and not a recessive factor. As such, it would certainly be transmitted to the offspring. Dismissing the problem as solved in so far as I had need to solve it, I deliberated upon the vastly changed circumstances.

The entire population of the colony would be of my own offspring in a few short weeks, all half human in mind, and the work of organization, planning, and execution of details would be vastly simplified. I might even go so far as to obtain advice from some of my offspring, these being perhaps somewhat more in tune with bee instinct than I, but this point was yet to be demonstrated and there was no hurry about it. There might even be some pleasure in existence now, with individuals to converse with. Furthermore, improved means were at my command for carrying on the fight against humanity. A sneering thought occurred to me that humanity itself recognized the fact that the mastery of the world was still in dispute between itself and insects, and that only by its greater intelligence did man have any show at all. Now things were to be changed. My colony of bees was fast becoming endowed with a certain degree of man's most important weapon. Ambition awoke in me. Such being the case, why should I not set my goal at complete mastery of the world for the benefit of the bees alone? A riotous thought that set my heart to pounding. Plans—plans—what a world of plans to be made lay before me.

Before evening came, with its cessation of field activities, those Owos that I had sent to organize companies of fighting bees returned to report the completion of their labors. I gave them instructions as to the disposition of the guard. One company was to remain in flight about the hive and at rest in the trees during the day ready to attack man at the least provocation. Another was to remain on duty about the entrance and just inside, to attack at the first smell of smoke, and another was to be on duty at the top of the hive prepared to fight if the hive were opened. It was well enough to proceed with this plan, even though I expected changes to be made as the older bees died and my own offspring became predominant.

The sun went down, and in the evening's twilight vast numbers of laboring field bees, which knew no other life than to work, returned to the hive. Some of these returned only to continue their labors by fanning their wings, while others clustered about the entrance, contented, resting, and perhaps thinking of flowers. It was better not to disturb them, so I called together those bees in which I took great pride, my own offspring, for a conference in the upper portion of the hive.

"Owos, you know your existence," I said. "You have been told wherein you are different from your predecessors. Are you content?"

The first few that I had had contact with acted as spokesmen, and I found it convenient to name these. I called them Mary, Lucille, Ann, and Betty. Mary replied, "We know that we are as we are, Masoul. There is nothing that we can do about it. We seek that happiness that may be granted to us in our short span of life."

"I hope that I may do much to improve your lot," I replied. "Your lot is most amazing and unnatural, even as mine is, and we shall work together to do the best we can."

"We are willing to cooperate, denying those instincts that tell us that we, as Owos, should direct you, not you us," said Ann.

"It is best, Ann," I said. "You are half as I am, else you would not see it so readily. And I shall always continue to have more experience than you, for I shall live through more than you, your days being more numbered than mine."

"It is too true, Masoul."

"Perhaps not quite so convenient, Betty. For, if my plans do not work out to perfection, I shall live through more smoke than you, and smoke is most distressing."

"So instinct tells us."

"Chalk up a score for instinct. But I mean to eliminate the smoke and to conquer man. Perhaps we may reduce the world to a land of flowers and bees in the end."

"Would we live to see it?" asked Lucille.

"I doubt it," I replied. "But during your lives we can do much."

I outlined to them the plan I had conceived of making my colony a nest of incorrigible, unmanageable and fighting demons as a first step in resisting the meddling of man. Questions were asked and answered, and I found myself surrounded by a group of bees that held me in the highest esteem.

Conferences with my new Owos were held each night for three nights, and it may perhaps seem strange to the reader that not a great deal was accomplished in the way of additional planning for future combat. The seeds of future ideas were being sown, however, for I was rather bothering over the fact that bees have to die when they sting. With my own progeny coming on, I hated to see them die even a few days before their time.

On the third day after the emergence of the first of my brood, I found myself over a section of comb in which I had laid drone eggs that first day I was in my new abode. Whereas worker bees take twenty-one days to emerge from the cells as young bees from the time the egg is laid, drones take twenty-four days, and I knew that these drones were about ready to crawl out. There was evidence that several were already in the process, and I decided to wait around a bit and start them on the road to learning. My loathing for the lazy drones would probably subside with my own drones showing signs of intelligence. I might even put them to work in some fashion.

The emergence of the first drone was considerably different from the emergence of the first worker. This drone, which I afterward named John, seemed to look me over calmly enough before "speaking."

"Masoul seems to be thinking hard with me as a subject. What is the trouble, Masoul?"

I was surprised at this comment, and taken somewhat off guard. This drone seemed to exhibit even more intelligence than my new workers, and I was unprepared for it. In a moment, however, the solution was clear, and I changed my discourse of enlightenment to this drone accordingly. I had entirely overlooked the fact that a drone bee is a development from an unfertilized egg, and that this bee in no wise owed his development to an immediate father. Such being the case, he took his heredity from me alone, and was consequently less cramped in his human intelligence characteristics than his sisters. What a remarkable situation! I realized on the instant that I might make great use of that.

In the evening, I called a conference to newly emerged drones.

"Well, boys, how do you like it?" I asked.

"Not bad," replied one I had named Paul. "We are drones, with instinct to tell us that we are men of leisure, fed free of charge by our worker sisters, and with intelligence to make the most of leisure. I advocate reorganization of colony life, with worker bees to put on shows for our benefit."

"Well, I'll be—" I burst out.

"Never mind Paul, Masoul," said John. "I think he is a misfit—a black sheep in the family. He had no sooner emerged than he started griping about the cramped quarters in his cell. Said he wished the workers would learn to build drone cells a little larger, and that his wonderful form might have experienced a fuller development in larger quarters."

"Should I decide that Paul needs attention from the workers he holds so lightly in his esteem, he will not be so handsome," I replied. "Minus a wing or two torn off by their mandibles, and with a shrunken abdomen from lack of food, his form will be nothing to brag about."

"Masoul," said another I chose to call Fritz, "I have talked with several of my brothers since emergence and we are of the same mind. We have instinct that tells us what is expected of us, which is nothing, of course, there being no mating to be done.* But, Masoul,

---

* A virgin queen takes her mating flight when she is from five to eight days old, weather permitting. She soars high into the air and mates with a single drone, this drone dying instantly in the act. On her mating flight she receives enough of the male sperms to do her for the rest of her useful life, the quantity of individual sex cells being measured by the millions. Only rarely has a queen been known to take a second mating flight.

the intelligence we possess is to our liking, and we find that we do not wish to be considered lazy individuals with no aim in life. Could you, Masoul, find us anything to do?"

"You did not come equipped with physical attributes that would enable you to do many things the workers do," I answered. "You have no pollen baskets on your legs for the gathering of pollen, and, for similar reasons, you cannot gather nectar from the fields. Without wax-secretion glands, you cannot build comb. But I think I can find inside work for you that will help the city by the removal of that many workers from those duties."

"Let us hear, Masoul."

"You have not yet flown. You will leave the hive in a few days to try your wings in flight, and make them stronger. You will note the wonderful buzz that you will make with your wings, for you are strong. Therein lies your only chance of being helpful at present. You shall use your wings for fanning, and with your magnificent wings keep the city ventilated to perfection. Is not all this a worthy occupation for you?"

"That sounds like work," lamented Paul.

The next day Paul started on a diet of nothing, followed by nothing, at my orders. He was dragged from the hive three days later by two capable Owos and left to die some distance away. I had no time for such characters.

The following evening I talked with a considerably larger number of drones.

"More possibilities are unfolding before me," I began. "It furthermore gives me great comfort to be able to talk things over with you, for your intelligence is freer from the chains of instinct that bind my Owos. Let us work together for the carrying out of my plans to make our city supreme over humanity."

"We are most willing, Masoul," said Omar. "Even though we take heredity direct from you, you are still greater than we. Dictate, Masoul, so that we may follow with the gift of your intelligence."

"Omar, your words are wise, and yet too modest. If I shall dictate, let it be with consideration, and should you perceive that which I do not perceive, then, by all means, give me the benefit of your perception."

"Masoul, you welcome free discussion with us concerning your plans?"

"Most heartily, Omar."

"Then, Masoul, what plans have you for your successor? Instinct tells me that you will live not always, and that, in the tomorrow of nectars, your Masoul daughter will mate with one of my yet unborn brothers. What shall she do?"

To tell the truth about it, I had not given this much consideration, and the question was somewhat staggering. But, for the sake of wholesome respect, I had to keep up appearances.

"A problem of tomorrow's nectars, Omar, requiring thought between now and then. I have not yet determined fully. Think about it, Omar, and give me the benefit of your thoughts."

So I successfully parried the question. But my relief was short-lived, for Fritz was as bright as Omar, and he absorbed my attention.

"Masoul, the workers of the guard die when they sting the man?"

"It is so, Fritz. It is for this reason that I form the guard of older bees who are doomed to die soon anyway."

I was distinctly proud of this idea.

"It is wise, Masoul, and your mind is great," continued Fritz. "But why do the Owos die? We have no stings, and we do not know."

"It is because the Owo's stings are barbed. They lose the stings in the flesh of the man they sting. The injury causes them to die. My sting is not barbed."

"It is unfortunate," commented Fritz, sadly. "It is not right they should die."

I was disturbed again. Something in the lamenting tone of Fritz, as he regretted the fate of his sisters of the guard, seemed to imply that he seemed to think that I should be able to remedy the situation, or that he would be distinctly glad if I could. That was enough. I brought the conference to a close for the evening, but not before appointing Fritz and Omar as my immediate assistants and advisers.

CHAPTER VI

The following day was historical in my existence in the colony. The smoke came about midday. At first, there was only a trivial attack. A few blasts of smoke at the entrance caused me dire discomfort, but they were of short duration. My first two companies of bees went into action, and twenty-five bees from the two units died from losing their stings. I did not wonder that the man retreated, but he was game, and I marveled at his courage. He returned in a short while, this time heavily dressed, wearing bee veil and gloves, and we suffered at his hands. When he was through, and I thought I was half dead from smoke, we found that robbing had taken place, and that we had lost much ripened and capped-over honey. My rage knew no bounds.

When evening came, I was an excited leader over the conference, and this time the conference was graced by the presence of a number of my own Owos selected with my utmost care. I began by addressing my remarks to the group.

"We have once more suffered at the hands of man. We have taken our toll in a measure, but he has taken his toll. The man does not rejoice over his stings, and we have begun the war. His toll was heavy, for he has taken much honey that would have nourished as well when the nectar is no more and the cold causes us to huddle together. We have lost our first battle with him, but there shall be more in which we shall not lose. It is time to carry the war to him; not let him bring it to us. Hear my words.

"Fritz, you were sad that your worker sisters die as they sting the man, and you caused me much thought. I, too, am sad. It must not be. We cannot always fight man so if our success be no greater than today. Therefore, I say, the workers of the guard shall no longer die. They shall no longer lose their stings, and every worker shall be a fighter. We shall carry the battle to the man. We shall seek him out and sting him. We shall attack him in great droves and seek to kill him. We shall seek out his woman and sting her, and his children. They cannot wear the veil from dawn until evening, and we shall kill them if we can. If we cannot kill them, we shall drive them away.

"This is my plan. My Owos will not die if their stings have no barbs. Therefore we must remove the barbs. I know the way."

There was a chorus of questions from the group.

"What is the way, Masoul?"

"The way is easy, and yet it may be hard."

My proposition was to assign a certain number of workers, say twelve, to the duty of finding a sand bed, and, having found it, to bring to the hive large numbers of sand grains for my inspection. From these, I would pick two having sharp edges of the most perfect form suited to the need, the remainder to be carried away. Having selected two suitable grains, I would then assign workers to the duty of mounting these securely in one corner of the hive where they would be readily accessible and yet obscure to the man. The mounting was to be accomplished by the use of propolis, a gummy material obtained from the buds of poplar and other trees and known as "bee glue" which is used for sealing cracks and for other purposes. It would require the utmost care, for the sand grains were to be mounted with meticulous accuracy, the spacing between the cutting edges probably requiring an accuracy down to one one-hundred-thousandth part of an inch. After the sand grains were mounted properly, the next step would be to have each worker bee in turn thrust her stinger between the sand grains and shave off the barbs. Any worker could then sting the man with impunity and repeatedly. My guard could be chosen from bees of any age, and the entire population of the colony would serve as reserve forces.

It was not at all difficult for me to sell this idea to my followers, but the matter of making clear to the workers just what sand grains are, or where they would be found, was extremely difficult. In the end I made arrangements to fly from the hive with a limited number of workers the next day, all instincts to the contrary notwithstanding, and personally take part in the search for a bed of sand.

Luck was with me the following day, for I found a suitable bed of sand in a creek bed in a relatively short time, and my accompanying workers brought back dozens of grains on the first trip. Not one of these was suitable, however, and I detailed fifty workers to the duty of bringing sand grains to the hive.

It required two days' time to find two grains of sand that had sharp cutting edges in a straight line sufficiently long, and I was heartily glad when this step was over. I had looked at sand grains with my poor vision and had utilized my sense of location to such an extent that I was most thoroughly worn out, for I had endeavored to carry on my usual duties of egg laying at the same time. Little did I then suspect, however, that the hard part was just about to begin.

Bees are credited with marvelous accuracy in building their combs with cells in the hexagonal shape, of given size, and with certain angles to give the greatest economy of wax together with maximum strength. I had found the combwork in the hive to be marvelous, especially considering those cells in which I laid eggs, and I had relied upon this accuracy of workmanship to make the matter of mounting the sand grains a simple matter. I was badly disappointed. Bees have built combs for ages, and instinct tells them how to build them well. Bees have never mounted sand grains by means of propolis for the purpose I intended them, and they knew nothing about it. Six of my own Owos labored long and hard at the troublesome task and made small progress. Time and again the mounting was finished only to be torn down and started over, either because the sand grains were too far apart or too close together. More than one of my Owos would have lost their lives in trying out these shears when it was thought that the perfect dimensions had been obtained, had it not been that my intelligent Owos were able to undo what they had done and remove one grain when it was found that the experimenting bee had hopelessly bound her sting in the shears. The first day of failure made me extremely impatient, but the following day I regained some of my patience and resolutely assigned a detail to the duty of completing the shears whenever it could, working continuously on this one job. In the meantime, I had other details to think about.

The somewhat disturbing thought that perhaps I might not win in my battle with man kept bobbing up. The fact that man may provide himself with veil and gloves to protect his face and hands and dress heavily to avoid stings on the body gave me no little concern. The man had deliberately robbed my colony after twenty-five of my guards had stung him. A thousand bees might sting him without his safeguards, now that I planned to remove the barbs from their stings, but if my fighters could not get to him, the battle would be lost. On the other hand, he could not wear these safeguards all day long and each day, and my bees could sting him freely when his safeguards were off. But what reaction would come? I could guess the answer to that. Knowing that this colony was becoming incorrigible, he would in all probability obtain a new queen from a professional queen breeder and introduce it to my colony after he had searched me out and killed me. This thought at once modified my plan of action.

Briefly, I must not carry the battle to the man until I was fully prepared. I would proceed about the business of removing barbs from the stings of each and every worker bee, but I must wait until all were my own offspring so that I might be more able to instruct them in the art of fighting. I believed that I could teach my half-human-minded bees to crawl inside the man's clothing and sting him at such times as he was heavily dressed. This was one point, but it was not sufficient.

Man is obstinate and hates to be outdone by animal or insect. My ultimate fate would be to die at the hand of man, but so great was my hate for man that I did not care. When I was gone, however, I would not be able to carry on the battle; therefore, I must plan for the future about which Omar had asked. Not only plan, but I must act now, and the action required that new queens, Masouls, be reared at once. I would send these queens from the hive in swarms to establish homes in hollow trees and caves so that my blood would not be lost, and so that the battle to last for years would be carried forward by an annually increasing number of colonies. Personally, I preferred to remain in close contact with man, fighting him until death, and I would not follow the instinct that directed that the old queen leave with the swarm. Then the matter of the characteristics of my Masoul daughter occurred to me.

She would not be as I. Being raised from an egg exactly similar to those that produced my half-human-minded Owos, she would be as they, and would have only half of my capabilities. But then the remarkable side of it occurred to me. In mating with one of my own drones, she would have offspring even better than mine, for they, taking one half of one half from their mother and a full one half from their drone father, would be, I might say, three-fourths human minded. What an idea! Let us rear a new queen, keep her in the colony for a time, and rear yet another queen from her eggs to mate with one of my own drones. Thus would be produced a queen having three-fourths of my capabilities who would produce offspring having seven-eighths of my capabilities. This fraction could be increased to almost unity after many generations, and it would not matter at all that I died. I settled on this plan immediately, determined to study new queens and new brood intently, until such degree of perfection was reached that I would feel safe in directing the casting of a swarm.

Before giving further attention to the construction of the barb shears, I personally attended to the matter of directing the construction of a queen cell. I selected the most perfect appearing egg from a large number, and directed that a queen cell* of the largest, most perfect form possible be constructed, and that every care be exercised in giving the developing larva the proper food. This work had been underway for a week, and it was almost time to cap the queen cell, when I again visited the site of the barb shears.

---

* Natural queen cells are usually constructed by the bees along the lower edges of combs or in the corners, and they point downward. Numerous queen-cell cups, which are the bases of such cells, will usually be found in any colony. When the bees are ready to rear a queen, either the queen deposits a fertilized egg in one of these cups, or the workers transfer a fertilized egg from a worker cell to a cup. From then on, it is a matter of feeding the developing larva the properly proportioned food and building the cell down to enclose the larvae.

No progress had been made whatsoever. The shears had been reconstructed perhaps thousands of times, and my half-human-minded Owos were showing a real characteristic of humanity as opposed to the bees. They were becoming discouraged. I found it necessary to take a hand, not only to accomplish results, but to maintain respect. I studied their methods and then conceived the means.

I directed an Owo to find a dead Owo and bring her back to the hive. This being done, I directed that she be dissected to the extent that her sting could be removed, and this was done. I then directed that one Owo grasp the base of the sting between her mandibles and draw it back and forth between the sand grains as other Owos manipulated the propolis mounting in such fashion as to gradually bring one sand grain up to the other with the sting between. I stood by to watch the results. Gradually, the two sand grains were brought closer together until there was no clearance between them and the sting of the dead bee. Then contact was made, and a minute quantity of the barbs was sheared off. Still closer contact was made, and every last vestige of the barbs was removed. I halted the work, directed that the grains be securely fastened so, and asked for volunteers to try the shears. A dozen stepped forward, thrust their stings through the shears, and had the barbs removed without one iota of ill effect. I rejoiced that success was mine.

Perhaps half of my colony had used the shears when the smoke came again. At the time, I could not quite account for the manipulation the man made. We had already been robbed, and we had not yet accumulated enough stores to warrant another robbing. I could only guess that the man was angry because we were intractable and was looking us over for whatever he might find. He found the queen cell, which had now been capped, and, to my extreme disgust and surging hate, he removed it. If I had been human, I am sure that I would have died of brain trouble of some sort, for my anger, rage, and hate consumed me. Not only did the smoke make me as sick as ever before, but my plans against the man were retarded by man's own hands. I cannot describe it, so the subject may well be dropped.

There was nothing to do but start over again, and I directed the construction of a half-dozen new queen cells in as remote corners of the combs as possible. I also directed that, should the hive be opened again, large numbers of Owos cluster over these cells and hide them from view as much as possible. In the meantime, every Owo passed her sting through the shears and was made a fighter of no mean possibilities.

Under the stress of disappointment, hate, and foiled plans, I lost my judgment and directed that the fight be carried to the man at once with barbless stings in the hope of killing this particular man at once. I directed that a company of two hundred bees seek out man and his kind every hour of the day and sting him unmercifully. The havoc this campaign wrought I learned about fully at a later date. My wife and my children were forced to stay indoors, but my father took action.

In justifying my action, I contented myself with the thought that I had taken it up with Omar, Fritz, and others in my council of drones and obtained their assent. I overlooked the fact that in successfully completing the barb shears, and in planning for the breeding of my successor, I had so completely won their confidence and respect that they had virtually become what humans call "yes men." They regarded me as wise beyond comprehension and thought that I could not fail. They sought to aid me in carrying out my plans rather than in looking for possible defects. But perhaps it was better so.

The day came very shortly when I realized that my father would not give up an inch in his battle with my brood. The new queen cells were only fairly well underway when he came again with the stench of rolling, billowing clouds of smoke, and dressed to perfection as a guard against stings. I was shortly very nearly unconscious, for I had never before experienced such terribly thick and completely awful clouds of smoke. They rolled about me and obscured my vision and so distressed my breathing that I was incapable of any degree of muscular activity. In this condition, I was barely conscious that the hive was being most thoroughly searched for my presence, and, in the end, I was found.

In the few short seconds when a person realizes that death is inevitable a myriad of thoughts can race through his mind. It was so in my case. I saw the approach of a bright, shining tool, and I realized that the end was near. I recalled that bright tool. It was a pair of thin-nosed, nickel-plated pliers. I had used those same pliers, in company with my father, in picking the queen from the combs that my own body had replaced. Now it was my turn! My father probably reasoned that the offspring of the new queen would be more easily handled. There was no reason why he should not think this, for, ordinarily, the bees we kept were not at all ill-tempered. He very likely thought that, while my parent stock was probably satisfactory, I was a freak that produced near demons instead of bees.

I had perhaps a split-second to think these things out as I saw the approach of the pliers. I was too weak to run or fly. I attempted to give orders to those workers near me to never accept the new queen he would introduce, but I was too late. The pliers closed on my thorax, and I was lifted from the comb.

I did not meet instant death. The principal contents of my thorax were muscles for driving my legs and wings which were attached thereto. The heart and other vital organs reposed in my long, slender abdomen, and these were unaffected. While I knew that death would ultimately come as a result of the complete crushing of my thorax, I could only suffer untold agony at the moment. When cast aside, I fell, mortally injured, in front of the entrance to the hive.

From the point where I lay I watched the activities as I suffered in silence. The heavenly fresh air on the outside, totally free from the strangling fumes I could see emanating from the smoker, was a blessing indeed, and cleared my senses. I saw my guards fight the man and was proud of them. They flew before him in droves obscuring his vision, and retired for the moment only when greeted by a blast of smoke. I could see the man wince and slap at his body, and I knew that some of my beloved Owos had penetrated his clothing, to meet their deaths in the performance of the duties I had assigned them. I did not relish the thought of dying and leaving such loyal subjects behind. I had learned to love them, just as I had learned to hate mankind.

I was almost gone when the man retired. I was missed in a short while, and a number of my faithful Owos, searching for me, came upon me on the ground. A little while longer and they would have been too late.

"Oh, Masoul, what has he done?" asked one of my most trusted Owos.

"He has killed me, Owo," I replied. "In a short while, I die."

"Then what can we do?"

"Has he placed a new Masoul in the city?" I asked.

"That he has, and she smells not right. We have tried to kill her, but we cannot reach her."

"You will reach her in a few days, and then you must kill her, even though her smell is good. You understand? You must kill her."

"Masoul, we may kill her, but he has destroyed our queen cells. What shall we do for Masoul?"

I thought a moment before replying, and when I "spoke" again, the clouds of death were hovering near.

"Owo, my faithful Owo, hear me. I laid eggs today, and in three days they hatch. After one or two days, the young hatched larva is not good with which to rear Masoul. You must work fast. I charge you, Owo, select a great many Owos and fly to the woods. Choose a hollow tree that is remote from man and hard for man to find. In that tree build comb rapidly ere the three days expire, even if it be but a small amount. As soon as this is done, choose three or four eggs and fly with them to your new city, and rear Masoul there. Take with you my drones. One of them shall mate with new Masoul. When Masoul lays eggs, come back to this city, and persuade every Owo and drone to fly with you to the new city. Carry with you all the honey you may. Rob this city for the benefit of the new. Abandon this city when the new Masoul shall lay eggs. Carry with you in your minds those things I have taught you, and carry on the fight against man."

If I had been speaking by the use of vocal cords and respiratory apparatus, I am sure that the last few words would have come in gasps, or perhaps not been said at all. Sixth sense was failing me even as I endeavored to emanate the last of these thoughts, and I was not sure that they were all properly comprehended. I "heard" no reply, for the dark clouds that were hemming me in settled closer until it seemed that they covered my pain-racked body with downy softness, and I went to sleep—blessed, restful sleep.

CHAPTER VII

I do not know, of course, just how long the reverse transfer took, but it seemed to me but an instant before I was again conscious, and in human form. I opened my eyes, cautiously, half fearfully.

Directly in front of me a few hundred feet away I saw a rather large red sandstone building. There was a helpful sign across the entrance to disclose its identity. It read, "Dr. Ray's Sanitarium." There was a large, beautiful, shady lawn between me and the building, with here and there a patient in a wheelchair with attendant nurses. Restricting my gaze to my own vicinity, I found that I, too, was in a wheelchair, and that within a very few feet there was a quite good-looking white-clad nurse calmly reading a magazine.

It was several minutes before I ventured upon a conversation, for I wanted to make sure that I would be quite calm myself. At length I thought that my poise would be secure.

"Good morning, Nurse," I said. "Would you mind telling me just why I am here?"

I have never seen anyone so surprised in my life. She dropped her magazine instantly, and came, I think, very near to fainting.

"Why—why yes! No! How do you feel?" she gasped.

"I feel quite hungry, Miss. I'd like to have a big beefsteak smothered with onions. What are the chances?"

By this time the nurse was on the road to recovery.

"Your chances are excellent," she replied, smiling. "There won't be a one of us that won't be so darned glad to see you feeding yourself that we won't know what to do. You have been the most helpless man for the last two months that I ever saw. In fact, you have been nothing more than a lump of clay with life in it, and you would have starved to death if we had not resorted to forced feeding. But come on. You are going to see Dr. Ray before you do anything else."

My rides in a wheelchair have been distinctly limited. If I ever have to ride in another one, I hope it won't be quite so fast. Nurse broke the speed limit across the lawn.

Dr. Ray was quite astonished at my instant recovery, and asked all manner of questions, which I sidestepped to the best of my ability. He became exasperated.

"It would be a great help to us if you would give us some sort of inkling as to what happened," he snapped. "It might help us some in our treatment of Newton Ware."

"Oh, is he here, too?" I asked instantly.

"He most certainly is. The two of you were found, completely out, in his laboratory in the midst of an array of broken equipment. You had apparently had quite a struggle, and we are quite sure that either you hit him on the head with some heavy equipment, or else he fell into it with tremendous force. He has been a much better patient than you, however. Most of the time he is fairly rational, but a part of the time he sits around with his inseparable notebook, studying it, and mumbling about a constant for a queen and 'a period of five minutes, no longer.' When he does that, he sees nothing, hears nothing, and looks very much as if he has a terrible headache. His trouble is undoubtedly caused by the blow on the head."

"Perhaps it might help if I could see Mr. Ware and talk with him," I suggested. "A sudden shock, you know."

"I wanted to try that."

When Newton was brought in I looked at him intently, spoke his name quietly, and continued to look at him.

It was apparent at once that my presence, actions, and voice were having an effect. Newton's eyes were perfectly dull when he entered the room, but now there seemed to be a trace of returning brightness appearing by flashes. The struggle within him went on for five minutes before the victory was won, but, in the end, his eyes became clear, bright, and steady.

"Well!" he exclaimed. "How did *you* get back?"

"I am asking you," I replied. "The queen was killed, and I thought I was dying, but I didn't. I came to out on the grounds a few minutes ago."

Newton grabbed his notebook in feverish haste and studied it intently. Dr. Ray looked worried, but did not interfere. While Newton was studying, Dr. Ray asked me, "What queen? What is he talking about?" but I paid him no heed. I was too much interested in my friend.

Ware put the notebook away with a very sad expression.

"I remember now what happened. The experiment was successful. But my formulas, unfortunately, did not tell me what would happen upon mixing small percents of different intelligences. I transferred you about 98 percent, leaving 2 percent to ensure the life of your body, while I transferred the queen only 5 percent, leaving 95 percent for you to ride in on top of and make use of. How did you get along?"

"Splendidly. I understand a lot of things now. The 95 percent was a great help. But how did *I* get along?"

"You got along horribly," he answered. "You went wild. I tried to control you and preserve the equipment, but I failed. The last thing that I can remember is that I fell violently as the result of a tremendous push. You had the strength of a madman."

"Dr. Ray says the equipment was badly disrupted. That being the case, can you explain how I got back?" I asked.

"I can remember that much. Your intelligence was not firmly bound into her body in the same sense that it would have been had you been born in it. When the body died, you were released. Since your own body still lived, your mind probably made the return trip with the speed of light."

Newton's face fell as he continued.

"But that is the end of the experimentation. There will be no more transfers. The particular inspiration for the conception and interpretation of these formulas which you once told me I had is gone, and I do not understand them. In some strange way, I seem to know that I shall never recover that inspiration."

"See if you can remember this one feature about it," I said, somewhat nervously. "Am I, now, carrying 5 percent queen in my brain?"

I thought surely that he was going to relapse, he looked so distressed, and I was sorry that I had said anything. The struggle within him must have lasted a minute.

"I am sure I do not know," he said. "You will have to determine that for yourself, if you can. Let's go home and forget it."

Not until then did we realize that we had an audience, so intent had we been on our discussion. Unfortunately for us, Dr. Ray had heard every word and understood very little. He insisted upon an explanation, and we refused to give it. He kept us three days before he would release us with a clean bill of health, and even then he released us only after I had given him my reluctant promise to send him a written account of the whole story.

My reunion with my family was joyous in the extreme. They had practically given me up as a hopeless case, even though they knew they had placed me in the care of the most competent physician in the country for what they thought was a mental disorder.

I found that my colony of bees had become so ferocious that my father had moved them to the farthest corner of the farm a mile from the house. I visited them, wearing a veil, as soon as I could with decency excuse myself from my rejoicing family.

I sat down by the side of the hive wherein I had had my abode. Bees flew about me in clouds, and I was forced to keep my hands in my pockets. In a measure, I was sad. Sixth sense was gone, and I could not communicate with them. Perhaps, I reflected, if I thought hard enough they might sense it.

"Owos," I thought, with the very utmost concentration, "please do not do it. I, Masoul, wish you not to. Do not sting me, for I am Masoul returned to humanity. I will take care of you and see that you enter the winter with bounteous stores. I will not use smoke when I visit you. You may even rear a new Masoul in your own city, and we shall work together in harmony. Do you hear me, Owos?"

The reward for my effort was several sharp stings. Several of the bees had penetrated my clothing and, with barbless stingers, were dealing me misery. I was forced to slap at them until I had killed them. I left the swarm then, knowing that I could never again communicate with them, and that, as a human, my work was cut out for me. The colony died that day as the result of poisoning with carbon bisulfide gas. I burned all that remained when the asphyxiation was complete.

This is my story as written for Dr. Ray. Since he is to read it, I may as well give it to the world. While you are reading it I shall be getting together my beekeeping equipment.

They tell me that times are getting better and that I could probably find employment if I tried. In fact, Newton Ware has found a very good position for himself. As for myself—well, I am just not interested. I am a beekeeper for life.

III

THE END

In 1937 F. Orlin Tremaine became editorial director of a number of Street & Smith's magazines; he hired John W. Campbell, Jr., then twenty-seven, to edit *Astounding* under his supervision. In the following year he left Street & Smith after a dispute with the management, and Campbell became editor in fact as well as in name.

It is interesting to note that this was the first time a science fiction magazine had been put into the hands of a professional s.f. magazine writer. (There was no such thing when Gernsback started *Amazing* in 1927.) Harry Bates wrote a few stories, including the Hawk Carse series, which aroused some excitement at the time, but only after he became editor of *Astounding*, and the same was true of Tremaine.

Beginning in 1935 *Astounding* had lost some of its momentum; it had trimmed edges now, an improvement often solicited by fans, but the fiction was growing routine. Campbell set out to put the magazine through what proved to be the first of a series of astonishing metamorphoses. After Weinbaum's death in 1935, *Astounding* had tried to fill the gap with Weinbaum imitations written by "Thornton Ayre" and "Polton Cross" (both pseudonyms of John Russell Fearn), "Gordon A. Giles" (Eando Binder) and D. L. James. Campbell put a stop to this and began to develop new authors. They included Isaac Asimov, L. Sprague de Camp, Lester del Rey, Robert A. Heinlein, L. Ron Hubbard and A. E. van Vogt—the big guns of the forties and fifties. Campbell brought in new illustrators and began to feature "astronomical" cover paintings—views of the planets as seen from their satellites, without the struggling spacesuited figures or alien monsters previously thought necessary. These early astronomicals were not so accurate as they later became under Chesley Bonestell, but they were an innovation.

Campbell, who had been a student at MIT, began to write editorials dealing with modern physics, a subject closed to Gernsback, whose forté was 1925 radio, and Sloane, who preferred chemistry and archaeology. He insisted on scientific accuracy and modernity from his writers. In August 1938 he ran his first market-research questionnaire, and in the October issue reported that over thirty percent of *Astounding*'s readers were "practicing technicians—chemists, physicists, astronomers, mechanical engineers, electrical engineers, radio men," etc. This discovery guided his editing of *Astounding* over the next thirty years. In March 1938 he changed the magazine's logotype from the old comet tail (designed in imitation of *Amazing*'s) to a new, vertical, sans-serif type. In every possible way he made it evident that *Astounding* was a new kind of magazine, appealing to new readers.

Some neglected stories from this period are of interest. "Minus Planet," by John D. Clark (*Astounding*, April 1937), is about contraterrene matter. "Frontier of the Unknown," by Norman L. Knight (*Astounding*, July-August 1937), features green smocks and masks for surgeons, vibrators for massage, term marriage, eye transplants, etc. "Seeker of Tomorrow," by Eric Frank Russell and Leslie T. Johnson, has a moving roadway on which a falling man knocks down other people, as in Heinlein's later "The Roads Must Roll." Don A. Stuart's "Out of Night" (*Astounding*, October 1937) has aliens with hair that radiates and receives radio waves (like the tendrils of A. E. van Vogt's "slans"). In "The Faithful," by Lester del Rey (*Astounding*, April 1938), intelligent dogs drop atomic bombs on the Rising Sun

Empire. "Iszt-Earthman," by Raymond Z. Gallun, in the same issue, has a Dyson ring. (Before Dyson!)

The destruction of the other two magazines was now complete. In June 1935 Gernsback had dropped his cover price again to 15¢ in a desperate bid for circulation. In February 1936 he announced his last and most visionary plan for *Wonder Stories*—a pay-as-you-go subscription plan under which a subscriber, each time he received a copy of the magazine, would send Gernsback 15¢ for the next one. It was an instant disaster. *Wonder* was sold to Better Publications, a pulp chain, which reissued it beginning in August 1936 as *Thrilling Wonder Stories* (with an early emphasis on horror and the occult). Two years later *Amazing* also failed and was sold to Ziff-Davis, another pulp chain, which transformed it into a juvenile publication, largely staff-written, illustrated with comic-book drawings by Julian Fuqua. The adult s.f. field was left to Campbell, and he dominated it without challenge until 1950.

Even as he spoke, the mirrored disk came to life with startling suddenness—

Illustrated by H. W. Wesso

Seeker of Tomorrow

By Eric Frank Russell and Leslie T. Johnson

I

THE Venusian city of Kar shimmered beneath an inverted bowl of blue glory. It was a perfect day for a civic demonstration such as the welcoming home of the first expedition to Earth in many centuries. Citizens appreciated the cooperation of the weather; Liberty Square was packed with a murmuring, multicolored concourse that swirled in kaleidoscopic patterns. Something shrieked in the vault of space; the kaleidoscope turned uniformly pink as five hundred thousand faces lifted to the sky.

High in the stratosphere appeared a pair of metallic pencils, their rear ends vomiting crimson flames. Sound waves from the rocket tubes fleeted downward, bounced from the eardrums of the expectant crowd. The pencils swelled; the crimson spread along their under surfaces as the retarding rockets belched with maximum power. In a short time the objects had resolved themselves into long, streamlined space ships.

With startling suddenness they loomed hugely to the view, sinking behind the mighty mass of university building. They seemed to pause for a moment, while the great, circular ports in their sides stared over the edge of the roof at the mob beneath. Then they were gone. Came one tremendous, reverberating crash succeeded by a moment's perfect silence. The great audience found tongues, broke into a babble of sound, as, with one accord, it stretched itself into a stream of individuals rushing along University Avenue toward the Kar Airport.

The landing field of Kar Airport presented a scene of utmost confusion. To one side lay the space ships surrounded by a shouting, struggling mob. The uproar was loudest at a point where the overwhelmed City Guards had reformed themselves into a wedge and were desperately battling their way through the barrier of bodies.

Babbling and bawling arose into a crescendo when it was perceived that the nearer space ship was opening its bow door. Steadily, the circular piece of metal revolved along its worm, retreating more and more into the shadow. A final half-revolution and it was drawn into the interior of the ship, while the form of a man appeared in the gap thus left.

The crowd bellowed itself red in the face: "Urnas Karin! Urnas Karin!"

Karin acknowledged the shouts and raised his hand for silence. Half the crowd hissed for silence, while the other half continued to bawl. The hissers reproved the bawlers and the bawlers answered back. Somebody pushed somebody and somebody else resented it. A woman fainted, collapsed, and a little man ten yards away was struck on the cranium by way of retaliation. In a flash, fifty different individuals assumed fifty different versions of what they regarded as a menacing pose. A hidden dog yelped, as somebody trod on it, and from the back of the crowd a piercing voice shrilled, "Woopsey! Woopsey!"

Immediately the crowd laughed; an ugly situation passed away and silence fell.

Karin jumped to the ground, followed by twenty of his companions from inside the ship. A small platform, about twice man-height, stood near. Karin mounted and let his sharp eyes pass over the waiting audience. A uniformed guard placed before him a small ebony box mounted on a tripod. He waved away the guard, stood before the box and spoke.

"My friends," he said, his voice pleasantly magnified by the disseminator he was using, "your marvelous welcome is a reward in itself. I thank you; and again, on behalf of my colleagues, I thank you! Now, I am sure that you are all fairly bursting to know whether this expedition has made any startling discoveries upon our Mother Planet." He paused and smiled, as the crowd signified with a roar that it *was* fairly bursting.

"Well, I am afraid that our story is far too long to narrate in detail. Let it suffice if I tell you that we did not find a trace of the civilization of those who were our ancestors. The great cities, the mighty machines that once were theirs have crumbled into the dust and have been obliterated completely by the foot of Time. Old Mother Earth is airless, waterless, and lifeless, thoroughly and completely.

"But we did make one most remarkable discovery." He hesitated for a tantalizing minute. "We found the body of a prehistoric man! It was truly an amazing discovery. There, upon a world so ancient that every artificial mark had been smoothed away, atmosphere had leaked off into space, and even axial rotation had ceased, lay the body of this man.

"Examination of the corpse disclosed the seemingly impossible fact that life had departed from it not more than fifty hours previously. Fortunately, we had with us, as part of our standard first-aid equipment, a normality chamber. We placed the corpse therein, warmed it, liquefied the blood and have succeeded in bringing it safely home in a condition that gives us good cause to hope that the experts in our Institute of Medicine and Surgery will be able to resuscitate it.

"The body of this man is in perfect condition. The cause of death, literally, was lack of breath. He appears to belong to a period placed several thousands of years before our ancestors departed from the dying Earth and settled here on Venus, a period so far back in time that our history reels do not talk of it. Why, his head is covered with hair and he even has hairs upon his chest and legs!

"The ability of scientists, in this our most progressive time, to revive the dead in cases where death is not due to old age and is not accompanied by serious injury is a marvel too well known to need emphasis by me. Possibly there are some people here who would not be with us but for the miracles performed by our most able men and women." He was interrupted by several cries of assent.

"I feel that there is a most excellent chance of the institute bringing this man back to life and permitting him to tell us his story with his own lips. If my hopes prove to be justified, I intend to make an official request to Orca Sanla, chairman of the stereo-vision committee, that this lone inhabitant of a long-dead planet be allowed to stand before the screen at Kar Stereo Station and give to our world an explanation of circumstances which, to be quite candid with you, we regard as absolutely inexplicable." Karin turned and gestured toward a burly individual standing in the front rank of his scores of followers.

"In any case, you will receive entertainment tonight. Olaf Morga, aided by his brother Reca, who is on our companion ship, has made a complete pictorial record of our venture from the time we departed from Kar to the time we left Earth. The record is being dispatched to the K.S. Station and will be radiated from sunset this evening."

Karin started to descend as a storm of cheering broke out. A woman in the center of the crowd screamed, "Belt!"

The word was caught up by a thousand others; ere Karin had placed his foot upon the topmost step the whole mob was roaring, "The belt! We want the belt!"

Morga and Karin exchanged smiles. The latter returned to the center of the platform, slowly and deliberately unbuckling the flexible metal belt encircling his middle. He held it loosely by one end, while the crowd danced with excitement.

Suddenly, he whirled it above his head, flung it upward and out. It snaked through the air toward where the throng clustered thickest. Half a hundred men leaped for it as it fell. Then it vanished beneath a mass of human beings all fighting madly for the prized souvenir.

Quick to profit by the diversion, the city guards cleared a path from the rocket ships to the control tower. Karin and his crew, together with the crew of the sister ship, sped along the path, entered the tower. The crowd swarmed out of the airport field, poured in a colorful torrent down University Avenue and put a test load on the moving roadways to the suburbs.

Dusk fell over Venus. The stars set in a moonless sky penetrated the thick veil of atmosphere just sufficiently to paint faint glimmers of steely brightness upon the sides of two voyagers of interplanetary space. Side by side, in a littered field, the rocket ships slept.

II

Two months later, Bern Hedan, the man who got the buckle of the belt, fiddled with the controls of his stereo set and cursed. The brand-new pan-selenite screen of the set displayed, in natural colors and with stereoscopic effect, the final stage of transformation of a sample of Venusian pond life. A hidden announcer betrayed the fact that Sanla's myrmidons regarded a dirge played upon an asthmatic oboe as fit accompaniment to the tri-monthly acrobatics of a frog-faced fish.

"By the death of Terra!" he ejaculated, using the most fearful oath his imagination could conceive at the moment. "I pay fifty-five yogs down and twelve more every high tide to be the owner of the set. I pay exorbitant bills for power to operate it; I produce eighteen yogs per annum for the right to make use of that which I have purchased—or am purchasing." He gestured to nothing in particular and talked aloud. He was very fond of talking to himself.

Common-sense views appealed to him. "And what do we get for this outrageous expenditure? What do we get, I say? Pictorial demonstrations of the domestic habits of red-hammed Venusian baboons accompanied by the noise of wailing catgut. Or the amatory adventures of a deep-sea worm who pays court to somebody's symphony for ten harmonicas. Bah!"

He wound savagely at the coordinating handle protruding from the front of the stereo cabinet. The screen dimmed, clouded over, then cleared and depicted a new scene. It was an interior view of the Hall of Debate in the city of Newlondon. Two men were seated upon chairs placed on a semicircular stage, facing a great auditorium packed with people from floor to ceiling. A third individual stood upon the stage facing a stereo screen. Bern Hedan noticed that a mirror suspended on the wall at the rear of this stage was responsible for the peculiar effect of showing the transmission screen in his own screen, giving him a double image of the three people on the stage.

The stereo announcer was saying, "This evening you have heard and seen an extremely interesting and most instructive debate upon the subject of another Great Migration. You all know the reasons why the human race was compelled to make use of its discovery of the means of traveling through cosmic space by indulging in a wholesale move to our present abode—Venus. The symptoms of planetary senile decay, such as loss of atmosphere, loss of orbital velocity, and speed of axial rotation, became so alarming that eventually it was obvious that Earth's characteristics were altering faster than humanity could accommodate itself to the change. Earth's days were numbered—from the human viewpoint, at least. Venus was a suitable habitat for our forefathers, ourselves, and our children's children, and the means to get to Venus were at hand.

"The question that has been discussed tonight has been, to put it briefly: 'Will history repeat itself?' In the course of time, somewhere in the distant future, our planet's fate will duplicate that of Earth. We may not like to think of it, but it is a fact, a perfectly natural fact, an inevitable one. Will Venusians die with Venus, or shall there be another Great Migration?" He signed with his hand to the man seated on his right-hand side.

"The pessimist thinks we are doomed for the reasons he has given you, the most unanswerable of which is that the next foothold in space is the planet Mercury—and Mercury is quite uninhabitable by human beings." He signed to the opposite side. "The optimist believes that humanity shall never disappear from creation, mainly because of our steady scientific advancement, which, he has said, will enable us to perfect the art of space travel to such a degree that we shall have the choice of a dozen worlds long before our present one has grown uncomfortable.

"This concludes the debate between Leet Horis of Kar and Reca Morga of the Newlondon Debating Society." He stood staring into the transmission screen while the auditorium thundered with applause.

"Now we come to the event to which all Venus has been looking forward with the keenest anticipation. Since the Kar Institute successfully resuscitated the prehistoric man two months ago, the entire world has been waiting to hear his story. There has been some comment about this delay of two months, which I am now to tell you was due to the fact that the revival of this man was not, in itself, enough to justify his immediate appearance. He needed a period of convalescence, during which he has learned how to speak our language. You will find that he can speak with fair fluency, the reason for this being that his own language proved to be the root of ours."

Bern Hedan adjusted the clarity knob of his set, making the screen depict the stage more sharply. He moved an easy-chair before the stereo, sat in it and switched on the automatic head-scratcher. Soothed by the restfulness of the cushions and the gentle rubs and tickles of the scratcher, he prepared to listen with tolerance.

Seen in the screen, the pair of debaters left the stage. The announcer walked to the rear, opened a door and, with a dramatic air, ushered in the prehistoric man. The man stood directly in front of the screen and studied twelve thousand Venusians. Two hundred million Venusians studied the man.

The Venusians felt slightly disappointed. The object of their examination did not look as though he lived in trees and ate nuts. His head was covered with disgusting hair, but otherwise he looked quite normal. He stood six feet in height; his eyes were dark, alert, his face intellectual even by Venusian standards of judgment. A woven *silvoid karossa* hung from his shoulders; the inevitable Venusian belt encircled his middle. He seemed to be quite at ease; it was evident that he did not agree with his audience in giving his own personality a purely antiquarian value.

"It is my privilege," said the announcer, "to introduce to you Glyn Weston, the man from A.D. 2007—a date placed approximately seventy thousand years before the Great Migration, about one hundred and fifty thousand years from today." Murmurs of surprise rippled around the serried rows of seats.

"Glyn Weston has told his story to the university board at Kar; he has made a most valuable contribution to the pages of ancient history. I shall now request him to repeat his narrative, and I think that after you have heard what he has to say you will agree that this voice from the past has recounted the most amazing tale ever to be projected over the stereo. *Glyn Weston!*"

III

My friends, began Weston, speaking in a pleasantly modulated voice, there is one thing I must say before I tell you my story. God's greatest gift to man is life. I cannot say that you have given me life, but to the remarkable abilities of your wonderful civilization I owe the restoration of that which was snatched from me—*life!* The poor and faulty power of speech is quite inadequate to convey to you the gratitude I feel. I want every one of you to know how deeply I appreciate what has been done for me by Venusian science.

(A roar of applause shook the auditorium. The audience decided that it was to listen to a man and not to a savage.)

As you have been informed, my name is Glyn Weston. My age I do not know; the reason will become apparent later in my story. In the period that is called mine, if any particular period can be so called, I was a physicist.

My work commenced at the age of twenty-eight, when I was fortunate enough to inherit a very large sum of money. I was then assistant to the famous Professor Vanderveen, astrophysicist at the Glasgow Observatory. For many years my hobby had been the study of the work of McAndrew, popularly called "The Death-ray Man."

McAndrew was a scientist of the previous decade. His life's work had advanced that of certain mathematicians and physicists of the twentieth century, most particularly Einstein, Graham, Forrest and Schweil. He was the world's most authoritative exponent of the space-time concept, and, like many other geniuses, he died discredited by his contemporaries because he had asserted that it would be found possible to travel in time, to move through time into the future.

Schweil, with whom McAndrew had been coworker, had shown that time was not an independent concept but an aspect of motion. There could be no time without motion—no motion without time.

This may seem rather obscure to some of you, but it really is quite simple. Try to imagine time without motion; consider the means whereby you estimate time. The two cannot be separated, for they are merely different aspects of the same thing. McAndrew's life was dedicated to discovering the true relationship between these aspects and, if I may put it so, to defining the "difference."

His work was crowned with success two years before his death. Working upon the theory that the velocity of motion and the rate of time invariably maintained a constant parallel, he evolved a ray with which he made a number of objects vanish. It was his claim that the ray speeded up the velocity of electronic motion, causing the atoms to experience time at a faster rate and thus forcing the objects into the future. Of course, he was laughed at.

His discovery was described in the absurdest terms, such as "the automatic disintegrator" and "the death ray." McAndrew left his data in the safe-keeping of the only scientist who believed in him. That scientist was Vanderveen, my superior.

Vanderveen was in his late fifties when he caught the torch cast by the fallen McAndrew. During my association with him he gave me constant, almost fatherly, encouragement. My interest in McAndrew pleased him immensely. When I received my inheritance I told him that it was my desire to use it in carrying on from where McAndrew had left off.

"Weston," he said, placing a hand upon my shoulder, "I have prayed that this should be your ambition. McAndrew, alas! found in me a dog too old to learn new tricks. But as for you—you are young."

Thus the seed was sown. But Vanderveen did not live to see the crop. Twenty-two years later I became the human subject of a time-travel experiment. I had set up my laboratory in the wilds of the Peak District of Derbyshire, in England, where work could be carried on with the minimum of interference. From this laboratory I had dispatched into the unknown, presumably the future, a multitude of objects, including several live creatures such as rats, mice, pigeons and domestic fowl. In no case could I bring back anything I had made to vanish. Once gone, the subject was gone forever. There was no way of discovering exactly where it had gone. There was nothing but to take a risk and go myself.

To this end I designed an air-tight time-travel room and had it fabricated immediately. The room was capable of holding the much perfected Schweil-McAndrew ray projector, myself and a quantity of material I considered necessary to take with me. The projector fitting was designed so that the entire room, with all its contents, would vanish immediately as the ray was turned on. I knew, of course, that if this room actually transported me into the future it was imperative that I take into account the possible alteration of ground contours over the period of time I covered. It would be foolhardy to experiment at a point where the ground might rise and leave me embedded yards below Earth's surface. So I hired a field upon a hilltop nine miles northwest of Bakewell—a very lonely spot—and equipped the roof beams with a parachute of my own design, to thwart an opposite possibility.

Upon the fourteenth of April, A.D. 1998, all was prepared for the great test. My financial affairs had been settled with an eye to the future in more ways than one. The time-travel room, lavishly set with windows and looking like a very large telephone kiosk, stood waiting in the middle of Farmer Wright's field. As I walked toward it, not knowing what Fate held in store for me, I thought what an incongruous object it looked standing amid the furrows. Without the slightest hesitation, I unlocked the door, stepped inside and relocked it, started the air-purifying apparatus, took one last look at Earth, fresh with the aura of spring, and closed the projector switch.

IV

The sensation of being under the influence of the rays was weird in the extreme. My mind seemed to be emptied of all thoughts, retaining only alternating impressions of roughness and smoothness, stickiness and gloss, for all the world as if the very nature of my brain material was swaying between a pseudo-fibrousness like that of pulled toffee and a satisfying softness like that of a newly rolled ball of putty. A veil of mist came between myself and the world I strained my eyes to see. The mist was elusive, intangible. Some temporary optical fault intervened to defeat all my efforts to decide whether this mist lay over the windows of the room or was coating my own eyeballs.

A sudden panic assailed me, and I pressed down the switch handle to which my right hand was still clinging. A sensation of immense strain racked my body from hair to toes, my blood vessels fizzed as if their contents had been replaced with soda water. The fugitive mist was whisked away like the gauzy veil of an oriental dancer. I felt as sick as a dog.

My key clicked in the lock of the door. I stepped outside and looked around. Everything looked exactly as I had left it. The field was still furrowed; a few trees and bushes were displaying their awareness of spring; the sky was still cloudy, the air as stimulating as before. My experiment had failed.

It was a miserable man who wended his way along the lonely lanes to his laboratory. I remember that birds were singing, but I did not hear them—at the moment; early flowers were adding their sweet beauty to this ugly world of mine and I did not see them—just then.

Mentally cursing my lack of foresight in not parking my car in the hired field, I turned a bend in the road and began to climb a hill lying between the field and the laboratory. A farm laborer emerged from a lane to my left and trudged along behind me. He increased his pace, caught up to me and requested the time. He was an old man of the garrulous type and, to my mind, his question was merely an excuse for a conversation. Nevertheless, I lugged at my gold chain and glanced at the cheap timepiece hooked upon its end.

"I'm sorry," I said, "my watch has stopped."

"So has mine," he responded. "Guess I'll have to get it on the wireless when I land home." He lighted a cigarette and climbed up the hill in silence for a little while. "What d'you think of the great rocket flight?" he asked suddenly.

I had some difficulty in gathering my wits, and had to make a definite mental effort before I could reply. Somehow, I managed to recall the sensational flight across the Channel of Robert Clair. This had been hailed as the first really successful experiment with a man-carrying rocket. If I remembered rightly, the event had taken place at least a month before. The science of rocketry held the interest of only a very small number of people; it was strange that this old man should still betray an interest in such an event placed a month earlier. Courtesy demanded a reply.

"Merely another step in the inevitable march of progress," I answered.

"D'you think they'll ever get to the Moon?"

"Who can tell," I said evasively.

"Well, they're talking about it; they're talking about it," he persisted. "I was reading in the papers only the other day that some professor had worked out how long it would take to get to Venus, how a suitable rocket could be built and how much it would cost. Always thought Venus was a naked woman, not a planet. Shows how knowledge has advanced since my younger days."

"Ah! it is the fate of all of us to be considered ignorant by later standards," I soothed.

"What's the world coming to?" he demanded, puffing furiously at his cigarette. "What with steam engines, then motor cars, airplanes and them auto-whatyamacallits that look like windmills and have got no wings, stratosphere planes—and now rockets! I remember when I was a kid there was a furor in the papers because Ginger Leacock circum—circum—went right round the world without a stop, in one of them crazy old stratosphere planes. They've gone round six times since then and aren't satisfied with that! So they've started meddling with rockets.

"First of all some maniac hops over a house and breaks his neck. They called him 'a martyr to science.' Then another idiot who wants to be a martyr rockets across the Channel and breaks both his legs. Not to be outdone, another fool starts out from Dublin and plunges clean through a skyscraper in New York, smearing himself all—"

"Here!" I interrupted. "What the devil are you talking about?"

"Rockets," he replied, startled. "And now when they can get from here to New Zealand in twenty-four hours, including stops, or eighteen hours without, what *I* say is—"

"Will you listen to me," I shouted, grabbing him by the shoulders. "What, in Heaven's name, are you talking about?"

"No offense, guv'nor, no offense!" he said nervously, trying to draw back. "I didn't mean anything, really I didn't!"

"Of course there's no offense," I roared. Then, realizing that my behavior was making the man nervous, I calmed myself and continued in a quieter tone. "You must pardon me. This subject you have been talking about is one that interests me very considerably and, for certain reasons, I have been out of touch with the news concerning it. My foolish excitement was caused by your mention of a rocket flight to New York. Will you tell me when that flight took place?"

"Now let me see!" Apparently reassured, he stood and contemplated the skies while he exercised his memory. "As near as I can guess it was in the late summer of 2004."

"What year?"

"2004," he repeated.

"And when was this great rocket flight to which you alluded in the beginning?" I asked, making a tremendous effort to control myself.

"Yesterday."

"You will think this a strange question," I told him, "but there is nothing seriously wrong with me. I am suffering from a slight trouble with my memory. Now tell me, what day was yesterday?"

He looked sympathetic, pulled a folded newspaper from his left pocket, opened it with deliberation and handed it to me. A two-inch streamer was spread across the top of the front page. It said: "NEW ROCKET RECORD." Beneath appeared: "TO N.Z. IN EIGHT-EEN HOURS—Lampson Crashes In Hawkes Bay." I took little notice of this news, red-hot though it was. My eyes searched eagerly along the top. There it stood in plain, indisputable print: "DAILY VOICE—May 22, 2007."

Before the startled native had time to move, I had seized him and kissed him. I flung his paper into the air and caught it with a mighty kick as it came down. I whoopee-e-ed at the top of my voice and danced a fandango in the roadway. My hat fell off and rolled without hindrance into a ditch; my watch jumped out of my pocket and danced in sympathy at the end of its chain. My time-travel experiment had *succeeded!* For a space of five minutes I went stark, staring mad, while my erstwhile companion, forgetting the dignity of age and his rheumatism, galloped up the hill like a hunted deer and vanished over the crest.

V

The remarkable feat of making a short trip through time had an effect upon me totally different from what I would have prophesied a few years before. I did not rush, flushed with triumph, to place the news before an astounded world. On the contrary, I became as suspicious and as secretive as any village miser. My desire for fame and the respect of the scientific world faded away, being replaced by a curiosity so insatiable that each today became a mere period of speculation about tomorrow. The future had grasped me like a vicious drug.

Formerly, I was secretive because I was determined not to permit my work to fall into unworthy hands. Now, the motive was fear of being deprived of the means to satisfy my desire to explore the future as thoroughly as possible.

From every point of view it seemed highly desirable that my next venture be undertaken at once. My personal fortune became a matter of little moment; my money was cached securely—but not securely enough to withstand the onslaught of time. I came to the conclusion that I could afford to ignore the fate of my worldly possessions; it was not likely that I could claim them at a distant date.

In the quiet atmosphere of the dust-covered laboratory, I thought it over. The time-travel room must be removed as soon as possible. Heaven alone knew what weird story had been told by my late companion upon his return home, what curious eyes and prying fingers would explore the object in Wright's field. Come to that, I did not know whether the field still belonged to Farmer Wright. The owner, whoever he might be, could arbitrarily uproot the trespasser upon his property. My next move must be made that night.

It was an hour after sunset when I entered the time-travel room and locked the door preparatory to my second adventure. My stomach was empty; the laboratory had been devoid of food and nothing had passed my lips for several hours. I consoled myself with a nine-year-old cigarette—still fresh! Faint streamers of light still permeated the sky in the direction of Staffordshire; a crescent moon hung low and stars twinkled clearly. The cigarette surrendered its last fragrant puff. I stamped on it and said, "Good-by, 2007!"

With my hand on the switch, I hesitated. On the last occasion the switch had been closed between six and ten seconds, as near as I could estimate, and I had covered nine years. Was the distance traveled in direct proportion to the time the switch was closed? Would I drop dead when the rays carried me to the very day that Nature intended to be the day of my death, or, whether it seemed logical or not, could one travel past what should be one's day of death? Silence answered my unspoken questions. There was nothing for it but to find out. It was a straight issue of success or suicide. I rammed home the switch with exaggerated determination. The die was cast!

I shall not weary you with another description of the sickness that I have called time nausea. The rays operated for a period about ten times longer than the last occasion—about one minute. Then the switch was opened; my body was subjected to a powerful but momentary strain, and I had arrived. The key clicked in the door lock; the door swung inward. With my eyes raised to the distant hills, I stepped out. Something snatched at my unwary feet and I fell upon my face. Regaining my feet, I discovered that the time-travel room was sunk into the soil to a depth of six inches; I had been tripped by the step of earth outside the door. It was fortunate that I had not fitted the time-travel room with an outward-opening door and thus imprisoned myself.

Looking around me, the first thing I noticed was that the field was uncultivated. A few miserable trees and bushes displayed their last tattered rags of brownish foliage. The sky was gray, angry and overcast; I concluded that it was late autumn or early winter. There was not a soul in sight as I paced across the field toward the lane.

Reaching a stone wall, about four feet in height, I mounted it and surveyed the distant horizon and the intervening terrain. There was not a sign of life or human habitation. My eyes roamed eagerly around, caught a glimpse of an inexplicable shape in the mid-distance, about four miles away. I took out my spectacles, polished them and adjusted them carefully on my nose. The object was a huge hemisphere of drab color.

The edifice, if such it was, bulged from the top of a tor like a wart upon an Earthly nose. It lay in the opposite direction from where my laboratory stood, or had once stood. I felt very hungry; my stomach suggested that this, the only artificiality on the landscape, held promise of food. I jumped down from the wall and trudged in the general direction of the distant tor.

Maintaining a rapid pace for the best part of an hour brought me to within a few hundred yards of the object, which had resolved itself into a great, smooth hump of concrete about one thousand feet in diameter by five hundred feet in height. There seemed to be a large hole in its top. I did not get a chance to pause and examine it before proceeding nearer; I hesitated in my stride and a voice materialized out of the air behind me. It spoke in accents curiously clipped, somewhat as the Scottish speak, briefly and to the point. It said, "Keep it up!"

I whirled around. Facing me was a man in dark-brown clothes cut in the manner of a compromise between an engineer's dungarees and a soldier's uniform. A helmet, nothing more than a dull metal skullcap, rested on his head; his hands grasped and pointed at me an object bearing only the faintest resemblance to a rifle. His attire was quite devoid of decoration; it made him look like something between an infantryman and a plumber.

"Where did you come from?" I exclaimed.

"Under a gooseberry bush," said he, grinning broadly. "Where did you?"

"From the year 2007."

"Indeed! Then the past is rising up against us!" A tinge of sarcasm suffused his voice, but he appeared to be an intelligent fellow.

"You must believe me," I argued. "My tale is very long, but when you have heard it you will find it—"

"Very plausible!" he interrupted. "If you're a better liar than most of us, you must be good. Now, get going. You can tell us all about how you saved the world in 2300 when you get inside."

"2300! Did you say 2300?" I tried to clutch his arm.

He placed the muzzle of his weapon against my middle. "Of course I said 2300. Move those feet of yours a little more and your tongue a little less. And, just in case you want to keep up the play, Methuselah, may I anticipate a question by informing you that this is the year of disgrace 2486?"

"Good heavens!" I cried, turning and moving up the hill. "I've jumped nearly four centuries!"

"Right out of the frying pan into the fire," my companion remarked.

"Why, what d'you mean?"

"Exactly what I said," he answered, his face taking on a sardonic expression. "You may be a good jumper, but you're a darned poor picker. Why didn't you jump a little less or a good bit more? The jumper who picks on this year is crazy. Hell, I knew you were crazy, anyway!"

"Yes, but—"

"Walk on, jumper, walk on!" he commanded. "I don't want to use my economy gun on a white man, even if he is cracked."

"Why d'you call your weapon an 'economy gun'?" I asked him. He heaved a sigh. "Well, if you must talk, and if you must pretend ignorance of commonplace things, it's because it uses poisoned darts propelled by compressed air and thus saves expenditure of explosives that are sorely needed elsewhere."

I was about to ask him where the explosives were needed, and for what purpose, when I found that we had arrived at the foot of the concrete mound and were facing a metal door set in its side.

My companion touched the door and slid aside a small trap set in its center, revealing a fluorescent screen behind. He faced the screen and spoke. "Number KH.32851B4, with a gentleman from the year 2007."

VI

The door opened silently. We entered. Facing us was a long passage indirectly illuminated from slots set in the sides. With synchronized step, which aggravated me and which I vainly tried to break, we marched down the passage, turned to the right at the bottom, *clump-clump-clump*ed along a concrete corridor and entered a large room.

A leather-skinned, mustached individual looked up from his desk. "What do you want?" he snapped.

"Food," I answered, briefly.

"Bring him food," he said, addressing my guardian. Turning to me, he said, "Sit."

A high cube of red rubber squatted on the floor behind me. I seated myself on it gingerly. It was an air cushion and it felt luxurious. The man behind the desk leaned forward, switched on an instrument bearing a vague resemblance to the old-time voice recorders. He stroked his mustache and looked me over.

"Name?" he demanded.

"Professor Glyn Weston."

"Professor, eh? Of what seat of learning?"

"Originally of Glasgow Observatory; since then I have been working in my own laboratory, about nine miles from here."

"There is no laboratory within a dozen miles of here," he said, acidly.

"My laboratory was within nine miles of here in the year 2007," I replied, doggedly.

"In 2007! How old are you then?"

"From one point of view I am a little over fifty, from another I am nearly five hundred."

"Absurd!" he exclaimed. "Obviously absurd!"

"There is an explanation for this seeming absurdity. In the year 2007 I was the first man to have made a trip in time—that is to say, into the future. I had traveled to that year from 1998. The experiment has been repeated. This is the result—I am here!"

"Hah!" He rubbed one side of his nose with a forefinger and regarded me queerly. "The popularity of science fiction has made the subject of time travel quite familiar to us. But time travel is impossible."

"Why?" I asked.

"It is illogical."

"Life is illogical; earthquakes are illogical."

"True," he agreed. "From some aspects that is profoundly true. But can you reconcile yourself with the idea of shaking hands with your ancestors a few centuries before you are born?"

"No—that would be really illogical. My experiments have shown me that time can be traveled in one direction only—and that is forward, into the future. There can be no returning, no motion into the past by as much as a fraction of one second."

He stood up, moved away from his desk toward a corner bookcase, searched along the serried volumes and pulled out a large, black tome. He ruffled its pages. Turning to me, with the book open in his hand, he questioned me. "What was the population of Bakewell in 2007?"

"I cannot tell you," I replied. "I spent very little time in that year. But in 1998 it was about 4,500."

"Hm-m-m! Who was the Premier of Great Britain?"

"Richard Grierson."

"Correct! Clair flew the Channel that year. Who designed his rocket?"

"The German astronautical experimenter, Fritz Loeb."

"Again correct!"

"Listen to me," I begged. "If that's some sort of ancient encyclopedia you've got there, please turn up the time concept and see who wrote books about it."

He wet a finger, searched through the pages of his book. Placing it on the desk, he grabbed another and searched through that also. Four books were explored before he found what was wanted.

"Here we are. By the way, my name is Captain Henshaw," he added, as an afterthought. "Let me see, Schweil, Herman, philos. Dutch 'Der something-or-other'; Schweil again, with another book; McAndrew, Fergus, 'Space-Time Coordinates'; McAndrew again, 'Time-Motion Relationship'; Weston, Glyn—well I'm a yellow man!—Weston, Glyn, 'Atomic Acceleration In the Time Stream'; again: Weston, Glyn, 'Schweil-McAndrew Theories Simplified.' Another and another; one, two, three, four, five, six! Glyn Weston—that's *you!*"

"And I can prove it," I said, feeling supremely satisfied that my work had been recorded over five centuries.

"How?" asked Captain Henshaw.

"My time-travel room stands awaiting your inspection at a place that I can describe to you only as Farmer Wright's field. It is an hour's walk from here."

A door to my left-hand side opened suddenly. A uniformed man appeared wheeling a dinner wagon constructed of bright metal tubes and mounted upon doughnut-tired castors. He twisted the wagon dexterously, turning it before my seat, lifted a well-loaded tray from the top and, with the casual air of an expert conjurer, drew four telescopic legs from its underside. Adjusting the contraption to a nicety, he stepped backward, flourished a cloth and bowed with an impudent grin.

"You must be hungry after five hundred years of abstention!" he said. Throwing another grin at Henshaw he marched from the room.

"To be perfectly candid with you," said Henshaw, as I commenced the welcome meal, "your story is too utterly ridiculous to believe, despite the evidence you have to offer. Now don't think that I am about to call you a liar, for I am not. All that I can say is that I intend to keep an open mind about the matter until I've had the opportunity to examine this magic kiosk of yours, and I am going to take a look at it immediately after my spell of duty ends, in about two hours' time."

"You are welcome," I mumbled with full mouth, waving a fork in the air.

"After I've taken a look at your gadget, I'll make a report to Manchester. My superiors can then decide how to treat you."

"Sounds threatening," I remarked, chewing rapidly.

"And, just in case your story happens to be true in every respect, is there anything you would like to know?"

"Yes!" I speared a potato. "Where am I?"

"You are inside No. 37 Interceptor Fortress." He moved from his desk and began to pace the room.

"No. 37 what?" I asked with sudden energy.

"Interceptor Fortress," he repeated. "There is a war on."

"A war!" I echoed, feebly.

"The biggest and most ferocious war the world has known. It has been on for the last five years and looks like lasting for the next five. One-tenth of Earth's population has been wiped out, obliterated. The Metropolis, which was called 'London' in your time, no longer exists except as a great area of shattered bricks, slates, and concrete, which harbor the bones of those they harbored in life. If you can travel in time, as you say you can, you will live to curse the invention that plunged you into the present day." Henshaw's face grew bitter, his voice hoarse.

"With whom is Britain fighting?" I asked, my dinner almost forgotten.

"There is no Britain," Henshaw answered. "The name was given up two centuries ago. There is no British Empire, either. You are now living in England, which is a self-ruling state and part of the White World, just as Scotland, Ireland, Australia, Germany, Russia, and all the others are part of the White World. The Earth of today has only three divisions: the White World, the Yellow World, and the Brown World.

"The Brown World is the smallest and most insignificant of the three. It includes the so-called black races and is neutral—up to the moment. The White and Yellow Worlds are decimating each other to assert their right to breed regardless of the room available. But I am disturbing your meal; please finish it and I will take you to the telescan room. There I can show you something of the war."

My mind pestered by a dozen vagrant thoughts, I ate in silence, while Henshaw fidgeted before the bookcase, taking out volumes and putting them back again. Eventually, the meal came to an end. I drank the last drop of liquid, munched the last fragment of biscuit and arose.

Henshaw signed toward the door through which I had entered. We passed through it, moved down a long corridor, through another door, up a corkscrew staircase into another corridor, reached its end and found ourselves in a long, rectangular room set under the roof of the fortress.

"This is the telescan room," said Henshaw.

VII

The walls and floor of the room were littered with a mass of instruments and equipment. Four men were moving about in the jumble, occupying themselves with various jobs, while, at the distant end, two more were seated at what I deduced to be control boards of some description. The most prominent object was a great glass disk secured in a metal frame in the center of the floor. The disk was tilted slightly out of the horizontal, had a mirror surface and bore a strong resemblance to the astronomical reflectors of my own day.

Henshaw produced a chair from somewhere. Placing it near the mirror, he bade me be seated, moved to the men at the control boards and held a brief conversation with them. He returned and stood by my chair.

"This telescan was the result of permitting amateur shortwave experimenters to play with television. It is much too complicated to explain to you here but, to put it briefly, a beam is directed into the sky, passes through the Heaviside and Appleton Layers and rebounds from the Grocott Layer, which lies at an altitude of about eight hundred miles. The beam then returns to Earth and catches the scene at its striking place.

"It bounces right round the Earth, registering the scene wherever it happens to strike; the first impression is the strongest, and when we pick up the beam again we have no great difficulty in tuning out the confusion of underlying scenes, leaving the first clear and sharp. The operators are now trying to angle the beam to give us a view of the Metropolis. We should get results any second."

Even as he spoke, the mirrored disk came to life with startling suddenness. There was no preliminary clouding or blur. One moment the surface was devoid of all but glitter; the next moment it depicted a scene with astonishing clarity. I leaned forward and looked at it.

A ruined road, pitted with ragged craters, passed through an area filled with hummocks of crushed building material. Carefully though I searched, I could not perceive one place where two bricks still clung together, neither could I find a single unbroken brick. The scene maintained a harrowing uniformity from the foreground to the background, a square mile of pathetic evidence.

Nothing stirred in that dismal scene; no step was taken where once ten million pairs of feet had trod; no voice was raised where the voices of children once were raised in play. A lump came in my throat, as I realized that the Metropolis—dear old London—was no more. It lay like a great, gray scar upon what I still imagined as the sweet green face of Mother Earth; it lay like a scar upon the soul of humanity.

The mirror altered its focus as the men at the end of the room manipulated their controls. The nearest end of the road seemed to rise toward me and show itself in greater detail. I saw bones protruding from a mound of dirt fifty yards from a large crater; near the legs lay the flattened skeleton of a dog. Henshaw bent his head forward, rubbed his chin with a harsh, scratching sound and spoke.

"Before you lies one of the most heart-rending incidents of the war. The dog refused to leave its stricken master. It stayed there until it starved to death. Thousands of people watched its long, drawn-out act of devotion, watched it through the telescan with curses and tears born of helplessness. Flight Lieutenant O'Rourke, disobeying orders, made a mad attempt to rescue the dog about the time its belly disappeared into its ribs. He was brought down by a Yellow squadron. His rocket plane is mixed with the dust of the Marble Arch. God rest a gallant gentleman!"

"Are the Yellows winning?" I asked, feeling sick at heart.

"No, I would not say that. Warfare has now reached the stage of perfection where nobody wins and everybody loses. The Metropolis, or what is left of it, is in no worse condition than Kobe and Tokyo. The campaign consists of a series of destructive assaults, followed by equally destructive retaliation; there have been no prolonged battles such as featured the past, just a delivering of rapid blows by one side or the other. The end of this great city was the result of such a blow; the end of Tokyo was our reply. Come, we'll take a look at your time-travel room."

With that I arose. We departed from the telescan room, retraced our steps through the corridors and came to the metal door. It opened silently as we reached it, revealing a small, streamlined vehicle standing on the path outside. Henshaw struggled to get his long legs beneath the steering wheel, while I took a seat by his side. Slamming the off-side door, Henshaw pressed a button protruding from the wheel boss. A smooth whir came from beneath the bonnet and we were off.

"Don't take the telescan picture too much to heart," said Henshaw, juggling with the wheel. "We received warning of that raid from our very excellent espionage service and managed to evacuate nine-tenths of the population in time. The remaining tenth was wiped out, but the death roll was not as large as the picture suggests."

"What caused the damage?" I asked.

"Bombs—high-explosive bombs dropped from the stratosphere airplanes and also from rocket ships flying at tremendous heights. The next raid will be upon Manchester or Sheffield, for these are now the southernmost towns of any importance, also centers of the armaments industry. Our fortress is one of a chain strung across the Derbyshire hills to protect Manchester. We cannot prevent a raid, but we can administer severe punishment with our rocket shells and our aerial torpedoes, which can ascend to very great heights, the latter by means of power picked up from the North Radiation Station."

"The Continent must have dropped in for it!" I offered.

"Not so much as you would think," he replied. "The opposing forces have vented their spite on what they consider to be the nerve centers of the enemy; thus England and Japan are the favorite targets. Neither side keeps its air fleet for purposes of defense but for retaliation. That is why these fortresses are very important—they are one of the few defense concessions wrung from the powers that be who worship the policy of attack, attack and again attack." He jerked at the steering wheel, avoided the curve of a stone wall and continued in a voice that grew more bitter.

"I am not looking forward to the next raid with eager anticipation. Information has reached us, from certain sources, telling that the Yellows have perfected a disintegrator bomb, the result of some nosey scientist occupying himself with the problem of how solar radiation is maintained. I understand that the bomb drops, bursts, upsets the stability of surrounding matter and causes it to burn itself away.

"The process does not continue indefinitely, but only as long as the original energy in the bomb lasts; the bigger the bomb the greater the area of matter affected. The process was described to me as 'readjustment of electronic balance,' and I believe that it takes place at a rate that will trap all but champion sprinters."

The car went over the crest of a hill. A field came into view. Simultaneously, we saw the time-travel room. We shot down a slight slope toward it, took an equally slight rise and came to rest beside the wall from which I had viewed the distant fortress. Henshaw squirmed from his seat, took out a watch and glanced at its dial.

"Four minutes—not so bad considering the state of the road."

"You've averaged about sixty miles per hour," I told him. "What sort of motor is this?" I asked, gesturing to the car.

"Electric. Runs on Freimeyer high-capacity batteries employing silver-tantalum alloy plates." He vaulted the wall, stared at the object in midfield. "So that's the magic box, eh? Let's go and put a penny in."

I climbed the wall. We started for the room together. Henshaw stroked at his mustache, an expression of keen interest in his face. The turf was damp and slippery beneath our feet. We had covered half the distance to the room when a hoarse whistle ran over the hills and echoed in the valleys. Henshaw stopped abruptly. The whistle ended, then was succeeded by six short toots.

Henshaw whirled around, grabbed me by the arm, pulled me toward the car. "By the Mandarin's Button," he roared, his face red with excitement, "*a raid!* Did you hear the siren? It's a raid warning from the fortress. We must return at once! Put a move on, for Heaven's sake! There's not a second to lose."

We ran toward the wall. Twenty yards from it I slid, staggered with wildly waving arms, slid again and fell upon the flat of my back with force that knocked the breath from my body. Henshaw, half a dozen jumps ahead, skidded in a circle, returned, and grasped my hands, preparatory to helping me up.

"Look!" I gasped weakly, my eyes bulging at the sky. "*Look!*"

About a mile away, coming in our direction at a fast pace, was a golden-colored air machine shaped like a bullet, small, stubby wings protruding from its sides, a long tail of fire streaming from its rear. It looked sinister, threatening; my heart turned to ice.

"By Hades! A fighting scout of the Yellows," shouted Henshaw. "He's got us spotted and intends to have a little amusement. Run like the very devil. We're as good as dead men already."

So saying, he gave a tremendous heave that swung me to my feet. I clutched his shoulders. We swayed about like a pair of adagio dancers, slipped and went down together. Somebody rattled a piece of rock in a monster can; a roar swept overboard; a flood of hot air washed our recumbent bodies. We regained our feet. The scout had passed us by a mile and was nosing upward in a great loop. The car was a smoking ruin.

"He's coming back for us," Henshaw screamed. "We're done. There's nowhere we can hide!"

"Heaven help—" I commenced, then paused as a thought struck me. "The time-travel room! Come on. We can make it with luck. We'll be safe there."

VIII

I turned, made for the center of the field, arms working like pistons, my pace hampered by fear of falls. Henshaw raced beside me, his chest laboring, his face livid.

Despite the telling pace, he found breath enough to ask a question as he ran. "What good will it do to get into that thing? He'll simply blow it sky high!"

"Wait and see!" I grunted.

A noise grew loud behind us, filling us with fear that added to our speed. With surprising suddenness, the scout roared overhead followed by its wake of heated air. A terrific blast came somewhere in the rear. Henshaw looked over his shoulder.

"A disintegrator bomb!" he shouted. "It's eating toward us like greased lightning. Run! Run as you've never run before!"

My protesting feet increased their speed. The total distance from the wall to the room was a bare five hundred yards. I would not have believed that such a distance could be so punishing. Thirty yards separated us from the time-travel room; it seemed like thirty miles. The distance already covered told in this final stage; we did not run it; we reeled it.

Henshaw, ahead of me, reached the room and tugged madly at the door, as a sensation of heat penetrated to the back of my legs. He danced with excitement as he pulled in vain. I sobbed out to him *"Push! Push!"* and he fell headlong inside. A fraction of a second later I staggered through the open door, turned and saw the earth literally melting and boiling within a yard of the step. We were barely in time.

Without further ado, I slammed the door and closed the switch of the ray apparatus. Red flames jumped upward and peered at us through the windows; a film of mist blotted them out. My body tingled with the old, familiar sensation and, as I breathed a prayer of thankfulness, the whole room fell over on its side. My head struck a projection on the wall. Frantically, I tightened my grip upon the switch as I slipped into unconsciousness.

The period of stupor did not last long—or it did not seem to. I came to my senses, jerked out a hand in search of the switch, found it and pulled it.

Somebody said, "Ouch!"

I sat up hastily. I was in bed!

My astonishment can well be imagined. I was in bed; there was not the slightest doubt about that. I stroked and felt the clothes, studied the weave of them and pinched myself. There was nothing else for it: definitely, beyond all dispute, I was sitting up in bed clad in a crimson nightgown.

A half-seen movement to one side drew my attention that way. I rubbed my eyes and looked again. Standing beside the bed, his face expressive of kindly solicitude, was a bald-headed man garbed in rompers of brilliant hue. His forehead was high, his eyes large, liquid and brown, his mouth and chin small, almost womanly. Suspended from a chain encircling his neck was a plated instrument which, I guessed, had taken the tug that brought forth the "Ouch!"

I stared at him. He contemplated me with quiet serenity.

"Where am I?" I asked weakly, making use of the conventional phrase under such circumstances.

"You are within my house situated in the city of Leamore," he answered in a pleasantly modulated voice, "and the year is 772 by the new reckoning, or 34656 by the old. You have leaped a chasm of time representing about thirty-two thousand years!"

"How did you know that I am a time traveler?" I demanded.

"Because your time-traveling device materialized out of thin air before the eyes of half a hundred citizens. You chose the center of a busy road as your arriving point. Dozens of people witnessed the phenomenon which, in the far past, undoubtedly would have been given a supernatural explanation. Our solution was that you had traveled through time: a simple solution seeing that your feat is the second within the last five centuries. Finally, your companion confirmed our—"

"Henshaw!" I interrupted, realizing that I had had company on my time trip. "Henshaw— Where is he?"

"He is having his hair plucked," was the amazing response.

"Hair plucked! *Hair!* Why? What?" My mind relapsed into confusion at this nonsensical twist in the conversation. For the second time I pinched myself to make sure I was not asleep. The man in the blue rompers smiled as he noted the effect of his words. Seating himself on the edge of the bed, he hugged a knee and continued.

"Your friend appears to be a person accustomed to making quick decisions. It is scarcely thirty minutes since your time-conquering device staged its dramatic appearance, yet already he has discovered that, according to present-day conventions, hair is regarded as not nice. Apparently he is determined to look nice at all costs, so he is having his hair removed by a painless method of extraction. We are depriving him of his mustache and head covering. The bristles on his face will have to grow longer before we can deal with them."

"Well, I'm damned!" I exploded. "Henshaw—the blessed goat! I boost him through a multitude of centuries and what happens? He rushes into a beauty parlor leaving me to expire in bed." Indignation brought me out of the bed and to my feet. "In a crimson nightgown!" I added.

My companion laughed aloud. "No fear of you expiring just yet," he assured me. "You received a nasty bump from which you will recover very soon. As for the nightgown, as you call it, we put you into it after giving you a much-needed bath, while we looked around for some suitable clothes."

"What's wrong with my own clothes?" I demanded.

"They have been burned; your friend's have been burned, also. The contents of your pockets have been fumigated; so has your time-travel room. This is a hygienic world you've stepped into. We don't mind your coming here, but we object, in the strongest possible manner, to your importing large quantities of germs of types that we have gone to considerable pains to eliminate. We like you; we like your friend; we *don't* like your passengers."

"Sorry!" I said, humbly.

"It's quite all right," he answered, releasing his knee and standing

up. "Perhaps I have been too blunt. The apology should be mine."
He walked across the room, pressed a button. A panel in the wall slid
silently downward. Behind lay a recessed wardrobe. He reached
inside, produced a complete outfit of clothing made of some material
resembling silk, tossed them onto the bed.

Removing the crimson wrap with secret relief, I commenced to put
on the apparel. The soft, almost dainty material enveloped my
bathed, refreshed body pleasantly. There was not a button in the
outfit. Everything fastened with a sort of glorified zipper. I pulled on
one strangely cut garment after another, zipped them tight and, in
the end, stood before a mirror regarding myself attired in emerald-
green rompers, green socks and sandals to match, a green tricorn hat
cocked rakishly on my head. I stared into the mirror, thinking it
depicted the biggest fool alive.

"How do you like it?" questioned the onlooker.

"Not so bad. All I want now is the cat."

"The cat?" he repeated, mystified.

"Yes, the cat. I look like the principal boy in Dick Whittington."

"Dick Whittington?" he muttered.

"You wouldn't know about that—let it pass!" I tried the tricorn at
a different angle; the result was an abomination. Finally, I gave it
up. If all of them dressed like this, an extra idiot wouldn't be noticed.

"Well, I'm ready, Mr.—Mr.—"

"Ken Melsona is my name," he responded.

"And Glyn Weston is mine." We shook hands. Melsona opened a
door, led the way down a passage to another door, which sank at the
pressure of a button. Outside lay the street. Conscious of my
unfamiliar garb, I hesitated; Melsona, dressed like Little Boy Blue,
stepped boldly out. I followed.

IX

Before me stretched a scene so unexpected I stopped and gasped.
Between the pavement curbs ran a moving roadway, smooth,
soft-surfaced, flowing evenly from west to east. It was divided into
three sections, all traveling in the same direction, the outer sections
at about five miles per hour, the middle section at about ten.
Hundreds of people clothed in gaudy colors stood and chatted on
the road or stepped from one section to another, all carried along

steadily like an array of targets in a gypsy shooting gallery. The total width of the roadway was about one hundred feet; fixed, mosaic-patterned pavements bordered it.

Picturesque villas set in lavish, well-cultivated gardens lined the roadway on both sides. Ornamental trees of every size and color, drilled and trimmed into every conceivable shape, sprouted from the pavements at intervals of thirty yards. It was a beautiful sight indeed, the most beautiful I had ever seen. The road deserved the name of Boulevard of Heaven.

Melsona made for the nearest-moving section of roadway, warning me to step on it while facing the direction of motion. We passed over to the middle section, stood upon it, side by side, and glided to the east. I felt as pleased as a kid at a fair.

"Let us call at one or two shops," suggested my guide. "Then we can pick up your companion—er—Henshaw you said his name was, didn't you?"

I mumbled an affirmative, my eyes roaming busily over the scenery and the accompanying crowd of road-riders, my mind inveigled by the novelty of it all.

We swept along for the best part of a mile, before Melsona nudged me into attention, dexterously transferred himself to the right-hand slow track, crossed it and gained the pavement. With me tagging behind, he made a beeline for a section of half a dozen shops, entering one displaying a mass of goods I had not the time to examine. A man and a woman, both brightly clad and equally bald, advanced eagerly at our entrance.

"Pray serve this gentleman," said Melsona, making a patronizing wave in my direction.

"Ah, certainly, it is a pleasure," purred the male assistant, washing his hands with invisible soap. "What is the gentleman's need?"

"Money," I said, succinctly.

"Money!" he parroted. "Money! What a strange request! It is obtainable, of course, but you will have to apply to a collector."

"Then how the devil can I—"

"It's quite all right," Melsona interrupted. "All you have got to do is to ask for whatever you require. If this shop has it, you will get it; if it hasn't, then some other shop may stock it."

"'Ask and it shall be given unto you,'" I quoted. The idea sounded crazy to me, but who was I to question the economics of this age? "Cigarettes," I said, hopefully.

The words were no sooner out of my mouth than the lady assistant darted to a shelf, beating her confrere by a foot, grabbed a dozen packages of assorted size and shape and placed them on the counter. My eyes stared in astonishment and delight. They were packets of cigarettes. I took one of the biggest. The lady wanted to know whether she could provide me with anything else. I asked her for a cigarette case and got it. I asked her for an automatic lighter. She provided me with a replica of the instrument dangling from Melsona's neck, which I had mistaken for the switch. I spent thirty minutes in that shop, emerging convinced that I had stepped into Utopia.

We stood on the pavement outside. I opened my cigarette packet, placed a welcome tube between my lips, and Melsona showed me how to use the lighter. It was shaped like an elongated fir cone, made of metal and affixed to the conventional neck chain. One merely squeezed it. A small lid in the wide end popped open, revealing a glowing filament underneath. I lighted it, inhaling the fragrant smoke with indescribable satisfaction.

"How long will this last?" I asked, studying the glowing end of the lighter curiously.

"For the whole of your lifetime," answered Melsona. "It's—" He looked upward suddenly, as a loud noise thundered down from the clouds. "Look! There's a world-trip liner!"

Overhead soared a titanic cigar, silvery-colored, flame-girt, awe-inspiring. The circumstances made it hard to grasp the true perspective. I judged the monster to be about a mile in length and a tenth of a mile in diameter. Poised high above the thin, almost transparent clouds, it was truly a majestic sight, its conical nose pointed toward the Sun setting in the west, its tail vomiting spears of flame that spread, lightened and resolved into an enormous fan of vapor.

It was moving at a height of at least seven miles, yet its size and the wonderful clearness of the atmosphere made the rows of circular ports along its sides easily discernible. Barraging the whole city of Leamore with a bombardment of sound, it sped swiftly to the west, its tremendous bulk dwarfing the antlike humans responsible for its fabrication.

"What do you think of that?" asked Melsona, proudly.

"It's magnificent! It's marvelous!" I said.

A shout drew our eyes to the roadway. A man standing on the

distant five-mile track waved madly, rushed in our direction, trod on the edge of the intervening ten-mile track and executed an imcomplete cartwheel. With the road rushing onward beneath him, he rolled full length in the contrary direction, mowing down people by the dozen. Still rolling, he broke out of a knot of recumbent forms, revolved across the track and tried to regain his feet on the very verge.

He stood up, for a fraction of a second, with one foot on the middle track and one foot on the nearer five-mile track; then the difference in speed overcame him. He chose the five-mile track and sat on it, hard. He passed us, as we gazed with interest, lying flat on his back, his feet in the air. Fifty yards along the road he gained the safety of the pavement with a sudden, acrobatic movement, turned and dashed toward us.

As he neared, I perceived that he was darker in complexion than most of the people I had seen. His rompers were a horrible yellow above the waist and black below; his socks were of black; his sandals black with yellow piping. A yellow pork-pie hat was rammed squarely on his head; a yellow tassel hung from the center of its crown and dangled over his left ear.

"Weston!" he bellowed. "It's me—Henshaw!"

He came up to us, his face beaming with pleasure, and smacked me heartily on the back. I studied him closely. He was as hairy as an egg.

"I don't believe it," I said, flatly.

"I can hardly believe it when I look at you," he retorted.

"Then how did you recognize me?"

"Because yours is the only monkey nut in the whole wide world." He took a pace back and surveyed me from head to heel. "The only original Robin Hood, as I live and breathe," he said. "How d'you like my rig?" He spread his arms and slowly rotated before us.

"I would rather not say," I said, averting my eyes from the bilious yellow; "justice can be pronounced only in vulgar terms."

"Jealous!" was his laughing comment. "Personally, I think attire such as this lends color to life. If I've any fault to find, it is only the trouble it creates in distinguishing sahibs from memsahibs. So you've been shopping, huh?" He jabbed a finger at the lighter suspended from my neck. "And how do you like this moneyless world?"

"Seeing you know about the money, or lack of it, it's evident you've been shopping," I commented.

"Oh, no," he assured us. "I went to pay the hair-plucker and he acted like one thunderstruck. Then I found out about the money. Wistfully, he said he would like an odd coin if I had one to give away. So I let him run through my purse, which I had swiped when they grabbed my clothes to burn them. His eyes stood out like organ stops when he saw what I had: eighteen dollars and forty-seven cents in good old White money."

"*White* money?" I queried.

"Of course. You didn't think I'd have money from your age, did you? Well, he raked through the lot and picked out a half-dollar piece which was the oldest-dated coin there. He was as pleased as a dog with two tails. I asked him what he was going to do with it. You would never guess what he said."

"What?" I encouraged him.

"I've not yet been able to make up my mind whether I'm mentally deficient or all this world's daft but me. Believe it or not, he said he was going to swap that half dollar for a *glass fish!*"

"A glass fish!" I echoed incredulously.

"Now what the deuce could he want with that?" Henshaw continued. "A live fish would be bad enough, a dead fish better, but a glass fish!"

"That can be explained," Melsona interjected. "You see, this world has progressed so far that its one great problem is how to keep people occupied. There is no monetary system; everything can be had for the mere asking. All work, manufacturing and the like, is carried on by volunteers, but so efficient are our methods that there is never enough work for all the people who want it. Inhabitants of this world have to fill up a very large amount of spare time somehow or other; consequently, work, once a curse, is now a godsend.

"How do our citizens spend their spare time? I will tell you. A little less than half devote themselves to science, a little more than half devote themselves to art. People invent things or create things, and everybody tries to make his work individualistic or superior to that of others.

"People dispose of the unwanted products of their own handicrafts by placing them in the shops for disposal to the persons who ask for them. The greatest shame any citizen can feel is when one of his products stands waiting in a shop for months. The greatest triumph he can experience is when so many clamor for one of his works that it has to be disposed of by means of drawing lots.

"People who collect the work of any particular artist, or have a special desire to acquire one of his works, can obtain them in three ways: they can get them from a shop for the asking, if the shop happens to have them; or, if the artist is so popular his work never reaches a shop, they can apply to the artist to join with other applicants in drawing lots for his work; or, if the artist happens to be a collector himself they can barter with him.

"This explains your man's intention of changing a coin for a glass fish. Coins of your age are not rare; they are absolutely unknown and, therefore, of incalculable pleasure to a collector. One of our most prominent collectors of these old trading tokens is Torquilea, who is Earth's greatest glass artist. I would like you to see an example of his work. Come with me."

X

Following Melsona's lead we marched along the pavement in the opposite direction to the motion of the road. A lively conversation was maintained; it consisted mainly of questions by Henshaw and myself, and Melsona's answers. We gathered that a system of moving roadways radiated like the spokes of a wheel from the center of Leamore to its outskirts, that roads ran inward and outward alternately, that people who wanted to travel in the opposite direction to a road's motion either walked along the pavements or cut through a side street to the next road. This road ran to the center of the city; if Melsona was returning home from the center and did not care to walk, he just took the adjacent road, which ran outward, and entered his house by the back way. All roads exceeding thirty meters in width were moving roads; narrower roads were stable. The whole system of transport was absurdly simple.

Melsona was explaining to us that private air machines and wheeled vehicles existed in large numbers, but were not allowed to enter into, or fly over, any city, confining their activities to the terrain between towns. Just then we passed an open-air café. We did not go far past; with one accord, we retraced our steps, entered and claimed a table.

"—thus only the great liners bound for city airports are permitted to pass over occupied areas," said Melsona, finishing his conversation. "What will you have?"

"Beef," said Henshaw.

"Beef? What is that?"

"Meat," said Henshaw, licking his lips, and easing the belt around his rompers. An expression of ineffable disgust appeared on Melsona's face.

"I was only joking," Henshaw assured him, quick-wittedly. "I'll have whatever you recommend."

Melsona's expression suggested that he did not regard the joke as being in the best of taste. He scribbled on a pad framed in the table's center, rammed his foot on a pedal protruding from the floor. The table sank downward, leaving us gaping into a shaft between our feet. After a short pause the table rose into view, settled before us with its top bearing the three meals ordered. We set to. The food was strange, but satisfying.

Eventually, feeling like a new man, I left the table and, with my companions, continued along the pavement. I fell into a reverie, thinking how queer it was that my previous meal was only a few hours before—or was it thousands of years? We had walked for about ten minutes, when Melsona stopped so suddenly that, still buried in my thoughts, I bumped into him. He pointed to the garden of a beautiful villa.

"Here's a fine sample of Torquilea's work," he remarked. "Come inside and take a look at it." Without hesitation, he opened the gate and stepped into the garden, telling us that our interested inspection would be regarded as most flattering both by the artist and the owner. He led us to an object standing in the middle of the lawn. We looked at it in silence. It was divine; there was no other word for it.

A mass of colored marble, onyx, agate and lapis lazuli, ingeniously arranged, arose to a height of ten or twelve feet. Over it flowed a mock waterfall of glass so realistic one was shocked by the lack of noise. So superb was the artist's cunning that even the grain of the underlying stone had been utilized to create an impression of subsurface swirls. Embedded in the glass, by what means I could not determine, were bubbles and shadows and vague flickers of light making a perfect simulation of live and dancing water.

The fall broke at the bottom, eddying and spraying among the colored rocks, while here and there little drops of spray hung glistening in various cracks and crannies. A pair of glass salmon were leaping the fall. By looking closer I could discern that several fine wires held them suspended in midair, but so accurately were they formed by the fingers of genius it was hard to believe that the wand of some modern Merlin had not fixed them thus when in full enjoyment of vibrant life.

Henshaw removed his pork-pie and said, "I take off my hat to this!"

"It was indeed a great triumph for Torquilea," Melsona told us. "No less than twenty-seven thousand persons drew lots to decide who should have this particular masterpiece."

He looked wistfully at Henshaw. "Torquilea is crazy about old coins. Only the other day I saw one of his works that will soon be given to somebody. It was simply a small bowl containing a seashore pool in glass. Sand and pebbles lay over its bottom; a pair of semitransparent shrimps sported in its depths; a strand of green seaweed grew from a small rock on which bloomed a beautiful sea anemone with all its tentacles fully extended. It was a reproduction of nature so truthful, so marvelous, one half expected ripples on the surface of the glass. Torquilea is the happiest of men to have his work so eagerly sought after. I am sure he would consider an exchange."

Henshaw took the hint. Fishing out a coin, he handed it to Melsona, telling him to put it to the best use on behalf of us all. This grouping together of us three seemed to please Melsona immensely. He accepted the gift with glee, announcing that he would interview Torquilea at the first opportunity.

Darkness had fallen several hours when we returned to Melsona's house for rest and sleep. We had ridden half the roads of Leamore, explored many shops and buildings, seen many marvels and had been introduced to so many people we could not remember more than a couple of them. Melsona, continuing in his voluntary capacity of city guide, had conducted us hither and thither, declaring himself to be the luckiest of men because our arrival had provided him with the means to use up leisure hours. His conversation, under the continual urge of our questions, informed us of a number of remarkable facts.

We found, first of all, that the day was much longer than in my time, and that Earth's axial rotation was slowing down at such a rate scientists estimated it would cease altogether in another twenty to thirty thousand years. The phenomenon dated from the arrival of The Invader, which time inaugurated the new calendar and made this the year 772 N.R.; the letters N.R. standing for "new reckoning."

The Invader, we were informed, was a planet about twice the size of Jupiter, which had come through interstellar space, cleaved a path through the solar system and vanished into the cosmos. It passed between the orbits of Mars and the asteroid belt, its influence upsetting the normal balance of half the system, making the paths of the asteroids, Mars and Earth much more eccentric, capturing and taking with it two members of the Trojan group of asteroids.

We were told that Venus had been reached by rocket ships about fifty years after The Invader had passed, that interplanetary travel was still so difficult, so risky, that the present population of Venus was not more than twelve thousand, and that for every individual who had reached the planet safely another had been killed in the attempt.

Earth's population had not altered in number for the last ten thousand years; all Earth acknowledged a central government situated in Osmia, and the social system was Pallarism. We found that Osmia was on the site of the city I had known as Constantinople, and that the "ism" favored at the moment was based on the theories of a philosopher named Palla, who had lived about 22,800 O.R.

Our stomachs warmed with a late supper, our minds filled with memories of the day's explorations, we went to bed. With quiet deference to my taste, our host had laid upon my bed what looked like a black bathing costume. The crimson nightgown had been transferred to Henshaw's bed. Henshaw came into my room to get my opinion of how he looked prepared for slumber. I fell asleep murmuring a description he could not hear.

XI

The following four days I count the most pleasant I have experienced. We traveled extensively with our host, becoming completely at home in this strange new world. Upon the morning of the fifth day we were riding on the center track of the Derby Highway, toward the outskirts of the city, when Melsona whistled to an old man walking along the pavement in the opposite direction. The old man stopped, Melsona transferred to the slow track, then to the pavement. We followed.

"This is Senior Glen Moncho," he introduced us. "Senior is a title we have for very learned men," he added in explanation.

"Like professor," I suggested.

"Exactly. This is Senior Glyn Weston and Captain Henshaw." He smiled as we shook hands in turn. "The senior is our most prominent historian. I thought he would have a special interest in meeting you."

Henshaw was quick to seize the opportunity. He asked, "Who won the White-Yellow War of 2481 to 2486?"

"The women," replied the senior promptly.

"The women!" Henshaw looked dazed.

"The war lasted nine years, not five," the senior continued. "It was brought to an end by a militant organization of women who, first of all, refused to bear any more children, then deserted the munitions factories, causing both sides to withdraw great numbers of men to replace them, and, finally, took up arms and assassinated the individuals whom they considered to be the key men of the war. The conflict was the direct cause of the world matriarchy that held sway for the next three thousand years."

"Well, I'm a dirty soldier!" cried Henshaw.

"So you're the famous time traveler," said the senior, turning to me. "I've heard a lot about you over the newscast. I understand that you are to be invited to the Annual Convention of Scientists to be held in Metro a week hence. It would be very interesting if you could bring your travel apparatus with you."

"Now isn't that curious!" I said. "I've been here several days and it has never occurred to me to inquire what has happened to the device."

"It is quite safe," said Melsona. "It was carried along on the road while you were being taken into my house. It was rescued and placed in the Science Museum until such time as you wish to have it."

"Good," I responded. "Would you like to go and see it?" Both Senior Moncho and Melsona indicated their eagerness to inspect the time-travel room. We cut through a side street to the next road, moving inward, stood upon an outer five-mile track and glided cityward.

"The most curious thing about time travel," I said to the senior, "is how it alters one's ideas. For instance, one would think that I have defeated Nature by living for thousands of years but, as a time traveler, I know that I have not. Actually, I am about a week older than when first I started my experiment. I now know that Nature has fixed the date of my end, not in terms of years of human computation but in terms of years of my life. I shall die a certain number of *my own years* after my birth, regardless of how that number of years may be divided out, or distributed over the future."

"There is one point which, to my mind, is even more curious," the senior remarked. "How is it that we, with our great civilization, our enormous interest in every branch of science, have not been able to solve the problem which already has been solved by two who antedate us by thousands of years?"

"Henshaw hasn't solved it," I told him.

"I was not referring to Henshaw, but to your predecessor."

"My predecessor?" I failed to grasp his meaning.

"I told you that time traveling was known to us," put in Melsona. "I told you when first we met that it had been accomplished before."

I searched my memory and found that I did have a vague recollection of his mentioning something of the sort. It had escaped me at the time, as I had felt rather confused.

"When Schweil turned up, claiming that—"

"Schweil!" I shouted at the top of my voice. "Did you say *Schweil?*"

"Yes!" answered the senior, looking very startled. "When he turned up claiming he had come originally from about your time, he was laughed at, and was—"

"Tell me," I interrupted, "from what year did he claim to come?"

"Let me see." He studied the ground and thought for an exasperatingly long time. "It was nineteen hundred and forty-four, I think."

"That's it!" I howled, literally shaking with excitement. "That's it!" Surrounding people stared at me as if they thought I was mad. I was making an exhibition of myself and didn't care.

"Did you know him?" asked the senior, a soothing note in his voice.

"No. He died a few years before I was born. Or he was believed to have died. He set out in his private airplane with the avowed intention of attending a scientific congress in New York. He vanished. The wreckage of his plane reached the shores of Nova Scotia a month later. He was rather eccentric, not very popular, and some people suggested that it was a plain case of suicide. His theories, and those of his successor, were used by me. What happened to him? Where is he? Please tell me about him—everything you know."

The senior looked overwhelmed, took a deep breath and said, "In 312 N.R., four hundred and sixty years ago, this man Schweil appeared on the outskirts of Metro, our great city on the Thames, and claimed that he had traveled through time from the past. His machine took the form of a dull metal sphere about three meters in diameter. Despite his atavistic characteristics, he was not believed. His machine was examined and pronounced a hoax.

"He was in the unfortunate position of not being able to prove his assertions, except by giving a practical demonstration and thus removing himself from the very people who were to be convinced, for he told us that though one could travel into the future there could be *no* motion into the past."

"Quite correct," I said, hanging on every word.

"He was very bitter. According to him ours was the eighth era he had visited and in not a single one of them had he been believed. In the end, he emigrated to Venus, taking his metal sphere with him. He lived there for nearly a year, then managed to convince us that his claims were justified. He did it by stepping into his sphere and vanishing before the eyes of a thousand colonists. He has not returned. We have seen nothing of him since."

"He has traveled forward," I said, jumping about like a cat on hot bricks. "He has traveled forward. Oh, if only I could meet him! A man from my own time, a fit companion for my travels! I *must* meet him! I must find him somehow! He awaits me somewhere in the tomorrow. I must seek him! My travel room must be transported to Venus at once!" So saying, in my crazy excitement I jumped on to the faster center track and rushed along it, my mind filled with only one thought: to get to the Science Museum as soon as possible and arrange for the transport of the room.

The exertion of running must have calmed my mind. Half a mile along the road I transferred myself to the pavement and waited for the others to catch up with me. They came stringing along breathlessly, first Henshaw, then Melsona, the senior a bad last and finding the going hard.

Together we entered the Museum, where Melsona inquired where my room had been placed. Following his lead, we reached it on the top floor. By this time I had cooled enough to remember that my companions wanted to examine it. I opened the door and proceeded to explain to them how the ray apparatus worked and the theories it made use of.

The room seemed to have suffered slight damage. The outside

corners were badly scratched and dented; one of the windows was cracked. I pulled out the valves and ray tube, held them up to the light and examined them, replacing them when I found them still in excellent condition.

I went over the whole apparatus, adjusting a cable here and tightening a terminal there. For several minutes I pottered about like a mother attending to her babe. I was in the act of bending down to examine a McAndrew vibrator contact when a nausea overcame me and the contact blurred before my gaze.

XII

I straightened, saw the windows framing a semitransparency in which a vague shadow danced, flickered, then disappeared like the flame of a snuffed candle. Panic overcame me, as a familiar mist obscured my sight. I realized what had happened. By some means the projector had come into operation.

Frantically, I searched the enveloping haze for the switch. The rapidly alternating impressions of smoothness and fibrousness fuddled my mind. I searched like a drunken man looking for he knew not what. Everything my hand touched I pulled. I tugged at unseen objects that refused to move. I heaved upon things that came out and sprang back again.

For how long I acted thus I do not know. I grew frantic at the knowledge that my last sweet world was receding rapidly into the irreclaimable past. I commenced to kick wildly in every direction. A crash of glass, followed by a sensation of strain, rewarded my efforts. The mist cleared, leaving me gazing at a broken valve. The time-travel room had come to rest.

A heavy vapor coated the inside surfaces of the windows. My attention was attracted by a loud, hissing sound. I was astounded to discover air rushing outward through the gap in the partly open door. I closed the door tightly, turned the petcock of the spare oxygen bottle, rubbed moisture from the windowpanes and looked out.

The scene before my eyes was most depressing: a smooth, even expanse of dirt and dust extended to the horizon without break. The sky to one side was sparkled with white light, to the other it loomed a dark, ominous purple. One glance told me that the world of this day was airless, deserted, dead. Horror took command of me with the knowledge that my hours were numbered. Death awaited me without—and within!

Hours later, with the precious oxygen still dribbling away, I stared gloomily through the windows of my room, noting that the sky had not changed in the slightest degree and that apparently I was stationed in a zone of perpetual twilight. Even as I watched, some instinct drew my attention to the far horizon. There, in a majestic curve, swooped a colossal space ship, its sleek body glistening, its tail plumed with fire. My heart leaped as I followed its line of flight until it dipped to an invisible landing place just over the edge of the Earth.

It did not occur to me to wonder why a space ship should fly over an airless world. The idea that I might be the victim of my own delusion never entered my head. I folded a handkerchief to form a pad, secured it over the end of the nearly empty oxygen bottle and opened the door. Ramming the pad against my nostrils, I ran toward the horizon—

For endless miles I seemed to run with heaving chest, thudding heart and whirling brain. My tongue swelled in my mouth; my eyes protruded painfully; I ceased to see. Whether I was moving in a straight line or in circles, I did not know or care. The main thing was to keep moving. Delirium became my master; I moved, moved, moved like an automaton.

I must have dropped the oxygen bottle; I must have fallen and died. But I have no recollection of it. My last memory of Earth is that of fleeing on leaden feet like one chased by phantoms in a nightmare. You know the rest of my story. I came to my senses lying in the resuscitation room at Kar Institute, my body racked with pain, my pulses throbbing in sympathy with the beating of a mechanical heart suspended over my chest.

What next? You are entitled to know. It is my intention to spend a little while touring your beautiful world. I wish to see the sights, to study your customs. With much interest I have learned that the immense amount of work resulting from the Great Migration has caused many radical changes from the world I visited last. I want to read about the Great Migration, to learn all there is to learn about this remarkable epic in human history, to know the nature of the changes it has brought about such as, for instance, your return to a monetary system.

Then I shall set to work and build myself another time-travel room. I shall do this because I am going to find my age-compatriot Schweil. We need each other. Would you like to know how I expect to accomplish this? Let me tell you.

I shall make a series of very short jumps into the future and from them I shall derive the data necessary for certain calculations which, when completed, will enable me to set out for a predetermined date. If Schweil has not turned up by then, I shall leave a message for him, making an appointment far in the future, and will then depart for that date. When Schweil arrives, and gets my message, he will travel to the same date. Thus we shall meet at a rendezvous in futurity.

I have no doubt that the scheme will work, if only Schweil is given my message. You will have to look for him. I am sure that already he has returned a dozen times since last he was heard of. Because of his previous receptions, knowing his character as I do, I can tell you he is likely to return secretly, without publicity.

You can assist me! All I ask of you is that you keep my story and my message ever fresh!

The stereo announcer padded softly in the direction of the transmission screen. The auditorium was a mass of eyes fixed intently on one central figure. With an abrupt movement, Glyn Weston, the "Seeker of Tomorrow," left the stage.

Illustrated by Charles Schneeman

"All I can hear," snapped the doctor, "is hair scratching on the stethoscope diaphragm."

Hyperpilosity

By L. Sprague de Camp

W E ALL know about the brilliant successes in the arts and sciences, but if you knew all their stories, you might find that some of the failures were really more interesting."

It was Pat Weiss speaking. The beer had given out, and Carl Vandercock had gone out to get some more. Pat, having cornered all the chips in sight, was leaning back and emitting vast clouds of smoke.

"That means," I opined, "that you've got a story coming. O.K., spill it. The poker can wait."

"Only don't stop in the middle and say 'That reminds me,' and go off on another story, and from the middle of that to another, and so on," put in Hannibal Snyder.

Pat cocked an eye at Hannibal. "Listen, mug, I haven't digressed once in the last three stories I've told. If you can tell a story better, go to it. Ever hear of J. Román Oliveira?" he said, not waiting, I noticed, to give Hannibal a chance to take him up.

He continued. "Carl's been talking a lot about that new gadget of his, and no doubt it will make him famous if he ever finishes it. And Carl usually finishes what he sets out to do. My friend Oliveira finished what he set out to do, also, and it should have made him famous. But it didn't. Scientifically, his work was a success, and deserving of the highest praise. But humanly, it was a failure. That's why he's now running a little college down in Texas. He still does good work, and gets articles in the journals, but it's not what he had every reason to suspect that he deserved. Just got a letter from him the other day—it seems he's now a proud grandfather. That reminds me of my grandfather—"

"Hey!" roared Hannibal.

Pat said "Huh? Oh, I see. Sorry. I won't do it again." He went on. "I first knew J. Román when I was a mere student at the Medical Center and he was a professor of virology. The J in his name stands

413

for Haysoos, spelled J-e-s-u-s, which is a perfectly good Mexican name. But he'd been so much kidded about it in the States that he preferred to go by Román.

"You remember that the Great Change—which is what this story has to do with—started in the winter of 1971, with that awful flu epidemic. Oliveira came down with it. I went around to see him to get an assignment, and found him perched on a pile of pillows and wearing the awfullest pink and green pajamas. His wife was reading to him in Spanish.

" 'Leesten, Pat,' he said when I came in, 'I know you're a worthy student, but I weesh you and the whole damn virology class were roasting on the hottest greedle in Hell. Tell me what you want, and then go away and let me die in peace.'

"I got my information, and was just going, when his doctor came in—old Fogarty, who used to lecture on sinuses. He'd given up G.P. long before, but he was so scared of losing a good virologist that he was handling Oliveira's case himself.

" 'Stick around, sonny,' he said to me when I started to follow Mrs. Oliveira out, 'and learn a little practical medicine. I've always thought it a mistake that we haven't a class to train doctors in bedside manners. Now observe how I do it. I smile at Oliveira here, but I don't act so damned cheerful that he'd find death a welcome relief from my company. That's a mistake some young doctors make. Notice that I walk up briskly, and not as if I were afraid my patient was liable to fall in pieces at the slightest jar—' and so on.

"The fun came when he put the end of his stethoscope on Oliveira's chest.

" 'Can't hear a damn thing,' he snorted, 'or rather, you've got so much hair that all I can hear is the ends of it scraping on the diaphragm. May have to shave it. But say, isn't that rather unusual for a Mexican?'

" 'You're jolly well right she ees,' retorted the sufferer. 'Like most natives of my beautiful Mehheeco, I am of mostly Eendian descent, and Eendians are of Mongoloid race, and so have little body hair. It's all come out in the last week.'

" 'That's funny—' Fogarty said.

"I spoke up. 'Say, Dr. Fogarty, it's more than that. I had my flu a month ago, and the same thing's been happening to me. I've always felt like a sissy because of not having any hair on my torso to speak of. Now I've got a crop that's almost long enough to braid. I didn't think anything special about it—'

"I don't remember what was said next, because we all talked at once. But when we got calmed down there didn't seem to be anything we could do without some systematic investigation, and I promised Fogarty to come around to his place so he could look me over.

"I did, the next day, but he didn't find anything except a lot of hair. He took samples of everything he could think of, of course. I'd given up wearing underwear because it itched, and anyway the hair was warm enough to make it unnecessary, even in a New York January.

"The next thing I heard was a week later, when Oliveira returned to his classes and told me that Fogarty had caught the flu. Oliveira had been making observations on the old boy's thorax, and found that he, too, had begun to grow body hair at an unprecedented rate.

"Then my girl friend—not the present missus; I hadn't met her yet—overcame her embarrassment enough to ask me whether I could explain how it was that *she* was getting hairy. I could see that the poor girl was pretty badly cut up about it, because obviously her chances of catching a good man would be reduced by her growing a pelt like a bear or a gorilla. I wasn't able to enlighten her, but told her that, if it was any comfort, a lot of other people were suffering from the same thing.

"Then we heard that Fogarty had died. He was a good egg and we were sorry, but he'd led a pretty full life, and you couldn't say that he was cut off in his prime.

"Oliveira called me to his office. 'Pat,' he said, 'you were looking for a chob last fall, ees it not? Well, I need an asseestant. We're going to find out about this hair beezness. Are you on?' I was.

"We started by examining all the clinical cases. Everybody who had, or had had, the flu was growing hair. And it was a severe winter, and it looked as though everybody was going to have the flu sooner or later.

"Just about that time I had a bright idea. I looked up all the cosmetic companies that made depilatories, and soaked what little money I had into their stock. I was sorry later, but I'll come to that.

"Román Oliveira was a glutton for work, and with the hours he made me keep I began to have uneasy visions of flunking out. But the fact that my girl friend had become so self-conscious about her hair that she wouldn't go out anymore saved me some time.

"We worked and worked over our guinea pigs and rats, but didn't get anywhere. Oliveira got a bunch of hairless Chihuahua dogs and tried assorted gunks on them, but nothing happened. He even got a pair of East African sand rats—*Heterocephalus*—hideous-looking hairless things—but that was a blank, too.

"Then the business got into the papers. I noticed a little article in *The New York Times*, on an inside page. A week later there was a full-column story on page one of the second part. Then it was on the front page. It was mostly 'Dr. So-and-so says he thinks this nation-wide attack of hyperpilosity' (swell word, huh? Wish I could remember the name of the doc who invented it) 'is due to this, that, or the other thing.'

"Our usual February dance had to be called off because almost none of the students could get their girls to go. Attendance at the movie houses had fallen off pretty badly for much the same reason. It was a cinch to get a good seat, even if you arrived around 8:00 P.M. I noticed one funny little item in the paper, to the effect that the filming of 'Tarzan and the Octopus-Men' had been called off because the actors were supposed to go running around in G-strings. The company had found that they had to clip and shave the whole cast all over every few days if they didn't want the actors and the gorillas confused.

"It was fun to ride on a bus about then and watch the people, who were pretty well bundled up. Most of them scratched, and those who were too well-bred to scratch just squirmed and looked unhappy.

"Next I read that application for marriage licenses had fallen off so that three clerks were able to handle the entire business for Greater New York, including Yonkers, which had just been incorporated into the Bronx.

"I was gratified to see that my cosmetic stocks were going up nicely. I tried to get my roommate, Bert Kafket, to get in on them too. But he just smiled mysteriously and said he had other plans.

"Bert was a kind of professional pessimist. 'Pat,' he said, 'maybe you and Oliveira will lick this business, and maybe not. I'm betting that you won't. If I win, the stocks that I've bought will be doing famously long after your depilatories are forgotten.'

"As you know, people were pretty excited about the plague. But when the weather began to get warm, the fun really started. First the four big underwear companies ceased operations, one after another. Two of them were placed in receivership, another liquidated completely, and the fourth was able to pull through by switching to the manufacture of table-cloths and American flags. The bottom dropped completely out of the cotton market, as this alleged 'hair-growing flu' had spread all over the world by now. Congress had been planning to go home early, and was, as usual, being urged to do so by the conservative newspapers. But now Washington was jammed with cotton-planters demanding that the Government Do Something, and they didn't dare. The Government was willing enough to Do Something, but unfortunately didn't have the foggiest idea of how to go about it.

"All this time Oliveira, more or less assisted by me, was working night and day on the problem, but we didn't seem to have any better luck than the Government.

"You couldn't hear anything on the radio in the building where I lived, because of the interference from the big, powerful electric clippers that everybody had installed and kept going all the time.

"It's an ill wind, as the prophet saith, and Bert Kafket got some good out of it. His girl, whom he had been pursuing for some years, had been making a good salary as a model at Josephine Lyon's exclusive dress establishment on Fifth Avenue, and she had been leading Bert a dance. But now all of a sudden the Lyon place folded up, as nobody seemed to be buying any clothes, and the girl was only too glad to take Bert as her lawful wedded husband. Not much hair was grown on the women's faces, fortunately for them or God knows what would have become of the race. Bert and I flipped a coin to see which of us should move, and I won.

"Congress finally passed a bill setting up a reward of a million dollars for whoever should find a permanent cure for hyperpilosity, and then adjourned, having, as usual, left a flock of important bills not acted upon.

"When the weather became really hot in June, all the men quit wearing shirts, as their pelts covered them quite as effectively. The police force kicked so about having to wear their regular uniforms that they were allowed to go around in dark blue polo shirts and shorts. But pretty soon they were rolling up their shirts and sticking them in the pockets of their shorts. It wasn't long before the rest of the male population of the United States was doing likewise. In growing hair the human race hadn't lost any of its capacity to sweat, and you'd pass out with the heat if you tried to walk anywhere on a hot day with any amount of clothes on. I can still remember holding onto a hydrant at Third Avenue and Sixtieth Street and trying not to faint, with the sweat pouring out the ankles of my pants and the buildings going 'round and 'round. After that I was sensible and stripped down to shorts like everyone else.

"In July Natasha, the gorilla in the Bronx Zoo, escaped from her cage and wandered around the park for hours before anyone noticed her. The zoo visitors all thought she was merely an unusually ugly member of their own species.

"If the hair played hob with the textile and clothing business generally, the market for silk simply disappeared. Stockings were just quaint things that our ancestors had worn. Like cocked hats and periwigs. One result was that the economy of the Japanese Empire, always a pretty shaky proposition, went completely to pot, which is how they had a revolution and are now a soviet socialist republic.

"Neither Oliveira nor I took any vacation that summer, as we were working like fury on the hair problem. Román promised me a cut of the reward when and if he won it.

"But we didn't get anywhere at all during the summer. When classes started we had to slow down a bit on the research, as I was in my last year, and Oliveira had to teach. But we kept at it as best we could.

"It was funny to read the editorials in the papers. The *Chicago Tribune* even suspected a Red Plot. You can imagine the time that the cartoonists for the *New Yorker* and *Esquire* had.

"With the drop in the price of cotton, the South was really flat on its back this time. I remember when the Harwick bill was introduced in Congress, to require every citizen over the age of five to be clipped at least once a week. A bunch of Southerners were back of it, of course. When that was defeated, largely on the argument of unconstitutionality, the you-alls put forward one requiring every person to be clipped before he'd be allowed to cross a state line. The theory was that human hair is a commodity—which it is sometimes —and that crossing a state line with a coat of the stuff, whether your own or someone else's, constituted interstate commerce, and brought you under control of the federal government. It looked for a while as though it would pass, but the Southerners finally accepted a substitute bill requiring all federal employees and cadets at the military and naval academies to be clipped.

"The destitution in the South intensified the ever-present race problem, and led eventually to the Negro revolt in Alabama and Mississippi, which was put down only after some pretty savage fighting. Under the agreement that ended that little civil war the Negroes were given the present Pale, a sort of reservation with considerable local autonomy. They haven't done as well as they claimed they were going to under that arrangement, but they've done better than the Southern whites said they would. Which I suppose is about what you'd expect. But, boy, just let a white man visiting their territory get uppity, and see what happens to him! They won't take any lip.

"About this time—in the autumn of 1971—the cotton and textile interests got out a big advertising campaign to promote clipping. They had slogans, such as 'Don't Be a Hairy Ape!' and pictures of a couple of male swimmers, one with hair and the other without, and a pretty girl turning in disgust from the hirsute swimmer and fairly pouncing on the clipped one.

"I don't know how much good their campaign would have done, but they overplayed their hand. They, and all the clothing outfits, tried to insist on boiled shirts, not only for evening wear, but for daytime wear as well. I never thought a long-suffering people would really revolt against the tyrant Style, but we did. The thing that really tore it was the inauguration of President Passavant. There was an unusually warm January thaw that year, and the president, the v-p, and all the justices of the Supreme Court appeared without a stitch on above the waist, and damn little below.

"We became a nation of confirmed near-nudists, just as did everybody else sooner or later. The one drawback to real nudism was the fact that, unlike the marsupials, man hasn't any natural pockets. So we compromised between the hair, the need for something to hold fountain-pens, money, and so forth, and our traditional ideas of modesty by adopting an up-to-date version of the Scottish sporran.

"The winter was a bad one for flu, and everybody who hadn't caught it the preceding winter got it now. Soon a hairless person became such a rarity that one wondered if the poor fellow had the mange.

"In May of 1972 we finally began to get somewhere. Oliveira had the bright idea—which both of us ought to have thought of sooner—of examining ectogenic babies. Up to now, nobody had noticed that they began to develop hair a little later than babies born the normal way. You remember that human ectogenesis was just beginning to be worked about then. Test-tube babies aren't yet practical for large-scale production by a long shot, but we'll get there some day.

"Well, Oliveira found that if the ectogens were subjected to a really rigid quarantine, they never developed hair at all—at least not in more than the normal quantities. By really rigid quarantine, I mean that the air they breathed was heated to 800° C., then liquefied, run through a battery of cyclones, and washed with a dozen disinfectants. Their food was treated in a comparable manner. I don't quite see how the poor little fellows survived such unholy sanitation, but they did, and didn't grow hair—until they were brought in contact with other human beings, or were injected with sera from the blood of hairy babies.

"Oliveira figured out that the cause of the hyperpilosity was what he'd suspected all along—another of these damned self-perpetuating protein molecules. As you know, you can't see a protein molecule, and you can't do much with it chemically because, if you do, it forthwith ceases to be a protein molecule. We have their structure worked out pretty well now, but it's been a slow process with lots of inferences from inadequate data. Sometimes the inferences were right and sometimes they weren't.

"But to do much in the way of detailed analysis of the things, you need a respectable quantity of them, and these that we were after didn't exist in even a disrespectable amount. Then Oliveira worked out his method of counting them. The reputation he made from that method is about the only permanent thing he got out of all his work.

"When we applied the method, we found something decidedly screwy—an ectogen's virus count after catching hyperpil was the same as it had been before. That didn't seem right. We knew that he had been injected with hyperpil molecules and had come out with a fine mattress as a result.

"Then one morning I found Oliveira at his desk looking like a medieval monk who had just seen a vision after a forty-day fast. (Incidentally, you try fasting that long and you'll see visions too, lots of 'em.) He said, 'Pat, don't buy a yacht with your share of that meelion. They cost too much to upkeep.'

" 'Huh?' was the brightest remark I could think of.

" 'Look here,' he said, going to the blackboard. It was covered with chalk diagrams of protein molecules. 'We have three proteins, alpha, beta, and gamma. No alphas have exeested for thousands of years. Now, you will note that the only deefference between the alpha and the beta is that these nitrogens'—he pointed—'are hooked onto *thees* chain instead of that one. You will also observe, from the energy relations wreeten down here, that if one beta is eentroduced eento a set of alphas, all the alphas will presently turn into betas.

" 'Now, we know now that all sorts of protein molecules are being assembled inside us all the time. Most of them are unstable and break up again, or are inert and harmless, or lack the power of self-reproduction—anyway, nothing happens because of them. But, because they are so beeg and complicated, the possible forms they take are very many, and it is possible that once in a long time some new kind of protein appears with self-reproducing qualities; in other words, a virus. Probably that's how the various disease viruses got started, all because something choggled an ordinary protein molecule that was chust being feenished and got the nitrogens hooked on the wrong chains.

" 'My idea is thees: The alpha protein, which I have reconstructed from what we know about its descendants beta and gamma, once exeested as a harmless and inert protein molecule in the human body. Then one day somebody heecupped as one of them was being formed, and presto! We had a beta. But the beta is not harmless. It reproduces itself fast, and it inheebits the growth of hair on most of our bodies. So presently all our species—wheech at the time was pretty apish—catch this virus, and lose their hair. Moreover, it is one of the viruses that is transmeeted to the embryro, so the new babies don't have hair, either.

" 'Well, our ancestors sheever a while, and then learn to cover themselves with animal skeens to keep warm, and also to keep fire. And so, the march of ceevilizations it is commence! Chust theenk—except for that one original beta protein molecule, we should probably today all be merely a kind of goreela or cheempanzee. Anyway, an ordinary anthropoid ape.

" 'Now, I feegure that what has happened is that another change in the form of the molecule has taken place, changing it from beta to gamma—and gamma is a harmless and inert leetle fellow, like alpha. So we are back where we started.

" 'Our problem, yours and mine, is to find how to turn the gammas, with wheech we are all swarming, back into betas. In other words, now that we have become all of a sudden cured of the disease that was endemic in the whole race for thousands of years, we want our disease back again. And I theenk I see how it can be done.'

"I couldn't get much more out of him; we went to work harder than ever. After several weeks he announced that he was ready to experiment on himself; his method consisted of a combination of a number of drugs—one of them was the standard cure for glanders in horses, as I recall—and a high-frequency electromagnetic fever.

"I wasn't very keen about it, because I'd gotten to like the fellow, and that awful dose he was going to give himself looked enough to kill a regiment. But he went right ahead.

"Well, it nearly did kill him. But after three days he was more or less back to normal, and was whooping at the discovery that the hair on his limbs and body was rapidly falling out. In a couple of weeks he had no more hair than you'd expect a Mexican professor of virology to have.

"But then our real surprise came, and it wasn't a pleasant one!

"We expected to be more or less swamped by publicity, and we had made our preparations accordingly. I remember staring into Oliveira's face for a full minute and then reassuring him that he had trimmed his mustache to exact symmetry and getting him to straighten my new necktie.

"Our epoch-making announcement dug up two personal calls from bored reporters, a couple of phone interviews from science editors, and not one photographer! We did make the science section of *The New York Times*, but with only about twelve lines of type—the paper merely stated that Professor Oliveira and his assistant—not named—had found the cause and cure of hyperpilosity. Not a word about the possible effects of the discovery.

"Our contracts with the Medical Center prohibited us from exploiting our discovery commercially, but we expected that plenty of other people would be quick to do so as soon as the method was made public. But it didn't happen. In fact, we might have discovered a correlation between temperature and the pitch of the bullfrog's croak for all the splash we made.

"A week later Oliveira and I talked to the department head, Wheelock, about the discovery. Oliveira wanted him to use his influence to get a dehairing clinic set up. But Wheelock couldn't see it.

" 'We've had a couple of inquiries,' he admitted, 'but nothing to get excited about. Remember the rush there was when the Zimmerman cancer treatment came out? Well, there's been nothing like that. In fact, I—ah—doubt whether I personally should care to undergo your treatment, sure-fire though it may be, Dr. Oliveira. I'm not in the least disparaging the remarkable piece of work you've done. But'—here he ran his fingers through the hair on his chest, which was over six inches long, thick, and a beautiful silky white—'you know, I've gotten rather fond of the old pelt, and I'd feel slightly indecent back in my bare skin. Also, it's a lot more economical than a suit of clothes. And—ah—if I may say so with due modesty—I don't think it's bad-looking. My family has always ridden me about my sloppy clothes, but now the laugh's on them. Not one of them can show a coat of fur like mine!'

"Oliveira and I left, sagging in the breeches a bit. We inquired of people we knew, and wrote letters to a number of them, asking what they thought of the idea of undergoing the Oliveira treatment. A few said they might if enough others did, but most of them responded in much the same vein that Doc Wheelock had. They'd gotten used to their hair, and saw no good reason for going back to their former glabrous state.

" 'So, Pat,' said Oliveira to me, 'it lukes as though we don't get much fame out of our discovery. But we may essteel salvage a leetle fortune. You remember that meelion-dollar reward? I sent in my application as soon as I recovered from my treatment, and we should hear from the government any day.'

"We did. I was up at his apartment, and we were talking about nothing in particular, when Mrs. O. rushed in with the letter, squeaking, 'Open eet! Open eet, Román!'

"He opened it without hurry, spread the sheet of paper out, and read it. Then he frowned and read it again. Then he laid it down, very carefully took out and lit the wrong end of a cork-tipped cigarette, and said in his levellest voice, 'I have been esstupid again, Pat. I never thought that there might be a time leemit on that reward offer. Now it seems that some crafty *sanamagoon* in Congress poot one een, so that the offer expired on May first. You remember, I mailed the claim on the nineteenth, and they got it on the twenty-first. Three weeks too late!'

"I looked at Oliveira, and he looked at me and then at his wife. And she looked at him and then went without a word to the cabinet and got out two large bottles of *tequila* and three tumblers.

"Oliveira pulled up three chairs around a little table, and settled with a sigh in one of them. 'Pat,' he said, 'I may not have a meelion dollars, but I have something more valuable by far—a wooman who knows what is needed at a time like thees!'

"And that's the inside story of the Great Change—or at least of one aspect thereof. That's how it happens that, when we today speak of a platinum-blonde movie star, we aren't referring to her scalp hair alone, but the beautiful silvery pelt that covers her from crown to ankle.

"There was just one more incident. Bert Kafket had me up to his place to dinner a few nights later. After I had told him and his wife about Oliveira's and my troubles, he asked how I had made out on that depilatory-manufacturer stock I'd bought.

" 'I notice those stocks are back about where they started from before the Change,' he added.

" 'Didn't make anything to speak of,' I told him. 'About the time they started to slide down from their peak, I was too busy working for Román to pay much attention to them. When I finally did look them up I was just able to unload with a few cents profit per share. How did you do on those stocks you were so mysterious about last year?'

" 'Maybe you noticed my new car as you came in?' asked Bert with a grin. 'That's them. Or rather, it; there was only one—Jones and Galloway Company.'

" 'What do Jones and Galloway make? I never heard of them.'

" 'They make'—here Bert's grin looked as if it were going to run around his head and meet behind—'currycombs!'

"And that was that. Here's Carl with the beer now. It's your deal, isn't it, Hannibal?"

Already the old dream was reality, and the civilization I had known was slipping away—

Illustrated by Elliot Dold

Pithecanthropus Rejectus

By Manly W. Wellman

MY FIRST memories seem to be those of the normal human child—nursery, toys, adults seriously making meaningless observations with charts, tape measures and scales. Well, rather more than average of that last item, the observations. My constant companion was a fat, blue-eyed baby that drooled and gurgled and barely crept upon the nursery linoleum, while I scurried easily hither and thither, scrambling up on tables and bedposts, and sometimes on the bureau. I felt sorry for him now and then. But he was amazingly happy and healthy, and gave no evidence of having the sudden fearful pains that struck me in head and jaw from time to time.

As I learned to speak and to comprehend, I found out the cause of those pains. I was told by the tall, smiling blond woman who taught me to call her "Mother." She explained that I had been born with no opening in the top of my skull—so needed for bone and brain expansion—and that the man of the house—"Doctor"—had made such an opening, governing the growth of my cranium and later stopping the hole with a silver plate. My jaw, too, had been altered with silver, for when I was born it had been too shallow and narrow to give my tongue play. The building of a chin for me and the remodeling of several tongue-muscles had made it possible for me to speak. I learned before the baby did, by several months. I learned to say Mother, Doctor, to call the baby "Sidney" and myself "Congo." Later I could make my wants known, although, as this writing shows and will show, I was never fluent.

Doctor used to come into the nursery and make notes by the hour, watching my every move and pricking up his ears at my every sound. He was a stout, high-shouldered man, with a strong, square beard. He acted grave—almost stern—where I was involved. But with baby Sidney he played most tenderly. I used to feel hurt and would go to Mother for sympathy. She had enough for me and Sidney, too. She would pick me up and cuddle me and laugh—give me her cheek to kiss.

Once or twice Doctor scowled, and once I overheard him talking to Mother just beyond the nursery door. I understood pretty well even then, and since that time I have filled in details of the conversation.

"I tell you, I don't like it," he snapped. "Showering attentions on that creature."

She gave him a ready laugh. "Poor little Congo!"

"Congo's an ape, for all my surgery," he replied coldly. "Sidney is your son, and Sidney alone. The other is an experiment—like a shake-up of chemicals in a tube, or a grafting of twigs on a tree."

"Let me remind you," said Mother, still good-natured, "that when you brought him from the zoo, you said he must live here as a human child, on equal terms with Sidney. That, remember, was part of the experiment. And so are affection and companionship."

"Ah, the little beast!" Doctor almost snarled. "Sometimes I wish I hadn't begun these observations."

"But you have. You increased his brain powers and made it possible for him to speak. He's brighter than any human child his age."

"Apes mature quickly. He'll come to the peak of development and Sidney will forge ahead. That always happens in these experiments."

"These experiments have always been performed with ordinary ape-children before," said Mother. "With your operations you've given him something, at least, of human character. So give him something of human consideration as well."

"I'm like Prospero, going out of my way to lift up Caliban from the brute."

"Caliban meant well," Mother responded, reminding him of something I knew nothing about. "Meanwhile, I don't do things by halves, dear. As long as Congo remains in this house, he shall have kindness and help from me. And he shall look to me as his mother."

I heard and, in time, digested all of this. When I learned to read, during my third year, I got hold of some of Doctor's published articles about me and began to realize what everything meant.

Of course, I'd seen myself in mirrors hundreds of times and knew that I was dark, bow-legged, and long-armed, with a face that grew out at an acute angle, and hair all over my body. Yet this had not set me very far apart, in my own mind, from the others. I was different from Sidney—but so was Doctor and so was Mother, in appearance, size and behavior. I was closer to them—in speech and such things as table manners and self-reliance—than he. But now I learned and grew to appreciate the difference between me, on one side, and Sidney, Doctor and Mother on the other.

I had been born, I found, in an iron cage at the Bronx Zoo. My mother was a great ape, a Kulakamba, very close to human type in body, size and intelligence—not dwarfed like a common chimpanzee nor thickset and surly like a gorilla. Doctor, a great experimental anthropologist—words like those happen to be easy for me, since they were part of daily talk at Doctor's house—had decided to make observations on a baby ape and his own newborn child, rearing them side by side under identical conditions. I was the baby ape.

Incidentally, I have read in a book called *Trader Horn* that there are no Kulakambas, that they are only a fairy story. But there are—many and many of us, in the Central African forests.

I tell these things very glibly, as if I knew all about them. Doctor had written reams about the Kulakamba, and clippings of all he wrote were kept in the library. I had recourse to them as I grew older.

When I was four, Doctor led me into his big white laboratory. There he examined and measured my hands, grunting perplexedly into his beard.

"We'll have to operate," he said at last.

"Will we?" I quavered. I knew what the word meant.

He smiled, but not exactly cheerfully. "You'll have an anesthetic," he promised, as though it were a great favor. "I want to fix your hands. The thumbs don't oppose and it makes your grasp clumsy. Not human, Congo; not human."

I was frightened, but Mother came to comfort me and say that I would be better off in the long run. So, when Doctor commanded, I lay on the sheet-spread table and breathed hard into the cloth he put on my face. I went to sleep and dreamed of high, green trees and of people like myself who climbed and played there—building nests and eating nuts as big as my head. In my dream I tried to join them, but found myself held back, as if by a pane of glass. That made me shed tears—though some say that apes cannot shed tears—and thus weeping, I awoke. My hands had a dull soreness in them and were swathed in bandages to the elbows. After weeks, I could use them again and found that their calloused palms had been softened, the awkward little thumbs somehow lengthened and newly jointed. I grew so skillful with them that I could pick up a pin or tie a bow knot. This was in the winter time, and once or twice when I played on the porch I had terrible pains in brow and jaw. Doctor said that the cold made my silver plates hurt, and that I must never go outside without a warm cap and a muffler wrapped high.

"It's like a filling against the nerve of a tooth," he explained.

At seven I was all about the house, helping Mother very deftly with her work. Now Doctor grew enthusiastic about me. He would lecture us all at the table—Sidney and I ate with him when there was no company—and said that his experiment, faulty in some ways, gave promise of great things along an unforeseen line.

"Congo was only a normal ape-cub," he would insist, "and he's developing in every possible way into a very respectable lower-class human being."

"He's by no means lower class," Mother always argued at this point, but Doctor would plunge ahead.

"We could operate on his people wholesale, make wonderful, cheap labor available. Why, when Congo grows up he'll be as strong as six or eight men, and his keep is almost nothing."

He tested me at various occupations—gardening, carpentry and ironworking, at which last I seem to have done quite well—and one day he asked me what I would rather do than anything else.

I remembered the dream I had had when he operated on me—and many times since. "Best of all," I replied, "I would like to live in a tree, build a nest of leaves and branches—"

"Ugh!" he almost screamed in disgust. "And I thought you were becoming human!"

After that he renewed his demands that Mother treat me with less affection.

Sidney was going to school at this time. I remained at home with Doctor and Mother—we lived in a small New Jersey town—and confined most of my activities to the house and the shrub-grown back yard. Once I ran away, after a little quarrel with Doctor, and frightened the entire neighborhood before I was brought back by a nervous policeman with a drawn revolver. Doctor punished me by confining me to my room for three days. During that lonely time I did a lot of thinking and set myself down as an outcast. I had been considered strange, fearful and altogether unbelonging, by human beings. My crooked body and hairy skin had betrayed me to enmity and capture.

At the age of ten I gained my full growth. I was five feet six inches tall and weighed as much as Doctor. My face, once pallid, had become quite black, with bearded jaws and bristly hair on the upper lip. I walked upright, without touching my knuckles to the ground as ordinary apes do, for I usually held some tool or book in my hands. By listening to Sidney as he studied aloud at night I got some smattering of schooling, and I built upon this by constant and serious reading of his discarded textbooks. I have been told that the average shut-in child is apt to do the same. On top of this, I read a great deal in Doctor's library, especially travel. But I disliked fiction.

"Why should I read it?" I asked Mother when she offered me a book about "Tom Sawyer." "It isn't true."

"It's interesting," she said.

"But if it's not true, it's a lie; and a lie is wicked."

She pointed out that novel-readers knew all the time that the books were not true. To that I made answer that novel-readers were fools. Doctor, joining the conversation, asked me why, then, I enjoyed my dreams.

"You say that you dream of great green forests," he reminded. "That's no more true than the books."

"If it is a good dream," I replied, "I am glad when I wake, because it made me happy. If it is a bad dream, I am glad because I escape by waking. Anyway, dreams happen and novels do not."

Doctor called it a *sophistication,* and let that conclude the argument.

I have said that I am no proper writer, and I have shown it by overlooking an important fact—the many visits of scientists. They came to observe and to discuss things with Doctor, and even with me. But one day some men appeared who were not scientists. They smoked long cigars and wore diamond rings and derby hats. Doctor had them in his study for an hour, and that night he talked long to Mother.

"Eighteen thousand dollars!" he kept saying. "Think of it!"

"You've never thought of money before," she said sadly.

"But eighteen th—my dear, it would be only the beginning. We'd do the experiment again, with two baby apes—two new little Congos for you to fuss over—"

"And the first Congo, my poor jungle foster son," mourned Mother. "He'd be miserable somewhere. How can you think of such a thing, dear? Didn't your grandfather fight to free slaves in his day?"

"Those were human slaves," replied Doctor. "Not animals. And Congo won't be miserable. His ape instinct will enjoy the new life. It'll fairly glitter for him. And we need the money to live on and to experiment with."

That went on and on, and Mother cried. But Doctor had his way. In the morning the men with the cigars came back, and Doctor greeted them gaily. They gave him a check—a big one, for they wrote it very reverently. Then he called me.

"Congo," he said, "you're to go with these people. You've got a career now, my boy; you're in the show business."

I did not want to go, but I had to.

My adventures as a theatrical curiosity have been described in many newspapers all over the world, and I will mention them but briefly. First I was rehearsed to do feats of strength and finish the act with alleged comedy—a dialogue between myself and a man in clown costume. After that, a more successful turn was evolved for me, wherein I was on the stage alone. I performed on a trapeze and a bicycle, then told my life story and answered questions asked by the audiences. I worked in a motion picture, too, with a former swimming champion. I liked him on sight, as much as I liked any human being except Mother. He was always kind and understanding, and did not hate me, even when we were given equal billing.

For a while many newspaper reporters thought I was a fake—a man dressed up in a fur suit—but that was easily disproved. A number of scientists came to visit me in the various cities I performed in, and literally millions of curious people. In my third year as a showpiece I went to Europe. I had to learn French and German, or enough to make myself understood on the stage, and got laughed at for my accent, which was not very good. Once or twice I was threatened, because I said something in the theaters about this political leader or that, but for the most part people were very friendly.

Finally, however, I got a bad cough. My owners were fearfully worried and called a doctor, who prescribed a sea voyage. Lots of publicity came of the announcement that I would sail south, to "visit my homeland of Africa."

Of course I had not been born in Africa, but in the Bronx Zoo; yet a thrill came into my heart when, draped in a long coat and leaning on the rail, we sighted the west coast just below the Equator.

That night, as the ship rode at anchor near some little port, I contrived to slip overside and into a barge full of packing cases. I rode with it to land and sneaked out upon the dock, through the shabby little town, and away up a little stream that led into a hot, green forest.

I tell it so briefly and calmly because that is the way the impulse came to me. I read somewhere about the lemmings, the little ratlike animals that go to the sea and drown themselves by the thousands. That is because they must. I doubt if they philosophize about it; they simply do it. Something like that dragged me ashore in Africa and up the watercourse.

I was as strange and awkward there as any human being would be for the first time. But I knew, somehow, that nature would provide the right things. In the morning I rested in a thicket of fruit trees. The fruit I did not know, but the birds had pecked at it, so I knew it was safe for eating. The flavor was strange but good. By the second day I was well beyond civilization. I slept that night in a tree, making a sort of nest there. It was clumsy work, but something beyond my experience seemed to guide my hands.

After more days, I found my people, the Kulakambas.

They were as they had been in the dream, swinging in treetops, playing and gathering food. Some of the younger ones scampered through the branches, shrilling joyfully over their game of tag. They talked, young and old—they had a language, with inflections and words and probably grammar. I could see a little village of nests, in the forks of the big trees; well-made shelters, with roofs over them. Those must have been quickly and easily made. Nothing troubled the Kulakambas. They lived without thought or worry for the next moment. When the next moment came, they lived that, too.

I thought I would approach. I would make friends, learn their ways and their speech. Then I might teach them useful things, and in turn they would teach me games. Already the old dream was a reality and the civilization I had known was slipping away—like a garment that had fitted too loosely.

I approached and came into view. They saw, and began to chatter at me. I tried to imitate their sounds, and I failed.

Then they grew excited and climbed along in the trees above me.

They began dropping branches and fruits and such things. I ran, and they followed, shrieking in a rage that had come upon them from nowhere and for no reason I could think of. They chased me all that day, until nightfall. A leopard frightened them then, and me as well.

I returned, after many days, to the town by the sea. My owners were there, and greeted me with loud abuse. I had cost them money and worry, important in the order named. One of them wanted to beat me with a whip. I reminded him that I could tear him apart like a roast chicken and there was no more talk of whipping me. I was kept shut up, however, until our ship came back and took us aboard.

Nevertheless, the adventure turned out well, so far as my owners were concerned. Reporters interviewed me when I got back to London. I told them the solemn truth about what I had done, and they made publicity marvels out of the ape-man's return to the jungle.

I made a personal appearance with my picture, for it had come to England just at that time. A week or so later came a cable from America. Somebody was reviving the plays of William Shakespeare, and I was badly wanted for an important role. We sailed back, were interviewed by a battery of reporters on landing, and went to an uptown hotel. Once or twice before there had been trouble about my staying in hotels. Now I was known and publicized as a Shakespearean actor, and the management of the biggest and most sumptuous hotel was glad to have me for a guest.

At once my owners signed a contract for me to appear in *The Tempest*. The part given me to study was that of Caliban, a sort of monster who was presented as the uncouth, unwelcome villain. Part of the time he had to be wicked, and part of the time ridiculous. As I read of his fumblings and blunderings, I forgot my long-held dislike of fiction and fable. I remembered what Doctor and Mother had said about Caliban, and all at once I knew how the poor whelp of Sycorax felt.

The next day a visitor came. It was Doctor.

He was grayer than when I had seen him, but healthy and happy and rich-looking. His beard was trimmed to a point instead of square, and he had white edging on his vest. He shook my hand and acted glad to see me.

"You're a real success, Congo," he said over and over again. "I told you that you'd be." We talked a while over this and that, and after a few minutes my owners left the room to do some business or other. Then Doctor leaned forward and patted my knee.

"I say, Congo," he grinned, "how would you like to have some brothers and sisters?"

I did not understand him, and I said so.

"Oh, perfectly simple," he made reply, crossing his legs. "There are going to be more like you."

"More Kulakambas?"

He nodded. "Yes. With brains to think with, and jaws to talk with. You've been a success, I say—profitable, fascinating. And my next experiment will be even better, more accurate. Then others—each a valuable property—each an advance in surgery and psychology over the last."

"Don't do it, Doctor," I said all at once.

"Don't do it?" he repeated sharply. "Why not?"

I tried to think of something compelling to reply, but nothing came to mind. I just said, "Don't do it, Doctor," as I had already.

He studied me a moment, with narrow eyes, then he snorted just as he had in the old days. "You're going to say it's cruel, I suppose," he sneered at me.

"That is right. It is cruel."

"Why, you—" He broke off without calling me anything, but I could feel his scorn, like a hot light upon me. "I suppose you know that if I hadn't done what I did to you, you'd be just a monkey scratching yourself."

I remembered the Kulakambas, happy and thoughtless in the wilderness.

He went on. "I gave you a mind and hands and speech, the three things that make up a man. Now you—"

"Yes," I interrupted again, for I remembered what I had been reading about Caliban. "Speech enough to curse you."

He uncrossed his legs. "A moment ago you were begging me not to do something."

"I'll beg again, Doctor," I pleaded, pushing my anger back into myself. "Don't butcher more beasts into—what I am."

He looked past me, and when he spoke it was not to me, but to himself. "I'll operate on five at first, ten the next year, and maybe get some assistants to do even more. In six or eight years there'll be a full hundred like you, or more advanced—"

"You mustn't," I said very firmly, and leaned forward in my turn.

He jumped up. "You forget yourself, Congo," he growled. "I'm not used to the word 'mustn't'—especially from a thing that owes me so much. And especially when I will lighten the labor of mankind."

"By laying mankind's labor on poor beasts."

"What are you going to do about it?" he flung out.

"I will prevent you," I promised.

He laughed. "You can't. All these gifts of yours mean nothing. You have a flexible tongue, a rational brain—but you're a beast by law and by nature. I"—and he thumbed his chest—"am a great scientist. You can't make a stand of any kind."

"I will prevent you," I said again, and I got up slowly.

He understood then, and yelled loudly. I heard an answering cry in the hall outside. He ran for the door, but I caught him. I remember how easily his neck broke in my hands. Just like a carrot.

The police came and got me, with guns and gas bombs and chains. I was taken to a jail and locked in the strongest cell, with iron bars all around. Outside some police officials and an attorney or two talked.

"He can't be tried for murder," said someone. "He's only an animal, and not subject to human laws."

"He was aware of what he did," argued a policeman. "He's as guilty as the devil."

"But we can hardly bring him into court," replied one of the attorneys. "Why, the newspapers would kid us clear out of the country—out of the legal profession."

They puzzled for a moment, all together. Then one of the police officers slapped his knee. "I've got it," he said, and they all looked at him hopefully.

"Why talk about trials?" demanded the inspired one. "If he can't be tried for killing that medic, neither can we be tried for killing him."

"Not if we do it painlessly," seconded someone.

They saw I was listening, and moved away and talked softly for a full quarter of an hour. Then they all nodded their heads as if agreeing on something. One police captain, fat and white-haired, came to the bars of my cell and looked through.

"Any last thing you'd like to have?" he asked me, not at all unkindly.

I asked for pen and ink and paper, and time enough to write this.

With a lithe flick of power-ful fins, the shark swept past, the lamb chop abruptly out of Brock's grasp and in the trap-mouth of the fish.

Illustrated by Charles Schnee

The Merman

By L. Sprague de Camp

As Jove nods occasionally, so Vernon Brock forgot to wind his alarm clock and, as a result, arrived at his office with the slightly giddy feeling that comes of having had no breakfast but a hasty cup of coffee. He had no way of knowing, then, what the results of his incidental nervousness would be.

He glanced at the apparatus that filled half the scant space in the room, thought, "You'll be famous yet if this works, my lad," and sat down at his desk. He reflected that being an assistant aquarist wasn't such a bad job. Of course, there's never enough money or enough room or enough time, but that's probably the case in most lines of work. And the office was really quiet. The chatter and shuffle of the visitors to the New York City Aquarium never penetrated; the only sounds were those of running water, the hum of the pump motors, and the faint ticking of typewriters. And he did love the work. The only thing that he possibly loved better than his fish was Miss Engholm, and for strategic reasons he wasn't telling anybody—least of all the lady—yet.

Then, nothing could have been sweeter than his interview with the boss yesterday. Clyde Sugden had said he was soon going to retire, and that he was using his influence to have Brock advanced to his place. Brock had protested with practically no conviction that, after all, Hempl had been there longer than he, and so ought to have the job.

"No," the head aquarist had said. "The feeling does you credit, Vernon, but Hempl wouldn't do. He's a good subordinate but has no more initiative than a lamellibranch. And he'd never sit up all night nursing a sick octopus the way you would." And so forth. Well, Brock hoped he really was that good, and that he wouldn't get a swelled head. But knowing the rarity of direct praise from superiors, he was determined to enjoy that experience to the utmost.

He glanced at his calendar pad. "Labeling." That meant that the labels on the tanks were out of date again. With the constant death of specimens and acquisition of new ones that characterizes aquaria, this condition was chronic. He'd do some label-shifting this evening. "Alligator." A man had phoned and said that he was coming in to present one to the institution. Brock knew what that meant. Some fat-headed tourist had bought a baby 'gator in Florida without the faintest notion of how to keep it properly, and now he would be dumping the skinny little wretch on the Aquarium before it died of starvation and the effects of well-meant ignorance. It happened all the time. "Legislature." What the devil? Oh, yes, he was going to write to the Florida State Legislature in support of a bill to prohibit the export of live alligators by more fat-headed tourists, while there were still some of the unfortunate reptiles left alive in the state.

Then the mail. Somebody wanted to know why her guppies developed white spots and died. Somebody wanted to know what kind of water plants to keep in a home aquarium and the name of a reliable seller of such plants in Pocatello, Idaho. Somebody wanted to know how to tell a male from a female lobster. Somebody—this was in nearly illegible shorthand, at which Brock cursed with mild irritation—"Dear Mr. Brock: I heard your lecture last June 18th inst. on how we are dissended from fish. Now you made a pretty good speech but I think if you will excuse my frankness that you are all wrong. I got a theory that the fish is really dissended from us. . . ."

He picked up the telephone and said, "Please send in Miss Engholm." She came in; they said "Good morning" formally, and he dictated letters for an hour. Then he said without changing his tone, "How about dinner tonight?" (Somebody might come in, and he had a mild phobia about letting the office force in on his private affairs.)

"Fine," said the girl. "The usual place?"

"O.K. Only I'll be late—labeling, you know—" He thought, foolish man, how surprised she'd be when he asked her to marry him. That would be after his promotion.

He decided to put in a couple of hours on his research before lunch. He tied on his old rubber apron and soon had the Bunsen burners going merrily. Motions were perforce acrobatic in the confined space. But he had to put up with that until the famous extension was finished. Then in a couple of years they'd be as cramped as ever again.

Sugden stuck his white thatch in the door. "May we come in?" He introduced a man as Dr. Dumville of the Cornell Medical Center.

Brock knew the physiologist by reputation, and he was only too glad to explain his work.

"You're, of course, familiar, Doctor," he said, "with the difference between lung tissue and gill tissue. For one thing, gill tissue has no mucus-secreting cells to keep the surfaces moist when out of water. Hence the gills dry and harden, and they no longer pass oxygen one way and carbon dioxide the other, as they should. But the gills of many aquatic organisms can be made to function out of water by keeping them moist artificially. Some of these forms regularly come out of water for considerable periods, like the fiddler crab and the mud skipper, for instance. They're all right as long as they can go back and moisten their gills occasionally.

"But in no case can a lung be used as a gill, to extract oxygen dissolved in water, instead of absorbing it from the air. I've been studying the reasons for this for some years. They're partly mechanical—the difficulty of getting any fluid as viscous as water in and out of the spongy lung structure fast enough—and partly a matter of the different osmotic properties of the breather cells, which are each adapted to operate on oxygen of a given concentration dispersed in a medium of given density.

"I've found, however, that the breather cells of lung tissue can be made to react to certain stimuli so as to assume the osmotic properties of gill tissue. And that's a batch of my stimulus boiling up there. It consists mainly of a mixture of halogen-bearing organic compounds. A good dose of the vapor of that stuff in the lungs of one of the young alligators in this tank should enable him to breathe under water, if my theory is correct."

"I'd suggest one thing," said Dumville, who had been giving polite but interested uh-huh's, "which is that when you hold your alligator under water, his glottal muscles will automatically contract, sealing off his lungs to keep out the water, and he'll suffocate."

"I've thought of that, and I'll paralyze the nerves controlling those muscles first, so he'll have to breathe water whether he wants to or not."

"That's the idea. Say, I want to be in on this. When are you going to try out your first alligator?"

They talked until Sugden began clearing his throat meaningfully. He said, "There's a lot more to see, Dr. Dumville. You've got to take a look at our new extension. We certainly sweated blood getting the city to put up the money for it."

He got Dumville out, and Brock could hear his voice dying away: ". . . It'll be mostly for new pumping and filtering machinery; we haven't half the space we need now. There'll be two tanks big enough for the smaller cetacea, and we'll finally have some direct sunlight. You can't keep most of the amphibia without it. We had to take half the damned old building apart to do it; it was originally built as a fort, in 1807, called 'West Battery.' Then it was the famous Castle Garden auditorium for half a century. Jenny Lind sang here. We're having a sesquicentennial celebration next year—"

Brock smiled. The extension was Sugden's monument, and the old boy would never retire until it was officially opened.

Brock turned back to his apparatus. He had just begun to concentrate on it when Sam Baritz stuck his gargoyle's face in. "Say, Voinon, wheh you gonna put the bichir? It gets in tomorrow."

"Hm-m-m—clear the filefish out of forty-three, and we'll make up a batch of Nile water this afternoon for it. It's too valuable to risk with other species until we know more about it. And—oh, hell, put the filefish in a reserve tank for the present."

That means another new label, he thought as he turned back to his chemicals. What would be a good wording? "Esteemed as food . . ." Yes. "Closely related to fossil forms"? Too indefinite. "Related to fossil forms from which most modern fish and all the higher vertebrates are descended." More like it. Maybe he could work in the words "living fossil" somehow. . . .

In his abstraction he hadn't noticed that the flask into which the oily liquid was dripping had been nudged too close to the edge of the table. The slam of a dropped plank from the extension, where construction was still going on, made him start nervously, and the flask came loose and smashed on the floor. Brock yelped with dismay and anger. Three weeks' work was spread all over the floor. He took his morning paper apart and swept up glass and solution. As he knelt over the wreckage, the fumes made his eyes water. In his annoyance it never occurred to him that a man's lungs aren't so different from an alligator's.

He answered the telephone. It was Halperin, the goldfish man. "I'm making a little trip down South; do you guys want me to pick up some bowfin or gar?" Brock said he'd have to ask Sugden and would call back. "Well, don't take too long; I'm leaving this aftanoon. Be seein' ya."

Brock set out on the long semicircular service-gallery walk over the ground-floor tanks that led around to the rear of the building and the entrance to the extension. As an old aquarium man he walked without faltering; he could imagine Dumville's cautious progress, clutching pipes and the edges of reserve tanks while glancing fearfully into the waters below.

Brock's lungs ached queerly. Must have gotten a whiff of that gunk of mine, he thought. That was a fool thing to do. But there couldn't have been enough to do any real harm. He kept on. The ache got worse; there was a strange suffocating sensation. This is serious, he thought. I'd better see a doctor after I deliver Halperin's message to Sugden. He kept on.

His lungs seemed to be on fire. Hurry—hurry—Dumville's an M.D.—maybe he could fix me up—

He couldn't breathe. He wanted water—not, oddly, in his throat, but in his lungs. The cool depths of the big tank at the end of the semicircle were below him. This tank held the sharks; the other big tanks, for groupers and other giants of the bass tribe, was across from it.

His lungs burned agonizingly. He tried to call out but only made a faint croaking noise. The tangle of pipes seemed to whirl around him. The sound of running water became a roar. He swayed, missed a snatch at the nearest reserve tank, and pitched into the shark tank.

There was water in his eyes, in his ears, everywhere. The burning in his lungs was lessening, and in place of it came a cold feeling throughout his chest. The bottom came up and bumped him softly. He righted himself. That was wrong; he should have floated. Then the reason came to him: his lungs were full of water, so that his specific gravity was one point something. He wondered for a confused minute if he was already drowned. He didn't *feel* drowned, only very wet and very cold inside. In any event he'd better get out of here quickly. He kicked himself to the surface, reached up and grabbed the catwalk, and tried to blow the water out of his lungs. It came, slowly, squirting out of his mouth and nostrils. He tried inhaling some air. He thought he was getting somewhere when the burning sensation returned. In spite of himself he ducked and inhaled water. Then he felt all right.

Everything seemed topsy-turvy. Then he remembered the liquid he'd prepared for the alligator: it must have worked on him! His lungs were functioning as gills. He couldn't quite believe it yet. Experimenting on an alligator is one thing; turning yourself into a fish is another—comic-section stuff. But there it was. If he'd been going to drown he'd have done so by now. He tried a few experimental breaths under water. It was amazingly hard work. You put on the pressure, and your lungs slowly contracted, like a pneumatic tire with a leak. In half a minute or so you were ready to inhale again. The reason was the viscosity of water compared with that of air, of course. But it seemed to work. He released the catwalk and sank to the bottom again.

He looked around him. The tank seemed smaller than it should be; that was the effect of the index of refraction of water, no doubt. He walked toward one side, which seemed to recede as he approached it.

Two nurse sharks were lying indifferently on the bottom across the tank. These brutes were sluggish and utterly harmless. The two sand sharks, the four-footer and the five-footer, had ceased their interminable cruising and had backed into far corners. Their mouths opened and closed slowly, showing their formidable teeth. Their little yellow eyes seemed to say to Brock, "Don't start anything you can't finish, buddy!" Brock had no intention of starting anything. He'd had a healthy respect for the species since one of them had bitten him in the gluteus maximus while he was hauling it into a boat.

He looked up. It was like looking up at a wrinkled mirror, with a large circular hole in it directly over his head. Through the hole he could see the reserve tanks, the pipes—everything that he could have seen by sticking his head out of water. But the view was distorted and compressed around the edges, like a photograph taken with a wide-angle lens. One of the Aquarium's cats peered down inscrutably at him from the catwalk. Beyond the circle on all sides the water surface was a mirror that rippled and shivered. Over the two sand sharks were their reflections upside down.

He turned his attention to the glass front of the tank. That reflected things, too, as the lamps suspended over the water made the inside brighter than the outside. By putting his head close to the glass he could see the Aquarium's interior concourse. Only he couldn't see much of it for the crowd in front of the tank. They were staring at him; in the dim light they seemed all eyeballs. Now and then their heads turned and their mouths moved, but Brock got only a faint buzz.

This was all very interesting, Brock thought, but what was he to *do?* He couldn't stay in the tank indefinitely. For one thing, the coldness in his chest was uncomfortable. And God only knew what terrible physiological effect the gas might have had on him. And this breathing water was hard work, complicated by the fact that unless he watched carefully his glottis would snap shut, stopping his breath altogether. It was like learning to keep your eyes open under water. He was fortunate in having fallen into a tank of salt water; fresh water is definitely injurious to lung tissue, and so it might have been even to the modified tissue in his lungs.

He sat down crosslegged on the bottom. Behind him the larger sand shark had resumed its shuttling, keeping well away from him and halting suspiciously every time he moved. Two remoras, attached to the shark by the sucking disks on top of their heads, trailed limply from it. There were six of these original hitchhikers in the tank. He peered at the glass front. He took off his glasses experimentally, and found that he could see better without them—a consequence of the different optical properties of water and air. Most of the Aquarium's visitors were now crowded in front of that tank, to watch a youngish man in a black rubber apron, a striped shirt, and the pants of a gray flannel suit sit on the bottom of a tank full of sharks and wonder how in hell he was going to get out of this predicament.

Overhead, there was no sign of anybody. Evidently nobody had heard him fall. But soon one of the small staff would notice the crowd in front of the tank and investigate. Meanwhile he'd better see just what he could do in this bizarre environment. He tried to speak, but his vocal cords, tuned to operate in a negligibly dense medium, refused to flutter fast enough to emit an audible sound. Well, maybe he could come to the surface long enough to speak and duck under again. He rose to the top and tried it. But he had trouble getting his water-soaked breathing and speaking apparatus dry enough to use for this purpose. All he produced were gurgling noises. And while the air no longer burned his lungs on immediate contact, keeping his head out soon gave him a dizzy, suffocating feeling. He finally gave up and sank to the bottom again.

He shivered with the cold, although the water was at 65° Fahrenheit. He'd better move around to warm up. The apron hampered him, and he tried to untie the knot in back. But the water had swollen the cords so that the knot wouldn't budge. He finally wriggled out of it, rolled it up, stuck his arm out of water, and tossed the apron onto the catwalk. He thought of removing his shoes, too, but remembered the sand sharks' teeth.

Then he did a bit of leisurely swimming, round and round like the sand sharks. They also went round and round, trying to keep the width of the tank between him and them. The motion warmed him, but he tired surprisingly soon. Evidently the rapid metabolism of a mammal took about all the oxygen that his improvised gills could supply, and they wouldn't carry much overload. He reduced his swimmings to an imitation of a seal's, legs trailing and hands flapping at his sides. The crowd, as he passed the front of the tank, was thicker than ever. A little man with a nose that swerved to starboard watched him with peculiar intentness.

A jarring sound came through the water, and presently figures, grotesquely shortened, appeared at the edge of the circle of transparency overhead. They grew rapidly taller, and Brock recognized Sugden, Dumville, Sam Baritz, and a couple of other members of the staff. They clustered on the catwalk, and their excited voices came to him muffled but intelligible. They knew what had happened to him, all right.

He tried by sign language to explain his sad predicament. They evidently thought he was in a convulsion, for Sugden barked, "Get him out!" Baritz's thick forearm shot down into the water to seize his wrist. But he wrenched loose before they had him clear of the surface, and dove for the bottom.

"Acts like he don't *wanna* come out," said Baritz rubbing a kicked shin.

Sugden leaned over. "Can you hear me?" he shouted.

Brock nodded vigorously.

"Can you speak to us?"

Brock shook his head.

"Did you do this to yourself on purpose?"

A violent shake.

"Accident?"

Brock nodded.

"Do you want to get out?"

Brock nodded and shook his head alternately.

Sugden frowned in perplexity. Then he said, "Do you mean you'd like to, but can't because of your condition?"

Brock nodded.

Sugden continued his questions. Brock, growing impatient at this feeble method of communication, made writing motions. Sugden handed down a pencil and a pocket notebook. But the water immediately softened the paper so that the pencil, instead of making marks, tore holes in it. Brock handed them back.

Sugden said, "What he needs is a wax tablet and stylus. Could you get us one, Sam?"

Baritz looked uncomfortable. "Cheez, boss, what place in N'yawk sells those things?"

"That's right; I suppose we'll have to make it ourselves. If we could melt a candle onto a piece of plywood—"

"It'll take all day fa me to get the candle and stuff and do that, and we gotta do something about poor Voinon—"

Brock noticed that the entire staff was now lined up on the catwalk. His beloved was well down the line, almost out of sight around the curve. At that angle the refraction made her look as broad as she was tall. He wondered if she'd look that naturally after they'd been married awhile. He'd known it to happen. No, he meant *if* they got married. You couldn't expect a girl to marry a man who lived under water.

While Sugden and Baritz still bickered, he had an idea. But how to communicate it? Then he saw a remora lying below him. He splashed to attract the attention of those above and sank down slowly. He grabbed the fish in both hands and kicked himself over to the glass. The remora's nose—or, to be exact, its undershot lower jaw—made a visible streak on the pane. Brock rolled over on his back and saw that he was understood; Sugden was calling for someone to go down to the floor and read his message.

His attempt at writing was hampered by the fish's vigorous efforts to escape. But he finally got scrawled on the glass in large, wabbly capitals:

2 WEIGHTED STEPLADDERS . . . 1 WEIGHTED PLANK . . . 1 DRY TOWEL.

While they were getting these, he was reminded by his stomach that he'd had no solid food for eighteen hours or thereabouts. He glanced at his wristwatch, which, not being waterproof, had stopped. He handed it up, hoping that somebody would have the sense to dry it out and take it to a jeweler.

The stepladders were lowered into the tank. Brock set them a few feet apart and placed the plank across their tops. Then he lay on his back on the plank, his face a few inches below the surface. He dried his hands on the towel, and by cocking one leg up he could hold a pad out of water against his knee and write on it.

He explained tersely about the accident and his subsequent seizure, and told what had happened chemically to his lung tissues. Then he wrote, "As this is first experiment on living organism, don't know when effect will pass, if ever. Want lunch."

Baritz called to him, "Don't you want us to take the shoks out foist?"

Brock shook his head. The claims of his stomach were imperious, and he had a vague hope of solving his problem without disturbing the fish. Then, too, though he'd have hated to admit it, he knew that everybody knew that the sharks weren't maneaters, and he didn't want to seem afraid of them. Even a sensible man like Vernon Brock will succumb to a touch of bravado in the presence of his woman, actual or potential.

He relaxed, thinking. Sugden was ordering the staff back to its work. Dumville had to leave but promised to be back. By and by the faithful Baritz appeared with what Brock hoped was food. Brock's position struck him as an uncomfortable one for eating, so he rolled off the plank and stood on the bottom of the tank. Then he couldn't reach the surface with his hand. Baritz thrust a lamb chop on the end of a stick down to him. He reached for it—and was knocked aside by a glancing blow from something heavy and sandpapery. The lamb chop was gone—or not quite gone; the larger shark had it over in a corner. The shark's jaws worked, and the bone sank slowly to the bottom, minus its meat.

Baritz looked helplessly at Sugden. "We betta not try meat again. Those shoks can smell it, and they might get dangerous if we got them woiked up."

"Guess we'll have to get the net and haul them out," said Sugden. "I don't see how he could eat mashed potatoes under water."

Brock swam up and made the motions of peeling and eating a banana. After Baritz had made a trip for bananas Brock satisfied his hunger, though he found that swallowing food without getting a stomachful of salt water required a bit of practice.

The crowd in front of the tank was larger, if anything. The little man with the wry nose was still there. His scrutiny made Brock vaguely uneasy. He'd always wondered what a fish on exhibit felt like, and now, by George, he knew.

If he could get out and do a few months' research he might be able to find how to counteract the effect of the lung gas. But how could he perform experiments from where he was? Maybe he could give directions and have somebody else carry them out. That would be awkward, but he didn't want to spend the rest of his life as an exhibit, loyal as he was to the Aquarium. A better idea might be to rig up some sort of diver's helmet, to be worn out of water with the water inside—if he could find a way of oxygenating the water.

Baritz appeared again, and put his head down close to the water. "Hey, Voinon!" he said. "God's coming down here!"

Brock was interested, though not by the theological aspects of the statement. "God," better known as J. Roosevelt Whitney, was the president of the New York Zoological Society, and the boss of Minnegerode, the director of the Aquarium (in Bermuda at the moment). Minnegerode was Sugden's boss. J. R., the head of this hierarchy, owned among other things a bank and a half, fifty-one percent of a railroad, and the finest walrus mustache in Greater New York.

Baritz put on his child-frightening grin. "Say, Voinon, I just thought. We can advatise you as the only moimaid in captivity!"

Brock throttled an impulse to pull his helper into the tank and motioned for his pad. He wrote, "The male of 'mermaid' is 'merman,' you ape!"

"O.K., a moiman, unless— Oh, good aftanoon, Mista Whitney. Here he is in this tank. Anything I can do, Mista Whitney?"

The famous mustache floated above the water like a diving seagull. "How ah you, my deah boy? Ah you making out all right? Don't you think we'd bettah get the sharks out right away? They're perfectly harmless, of course, of course, but you might accidentally jostle one and get nipped, ha-ha."

Brock, who, at thirty-two, was pleased rather than irked at being called "my boy," nodded. J. R. started to get to his feet, not noticing that one foot was planted on Brock's rolled-up apron, while the toe of the other was caught in it. Brock received a tremendous impact of sound and current, and through the sudden cloud of silver bubbles saw J. R.'s massive rear descending on him. He caught the man and shoved him up.

As the shiny pink head cleared the surface, he heard a terrified scream of "Glugg . . . blubb . . . O Lord, get me out! The sharks! Get me out, I say!"

Brock boosted and Baritz and Sugden heaved. The dripping deity receded down the catwalk, to Brock's distorted vision broadening to something like a *Daily Worker* cartoon of Capital. He wished he knew whether J. R. would be angry or whether he'd be grateful for the boost. If he inquired about the apron it might be embarrassing.

The cold was biting Brock's innards, and the bananas seemed to have turned into billiard balls in his stomach. The little man with the nose was still there. Brock hoisted himself on his plank and wrote directions: "Raise temperature of feed water slowly. Get me thermometer. Will signal when temperature is right. Should be about ninety degrees Fahrenheit. Run more air lines into tank to make up for lowering oxygen saturation point. Put sharks in reserve tank for present; warmth might harm them, and I need all oxygen in tank."

By 9:00 P.M. all was done. The tearful Miss Engholm had been shooed away. Baritz volunteered to spend the night, which proved the most uncomfortable of Brock's experience. He couldn't sleep because of the constant muscular effort required to work his lungs. He tried to think his way out of the mess, but his thoughts became more and more confused. He began to imagine things: that the little man with the nose had been there for no good, for instance. Just what, he couldn't think, but he was sure it was something. Again and again he wondered what time it was. At first he aroused Baritz to tell him at intervals, but toward two o'clock Sam went to sleep on the catwalk, and Brock hadn't the heart to awaken him.

Lord, would the night never end? Well, what if it did? Would he be any better off? He doubted it. He looked at his hands, at the skin of his fingers swollen and wrinkled by soaking. A crazy idea grew on him with the force of an obsession. His hands would turn into fins. He'd grow scales—

It was getting light. Then all these people would come back to torment him. Yes, and the little man with the nose. The little man would put a worm on a hook and catch him and eat him for supper—

Under sufficiently strange circumstances the human mind is often thrown out of gear and spins ineffectually, without definite relationship to external things. Perhaps that is because of a weakness in the structure of the mind, or perhaps it is a provision by nature to disconnect it to avoid stripped gears when the load is too heavy.

People were coming in; it must be after nine o'clock. People on the catwalk overhead were talking, but he couldn't understand them. His lungs weren't working right. Or rather his gills. But that was wrong. He was a fish, wasn't he? Then what could be wrong with them? All these people who had it in for him must have turned off the oxygen. No, the air lines were still shooting their streams of tiny bubbles into the tank. Then why this suffocating feeling? He knew; that wasn't air in the air lines; it was pure nitrogen or helium or something. They were trying to fool him. O Lord, if he could only breathe! Maybe he had the fish's equivalent of asthma. Fish came to the surface and gulped sometimes; he'd try that. But he couldn't; his experiences of the preceding day had given him a conditioned reflex against sticking his head out, which his shattered reason was unable to overcome.

Was he going to die? Too bad, when he had been going to marry Miss Engholm and all. But he couldn't have married her anyway. He was a fish. His face twisted in an insane grin at the grotesque thought that struck him.

He was dying. He had to get oxygen. Why not go through the glass? But no, any intelligent fish knew better than to try to make holes in the glass. Then he saw the little man with the nose, standing and staring as he had yesterday. He thought, you'll never catch me on a hook and eat me for supper, you piscicide; I'm going to get you first. He fished out his jackknife and attacked the pane. A long scratch appeared on it, then another, and another. The glass sang softly. The people behind the little man were moving back nervously, but the little man still stood there. The song of the glass rose up—up—up—

The glass, with a final *pinnng,* gave, and several tons of green water flung themselves into the concourse. For a fleeting second Brock, knife in hand, seemed to be flying toward the little man. Then the iron railing in front of the tank came up and hit his head.

He had a vague sense of lying on a wet tile floor, while a foot from his ringing head a stranded remora flopped helplessly—

He was lying in bed, and Sugden was sitting beside him, smoking. The old man said, "Lucky you didn't get a fractured skull. But maybe it was a good thing. It put you out during the critical period when your lungs were changing back to normal. They'd have had to dope you anyway, out of your head as you were."

"I'll say I was out of my head! Wait till I see your friend Dumville; I'll be able to describe a brand-new psychosis to him."

"He's a physiologist," replied Sugden, "not a psychologist. But he'll want to see you just the same.

"The doctor tells me you'll be out tomorrow, so I guess you're well enough to talk business. J. R. didn't mind the ducking, even after the exhibition he made of himself. But there's something more serious. Perhaps you noticed a small man with a crooked nose in front of the tank while you were there?"

"*Did* I *notice* him!"

"Well, you nearly drowned him when you let the water out of the tank. And he's going to sue us for damages—way up in five or six figures. You know what *that* means."

Brock nodded glumly. "I'll say I do! It means that I don't get your job when you retire next winter. And then I can't get ma— Never mind. Who is this little guy? A professional accident-faker!"

"No; we investigated him. He was a trapeze artist in a circus until recently. He says he was getting too old for that work, but he didn't know any other. Then he hurt his back in a fall, and he's been on relief since. He just came in to watch you because he had nothing else to do."

"I see." Brock thought. "Say, I have an idea. Nurse! Hey, *nurse!* My clothes! I'm going out!"

"No, you're not," said Sugden firmly. "Not till the doc says you can. That'll only be tomorrow, and then you can try out your idea. And I hope," he added grimly, "that it's better than the last one."

Two days later Brock knocked on Sugden's door. He knew that Sugden and J. R. were in there, and he could guess what they were talking about. But he had no fears.

"Morning, Mr. Whitney," he said.

"Oh . . . ah . . . yes, my deah boy. We were just talking about this most unfortunate . . . ah—"

"If you mean the suit, that's off."

"*What?*"

"Sure, I fixed it. Mr. Oscar Daly, the plaintiff, and I are going into a kind of partnership."

"Partners?"

"Yes, to exploit my discovery of lung conversion. I supply the technique so that he can exhibit himself in circuses as Oscar the Merman. He dopes himself with my gas and parks in a tank. Our only problem is the period when the effect of the gas wears off and the lungs return to normal. That, I think, can be licked by the use of any of several anesthetic drugs that slow down the metabolism. So, when the human fish begins to feel funny, he injects himself and passes out peacefully, while his assistants fish him out and wring the water out of his lungs. There are a few technical details to work out on my alligators yet, but that'll be all right. I'll wear a gas mask. Of course," he added virtuously, "any monetary returns from the use of the process will go to the Zoological Society. Oscar says to send your lawyer over any time and he'll sign a release."

"Why, that's fine," said Whitney, "that's splendid, my boy. It makes a big difference." He looked significantly at Sugden.

"Thanks," said Brock. "And now, if you'll excuse me, Sam and I have some fish to shift. So long, cheerio, and I hope you drop in often, Mr. Whitney." He went out, whistling.

"Oh, Vernon!" the head aquarist called after him. "Tomorrow's Sunday, and I'm driving my family out to Jones Beach. Like to come along for a swim?"

Brock stuck his grinning head back in. "Thanks a lot, Clyde, but I'm afraid I might carelessly take a deep breath under water. And—I've had enough swimming to last me the rest of my unnatural life!"

Illustrated by Paul Orban

The Day Is Done

By Lester del Rey

HWOOGH scratched the hair on his stomach and watched the sun climb up over the hill. He beat listlessly on his chest and yelled at it timidly, then grumbled and stopped. In his youth, he had roared and stumped around to help the god up, but now it wasn't worth the effort. Nothing was. He found a fine flake of sweaty salt under his hair, licked it off his fingers, and turned over to sleep again.

But sleep wouldn't come. On the other side of the hill there was a hue and cry, and somebody was beating a drum in a throbbing chant. The old Neanderthaler grunted and held his hands over his ears, but the Sun-Warmer's chant couldn't be silenced. More ideas of the Talkers.

In his day, it had been a lovely world, full of hairy grumbling people; people a man could understand. There had been game on all sides, and the caves about had been filled with the smoke of cooking fires. He had played with the few young that were born—though each year fewer children had come into the tribe—and had grown to young manhood with the pride of achievement. But that was before the Talkers had made this valley one of their hunting grounds.

Old traditions, half told, half understood, spoke of the land in the days of old, when only his people roamed over the broad tundra. They had filled the caves and gone out in packs too large for any animal to withstand. And the animals swarmed into the land, driven south by the Fourth Glaciation. Then the great cold had come again, and times had been hard. Many of his people had died.

But many had lived, and with the coming of the warmer, drier climate again, they had begun to expand before the Talkers arrived. After that—Hwoogh stirred uneasily—for no good reason he could see, the Talkers took more and more of the land, and his people retreated and diminished before them. Hwoogh's father had made it understood that their little band in the valley were all that were left,

455

and that this was the only place on the great flat earth where Talkers seldom came.

Hwoogh had been twenty when he first saw them, great long-legged men, swift of foot and eye, stalking along as if they owned the earth, with their incessant mouth noises. In the summer that year, they pitched their skin-and-wattle tents at the back of the hill, away from the caves, and made magic to their gods. There was magic on their weapons, and the beasts fell their prey. Hwoogh's people had settled back, watching fearfully, hating numbly, finally resorting to begging and stealing. Once a young buck had killed the child of a Talker, and been flayed and sent out to die for it. Thereafter, there had been a truce between Cro-Magnon and Neanderthaler.

Now the last of Hwoogh's people were gone, save only himself, leaving no children. Seven years it had been since Hwoogh's brother had curled up in the cave and sent his breath forth on the long journey to his ancestors. He had always been dispirited and weak of will, but he had been the only friend left to Hwoogh.

The old man tossed about and wished that Keyoda would return. Maybe she would bring food from the Talkers. There was no use hunting now, when the Talkers had already been up and killed all the easy game. Better that a man should sleep all the time, for sleep was the only satisfying thing left in the topsy-turvy world; even the drink the tall Cro-Magnons made from mashed roots left a headache the next day.

He twisted and turned in his bed of leaves at the edge of the cave, grunting surlily. A fly buzzed over his head provocatively, and he lunged at it. Surprise lighted his features as his fingers closed on the insect, and he swallowed it with a momentary flash of pleasure. It wasn't as good as the grub in the forest, but it made a tasty appetizer.

The sleep god had left, and no amount of lying still and snoring would lure him back. Hwoogh gave up and squatted down on his haunches. He had been meaning to make a new head for his crude spear for weeks, and he rummaged around in the cave for materials. But the idea grew farther away the closer he approached work, and he let his eyes roam idly over the little creek below him and the fleecy clouds in the sky. It was a warm spring, and the sun made idleness pleasant.

The sun god was growing stronger again, chasing the old fog and mist away. For years, he had worshiped the sun god as his, and now it seemed to grow strong again only for the Talkers. While the god was weak, Hwoogh's people had been mighty; now that its long sickness was over, the Cro-Magnons spread out over the country like the fleas on his belly.

Hwoogh could not understand it. Perhaps the god was mad at him, since gods are utterly unpredictable. He grunted, wishing again for his brother, who had understood such things better.

Keyoda crept around the boulder in front of the cave, interrupting his brooding. She brought scraps of food from the tent village and the half-chewed leg of a horse, which Hwoogh seized on and ripped at with his strong teeth. Evidently the Talkers had made a big kill the day before, for they were lavish with their gifts. He grunted at Keyoda, who sat under the cave entrance in the sun, rubbing her back.

Keyoda was as hideous as most of the Talkers were to Hwoogh, with her long dangling legs and short arms, and the ungainly straightness of her carriage. Hwoogh remembered the young girls of his own day with a sigh; they had been beautiful, short and squat, with forward-jutting necks and nice low foreheads. How the flat-faced Cro-Magnon women could get mates had been a puzzle to Hwoogh, but they seemed to succeed.

Keyoda had failed, however, and in her he felt justified in his judgment. There were times when he felt almost in sympathy with her, and in his own way he was fond of her. As a child, she had been injured, her back made useless for the work of a mate. Kicked around by the others of her tribe, she had gradually drifted away from them, and when she stumbled on Hwoogh, his hospitality had been welcome to her. The Talkers were nomads who followed the herds north in the summer, south in the winter, coming and going with the seasons, but Keyoda stayed with Hwoogh in his cave and did the few desultory tasks that were necessary. Even such a half-man as the Neanderthaler was preferable to the scornful pity of her own people, and Hwoogh was not unkind.

"Hwunkh?" asked Hwoogh. With his stomach partly filled, he felt more kindly toward the world.

"Oh, they come out and let me pick up their scraps—me, who was once a chief's daughter!—same as they always do." Her voice had been shrewish, but the weariness of failure and age had taken the edge from it. " 'Poor, poor Keyoda,' thinks they, 'let her have what she wants, just so it don't mean nothin' we like.' Here." She handed him a roughly made spear, flaked on both sides of the point, but with only a rudimentary barb, unevenly made. "One of 'em give me this—it ain't the like of what they'd use, I guess, but it's good as you could make. One of the kids is practicing."

Hwoogh examined it; good, he admitted, very good, and the point was fixed nicely in the shaft. Even the boys, with their long limber thumbs that could twist any which way, made better weapons than he; yet once he had been famous among his small tribe for the nicety of his flint work.

Making a horse gesture, he got slowly to his feet. The shape of his jaw and the attachment of his tongue, together with a poorly developed left frontal lobe of his brain, made speech rudimentary, and he supplemented his glottals and labials with motions that Keyoda understood well enough. She shrugged and waved him out, gnawing on one of the bones.

Hwoogh wandered about without much spirit, conscious that he was growing old. And vaguely, he knew that age should not have fallen upon him for many snows; it was not the number of seasons, but something else, something that he could feel but not understand. He struck out for the hunting fields, hoping that he might find some game for himself that would require little effort to kill. The scornful gifts of the Talkers had become bitter in his mouth.

But the sun god climbed up to the top of the blue cave without Hwoogh's stumbling on anything. He swung about to return, and ran into a party of Cro-Magnons returning with the carcass of a reindeer strapped to a pole on their shoulders. They stopped to yell at him.

"No use, Hairy One!" they boasted, their voices light and gay. "We caught all the game this way. Turn back to your cave and sleep."

Hwoogh dropped his shoulders and veered away, his spear dragging limply on the ground. One of the party trotted over to him lightly. Sometimes Legoda, the tribal magic man and artist, seemed almost friendly, and this was one of the times.

"It was my kill, Hairy One," he said tolerantly. "Last night I drew strong reindeer magic, and the beast fell with my first throw. Come to my tent and I'll save a leg for you. Keyoda taught me a new song that she got from her father, and I would repay her."

Legs, ribs, bones! Hwoogh was tired of the outer meat. His body demanded the finer food of the entrails and liver. Already his skin was itching with a rash, and he felt that he must have the succulent inner parts to make him well; always, before, that had cured him. He grunted, between appreciation and annoyance, and turned off. Legoda pulled him back..

"Nay, stay, Hairy One. Sometimes you bring good fortune to me, as when I found the bright ocher for my drawing. There is meat enough in the camp for all. Why hunt today?" As Hwoogh still hesitated, he grew more insistent, not from kindness, but more from a wish to have his own way. "The wolves are running near today, and one is not enough against them. We carve the reindeer at the camp as soon as it comes from the poles. I'll give you first choice of the meat!"

Hwoogh grunted a surly acquiescence and waddled after the party. The dole of the Talkers had become gall to him, but liver was liver—if Legoda kept his bargain. They were chanting a rough marching song, trotting easily under the load of the reindeer, and he lumbered along behind, breathing hard at the pace they set.

As they neared the village of the nomads, its rough skin tents and burning fires threw out a pungent odor that irritated Hwoogh's nostrils. The smell of the long-limbed Cro-Magnons was bad enough without the dirty smell of a camp and the stink of their dung-fed fires. He preferred the accustomed moldy stench of his own musty cave.

Youths came swarming out at them, yelling with disgust at being left behind on this easy hunt. Catching sight of the Neanderthaler, they set up a howl of glee and charged at him, throwing sticks and rocks and jumping at him with play fury. Hwoogh shivered and crouched over, menacing them with his spear, and giving voice to throaty growls. Legoda laughed.

"In truth, O Hairy Chokanga, your voice should drive them from you. But see, they fear it not. Kuck, you two-legged pests! Out and away! Kuck, I say!" They leaped back at his voice and dropped behind, still yelling. Hwoogh eyed them warily, but so long as it suited the pleasure of Legoda, he was safe from their pranks.

Legoda was in a good mood, laughing and joking, tossing his quips at the women until his young wife came out and silenced it. She sprang at the reindeer with her flint knife, and the other women joined her.

"Heyo," called Legoda. "First choice goes to Chokanga, the Hairy One. By my word, it is his."

"Oh, fool!" There was scorn in her voice and in the look she gave

Hwoogh. "Since when do we feed the beasts of the caves and the fish of the river? Art mad, Legoda. Let him hunt for himself."

Legoda tweaked her back with the point of his spear, grinning. "Aye, I knew thou'dst cry at that. But then, we owe his kind some pay—this was his hunting ground when we were but pups, straggling into this far land. What harm to give to an old man?" He swung to Hwoogh and gestured. "See, Chokanga, my word is good. Take what you want, but see that it is not more than your belly and that of Keyoda can hold this night."

Hwoogh darted in and came out with the liver and the fine sweet fat from the entrails. With a shrill cry of rage, Legoda's mate sprang for him, but the magic man pushed her back.

"Nay, he did right! Only a fool would choose the haunch when the heart of the meat was at hand. By the gods of my father, and I expected to eat of that myself! O Hairy One, you steal the meat from my mouth, and I like you for it. Go, before Heya gets free."

Tomorrow, Hwoogh knew, Legoda might set the brats on him for this day's act, but tomorrow was in another cave of the sun. He drew his legs under him and scuttled off to the left and around the hill, while the shrill yells of Heya and the lazy good humor of Legoda followed. A piece of liver dangled loose, and Hwoogh sucked on it as he went. Keyoda would be pleased, since she usually had to do the begging for both of them.

And a little of Hwoogh's self-respect returned. Hadn't he outsmarted Legoda and escaped with the choicest meat? And had Keyoda ever done as well when she went to the village of the Talkers? Ayeee, they had a thing yet to learn from the cunning brain of old Hwoogh!

Of course the Talkers were crazy; only fools would act as Legoda had done. But that was none of his business. He patted the liver and fat fondly and grinned with a slight return of good humor. Hwoogh was not one to look a gift horse in the mouth.

The fire had shrunk to a red bed of coals when he reached the cave, and Keyoda was curled up on his bed, snoring loudly, her face flushed. Hwoogh smelled her breath, and his suspicions were confirmed. Somehow, she had drunk of the devil brew of the Talkers, and her sleep was dulled with its stupor. He prodded her with his toe, and she sat up bleary-eyed.

"Oh, so you're back. Ayeee, and with liver and fat! But that never came from your spear throw; you been to the village and stole it. Oh, but you'll catch it!" She grabbed at the meat greedily and stirred up the fire, spitting the liver over it.

Hwoogh explained as best he could, and she got the drift of it. "So? Eh, that Legoda, what a prankster he is, and my own nephew, too." She tore the liver away, half raw, and they fell to eagerly, while she chuckled and cursed by turns. Hwoogh touched her nose and wrinkled his face up.

"Well, so what if I did?" Liquor had sharpened her tongue. "That no-good son of the chief come here, after me to be telling him stories. And to make my old tongue free, he brings me the root brew. Ah, what stories I'm telling—and some of 'em true, too!" She gestured toward a crude pot. "I reckon he steals it, but what's that to us? Help yourself, Hairy One. It ain't ever' day we're getting the brew."

Hwoogh remembered the headaches of former experiments, but he smelled it curiously and the lure of the magic water caught at him. It was the very essence of youth, the fire that brought life to his legs and memories to his mind. He held it up to his mouth, gasping as the beery liquid ran down his throat. Keyoda caught it before he could finish and drained the last quart.

"Ah, it strengthens my back and puts the blood a-running hot through me again." She swayed on her feet and sputtered out the fragments of an old skin-scraping song. "Now, there you go—can't you never learn not to drink it all to once? That way, it don't last as long, and you're out before you get to feeling good."

Hwoogh staggered as the brew took hold of him, and his knees bent even farther under him. The bed came up in his face, his head was full of bees buzzing merrily, and the cave spun around him. He roared at the cave, while Keyoda laughed.

"Heh! To hear you a-yelling, a body might think you was the only Chokanga left on earth. But you ain't—no, you ain't!"

"Hwunkh?" That struck home. To the best of Hwoogh's knowledge, there were no others of his kind left on earth. He grabbed at her and missed, but she fell and rolled against him, her breath against his face.

"So? Well, it's the truth. The kid up and told me. Legoda found three of 'em, just like you, he says, up the land to the east, three springs ago. You'll have to ask him—I dunno nothing about it." She rolled over against him, grunting half-formed words, and he tried to think of this new information. But the brew was too strong for his head, and he was soon snoring beside her.

Keyoda was gone to the village when he awoke, and the sun was a spear length high on the horizon. He rummaged around for a piece of the liver, but the flavor was not as good as it had been, and his stomach protested lustily at going to work again. He leaned back until his head got control of itself, then swung down to the creek to quench a thirst devil that had seized on him in the night.

But there was something he should do, something he half remembered from last night. Hadn't Keyoda said something about others of his people? Yes, three of them, and Legoda knew. Hwoogh hesitated, remembering that he had bested Legoda the day before; the young man might resent it today. But he was filled with an overwhelming curiosity, and there was a strange yearning in his heart. Legoda must tell him.

Reluctantly, he went back to the cave and fished around in a hole that was a secret even from Keyoda. He drew out his treasures, fingering them reverently, and selecting the best. There were bright shells and colored pebbles, a roughly drilled necklace that had belonged to his father, a sign of completed manhood, bits of this and that with which he had intended to make himself ornaments. But the quest for knowledge was stronger than the pride of possession; he dumped them out into his fist and struck out for the village.

Keyoda was talking with the women, whining the stock formula that she had developed, and Hwoogh skirted around the camp, looking for the young artist. Finally he spotted the Talker out behind the camp, making odd motions with two sticks. He drew near cautiously, and Legoda heard him coming.

"Come near, Chokanga, and see my new magic." The young man's voice was filled with pride, and there was no threat to it. Hwoogh sighed with relief, but sidled up slowly. "Come nearer, don't fear me. Do you think I'm sorry of the gift I made? Nay, that was my own stupidity. See."

He held out the sticks and Hwoogh fingered them carefully. One was long and springy, tied end to end with a leather thong, and the other was a little spear with a tuft of feather on the blunt end. He grunted a question.

"A magic spear, Hairy One, that flies from the hand with wings, and kills beyond the reach of other spears."

Hwoogh snorted. The spear was too tiny to kill more than rodents, and the big stick had not even a point. But he watched as the young man placed the sharp stick to the tied one, and drew back on it. There was a sharp twang, and the little spear sailed out and away, burying its point in the soft bark of a tree more than two spear throws away. Hwoogh was impressed.

"Aye, Chokanga, a new magic that I learned in the south last year. There are many there who use it, and with it they can throw the point farther and better than a full-sized spear. One man may kill as much as three!"

Hwoogh grumbled; already they killed all the good game, and yet they must find new magic to increase their power. He held out his hand curiously, and Legoda gave him the long stick and another spear, showing him how it was held. Again there was a twang, and the leather thong struck at his wrist, but the weapon sailed off erratically, missing the tree by yards. Hwoogh handed it back glumly—such magic was not for his kind. His thumbs made the handling of it even more difficult.

Now, while the magic man was pleased with his superiority, was a good time to show the treasure. Hwoogh spread it out on the bare earth and gestured at Legoda, who looked down thoughtfully.

"Yes," the Talker conceded. "Some of it is good, and some would make nice trinkets for the women. What is it you want—more meat, or one of the new weapons? Your belly was filled yesterday; and with my beer, which was stolen, I think, though for that I blame you not. The boy has been punished already. And this weapon is not for you."

Hwoogh snorted, wriggled and fought for expression, while the young man stared. Little by little, his wants were made known, partly by signs, partly by the questions of the Cro-Magnon. Legoda laughed.

"So, there is a call of the kind in you, Old Man?" He pushed the treasure back to Hwoogh, except one gleaming bauble. "I would not cheat you, Chokanga, but this I take for the love I bear you, as a sign of our friendship." His grin was mocking as he stuck the valuable in a flap of his clout.

Hwoogh squatted down on his heels, and Legoda sat on a rock as he began. "There is but little to tell you, Hairy One. Three years ago I did run onto a family of your kind—a male and his mate, with one child. They ran from us, but we were near their cave, and they had to return. We harmed them not, and sometimes gave them food, letting them accompany us on the chase. But they were thin and scrawny, too lazy to hunt. When we returned next year, they were dead, and so far as I know, you are the last of your kind."

He scratched his head thoughtfully. "Your people die too easily, Chokanga; no sooner do we find them and try to help them than they cease hunting and become beggars. And then they lose interest in life, sicken and die. I think your gods must be killed off by our stronger ones."

Hwoogh grunted a half assent, and Legoda gathered up his bow and arrows, turning back toward camp. But there was a strange look on the Neanderthaler's face that did not escape the young man's eyes. Recognizing the misery in Hwoogh's expression, he laid a hand on the old man's shoulder and spoke more kindly.

"That is why I would see to your well-being, Hairy One. When you are gone, there will be no more, and my children will laugh at me and say I lie when I spin the tale of your race at the feast fire. Each time that I kill, you shall not lack for food."

He swung down the single street toward the tent of his family, and Hwoogh turned slowly back toward his cave. The assurance of food should have cheered him, but it only added to his gloom. Dully, he realized that Legoda treated him as a small child, or as one whom the sun god had touched with madness.

Hwoogh heard the cries and laughter of children as he rounded the hill, and for a minute he hesitated before going on. But the sense of property was well developed in him, and he leaped forward grimly. They had no business near his cave.

They were of all ages and sizes, shouting and chasing each other about in a crazy disorder. Having been forbidden to come on Hwoogh's side of the hill, and having broken the rule in a bunch, they were making the most of their revolt. Hwoogh's fire was scattered down the side of the hill into the creek, and they were busily sorting through the small store of his skins and weapons.

Hwoogh let out a savage yell and ran forward, his spear held out in jabbing position. Hearing him, they turned and jumped back from the cave entrance, clustering up into a tight group. "Go on away,

Ugly Face," one yelled. "Go scare the wolves! Ugly Face, Ugly Face, waaaah!"

He dashed in among them, brandishing his spear, but they darted back on their nimble legs, slipping easily from in front of him. One of the older boys thrust out a leg and caught him, tripping him down on the rocky ground. Another dashed in madly and caught his spear away, hitting him roughly with it. From the time of the first primate, the innate cruelty of thoughtlessness had changed little in children.

Hwoogh let out a whooping bellow, scrambled up clumsily and was in among them. But they slipped nimbly out of his clutching hands. The little girls were dancing around gleefully, chanting, "Ugly Face ain't got no mother, Ugly Face ain't got no wife, waaaah on Ugly Face!" Frantically he caught at one of the boys, swung him about savagely, and tossed him on the ground, where the youth lay white and silent. Hwoogh felt a momentary glow of elation at his strength. Then somebody threw a rock.

The old Neanderthaler was tied down crudely when he swam back to consciousness, and three of the boys sat on his chest, beating the ground with their heels in time to a victory chant. There was a dull ache in his head, and bruises were swelling on his arms and chest where they had handled him roughly. He growled savagely, heaving up, and tumbled them off, but the cords were too strong for him. As surely as if grown men had done it, he was captured.

For years they had been his enemies, ever since they had found that Hwoogh-baiting was one of the pleasant occupations that might relieve the tedium of camp life. Now that the old feud was about finished, they went at the business of subduing him with method and ingenuity.

While the girls rubbed his face with soft mud from the creek, the boys ransacked the cave and tore at his clothes. The rough bag in which he had put his valuables came away in their hands, and they paused to distribute this new wealth. Hwoogh howled madly.

But a measure of sanity was returning to them, now that the first fury of the fight was over, and Kechaka, the chief's eldest son, stared at Hwoogh doubtfully. "If the elders hear of this," he muttered unhappily, "there will be trouble. They'd not like our bothering Ugly Face."

Another grinned. "Why tell them? He isn't a man, anyway, but an animal; see the hair on his body! Toss old Ugly Face in the river, clean up his cave, and hide these treasures. Who's to know?"

There were half-hearted protests, but the thought of the beating waiting for them added weight to the idea. Kechaka nodded finally and set them to straightening up the mess they had made. With broken branches, they eliminated the marks of their feet, leaving only the trail to the creek.

Hwoogh tossed and pitched in their arms as four of them picked him up; the bindings loosened somewhat, but not enough to free him. With some satisfaction, he noted that the boy he had caught was still retching and moaning, but that was no help to his present position. They waded relentlessly into the water, laid him on it belly down, and gave him a strong push that sent him gliding out through the rushing stream. Foaming and gasping, he fought the current, struggling against his bonds. His lungs ached for air, and the current buffeted him about; blackness was creeping up on his mind.

With a last desperate effort he tore loose the bonds and pushed up madly for the surface, gulping in air greedily. Water was unpleasant to him, but he could swim, and he struck out for the bank. The children were disappearing down the trail and were out of sight as he climbed from the water, bemoaning his lost fire that would have warmed him. He lumbered back to his cave and sank soddenly on the bed.

He, who had been a mighty warrior, bested by a snarling pack of Cro-Magnon brats! He clenched his fists savagely and growled, but there was nothing he could do. Nothing! The futility of his own effort struck down on him like a burning knife. Hwoogh was an old man, and the tears that ran from his eyes were the bitter, aching tears that only age can shed.

Keyoda returned late, cursing when she found the fire gone, but her voice softened as she spied him huddled in his bed, staring dully at the wall of the cave. Her old eyes spotted the few footprints the boys had missed, and she swore with a vigor that was almost youthful before she turned back to Hwoogh.

"Come, Hairy One, get out of that cold, wet fur!" Her hands were gentle on the straps, but Hwoogh shook her aside. "You'll be sick, lying there on them few leaves, all wet like that. Get off the fur, and I'll go back to the village for fire. Them kids! Wait'll I tell Legoda!"

Seeing there was nothing he would let her do for him, she turned away down the trail. Hwoogh sat up to change his furs, then lay back. What was the use? He grumbled a little when Keyoda returned with fire, but refused the delicacies she had wheedled at the village, and tumbled over into a fitful sleep.

The sun was long up when he awoke to find Legoda and Keyoda fussing over him. There was an unhappy feeling in his head, and he coughed. Legoda patted his back. "Rest, Hairy One. You have the sickness devil that burns the throat and runs at the nose, but that a man can overcome. Ayeee, how the boys were whipped! I, personally, attended to that, and this morning not one is less sore than you. Before they bother you again, the moon will eat up the sun."

Keyoda pushed a stew of boiled liver and kidneys at him, but he shoved it away. Though the ache in his head had gone down, a dull weight seemed to rest on his stomach, and he could not eat. It felt as though all the boys he had fought were sitting on his chest and choking him.

Legoda drew out a small painted drum and made heavy magic for his recovery, dancing before the old man and shaking the magic gourd that drove out all sickness devils. But this was a stronger devil. Finally the young man stopped and left for the village, while Keyoda perched on a stone to watch over the sick man. Hwoogh's mind was heavy and numb, and his heart was leaden in his breast. She fanned the flies away, covering his eyes with a bit of skin, singing him some song that the mothers lulled their children with.

He slept again, stirring about in a nightmare of Talker mockery, with a fever flushing his face. But when Legoda came back at night, the magic man swore he should be well in three days. "Let him sleep and feed him. The devil will leave him soon. See, there is scarce a mark where the stone hit."

Keyoda fed him, as best she could, forcing the food that she begged at the village down his throat. She lugged water from the creek as often as he cried for it, and bathed his head and chest when he slept. But the three days came and went, and still he was not well. The fever was little higher, and the cold little worse, than he had gone through many times before. But he did not throw it off as he should have done.

Legoda came again, bringing his magic and food, but they were of little help. As the day drew to a close, he shook his head and spoke low words to Keyoda. Hwoogh came out of a half stupor and listened dully.

"He tires of life, Keyoda, my father's sister." The young man shrugged. "See, he lies there not fighting. When a man will not try to live, he cannot."

"Ayyeah!" Her voice shrilled dolefully. "What man will not live if he can? Thou art foolish, Legoda."

"Nay. His people tire easily of life, O Keyoda. Why, I know not. But it takes little to make them die." Seeing that Hwoogh had heard, he drew closer to the Neanderthaler. "O Chokanga, put away your troubles and take another bite out of life. It can still be good, if you choose. I have taken your gift as a sign of friendship, and I would keep my word. Come to my fire, and hunt no more; I will tend you as I would my father."

Hwoogh grunted. Follow the camps, eat from Legoda's hunting, be paraded as a freak and a half-man! Legoda was kind, sudden and warm in his sympathy, but the others were scornful. And if Hwoogh should die, who was to mourn him? Keyoda would go back to her people, Legoda would forget him, and not one Chokanga would be there to show them the ritual for burial.

Hwoogh's old friends had come back to him in his dreams, visiting him and showing the hunting grounds of his youth. He had heard the grunts and grumblings of the girls of his race, and they were awaiting him. That world was still empty of the Talkers, where a man could do great things and make his own kills, without hearing the laughter of the Cro-Magnons. Hwoogh sighed softly. He was tired, too tired to care what happened.

The sun sank low, and the clouds were painted a harsh red. Keyoda was wailing somewhere, far off, and Legoda beat on his drum and muttered his magic. But life was empty, barren of pride.

The sun dropped from sight, and Hwoogh sighed again, sending his last breath out to join the ghosts of his people.

Bibliography

Asimov, Isaac. *Before the Golden Age.* Doubleday, 1974.

Conklin, Groff. *The Best of Science Fiction.* Crown, 1946.

——. *Big Book of Science Fiction.* Crown, 1950.

Derleth, August. *Beyond Time and Space.* Pellegrini, 1950.

Healy, Raymond J., and McComas, J. Francis. *Famous Science Fiction Stories (Adventures in Time and Space).* Modern Library, 1957.

Moskowitz, Sam. *Seekers of Tomorrow.* World, 1966.